Acclaim for Amanda Brookfield's novels:

'The novel walks a line between comedy and wrenching sadness. It is fluently written and its deception of domestic chaos and a man's bewilderment when unexpectedly faced with a young son's needs is all too recognisable'
     Elizabeth Buchan, *The Sunday Times* on *A Family Man*

'Recounted with compassion and humour'
                         *Family Circle* on *A Family Man*

'Superb in its minute observation'
                              *Northern Echo* on *The Lover*

'Amanda Brookfield writes about the quiet crises of life; the pivotal points'
                       *Daily Telegraph* on *Single Lives*

'A perceptive and very readable account of the strains of marital breakdown'
                             *The Times* on *Walls of Glass*

'Amanda Brookfield's assurance and intelligence make *Alice Alone* stand out ... A strong sense of humour, a natural narrative gift and controlled, understated characterisation signify a promising debut'
                      *Evening Standard* on *Alice Alone*

*Also by Amanda Brookfield*

Walls of Glass

A Summer Affair

Alice Alone

A Cast of Smiles

The Godmother

Marriage Games

Single Lives

The Lover

A Family Man

## About the Author

Amanda Brookfield gained a First Class Honours degree from Oxford before working at an advertising agency for several years. She wrote her first novel while living in Buenos Aires with her diplomat husband, and her second while in Washington, D.C. She has two young sons and now lives in London, dividing her time between writing fiction and looking after her family.

AMANDA BROOKFIELD

# Sisters and Husbands

CORONET BOOKS
Hodder & Stoughton

Copyright © 2002 by Amanda Brookfield

First published in Great Britain in 2002 by Hodder and Stoughton
A division of Hodder Headline

The right of Amanda Brookfield to be identified as the Author
of the Work has been asserted by her in accordance with the
Copyright, Designs and Patents Act 1988.

A Coronet Paperback

4 6 8 10 9 7 5

A CIP catalogue record for this title is available from the British Library

ISBN 0 340 77012 0

Typeset in Plantin Light by Palimpsest Book Production Limited,
Polmont, Stirlingshire

Printed and bound in Great Britain by
Mackays of Chatham plc, Chatham, Kent

Hodder and Stoughton
A division of Hodder Headline
338 Euston Road
London NW1 3BH

For Andy and Jacky

# I

The best part of the dream was slipping from her grasp, buckling under the pressure of an uncomfortable urgency connected to the outside world, a dim sense of guilt. Becky pressed her face more tightly into the pillow, willing the delicious abstraction to return, but aware already that the once clear images were becoming garbled and inexplicable. There had been vivid colours and comfort, something to do with numbers and warmth and melting. She made a fresh effort to sink back into it, only to feel her mind snag again, more forcefully this time, on the quiet electronic tick of Joe's alarm clock.

Opening her eyes, she saw to her horror that it was half past eight. By such an advanced hour she should in theory be seated at her desk, ready to tackle the typing, photocopying and meter-feeding requirements of the five-strong executive team at Takoma Designs, a website design company founded and led by a charismatic ex-advertising man called Michael Hadfield. A wealthy divorcee in his forties, full of angst and ideology about his fledgling company, he would have been at his own desk for hours. Like the rest of his team he would assume that their chief office dogsbody was on the verge of arrival, nose-to-armpit somewhere during the latter stages of her commute from Balham to Hammersmith, held up perhaps by a faulty escalator or a Monday-morning suicide.

Feeling like an animal being forced out of hibernation, Becky trailed into the bathroom with the duvet round her shoulders and slumped down onto the toilet to consider her options. She was so late already the prospect of hurrying seemed pointless. Getting up from the toilet, she slipped her fingers between the wooden slats of the bathroom blind and peered outside. The row of shabby terraced houses across the street, a mirror image of the ones on their side, were looking somehow polished and pleased with themselves under the glare of the morning sun. Even the road, pitted with patches and lumps, shone with all the allure of dark treacle. Four doors down a window cleaner was at the top of his ladder, leaning precariously to reach an upper pane, whistling something tuneless in a shrill vibrato. As she watched, the old man opposite shuffled out of his front door in slippers and a string vest, a small knotted bag of rubbish swinging from the little finger of his left hand. Lifting the lid of his dustbin, he paused to glance with evident satisfaction at the cloudless state of the sky before releasing his modest deposit and tottering back indoors.

Letting the slats fall, Becky trudged back into the bedroom, tugging the bedding after her. Before reaching for the telephone she practised speaking out loud, pleased to hear that her voice retained the suggestively ailing croak of early morning. She dialled the numbers slowly, willing Juliette, the other, even more menial secretarial assistant who sat opposite her, to answer.

'Takoma Designs – Mike Hadfield speaking.'

'Oh, Mike . . . I . . . it's me, Becky—'

'Ah, Rebecca, you sound . . . distant. Are you on your mobile?'

'No . . . in fact I'm at home . . . not feeling too great to be honest . . .'

'Food poisoning?'

'Pardon? Er . . . no, a touch of flu I think – sore throat, temperature, that sort of thing.'

'Summer flu then?'

'I guess. Sorry Mike, I know it's inconvenient. I'll speak to Juliette, make sure she knows the most important things . . .'

'Don't worry, indispensable as you are, I expect we'll all struggle through the day somehow.'

Distrusting the dry tone of his voice, but fearful that pressing the severity of her symptoms any further might fuel any lurking suspicions as to the authenticity of her condition, Becky offered a last rasp of an apology before hanging up and flinging herself back amongst the bed covers. A rush of exultant relief followed, reminiscent of innumerable successful school truancy episodes during her teens: time snatched; illicit, secret, borrowed time, with no one to answer to but herself. She stretched luxuriously, pointing her toes and reaching her arms up to the ceiling. She deserved a day off. For a woman who had always nurtured an unfashionable reluctance to pursue a career of any kind, she worked bloody hard. And she was nearly thirty. The recollection of this now imminent birthday popped into Becky's head like an unwelcome face at a window, stopping all the exultation in its tracks. Almost worse than anything, she scolded herself, beating air into a flattened pillow, was allowing herself to succumb to the cliché of minding about such a thing. Practically everybody she knew was thirty already. Her sister Anna, who had passed the same milestone three years previously, had asserted many times that it was just something to be got through, like A levels or losing your virginity.

And it wasn't as if she felt old, Becky decided, raising one leg in the air in order to admire the delicate gold ankle chain Joe had given her a couple of years before, liking the way it fell around the curve of her ankle bone. It was more a question of a dim impatience, a mounting desire to get on with attaining all those things she imagined should rightfully be hers by such a ripe old age; not the hugely aspirational things which Anna already had – career success, a beautiful home, a fast car – but dull conventional stuff, such as a manageable overdraft and at least the possibility of starting a family. Opening her eyes and seeing the eager face of her husband beaming at her from the picture frame on her bedside table, Becky experienced a confused but familiar rush of shame and reassurance. Joe worked harder than anyone she had ever met. Burdened with alimony payments to an ex-wife and child, he had nonetheless had the courage to pack in a loathed career in accountancy and set about reinventing himself as a restaurateur. After a couple of years juggling an MBA with countless cookery courses, he had recently taken the first big step towards achieving this ambitious objective by landing the job of chef at a place called Le Moulin in Clapham. The shifts were long and hard and made no easier by the fact that he got up at dawn to help collect and deliver produce for a friend who ran an organic food delivery business. Two more years, he had promised recently, breaking the news of a small but very welcome pay rise, and he would be sufficiently on his feet for Becky to show Takoma Designs the finger and do something she really wanted instead, like redecorating the house or making babies. Looking again at the photograph, seeing the gentle smile and striking grace of her husband's broad frame, Becky felt her confidence in such a scenario return. The tenderness of the love Joe showed towards his daughter Jenny, the disarming gentleness with which he handled her, had from the start been a vital element in his appeal, making Becky decide, quite deliberately – instead of subconsciously as the sociologists said was supposed to happen – that she had met the ideal man one day to father her own offspring. Any impatience as to when such a day might finally dawn was something Becky had done her best to keep to herself. Partly because Joe had enough pressures to contend with and partly because she suspected, deep down, that her keen but sporadic maternal yearnings stemmed not so much from buried earth-mother tendencies as the appealing prospect of giving up work.

Rolling onto her back, Becky studied the crack overhead, which for as long she could remember had been zigzagging its way from the door lintel, round the light fitting and towards the curve of the bay window facing the street. Since her last proper look it appeared to have developed a new lightning strike of a tributary, cutting into the hitherto unaffected region above the bathroom door. Anna, consulted at some early stage about the problem, had murmured gravely about subsidence, recounting the time she and David had had concrete poured under a back window in Pimlico. But when Becky relayed her sister's fears to Joe he had merely laughed, saying there had been cracks ever since he and Ruth had bought the place, and that there was no point in worrying because they didn't have subsidence cover anyway. And the cracks in Anna's and David's place had been so huge you could stick your fist in them, Becky consoled herself, tossing uncomfortably now amongst the sheets, her skin clammy both from these small bursts of worry and the heat of the day beginning already to seep into the room. Joe, she reminded herself, in a further bid for comfort, had no qualms about sleeping with this Damoclean network of crevices over the marital bed. When she had raised the subject again that weekend he merely joked that it was such a perfect example of the river basins Jenny was studying in Geography that he would point out the delta and meanders next time she stayed.

Becky closed her eyes and tried to concentrate on the scenes going on at work, wanting to savour every last morsel of satisfaction at having to play no part in them. A pitch for an important client loomed, as it always seemed to. The place would be in its usual frenzy of self-examination and preparation, with Mike saying, as he always did, that this was the big one and could they pull all the stops out. Sometimes she longed for the easy impersonality of the job she had had before, amongst a pool of secretaries in a large Lloyds insurance firm. There the only daily challenge had been boredom and jamming photocopiers. Crises occurred, but behind sealed doors where menial employees had neither to witness nor worry about them. This dull but cushy existence had been brought to an end by one of a string of take-overs then sweeping through the insurance industry. Aware that many like her were facing redundancy, and with Joe only halfway through his career switch, Becky had swept her cardboard box off her desk and gone straight to a temping agency recommended by a friend. The very next morning she had been asked to report for a week's work at Takoma Designs where she had remained ever since, persuaded into full-time employment by a combination of Mike Hadfield's indubitable charm and the offer of a reasonable pay package.

Further from sleep than ever and with her holiday mood in tatters, Becky threw back the covers and swung her legs out of bed. Joe had left her a cup of tea, she noticed, full to spilling and far too weak as always. Touched nonetheless by the offering, she took a sip, scowling because it was cold and marvelling at how five years of cohabitation, not to mention months of honing skills with soufflés and hollandaise sauce, should have made no inroads into her husband's ability to do the right thing with a tea bag. In retaliation, he maintained that she made diabolical coffee, even when she followed his advice about letting the contents of the cafetière rest instead of whisking them into a frenzy with a spoon.

Before going downstairs Becky returned to the bathroom to wash the sleep out of her eyes. Leaning against the basin, she turned the hot tap on full, drumming her fingers against the familiar chipped edge of the porcelain while waiting for the water to get hot. Through the flimsy wall of the cupboard next to her she could hear the hot-water cistern belching its usual reluctance at being called upon to fulfil the duty for which it had supposedly been designed. I'm depressed, she thought suddenly, glancing at her reflection in the mirror above the basin, surprised at the notion and seeking some physical evidence of it in her features. She looked normal enough: her face slightly puffy from sleep but otherwise its usual pale self, contrasting starkly with her heavy black hair. Seizing a bunch of tresses in both hands, she tried piling it on top of her head, tipping her face this way and that in a bid to imagine what it would look like short, cut up round her ears like Anna's. But then her sister had soft fair waves, she reminded herself, letting the hair fall back onto her shoulders – hair that held a style instead of dropping out like weighted curtains, lengthening features which were on the long side anyway. When the water was still only tepid she put the plug in and plunged her face into the basin, screwing up her eyes and holding her breath till her lungs ached.

Downstairs in the kitchen the drainer was piled high with evidence of Joe's noble attempts to clear up the debris from the weekend. Perhaps in reaction to the disciplines of his new line of work, he remained incapable of cooking anything at home without creating a tidal wave of destruction in his wake, especially not if he was experimenting with ingredients as he had been the day before. Pasta, pine kernels, raisins, parmesan and several pungent herbs; the dish hadn't really worked; although Becky hadn't quite said as much, experience having taught her that what her husband presented as a desire for criticism was invariably a thinly disguised plea for encouragement.

Poised with a wedge of butter over her toast when the phone rang, she decided to let the answering machine screen the caller before deciding whether to pick up. She smoothed the butter in thick swirls, tensing only slightly as the familiar voice of her husband's ex-wife broke the silence of the kitchen.

*'Joe, it's Ruth. Just calling to ask whether Jen could come and stay this weekend instead of next. I won't go into the ins and outs but it would help me out enormously if she could. Oh and have you come across her pink hairband? Elastic with four white flowers across the top – it's the current favourite and we're frantic. I wondered if she'd left it last time she stayed. Could you call as soon as? Thanks so much.'*

Even after six years the cheerful-in-spite-of-it-all tone – the unmistakable twang of martyrdom – made Becky's stomach clench. Sometimes she had to remind herself that it was Ruth who had walked out on Joe, putting him through the torture of separation from his baby daughter and all for a relationship which had folded within a couple of years. That all the subsequent arrangements, financial and otherwise, had been managed so amicably – and so generously – was a powerful testimony both to the monumental patience of the man she had married and the strength of his commitment to his child. Theoretically he had unlimited access to Jenny. In practice this usually meant fitting in with Ruth's social life, a fact about which Joe never complained, refusing to mind – as Becky did on his behalf – that he was often thus consigned to the role of fall-back baby-sitter, and a free one at that.

Taking a cup of tea and her toast upstairs, Becky cast an eye round Jenny's bedroom for any sign of the missing hairband. The room, as usual, was very tidy, not because Becky had cleared up after the last visit but because Jenny left it that way. Her ten-year-old stepdaughter had an uncanny habit of creating almost no mess at all. Almost as if she wanted to slip through life unnoticed, Becky mused sadly, taking a bite of toast as she surveyed the orderly shelves and stacked toy boxes, aware that such spurts of sympathy were rather harder to come by when actually in the presence of Jenny herself. Early heady ambitions of defying the traditionally dark mould of the stepmother, of developing a warm and open relationship with her husband's young daughter, had been quickly drummed out of being by the resolutely cool attitude of the child herself. Although seldom overtly rude or difficult, she had made it clear, even at the tender age of five, that her father's new wife was an interloper, something to be tolerated rather than enjoyed. Recently, with Joe working at Le Moulin and the frequency of Jenny's visits suffering in consequence, the distance between the two of them seemed to have reached a new extreme. So much so that Becky sometimes wondered whether their limited communications arose solely out of a tacit mutual desire not to upset Joe. Watching a video during her last stay, with Joe planted in the middle of the sofa, one arm firmly across each of their backs, she had wondered whether he too felt the precarious balance of it all, whether it occurred to him that his broad shoulders were the only thing holding it together.

Becky tugged the creases out of the duvet cover with a heavy sigh and checked behind the curtains for the hairband. The window cleaner was still up his ladder several doors down, his shaved head shiny in the morning sun. He had rung their bell once, she remembered, catching her as she left for work and offering to do back and front for fifteen pounds. Not on our budget, she had laughed, slamming the door with a toss of her head, wishing not for clean windows but the freedom to choose to spend so measly a sum without a second thought.

Back in her own bedroom, Becky settled herself amongst the covers with tepid tea and the brittle remains of her toast and then reached for the telephone.

'It's me. I'm at home.'

'Why?'

'I overslept. So I rang in and said I wasn't feeling well and now I don't think I am.'

'What?'

'Feeling well.' Becky could tell that he wasn't really listening. He sounded faintly out of breath and in the background she could hear the voices of several other people. 'You're busy, I'll let you go. Just wanted you to know I'm at home, so you don't ring work and sound surprised when I'm not there.'

'Right, I see,' he said, sounding hurried and distracted, as if he didn't see anything at all. 'Catch you later then.'

'You're not working tonight are you?'

'No, but I've got my wine-tasting course. It's Monday, remember?'

'Oh yes. Of course.'

'I might be quite late.'

'Right.'

'Sorry love. Only a couple more weeks to go. You know I wouldn't be doing it if I didn't think it was important.'

'No, I know.'

'Hope you feel better.'

'Thanks.'

Becky replaced the phone and felt round her throat with her fingertips to see if the dryness spreading in the region of her tonsils might be connected to her glands. And there was a headache coming too, she decided, swiping ineffectually at the toast crumbs scattered amongst the bedding, forlorn suddenly to the point of tears.

# 2

Anna threaded her way through the Oxford Street crowds, swinging her bare arms and staring straight ahead, her gaze fixed quite happily on nothing in particular. She had always loved the West End, ever since her first trip there with her mother as a young girl, after the move back from France when they had come in search of uniform and hockey boots for their new school. Even at the tender age of thirteen she had relished the buzz of tourists and shoppers, the liberating anonymity that being part of such a dense and varied canvas allowed.

Pressing her sunglasses more firmly into the bridge of her nose, Anna tilted her head slightly so as to feel the full force of the sun on her face. She had known even at six thirty that morning, hurrying out of the house to race her new Saab round the curling country lanes to the station, that it would be hot. Waiting for the train, she had stood near the edge where the platform caught the sun, shivering slightly in her thin linen jacket. Though fresh there had been a stillness to the air which she associated with high summer, as if the heat was coiled inside, waiting to seep into the day. Nothing stirred in the scrubby grass lining the tracks, nor in the woodland ranged further behind. As if the world was literally holding its breath, Anna had mused, in awe at the unfolding of such a glorious day, feeling a burst of fresh confidence in the still relatively new business of seeing verdant Dorset countryside on her way to work instead of smudgy concrete and graffiti.

On the train it had taken some considerable effort to drag her gaze from the sunny green drama unfolding through the window and concentrate on her notes for *Fashion Focus*, the thirty-minute radio programme she devised and presented live for the BBC on Monday mornings. The subject that day had been shoes, a theme which had proved surprisingly rich in possibilities, in spite of her producer's initial scepticism. After a somewhat sticky start, the guests had got very lively, particularly a model suing her ex-employers for a back injury caused by a fall from eight-inch platforms and a designer whose creations resembled scale models of experiments in modern architecture. The other two programmes with which she was involved, a consumer series and a general health round-up, were pre-recorded and therefore not nearly as stressful. And ultimately not quite so sharp, Anna reflected, pausing to fish for her mobile which was bleeping somewhere in the bottom of her handbag. There was an edge to doing live radio which made her both very excited and very afraid, something connected to the relentless possibility of silence and the uncertainty as to what anyone, herself included, might say next.

The phone revealed a text message from Becky saying that she was running late and wouldn't make their lunch rendezvous until half past one. Anna quickened her stride, shaking her head in affectionate exasperation, wondering if the extra thirty minutes would be enough to choose a shower curtain and four lampshades from John Lewis. David, for all his new found freedom as an ex-captain of industry, with almost limitless time to trawl round department stores, remained somewhat unreliable when it came to having an eye for such items. His forte, as with sorting out companies, was more on the visionary side of things, a knack for seeing the big picture. Like for instance spotting the potential of the barn, now a stunning conversion of glass and stone which served as his studio. He had contributed so much to the original design that Anna had at times wondered why they bothered to pay the architect. The finishing touches however, the rainbow brilliance of the Bolivian rugs, the black leather sofa, so cool and smooth next to the plain tall-backed Shaker rocking chair, had been all her own.

In truth, Anna had been rather looking forward to a lunch hour in John Lewis. Becky calling and begging to meet had thrown the whole morning out of kilter; but then Becky had a habit of doing that. It was one of her charms, putting the spanner in the works, never doing what was expected and always at the last minute. Like falling for Joe, just when she was all set to marry Cliff, who was not only sweet and steady but also unencumbered by the baggage of an ex-wife and child; or walking out midway through her degree and doing a secretarial course instead; or taking the day off because she'd overslept and felt a little off-colour. Anna, now flicking through a stand of plastic shower curtains, shook her head, wondering as she had countless times in the past, at her younger sister's ability to attract complications, to make life hard when it could be so very easy.

'Were you wanting help?' The shop assistant approached gingerly, as if compelled to do so only by the drill of Anna's gaze.

'I like the seahorse one but it looks too short. Do you do the same design but longer?'

The young man shook his head gloomily. 'That's all we've got in the longer style.' He pointed at two curtains on the very end, one lime green and the other transparent.

No more attractive than a large plastic bag, decided Anna, thinking of the now virtually complete L-shaped ensuite in Dorset, with the white sea horse tiles moulded in amongst the soft brown stone walls and the arched niche above the towel rail where the coral and sea urchins they had brought back from the Seychelles sat as prettily as they had on the seabed. 'I think I'll leave it in that case, thank you.'

'We've got a delivery coming in on Friday, if you'd like to come back then.'

'I'll see, thanks.' Irritated, and with very little time left, she managed to find a tangerine silk lampshade which would do for the top spare bedroom, before trotting back out into the street and turning right towards St Christopher's Place, which housed the small bistro where she was due to meet her sister.

She spotted Becky at once, sitting at a square glass table in a far corner, studying the menu card with her fingers in her mouth, absently chewing the already chewed edges of her fingertips. Hanging off her chair were several bulging shopping bags displaying the brand names of a clutch of fashionable high street outlets. She was wearing a black T-shirt Anna hadn't seen before, with the words, *fcuk you*, emblazoned across the chest and baggy white shorts, full of zips and pockets.

'Hey you.' Becky's face lit up at the sight of her elder sister, edging her slim hips between the backs of the other diners' chairs. 'I tried to get one outside but everybody had booked. You look fab,' she added, beaming in genuine and unbridled admiration at the familiar star quality looks of her sibling, having long ago accepted the fact that Anna had somehow secured all the classic feminine charms from those available in the gene pool, leaving her to make the best of all the less obvious ones, most of them rooted in her father. And there's the scar, she thought, as she always did, seeing the jagged white zip running from the back of Anna's left hand to her forearm. Testimony to a serious car crash in her late teens, it was a defect which had always seemed to Becky to have the curious effect of heightening her sister's physical charms rather than undermining them; perhaps because of its hint of drama and vulnerability. Or perhaps, more simply, because the slender and smooth perfection of the rest of her appeared all the more striking in comparison.

'I thought you weren't feeling well,' said Anna, sliding into her seat. 'I thought you were dragging yourself into town through a haze of analgesics. When instead,' she continued, giving the laden back of Becky's chair a pointed stare, 'it looks as if you've been rather busy.'

'Retail therapy,' quipped Becky, ignoring the leap in her stomach at the thought both of what Joe would say when he saw the credit card bill and the recollection of several small items, a vest top, some mascara and a belt, which had made it out of their respective shops without the traditional process of being scanned through a till beforehand. 'I'm feeling heaps better. Hot though, isn't it?' she murmured, blushing a little as she ran both hands through her heavy dark hair, aware that in some deep, indefinable way Anna's predilection for playing the role of admonisher was something on which she relied. 'I've been a bit mad, I know.'

'Well, we all need to go a little mad sometimes,' conceded Anna, her expression softening. 'Can we order? I'm starving – haven't eaten since the train—'

'How's it going – the commuting, the house, David's pottery? I keep thinking you're still in Kensington – I mean I can't believe that you've actually done it.'

'Neither can I sometimes.' Anna smiled. 'But it's wonderful. We're all but there on the decorating and I've got used to the journey. When things go smoothly I can be out of Broadcasting House by four.'

'And David's still enjoying the freedom of early retirement, is he?'

'I've never seen him happier,' confided Anna with a sigh. 'And he's so good too, some of the pieces he's producing, it's sickening.' She rolled her eyes. 'If he wasn't mine I'd hate him.'

'You'll be getting a black Labrador next,' quipped Becky, a little hurriedly, feeling as she always did when it came to the remarkable capabilities of her brother-in-law, a confusing combination of admiration and mild antipathy. 'To complete the rural idyll – green wellies and long walks in the woods.'

'Oh no we won't.' Anna laughed. 'Neither of us are ready for any of that sort of thing – far too much of a tie. Now that he's got the time David's planning so much – not just artistically either. He's got a friend who's promised to teach him how to fly and – oh yes – he said something the other day about wanting to charter a boat in the Caribbean . . . but enough of us.' She broke off, urging in a different, more tender voice, 'How are you, Becks? You did sound a bit low on the phone.'

'Did I?' Becky frowned, recalling her peculiar mood that morning. 'Yeah, well I really did think I was going down with something, but then I had another snooze and it sort of went away. Mid-life crisis probably.' She grinned ruefully. 'Two weeks and counting.'

'Oh God, not that again.' Anna speared a tidy package of ravioli and a salad leaf onto her fork and popped it into her mouth. 'Being thirty is no big deal,' she continued, speaking with her mouth full, 'how many times do I have to tell you and besides . . .'

'What?'

'Nothing.

'Oh, don't give me that. What were you going to say?'

'It's just that . . . well I think Joe might be planning something. I shouldn't tell you, but he – well a few weeks back he phoned to ask if I had any idea where you might keep your passport.'

'You're joking,' squealed Becky, dropping her cutlery with

a clatter and clapping both hands to her face. 'My passport – ohmyGod – and there was me thinking we'd end up getting a takeaway curry.' She flung her arms wide as if about to hug her sister across the table. 'Thank you, darling Anna, for telling me . . .'

'I haven't told you anything,' she insisted a little sternly, in truth somewhat concerned at Becky's exuberance. 'Forget I said a word. He's very kind your husband,' she added after a pause, 'one of those people who always tries to do the right thing.'

'I'm married to a saint,' agreed Becky heavily, the delight seeping out of her, 'which can be hard at times, believe me. And a fat lot of good it's done Joe himself,' she continued, warming to her theme, 'I mean, being kind is no recipe for success, is it? And I'm not just talking about his work. He lets Ruth walk all over him, and Jenny too these days, winds him round her little finger – she can be a right little cow when she wants, turning on the taps to get his sympathy, asking for hand-outs when he's already given most of his savings and practically every penny he earns to her mother . . .'

'It must be hard for Jenny,' said Anna quietly, familiar with such complaints and ready to deliver the usual sympathies.

'Well, it's hard for me too,' retorted Becky, throwing her napkin onto her side plate and giving up on her steak which was overcooked and streaked with gristle. 'All I want is our own life, Joe and me, it's all I've ever wanted . . . only the years roll by and it never seems to get any closer to coming true.'

'Becks? Are you okay? You're not, are you? I knew you weren't,' she murmured, fishing in her handbag for a clean tissue and offering it across the table.

But Becky was already dabbing at her eyes with her paper napkin. 'God . . . sorry. Just a bit fed up. Looking back over three decades and wondering what the fuck I've got to show for it.' She blew her nose and dropped the damp remains of her napkin onto her slab of half-eaten meat. 'There we are. Better already. What a dope.'

'Not a dope at all, although you do talk a lot of nonsense sometimes. You've got loads to show for yourself – a good job, a nice home and Joe, who's a treasure, and so close now to getting himself sorted – I mean to go and do what he's done takes courage and he's almost there, isn't he? That place he's working at . . .'

'Le Moulin.'

'That's it. I meant to tell you I read a review of it the other day – I can't quite remember where – but it's well thought of, you know Becks, the kind of place that's brilliant for the CV of any chef, let alone one like Joe who's so committed and so good. You just wait, one day you'll have two point two kids and no mortgage and wonder what all the fuss was about.'

'Yeah, right,' Becky murmured, unconvinced but comforted nonetheless.

'Look, why don't you come and stay this weekend – have a break in the country? It's months since we all got together. The boys can talk about the traumas of changing careers.' Anna paused, adding thoughtfully, 'Quite something, don't you think, that both our husbands, both in their late thirties, should change course so dramatically in the space of three years?'

'Yeah, I guess,' Becky conceded, thinking that there was in fact very little to compare an ex-company director millionaire retiring to pursue exotic hobbies and a man sweating it out in kitchens to try and secure a foothold in the impossibly competitive world of haute cuisine. Although she wouldn't have wanted Joe to return to accountancy for anything, she sometimes wished he could have chosen an alternative vocation that was a little better paid, with a clearer greasy pole to climb. 'I would like to, really I would, but Ruth has asked us to have Jenny and . . .'

'Well bring her too, for heaven's sake.'

'I'll talk to Joe. See what he says. Thanks Anna.'

There were traces of defeat in the gratitude, Anna noticed, sitting back in her chair and observing her sister with the protective concern which had characterised their relationship for as long as she could remember. It occurred to her in the next instant that she should probably have consulted David before inviting them. Since the departure of the builders he seemed to relish having both the house – and her – to himself at weekends, seeking her attention in a way he hadn't for years. So much so that at times, after a busy week, delivering the desired response could feel like quite a drain on her energies. Looking across the table at Becky, now stirring heaps of brown sugar into a large coffee, Anna caught herself toying with the notion of voicing this one small gripe of her own out loud. Which was unusual, because she rarely confided such minutiae to Becky – or anyone else for that matter. Such emotional blips normally ironed themselves out with time, she had discovered, if ignored stoutly enough. That David was equally self-contained – someone who got on with life rather than analysing it too deeply – was one of the many vital ingredients of their marital contentment. Fortified by a slice of cheesecake from the dessert trolley, she turned instead to the invariably tricky subject of their mother, Stella, who lived on her own in Amersham.

'Just a card, Becks, to say you're thinking of her.'

'I do cards at birthdays and Christmas.'

'But it's August, the anniversary, she's always bad then.'

'Jesus, Anna, it's twenty years. She's got to let it go, like we've done. I mean, why hasn't she been sending us commiseration cards all these years, then? We lost him too. It wasn't just her.'

'Just a card,' persisted Anna, 'it's not just remembering Dad, she's not been well . . .'

'What, again? What was it this time? There are just so many scares you can have, Anna, don't you think? Just so many times we can all be led to the brink of fearful expectation and then spring back to a state of normality upon discovering that it was yet another false alarm . . . oh okay, sorry, sorry, sorry.' She raised her arms in apology, relenting both at the hurt expression on her sister's face and the knowledge that she was, as always when it came to their mother, being spiteful. 'A card it is. Thinking of you, all my love. From Becky, irksome daughter and hypocrite . . .'

'Sometimes being a hypocrite is fine,' put in Anna quietly, 'when it involves saying what someone badly needs to hear.'

Becky was on the point of giving this remark serious thought when the sight of a familiar figure on the far side of the restaurant sent her ducking behind her hands instead. 'Oh fuck . . . no, don't turn round, don't look, stay exactly as you are. He might not have seen me.'

'Who?' asked Anna, half turning in spite of herself and glimpsing the backs of two businessmen leaving the restaurant.

'Mike bloody Hadfield, that's who.' Becky dropped her hands with a groan. 'Oh God, do you think he saw me?'

'He would have come over if he had, wouldn't he?'

'Would he? Oh God, I don't know. Bloody hell, of all the places in this entire bloody city . . . he must have been sitting round the corner all this time . . . he could have spotted me hours ago – and with all this shopping too, he won't be fooled . . . oh Jesus, I'm going to be in such deep shit tomorrow.'

It took some considerable time for Anna to calm her down, with reassurances which in truth she struggled to feel herself. Was bad luck something that just dogged certain personalities? she wondered, aware of Becky's stricken expression as she settled the bill. Or did it merely arise from flawed decision-making, acting on impulse instead of thinking things through. Out in the street, she gave her younger sister an especially fond hug of a farewell, commanding her to look after herself and reminding her not to say a hint of anything about the passport business to Joe.

'Not a word,' Becky promised, still glancing nervously about her, as if half expecting her boss to spring from the crowds and accost her in the street. 'But thanks again for telling me – it's just brilliant to have something to look forward to. And I'll give you a call about the weekend,' she added, before spotting a bus and sprinting after it, her bags flapping awkwardly against her legs.

Hopping off two bus changes later by the garage near her road, Becky felt sufficiently taxed by the day's events to justify the purchase of a packet of ten Camel Lights and a box of matches. Knowing how disappointed Joe would be if he detected even a whiff of smoke in the house – he had been the powerhouse of encouragement and support behind the unprecedented act of self-discipline it had taken to give the habit up – she retreated to their small scrubland of a back garden before lighting up. She puffed till her throat was raw, huddling between a pot of something limp and green and the fence, self-loathing at what she was doing causing her to seek total concealment, even though their neighbours barely knew her and almost certainly wouldn't give a damn if they did. Afterwards she rushed straight up to the bathroom to clean her teeth and scrub at her fingers. Glancing up as she did so, she caught a glimpse of her flushed guilty face in the mirror and froze, arrested momentarily by the unsettling notion that she had never moved on from being an irksome misbehaving child and never would. Returning her attention to her hands, she rubbed with renewed ferocity, some dim part of her aware that she might be scrubbing at something that went rather deeper than the smell of smoke.

# 3

Joe steered his motorbike up onto the pavement and in through the front gate, scraping his left hand on the rough metal as he struggled to negotiate the handlebars through the narrow opening. He took off his helmet and wiped his hand across his face, suddenly damp with sweat now he had stopped moving. Before going inside he paused, breathing deeply and stretching his neck. The night was airless and so heavily clouded that it felt as if the sky was pressing its full weight down towards the earth. The only illumination came from the sickly orange glare of the street lamp, where several fat moths danced in small circles, throwing themselves against the thick glass and bouncing back again. Seeing no hint of light behind the curtains in the front bedroom, he wondered if Becky would turn out to be properly asleep or just sulky and pretending, making a point about the lateness of the hour and the fact that an impromptu drink with his course mates had meant that she had spent the entire evening alone. Joe sighed, for a moment lamenting how such considerations should become entwined in the woof of any long-term cohabitation, no matter how much love had got the thing off the ground.

Stepping into the house, he slid his helmet out of the way under the hall table before going on through to the kitchen at the back. A lamp had been left on, positioned so as to present a clear view of a piece of paper containing a few brief sentences in Becky's typically energetic short-hand style.

*Crap day – thk rlly am ill. R wants J to stay w/e. A and D have invited us to rural palace in Dors. B.*

Joe yawned deeply, stretching his arms so high above his head he could feel small clicks along his spine as the vertebrae realigned themselves. The muscles round his shoulderblades felt especially tight, as if they had spent so long clenched in one position that they had lost the ability to relax out of it. Though keen as ever to be of use to his friend, Adrian's boxes of organic produce had felt particularly heavy that morning. Ten years younger and full of the optimistic zeal which Joe recalled from his own twenties, Adrian himself never seemed to get tired. Almost as soon as he had completed the MBA course where the pair of them had met, he had launched his own business on the back of nothing more than a small bank loan and a spacious garage. In the intervening two years he had built up an impressively long customer list, but remained on the cusp of proper success. Although Joe knew he couldn't go on helping him indefinitely, the extra cash was useful, as were the bagfuls of fresh and excellent food which he got in return. It was also fun to meet members of the eclectic and dynamic group of friends forever turning up on Adrian's doorstep. Just that morning he had got chatting to a man called Gary, who said that anyone interested in owning a restaurant south of the river should take a look at some premises currently housing a pizza parlour down one of the side streets off Acre Lane in Brixton. It would probably be sold before the For Sale sign went up, he had warned, going on to talk, somewhat less interestingly, of his many contacts in the property world. Joe had been sufficiently interested to take a detour there on his way home, finding a tattered green and white striped canopy under a dusty but solid-looking Victorian front. That the place was on its last legs was evident from the patchy paintwork, the faded lettering of the word 'Pizzeria' across the front door and the brown-stemmed flowers trailing out of the window boxes, drooping over the edges as if in a last exhausted gasp for air. To Joe's eyes however, the potential of the building was immediately self-evident; it was not just stalwart, but attractive, within walking distance of shops and bordered by lines of orderly houses. During the course of the ride home he was already imagining the price it might go for and the viability of taking it on. He pictured how the inside might look, painted a vivid yellow, or possibly blue, with sleek chrome uplighters on the walls, casting pretty shadows across the white linen tablecloths and polished cutlery . . .

Joe was woken by the jerk of his own head as it pitched forward onto his chest. He opened his eyes to find that he was still sitting at the kitchen table, Becky's note in his hand. He had been on his feet for sixteen hours, he realised, not just that day, but every day of the previous week as well, and the one before that, and the one before that. Feeling his eyelids closing again, he pressed both palms onto the table and heaved himself to his feet for the journey upstairs. He would give up the Adrian business soon, he vowed a few minutes later, sliding in beside Becky's motionless frame as smoothly as he could, holding his breath as the bed springs creaked under his weight.

'Joe?'

'Mm sweetheart.' He was already on the verge of sleep, sliding into a deep warm crevasse.

'Joe, where've you been? It's so late.'

'Sorry. Had a drink . . . after the course, sorry darling.' He pulled her to him, dimly considering and rejecting the idea of mentioning any of his new grand plans, not wanting to get her hopes up. 'How are you feeling?' he managed, clinging now to consciousness like a drowning man.

'Not great . . . that is, I *was* feeling a bit better, so I met Anna for lunch, which could have been nice except that Mike Hadfield happened to be in the same bloody restaurant – I don't know for sure that he saw me, but I think he must have. So I'm dreading tomorrow. You know what he's like – he'll play it for all it's worth . . .' Becky rolled over and slipped her head under the crook of Joe's arm, fighting a sudden temptation to fish for clues about her birthday surprise. Joe tightened his grip on her, briefly stroking her forearm with his fingertips. Feeling protected, loved and therefore very brave, Becky launched into a confession about some of the less edifying aspects of her day: 'And Joe, you might as well know that I had a bit of a spree, bought a few more bits and pieces than I should have, because I was feeling sorry for myself, I guess, and because it felt like ages since I'd bought anything just for the hell of it. And then I just felt really guilty and empty, especially after the Mike business, so I bought some cigarettes and smoked five in a row even though they tasted foul. And of course that just made me feel worse so I chucked the rest of the packet in the bin. It was just a lapse, Joe, a bad day. I feel so much better now I've told you about it. Joe?' Becky listened hard, imagining disapprobation in his silence before gathering from the small regular breathing sounds that he had in fact fallen asleep. For a few moments she didn't move, marvelling at the grip of his arm, wondering if it indicated that while apparently dispensable in real life, she was a vital accoutrement to his dreams. Then, irritated that her grand confession had fallen on deaf ears and the realisation that she was unbearably hot, she wriggled free and tiptoed across to lean out of the open window on the far side of the room. Below she could just make out the chrome wheel guard of Joe's motorbike, sticking out from under its protective plastic cover. Apart from a fox crossing the road, trotting jauntily on its toes, the street looked sinister and empty. Wide awake and shivering suddenly, thinking how different the same view had looked in the morning sunshine, she crept back past the bed and out of the room.

Downstairs it was much cooler. She poured herself a glass of orange juice and drank it in one go standing next to the fridge. Taking the glass and carton of juice with her, she then decamped to the sitting room with the intention of soothing herself back to sleepiness with the aid of the television. Before reaching for the remote however, overtaken by an impulse to do at least one virtuous thing in an otherwise thoroughly unvirtuous day, she rummaged for a box of notelets from amongst the piles of papers scattered across the chipped Formica table that passed for a desk and set about composing a few words to her mother. To fill some of the space she wrote her address first and then the date. *Monday 24th August.* Then she paused, sucking the end of her Biro and frowning at the realisation that it was past midnight and therefore already Tuesday 25th August, the exact day on which her father had died. A ripple of mild anger followed, aimed partly at her mother's neediness and partly at Anna for having reminded her of something that she had grown rather practised at forgetting. In Becky's experience grief was something one could visit, a space with a door one could choose to unlock, or not, as the case may be. But sitting there in the half dark, pen poised over a blurred impressionist print of bluebells and poppies, with the date jumping out at her like that, she felt the door slide open of its own accord, taking her back to the afternoon twenty years before beside a river in France, with the tartan picnic rug, Anna doing handstands in her green shorts, her blonde curls falling over her eyes, and their mother lying on her side with a book, picking idly at a bunch of fat purple grapes. Becky had been by the river, hopping up and down on the waterlogged bank, enjoying the feel of mud pushing between her toes, squealing with delight at the antics of her father who had already swum across and was on the far bank, pretending to fall in, and just saving himself every time. The stretch of river was one they had not visited before, fuller and somewhat murkier than their usual spot. Small armies of gnats hovered above its surface, easy prey for the dragonflies which swooped amongst them, their slender bodies flashing like tiny blue lights. When her father at last steadied himself for a proper dive, Becky, in truth a little tired of laughing, had been relieved. She had shouted, *one two three*, and clapped her hands as he jumped, arching his back and spreading his arms in a dramatic swallow-dive of an entry into the water. And when he didn't surface she had clapped again, laughing at the new game.

*I am sorry you've not been well*, she wrote to her mother, her hands so clammy that her fingers slid to the very tip of the pen. And I'm sorry you're missing Dad, she thought, but did not write because deep down she had always believed that bereavement was a role her mother chose to play, out of a desire for attention and sympathy, rather than something truly felt. At ten she had been old enough to perceive the steel of real antagonism in her parents' arguments, to understand that her mother hated France almost as much as the renovating of holiday properties that kept them there. Fuelled by the clouds of white dust and paperwork scattered around their own half-renovated home, while her husband, Colin, bounced happily around the undulating countryside of the Gers in his beaten up Ford, Stella's dissastisfaction and resentment had been a palpable force in all their lives. The picnic by the river had constituted an increasingly rare show of family unity, a brief suspension of hostilities in the running parental battle as to when – if ever – they could look forward to transplanting themselves back to England. They had argued fiercely on the way to the river, Becky remembered now, picturing the back of her parents' heads in the car as they sliced the air with their sentences, her father drumming his fingers on the steering wheel.

*Love from Becky*. After another pause, remembering what

Anna had said about hypocrisy being okay sometimes, she wrote, *PS Will ring soon*, before sealing the card into the envelope and flicking on the television. The night if anything seemed to be getting hotter. Buried amongst sofa cushions, blinking at the TV screen, Becky could feel the prickle of heat across her scalp and under her arms. When she couldn't bear it a moment longer she went in search of the ice tray and some clips to pin up her hair, which was sticking to the back of her neck. She managed a cumbersome bun in front of the mantelpiece mirror, before – irritation mounting – lunging for some scissors off the top of the desk and giving some extravagant snips to her fringe. She then retreated to the sofa, ignoring the mess of hair, scattered across the floorboards like dark needles. Flicking on the television, she found Cary Grant on his knees at the feet of a watery-eyed Ingrid Bergman, telling her in his curious clipped tones that he loved her and always had, that they would live happily ever after or there would be hell to pay. Becky observed the scene impassively, unable to make the leap of faith required to believe in it. Love mattered but so did money, she reflected grimly, recalling with some discomfort her spurt of kleptomania that morning. Letting her gaze drift from the screen, she plucked an ice cube out of her glass and began rolling it slowly across her cheeks and forehead. Feeling soothed and suddenly rather sleepy, she then slid the shrinking pebble of ice down her neck and across her chest, watching with detached interest as drops of water began to trickle between her breasts and soak the faded blue edging of her nightshirt.

# 4

The weather in London broke the following Friday. Overcast grey skies which had for days been belting a stifling heat, suddenly released sheeting fat dollops of rain instead, reducing the already slow Bank Holiday traffic to a virtual standstill and reminding everybody that summer was at an end and a good seven months of dreariness lay ahead. Or so it seemed to Becky, sitting on the windowsill near her desk during her lunch hour, skim-reading the paper as she ate her way through a sausage sandwich delivered by the girl from the deli across the road, who took orders from most of the offices in their block.

After considerable discussion it had been decided that she should accept Anna's invitation to go to Dorset for two nights on her own. Ruth was due to retrieve Jenny on Sunday morning and Joe didn't have to work on Monday, which meant they would have the rest of the long weekend to themselves. Joe had been extremely insistent and tender about these arrangements, instructing Becky, in spite of the dark bags under his own eyes, that a break from London would do her the world of good and that he would juggle Jenny and his cooking shifts fine without her aid.

'I just don't know how you do it.'

Becky glanced up sharply, somewhat dismayed to have the companionable silence of the lunch hour broken by conversation. The remark had been delivered by Juliette, her secretarial colleague, who was seated at her desk on the other side of the room, picking desultorily at a tub of salad with a plastic fork.

'Do what?'

'Eat sausage sandwiches. I love sausages. But they're three hundred and fifty calories each, and that's only chipolatas and not counting the bread and butter. I'm already over my count for the day because I had a croissant on the way to work and they're off the scale when it comes to points.' She stared glumly at the food on her lap. 'This has got loads of celery in and I hate celery.'

Becky, who really wanted to be left alone and who, apart from an experimental phase of starving herself in her teens, had always eaten when and what she liked with no ill-effects, tried to look sympathetic. 'You don't need to diet. Just eat when you're hungry.'

Juliette's eyes widened. 'If I did that I'd be the size of a house. I'm *always* hungry.'

'Perhaps because you're thinking about it all the time,' suggested Becky kindly, posting the last of her sandwich into her mouth and shaking out the newspaper in a bid to communicate that she wished to spend the last ten minutes of her lunch break in peace. All their employers were out, either meeting clients or because they were involved in the new business pitch taking place on the other side of town. It was rare to have the place to themselves, to be able to keep their fingers from the keyboards without feeling guilty. Becky had worked particularly hard that week, partly because that day's presentation had demanded it, and partly in a vague bid to make up for playing truant on Monday. After rehearsing a variety of explanations for Mike on the way in on Tuesday morning, she had been pleasantly surprised to find herself subjected to no quizzing on the matter at all. Not even one tiny sly, dry hint.

'What's mine say then?' persisted Juliette.

'Your what?'

'Horoscope. I'm a Gemini – sunny-natured but lacking in confidence. Go on, let's hear what I've got in store for the weekend.' Having tipped the empty plastic box to her mouth to get the last of the salad dressing, Juliette had begun, slowly and somewhat reverentially, to peel the silver foil off a small chocolate bar. 'Geminis' ideal partners are supposed to be Pisces but Pete's a Taurus and we get along fine. Well . . . mostly. Like everybody. Nothing's perfect is it?'

'No, it isn't,' murmured Becky, watching in some fascination as her companion closed her eyes to savour her first bite of chocolate, clearly deriving a satisfaction that went way beyond the artless chomping with which Becky herself tackled confectionery. She noted too that the girl had no serious need to count calories. Her figure was on the large side, but in a buxom, motherly way that suited her generous features: with airy auburn hair, large green eyes and a wide mouth, curling prettily at the corners in a manner suggestive of a state of perpetual merriment, she was attractive in a way that bore no relation to her size.

'Go on then, let's hear it,' pleaded Juliette, starting to fold away the remains of the chocolate but then changing her mind and taking another bite. 'And then you can read me yours if you want. What did you say you were?'

'Virgo,' replied Becky, struggling now to hide the weariness in her tone, wishing her young colleague had defied the rain and gone for one of her usual Friday lunches with a girlfriend instead. 'Gemini. Here we are. It says you have some big decisions to make during the next few days—'

Juliette nodded gravely. 'That'll be with Pete. Whether to make it permanent or not. When you've been together as long as we have it seems only common sense, doesn't it? I mean, you might as well.'

Becky managed a bland smile, thinking with a stab of

nostalgia of her decision to leave Cliff and align herself with Joe five years before, how it had been prompted by something far too giddy and lunatic to bear even the remotest connection to common sense. 'And a period of uncertainty will be brought to an end,' she continued returning her attention to the paper and then breaking off at the sight of their boss, bursting through the door, his glasses specked with rain, his greying sandy hair sticking to his forehead. 'Ladies, would you like to go home?'

Becky and Juliette exchanged looks of astonishment.

'By way of a celebration,' he explained, clearly enjoying their startled faces. 'The biggest publishing house in London and they want us to design their website – sites for every department, every author . . .' He rubbed his hands with schoolboyish glee. 'Can't remember when I was more pleased. I'm telling everyone to take the afternoon off. Geoff and Tony have already gone.' He clapped his hands. 'Go on, get out of here.' Not needing to be told again, Becky and Juliette switched off their PCs and began scrambling for their handbags.

'Blimey,' said Juliette, as they coincided at the basins in the Ladies a few minutes later. 'Talk about a surprise.'

'Yeah, amazing,' murmured Becky, stabbing at her new stump of a fringe with a comb, wishing it had at least an echo of sophistication, instead of looking like a rash act of self-disfigurement.

Outside in the hallway she almost tripped over Mike Hadfield who was hovering by the door, rubbing at the lenses of his spectacles with a handkerchief. 'Rebecca – would you mind – could we have a quick word in my office before you go?'

'Cheerio then,' trilled Juliette, appearing behind them and unpopping her umbrella. 'Have a nice weekend.'

'Thanks. Bye.' Becky watched enviously as the lift doors slid shut behind her. Mike Hadfield was already striding down the corridor towards his office. She turned to follow him with a heavy heart, studying the white flecks in the carpet and chiding herself for ever having imagined that he would let Monday's fiasco pass without comment.

By the time she reached the open door to his office he was already sitting behind his desk. His glasses were back in place and his elbows were planted firmly on the broad arms of his chair. He had made a pyramid of his hands and was resting his chin, lightly, but somehow imposingly on the very top of his fingertips. Like some sort of headmaster with a list of reprimands, Becky thought gloomily, pausing in the doorway to compose herself.

'Sit down.' He pointed at the chair in front of his desk, frowning. 'I've been waiting for the chance to have a word.'

Becky perched stiffly on the edge of the soft leather, making a big show of meeting his gaze by way of camouflage for the fact that she longed only to turn and run from the room. She opened her mouth to speak first but then dried up at the daunting prospect of justifying a high street spending spree when supposedly summoned from her sick bed to deal with a family calamity. But then, maybe he hadn't noticed the shopping bags, she thought wildly. Men often didn't notice the obvious things, like flowers on a table or a new hairstyle. Even her hacked fringe had failed to trigger a comment from Joe until she swivelled his head and commanded him to study her face, holding it there until he conceded that something looked a bit different, stumbling finally to the generous observation that the new cut drew more attention to her eyes.

When Mike started speaking it was a while before Becky allowed herself to focus on what he was saying. It was a trick she had developed in her youth, a way of mentally removing herself from a situation so as to minimise the pain. As a

33

schoolgirl, hauled before countless scolding authorities, she had sometimes managed to feel so closed down inside as to be almost sleepy. She was prevented from reaching such extremes on this occasion however, by the gradual realisation that the dressing down for which she had been bracing herself was not taking place.

'In short,' Mike was saying, raising his chin from his fingertips and pressing his palms together, 'what I am offering you is the chance to cross from the secretarial to the executive side of the business. Our very own in-house trainee. It's quite clear that you've got the ability and after two years it's also quite clear that you've picked up on many aspects of what such a role would entail. As I say, I had been thinking about it for some time, but with today's news – the acquisition of another big account – we are going to need a little more manpower on the executive front and I prefer the idea of promoting you and drafting some assistance for Juliette . . . Rebecca, are you with me so far?'

'Oh yes, thank you,' Becky managed, aware that she was looking appalled when what the man had probably expected was something more along the lines of unbridled jubilation. 'But if you could just stop there . . . you see, the thing is, I'm not exactly what you would call the career type.'

He sat back in his chair and folded his arms, looking amused. 'Really? And what type would that be exactly?'

'I mean, I like to do my job and go home.'

'So do I.'

'No you don't, you're here till all hours, every day.'

'Perhaps that's because I don't have much of a home to go to.'

'Oh.' Somewhat nonplussed, Becky sought a new line of defence. 'And I don't want pressure – I know you're supposed to – I've got a sister who lives and breathes the stuff, makes live radio programmes, timing sentences to seconds and ad

34

libbing when a guest dries up or a wrong tape gets put on – but . . . to be perfectly frank, all I really want to do is not to have to go to work at all.'

Her boss laughed hard for several seconds. 'Nothing if not honest . . . though you might want to consider toning down some of that straight-talking with clients,' he added, clearly not sufficiently impressed by her honesty to consider it significant. Getting up from his chair, he went to stand at the window behind, nodding at its view of greying housing and office blocks, veiled under a mist of rain. 'No hurry.' He thrust both hands deep into his trouser pockets, still not looking at her. 'As obviously I shall need time to employ more secretarial help and to have a proper consultation with my colleagues, who would assume the greater part of the burden of training you. Your starting salary, incidentally, would be twenty-eight thousand, or twenty-four five and a company car, depending on how you chose to take the package. My guess is you would take the money.' He turned and cocked his head at her, raising one eyebrow. 'Don't tell me you're not going to think about it.'

He then smiled, so broadly and smugly that Becky felt sure some radar detection service had given him a clear view of the pitiful state of her bank account. Hating the notion of being so readable, so financially hamstrung that she could afford to exercise no choice over the matter, she almost delivered a flat refusal on the spot. Then she thought of having several more hundred pounds each month and smiled back at him instead. 'Thank you, I will. And . . . well I'm sorry not to appear more grateful and so on . . . I mean, obviously I'm deeply flattered. When you said you wanted to see me . . . well, it's not what I was expecting at all.'

'You mean you thought I was going to ask about Monday.'

'I beg your pardon?'

35

'About Monday.' He was smiling again, but less smugly.

'Monday?' Becky felt herself go pale.

'You know I saw you. In the restaurant.'

'I can explain about that – it was a . . . crisis . . . a family thing . . . I had to meet my sister . . . I mean, I . . . and I was feeling ill, honestly . . .'

'So that was your sister, was it?' he continued, not picking up on the family crisis defence at all and sounding not so much cross as interested.

'Yes.' Becky studied her fingers, knitted together in her lap.

'One would never guess. You look so different.'

'Everyone says that,' she muttered. 'Beauty and the beast.'

'Not at all, no.' He sounded genuinely indignant. 'Just different. But in future if you need a day off,' he added, his voice hardening. 'I'd prefer you to ask for it officially, even if it's at the last minute. I can come across as something of a workaholic myself, but I've seen enough to know that the happiest employees are the most efficient. Now go and enjoy your weekend and think about what I've said.'

'Right, thanks.'

'Oh and Rebecca.'

'Yes?' She stopped at the door.

'It's a Bank Holiday so you get Monday off legitimately this time.' He broke into laughter at his own joke, so volubly that Becky could still hear it at the end of the corridor.

# 5

David held his hands low in the deep white enamel sink, watching as the jet of water chiselled off the soft grey clay coating his fingers. It dropped in small clods which took a while to dissolve, leaving smears across the smooth bottom of the sink. With his fingers clean but still wet, he undid the knot of the bandana round his head, fixed not as a fashion statement, but to keep his hair out of his eyes. Not paying monthly trips to the barber's was one of the more trivial pleasures of early retirement. Absently scratching his scalp, musing that with a few more weeks' neglect he would be sufficiently hirsuite to fix his unruly fair mop into a decent ponytail, he stepped back into the studio for a fresh appraisal of his day's efforts. There was still a long way to go. A very long way, he decided, walking round the bust, which was supposed to be of his own head, and frowning at the difficulty of the task he had set himself. On a wheel there was at least a centre point, a guiding core, even when the edges took on a life of their own. Sculpting from a raw lump of nothing was quite another matter, especially if searching for the elusive likeness of one's own features. If it failed he would throw the thing away, he vowed, slipping a damp coth over the still shapeless mass and stowing it at the back of a cupboard. Even though Anna sweetly claimed to be impressed by every single one of the innumerable bowls and vases already lining the shelves of his studio he wanted his Christmas present to be really special. Something that truly marked this new departure in his life. He had once been quite good. Good enough probably to have gone to art college. But then he had been good at maths too, and physics and business studies, and at nineteen the idea of being a penurious student for the rest of his life had held little appeal.

David retrieved his watch from his jeans pocket and slipped it onto his wrist, noting with a twist of resentment that with Becky's last-minute alteration to her travelling plans only half an hour remained before he would have to set out for the station. When he had agreed to her coming to stay he had not envisaged the commitment breaking into his afternoon; a precious afternoon, still brilliant with the sort of daylight that the strip lighting above his work benches would have to manufacture artificially for most of the six months that lay ahead. Above him, great shafts of buttery afternoon sun were still streaming in through the huge panels of glass laid into the tiled roof of the barn, crisscrossing the quarry floor like the beams of a hundred torches. Although hot outside, the high ceiling and stone walls ensured that none of the heat's oppression filtered into the studio. The air remained cool and dry, smelling faintly still of paint and fresh wood. The two huge ceiling fans, installed between the rafters as a precaution against the greenhouse effect of so much glass, had hung unused all summer, looking like the propellers of small aircraft.

Stepping outside, David felt the warmth of the afternoon punch his chest. Though the radio had reported torrential rain in London, it had yet to affect the West Country. Crossing the courtyard to the garage, green and yellow specks danced in front of his eyes until he slipped on his sunglasses, which bestowed a gentle bluish tinge on everything instead, even the metallic silver of his Mercedes. It was a relief to get inside, to switch on the engine and feel the icy draughts of air-conditioning dry the moisture from his skin. He accelerated a little recklessly down the drive, enjoying as always the crunching resistance of the gravel under the car wheels, made somehow more dramatic by the burst of music from the CD player. It was Mozart, a passage he was getting to know rather well, even if he didn't exactly like it, not yet anyway. Teaching himself to like opera was something about which he felt rather determined. With the time now for such indulgences he had even bought a self-help book on the subject which was full of advice about listeners letting the passion of the music wash over them and not worrying about the daftness of the plot.

Preoccupied by such endeavours, David braked sharply to avoid a waddling figure in a voluminous pink T-shirt and white track-suit bottoms, whom he recognised a little belatedly as Mrs Costa, the woman from the village employed by Anna to clean their house. She was clearly in a hurry, walking as quickly as her round frame and wide flip-flops would allow. Pulled low over her head was a fluorescent pink baseball cap, from the back of which sprouted, as if growing independent of its owner, threads of stringy bleached hair. On hearing the roar of the car, she looked up in horror and took a small leap sideways, almost toppling into the ditch which ran along the verge.

'I was just on my way to yours,' she exclaimed, recovering herself as David switched off the tape and wound down the window to apologise. 'I know I said I'd be there this morning but Bella – that's my daughter – came down from London yesterday. She arrived ever so late – right out of the blue as well – and so I didn't like to rush off first thing. And then we had some lunch and the day sort of slipped me by . . . still I'm here now and that's what matters. I'll scoot round in no time, have the place looking nice for the weekend. I'll need the key though, of course, unless Mrs Lawrence is in that is . . .' She broke off, some of her certainty faltering at the look on David's face. It was a look of deep irritation, reflecting both his failure to remember the weekly clean and a strong disinclination either to wrest the front door key from his key ring or to return to the house in order to let her in himself.

'You should have called,' he said testily. 'I'm in a hurry to meet a train – my wife's sister is coming for the weekend. In fact it really isn't terribly convenient for you to start cleaning now.' He looked pointedly at his watch. It was almost four o'clock. Becky's train was due in at ten past.

'I see.' She withdrew her face from the frame of the open window, evidently affronted.

'Hang on a minute, I didn't mean . . .' David had to lean across the passenger seat to recapture her attention. As he did so he noticed a large farm vehicle approaching from behind. Aware of the need to pull over and fearful that he might run his employee down in the process, he gestured at her to get in the car. A few moments later the vehicle lumbered past, showering them and the road with handfuls of dusty hay.

'Oh, I say, this cold air is just lovely, isn't it?' Mrs Costa, now beaming in appreciation, all affrontery forgotten, was holding both hands towards the cold air jetting out of the air-conditioning vent in front of her. Seen close to, David could not help noticing that the skin across her cheeks and nose was a riotous map of broken blood vessels, while the rest of her exposed flesh looked loose and mottled. Although probably in her thirties – Anna said the daughter was in her late teens – she looked considerably older, in spite of the bold chemical whiteness of her hair.

'Now where were we?' He had to make an effort to sound friendly, to suppress not just impatience but a cruel reflex of distaste. Physical beauty, in all its manifestations had always mattered deeply to him. How a person presented themselves to the outside world in his view spoke volumes both about their capabilities and state of inner well-being. Seeing the puffy moist face of the woman next to him, the rings wedged into her fleshy fingers, the eye-pouches and blotchy complexion, he felt he already knew more than he ever wanted to about the ugly minutiae of her life. Just as, in contrast, the first glimpse of Anna a decade before, at a party given by mutual friends, had told him that he was in the presence of a woman with whom he would be prepared to consider sharing the rest of his life. Not just because of the effortless elegance of her slim limbs, the lustre of her eyes and hair, of which he believed at once that it would be impossible to tire, but because she had the rare gift of one who seemed to glow from the inside, who managed to light up a room even when she was standing in its furthest, darkest corner. He had wanted instantly and overwhelmingly, to know more about her, to receive the full beam of her attention, not only to bask in her beauty, but to be the accoutrement that completed it. Though the other vital things – being on the same wavelength and sharing similar ambitions – had come later, they remained, even after a decade together, so deeply interwoven with the strong and glowing image the pair of them presented to the world that David would have found it hard to separate the two.

Beside him, Mrs Costa, now apparently in a state of deep relaxation, had closed her eyes and was absently picking at a small scab on the bridge of her nose. Tempted though David was to deposit her back outside her own front door, to leave the house in its state of mild disarray until the following week, he knew that Anna would find such a decision deeply disappointing. After months of shaking workmen's dust out of clothes and tea cups, she liked to arrive home on a Friday to a clean and tidy house. And who could blame her? he reasoned, shooting Mrs Costa an encouraging smile as he succumbed to the inevitable necessity of switching

41

off the engine in order to extricate his door keys from the key-ring.

'If I had my own set . . .' she ventured slyly.

'Yes, but as we've discussed before, there's really no need, with me at home, is there?' David interjected, keeping the smile in place. 'And if you could begin with the guest room – the yellow one with the ensuite – that would be marvellous. Now, I'm afraid I've got to hurry or my sister-in-law will think I've abandoned her.'

A few minutes later he swung the Mercedes into Balcombe Station's tiny car park. Becky, looking far from abandoned, was sitting outside the main entrance, leaning up against a bulging holdall, her face tipped up towards the sun. As usual, she was dressed in what David regarded as the wardrobe of a teenager, comprising on this occasion a pair of large combat-style shorts and a sleeveless white T-shirt which finished somewhere around her rib cage. Seeing her, he paused for a moment, marvelling as he always did at the depth of the contrast between the sisters, one so slight and dark, the other so blooming and golden-skinned. Though youthful photos of his mother-in-law and a few blurred images of the father made it clear how such features originated, it still struck him as remarkable that there seemed to have been so little fusion between the two sides of the family. In contrast, people had always known at once that he and Jonathan were brothers; although snaps from Canberra, where his sibling now resided, showed that age and environment were at last taking their toll, there had once been such a physical likeness that they had occasionally been mistaken for twins.

'Hi, sorry I'm a bit late. Contretemps with a farm truck and a cleaning lady – a deadly combination, believe me.' He grinned, rolling his eyes, secretly musing upon the curious fact that the reality of talking to his sister-in-law always caused him much more pleasure than the prospect of having to do so.

'Oh, hi David. You look well. Country life obviously suits you.' Becky got to her feet slowly, holding one hand to her eyebrows and squinting in a bid to fend off the glare of the sun. With it raining so badly in London she hadn't thought to pack her sunglasses. 'Or maybe it's just being a man of leisure.'

'A man of leisure, bollocks.' He laughed smoothly, bending down to kiss her cheek and then slinging her bag over his shoulder. 'I don't know how I ever found time to go to the office.'

'New car,' she murmured, following him down the path to the car park.

He nodded. 'New model. Always trade up every year.'

'Right.' Becky stood and watched as he stowed her bag in the boot, noting the even crease in his jeans and the crisp white T-shirt, stretched becomingly across the broad chest and flat stomach, developed, as she knew from Anna, over years of private and conscientious exercise.

'I like the hair by the way, very Ally McBeal.'

'Thanks.' She grinned, so pleased and caught off guard by the compliment that she found herself blurting, 'And yours looks good too – long like that – very Bohemian,' when in fact she thought it looked dreadful.

David pulled a comical face, which metamorphosed into a scowl as Becky responded to the empty dappled lanes stretching ahead of them by winding down the window and sticking her head into the onrush of air like an eager dog. 'We could have the air-con on,' he ventured, raising his voice above the noise.

'No, I like this,' she shouted back, enjoying the whip of her hair across her mouth and eyes. 'The train was so stuffy . . . and London . . .' She twisted her face. 'Sorry again by the way, about dumping myself on you early, but I had all my gear for the weekend at work and so when I got given the afternoon off . . .'

'No problem.'

'When will Anna get back?'

'She's due in on the seven thirty-eight. It's usually earlier but she's got some meeting or other with a new producer, about this new phone-in programme she's planning . . . I say, do you mind if I just . . . ?' He pressed a button on a panel between their two seats, causing the window under Becky's elbow to rise upwards. 'There, that's better.' He raked the hair back off his face. 'Now I can see the road and hear what you're saying. We've put you in the yellow room, by the way – I hope you'll like it.'

'I'm sure I will,' replied Becky drily, resuming her study of the coloured bands of countryside streaking past her, unable to feel as enthusiastic about them now that they were hermetically sealed behind the car window.

Some ten minutes later, half a mile beyond the end of Balcombe village, David slowed for the final turn towards the house. The drive had received fresh layers of gravel since Becky's last visit and was bordered on either side by huge and vividly flowering shrubs. Up ahead the honey-coloured stone of the house, now free of scaffolding and skips, glowed a golden brown in the afternoon sunshine, the lawns surrounding it as spruce and smooth as golfing greens.

'It's like something out of a glossy magazine,' she exclaimed to Joe, describing the scene on her mobile a short while later, taking the chance to call from the relative privacy of her yellow bedroom. 'I mean, the whole place is so unbelievably *perfect*, it's unreal. You should see his studio – the old barn – it is just immaculate, I swear I could be a brilliant potter if you put me in there. And the stuff he's making – there are shelf-loads of pots and vases and some tea cups with big handles – is really good – though I didn't rave too much because I just couldn't bring myself to make him feel any more pleased with himself than he does already . . .'

'So you're having a good time then?' Joe laughed, pleased to hear some of the old exuberance in his wife's tone. 'How come you're there so bloody early anyway?'

'Oh yes, I meant to tell you. The most amazing thing happened today. Well, two amazing things. Mike swanned in to say they'd won this massive new account and then told Juliette and me to take the afternoon off.'

'Brilliant.'

'So I caught an earlier train,' she rushed on, deciding at the last minute to keep the business of the job offer to herself for the time being. Partly because the crackle on her mobile was not exactly oiling the wheels of the conversation and partly because she was not yet straight in her own mind as to how to respond to it.

A soft knock at her door was followed by David's head appearing round the corner. 'Just to say, tea in the garden when you're ready,' he whispered, gesturing apologetically when he saw she was on the phone.

'Look, Joe, I've got to go.'

'Me too. Ruth and Jenny are due any minute. Have a nice evening – I'll call tomorrow.'

Before going downstairs Becky had a final tour of her bedroom, stroking the luxurious furnishings and admiring the prints on the walls. The house in Kensington had been lovely, but on nowhere near so grand a scale. Next to the door were some framed before-and-after photographs of the building work. In one Anna, wearing dungarees and a hairband, posed with a huge hammer, pretending to swing it at the wall, her brow creased in mock exertion. In another she stood with her arm round David; the pair of them were smiling at each other, their handsome faces radiating deep and mutual satisfaction at the structural transformations taking place around them. Like actors on a set, Becky mused, thinking at the same time that people's houses were indeed a sort of stage, full of props that reflected how they lived. Or how they wished to live. Or how they wished to be judged to live, she pondered, thinking with a spurt of fondness of her own home, which for all its cracks had the comfortable used feel of a pair of favourite jeans. Crossing to the window, she spied David in the garden below, sitting with a tray of tea things on the verandah of a hexagonal summerhouse, set on the back edge of the lawn where the grass lengthened round the feet of several fruit trees and a small weeping willow.

'How on earth do you decide where to put yourself?' she exclaimed, joining him a couple of minutes later, curling her bare legs under her as she sank into a wide-backed wickerwork chair.

'What do you mean? Tea? Or a soft drink? I've brought nettle cordial and some fizzy water, cold I promise.' He touched the bottle of water, which was dark blue and as elegantly shaped as one of the vases in his studio. Leaning forwards, catching a fleeting glimpse of her reflection in the curve of the glass, Becky was struck by the realisation that wealth allowed the mundane to be made beautiful. In her household water came out of a tap or ugly plastic bottles, the make depending on offers in the supermarket. 'Tea please. Not too much milk. I just mean that you've got so many places to choose from – the kitchen, the sitting room, the den, the conservatory, or this lovely little house – how on earth do you decide where to put yourself?' She laughed, fearful suddenly that the question sounded impertinent. She had known for years that David and Anna were raking it in, but had never before seen the spoils of their labours on such obvious display.

'Strict rotation,' he quipped, looking pleased rather than offended, 'or whichever location keeps me furthest from the creature currently knocking chunks out of the furniture with a hoover. Mrs Costa. Our very own local treasure.' He made a face. 'To be avoided at all costs. You'd have thought with all the talk of rural unemployment you could get someone decent, wouldn't you? But Anna assures me she's the best money can buy. She's done your room though,' he added with a quick smile, 'so you're safe. What did you think, by the way? Do you like it?'

Becky took a sip of her tea, happy to note that it was not only the perfect temperature but also the perfect shade of brown. 'I think,' she said slowly, 'that the pair of you have made this into one of the most lovely places on the planet and if you're not careful I might seriously consider staying full-time. I'm good at hoovering, I could do Mrs Costa's job. And Joe could cook. How about that for a cool idea?'

David laughed easily. 'Sorry, no vacancies at present. Mrs Costa needs to keep herself in sherry and cigarettes and Anna still claims that cooking relaxes her, which is just as well as I'm crap at it. Thinking of taking a course actually, I was going to consult Joe . . . how is he, by the way? How's it going at the place in Clapham? I keep telling Anna that next time we need to eat out in town we must go there. We're having a housewarming, by the way,' he added, switching subjects in midstream, 'Anna's idea entirely – October 17th – invitations to be issued shortly—'

'I think your local treasure wants you,' Becky interrupted with a giggle, catching sight of a large woman lumbering towards them across the lawn. David rose to go and meet her but she waved him back with a duster.

'Took a phonecall,' she gasped, wheezing audibly as she arrived at the summerhouse and leaning on one of the wicker chairs to catch her breath. 'Mrs Lawrence – the trains are all up the spout and could you put the pheasant in – seven thirty at a hundred and eighty – I think that was it.' She tugged off her hat and began batting it at her face like a fan. 'Gawd, this heat, really gets you doesn't it?'

47

'It certainly does,' agreed Becky, feeling a faint need to make up for the fact that David was looking not so much grateful as irritated.

'I could have spoken to Anna myself if you'd called me,' he said, ignoring Becky's efforts.

'She said just to pass on the message,' retorted his employee, turning on her heel and setting off back towards the house with all the look of someone embarking on a hike to the top of a high mountain.

'I really must get onto having a phone connection put down here,' David muttered, standing on the lawn staring after her, clicking his fingers in annoyance. 'Bollocks. It's the pheasant I'm worried about,' he added gravely, 'Anna does it marvellously, I'm bound to fuck it up.'

'We'll attack the problem together,' Becky promised. 'And I'm a dab hand at roast potatoes, even Joe says so.' She reached out of her creaky chair to pour more tea, unable to suppress the thought that if she lived in a palace with cleaning ladies and summerhouses it would take a lot more than a poxy roast dinner or a late train to get her annoyed.

# 6

Why was it, Becky wondered, tossing amongst feather pillows during the dawn hours of Saturday morning, that whenever she was presented with the opportunity of a long sleep, something intervened to prevent it. On this occasion a set of wind chimes had been the culprit, a delicate mobile of thin white birds which she remembered seeing that afternoon, hanging from the branch of a small apple tree by the kitchen door. Innocent in the stillness of the afternoon, they had begun emitting a maddening, tuneless jangle during the night, stirred into activity by the stiff breeze blowing in the bad weather predicted by the forecasters. To compound the interruption, the canary yellow curtains, so appealing a panoply of colour across the bedroom windows, had proved remarkably ineffectual when it came to the business of keeping out light. By five o'clock the first silver rays of morning were slanting through the flimsy material and directly onto the bed, driving Becky to try the impossibly suffocating challenge of sleeping with the covers pulled over her head.

Anna had eventually got home at eight thirty, the beam of her Saab headlights across the windows causing a flurry of last-minute activity with cutlery and basters in the kitchen. She had sailed into the house a few seconds later and taken charge, whisking the lumps out of the gravy and directing David to a drawerful of clean napkins and table mats. The pheasant was tasty, if a little dry and had been followed by a fruit tart which Anna had transported all the way from some delicatessen in

London. The conversation flowed smoothly, covering a range of untaxing topics, from plans for the housewarming to the limitations of the national rail service. That it was a little dull did not bother Becky unduly. She had long since accepted that she would never have particularly meaningful exchanges with Anna in the presence of their husbands, or anyone else for that matter. As close sisters there was too much shared and private territory for outsiders to be satisfactorily absorbed into the loop. Much as there was between married couples, she had reflected, watching David and Anna discuss, rather stiffly, the necessity of getting a phoneline installed in the summerhouse and wondering how different the exchange would have been had she not been there to witness it.

After the meal David made a big to-do of being allowed to clear the plates and load the dishwasher, before herding them into the sitting room with a tray of coffee. He sat with his arm round Anna on the sofa, leaving Becky to face them in the armchair, feeling for the first time since her arrival the surfacing of the faint, but ever-present proprietorial tension that had always existed between her and her brother-in-law.

'Well, night then,' she had ventured at last, judging from the determined grip of David's arm and Anna's suppressed yawns that there was little chance of a sisterly heart-to-heart that night, 'I'll retire to my buttercup haven in the west wing.' Once in bed, she had lain stiff and alert between the crisp unfamiliar linen, unable to relax until she had heard the creak of footsteps on the landing, followed by the soft closing of their bedroom door. Creaking of a different kind a little while later however, barely audible but persistent through the wall separating their bedrooms, caused the next set-back to her hopes of a peaceful and uninterrupted night. Once identified, she could not block the sound from her mind, nor the images accompanying it. The thought of Anna being shagged senseless was not appealing. Almost as bad as parents, Becky decided, pulling the pillow over her head in a bid to muffle the noise but only to find an ancient memory bursting inside her head, of her father arched over her mother, his bottom pasty white, his head swivelled round staring at her in surprise. Aged just ten, standing bleary with sleep in the doorway, it had been the awkwardness of the pose that had struck her most, the fact that her mother was half pressed up against the wall with her father slanted over her, when all her as yet limited imaginings about the sexual act had envisaged something balletic and symmetrically composed, like swimming or doing a star jump.

When the orchestra of wind chimes was joined by the Balcombe dawn chorus, a sound on a scale far exceeding anything managed by the motley creatures inhabiting the straggling trees of Balham, Becky gave up and flung herself out of bed. Tiptoeing past David and Anna's door, she made her way downstairs with the intention of fixing herself a cup of tea and possibly even browsing herself back to sleepiness with the aid of one of the glossy magazines Anna kept in a rack next to the kitchen sofa. In the hall she paused, straining for sounds beyond the tick of the mahogany wall clock, its huge white face offering the grim reminder that it was still only half past five. A moment later an ear-splitting wail exploded around her, followed closely by the sound of racing footsteps and concerned voices from the landing. She looked up to see both David and Anna at the top of the stairs, their hair wild, their dressing-gowns still half round their shoulders.

'It's all right, it's only Becky,' Anna shouted, somewhat unnecessarily, Becky felt, given that she was standing right in front of them.

'I'll call the police,' David shouted back, turning and disappearing in the direction of the bedroom.

'The police? Why?' Becky gasped, still rooted to the spot, feeling like a rabbit caught in headlights. Anna hurried past her and began punching at a panel of numbers in a small cupboard by the front door.

'They'll come otherwise, you dope.'

'Sorry.' Even with the alarm turned off its piercing ring seemed to echo in the silence. 'Sorry,' Becky said again, her voice small. 'It was those fucking wind chimes, they woke me up.'

To her relief Anna giggled, sinking onto the bottom stair and running her hands through her hair. 'Never mind.'

A moment later David reappeared on the landing, growled some sort of greeting and disappeared again.

'God, he's furious, isn't he?' Becky whispered, sinking down onto the stairs next to her sister.

'No, he doesn't get furious. It's one of the reasons I married him . . . we each keep our fury to ourselves . . .' She yawned deeply. 'Cup of tea?' As she made the suggestion she stood up, tightening the cord of her dressing-gown.

'Go back to bed, for God's sake, I feel guilty enough already.'

'I was awake anyway. And it's our fault – we should have warned you about the alarm. We only had it installed a couple of months ago.'

A few minutes later they were sitting end to end on the wide sofa in the sitting room, their hands round their mugs of tea and a plate of digestives balanced on a cushion between them. Pleased to find herself with exactly the opportunity for which she had been hoping just a few hours before, Becky tucked her legs right up under her nightie and launched into an account of the events at work the previous afternoon.

'That's absolutely brilliant, you clever *clever* girl . . . but you're not sure whether you want it, are you?' Anna added at once, interpreting correctly the confusion of pleasure and perplexity in her sister's face.

'Exactly. I know I *ought* to want it . . .'

'What does Joe say?'

'I haven't had a chance to tell him.' Becky sighed. 'More money would be fantastic, obviously, and of course it is kind of flattering, and Joe says things aren't going to be straight on his front for at least two more years . . . so I guess I might as well accept it and see what happens.'

'Two years is a long time,' said Anna quietly, 'to be doing something you don't want, I mean.'

'That's true.' Becky sighed again, absently nibbling the edge of her biscuit, noting with mild interest that Anna was on her fourth. 'As things are, Joe and I hardly ever see each other. I tell you, this restaurant business has about the crappiest hours any job could possibly have; they call it split shifts, but by the time you've got home after the lunch session it's time to go back again . . . Anna, are you okay? You look sort of . . . weird.'

'Fine . . . breathing . . . give me a minute.' She had folded her long legs into a yogic position and was inhaling noisy gulps of air and then making comical pouts to let it out again, hollowing her cheeks and mouth like someone expelling smoke rings.

Becky watched, fascinated. 'Is it something you should teach me? I mean, are you on a higher plane of being or something?'

'No.' She let out one long last breath and turned to look at her sister. 'I'm pregnant. And before you say anything,' she held up her hand to forestall the possibility of Becky disobeying the instruction, 'no, I am not pleased, no, David doesn't know and no, I'm not going to keep it. I only had it confirmed yesterday – it was a meeting with a doctor not a producer that made me so late last night.' She reached for the last biscuit, broke it in two and offered one half to Becky, who, still mute with shock, shook her head. 'I'm a very rare bird, apparently . . . I went onto a low dosage minipill thing last year; one per cent failure rate, looks like I'm the one per cent.'

'But Anna, shouldn't you at least think about it or talk to—'

'I have thought about it. A lot. Neither of us is ready for children. David's given up his job to enjoy his freedom and I want him to be able to do just that without being shackled either with a baby or the guilt of having decided to be selfish and not have one. And my job is just going brilliantly at the moment – I couldn't – I won't compromise that.' She was clenching her empty tea mug, Becky noticed, although her voice was cool and very composed. 'I don't want it to be a big deal, Becks, I've told you because you're you and because I had to tell *somebody*.' She smiled. 'I don't feel remotely sad about it. I'm in control of my life and have every intention of staying that way. I want to get my career sorted and then see how I feel about babies.'

'But won't David guess?' Becky ventured after a few moments, impressed in spite of herself at this new evidence of a strength of will on which she herself had relied many times in the past. 'I mean . . . well, you do look a bit pale and if you carry on like that . . .' She looked pointedly at the empty plate.

Anna laughed and Becky found herself joining in. 'I get a bit nauseous and eating helps, but I'm not actually being sick. And anyway, it won't be for long. For a termination you have to have consultations and so on first, but I should be back to normal in no more than a couple of weeks.'

'Great,' said Becky, still shaken but recognising from years of acquaintance with such matters that Anna's tone of voice precluded any invitation to discuss the matter further. 'God, look it's raining.' They both turned to stare out of the window where grey flecks of moisture were sliding silently down the panes of glass. 'A wet Bank Holiday. It must have followed me from London,' Becky groaned, feeling dimly – perversely – responsible.

'I think it's rather nice,' murmured Anna, curling deeper into her corner of the sofa and closing her eyes. A few minutes later she was sound asleep, both hands under her cheek to cushion her face. Becky, who could only sleep horizontally, in a bed with a pillow, watched in some fascination. Free now from the burden of having her reactions scrutinised, she was aware too of a quickening of something beneath the emotions she had expressed out loud. Something dark and faintly celebratory; something connected to the fact that for Anna to have a baby on top of all the other blessings in her life would have been a surfeit of riches indeed. Sisterly quips on the subject over the years had always been based on the assumption that Becky would be the first to reach the milestone of motherhood. An assumption which Becky had not only done nothing to dispel but also come to regard along the lines of a God-given right.

Which was irrational, foolish and also very mean, Becky scolded herself, carefully swinging her legs to the floor and slipping off her dressing-gown. Anna stirred, pressing her lips together as if about to speak, but uttering no sound. Becky gently draped the dressing-gown over her, unable to resist noting as she did so the striking flatness of the stomach beneath the white cotton nightie, thinking to herself that it looked barely capable of accommodating a square meal, let alone a baby.

# 7

A hundred and fifty miles away Becky and Anna's mother, Stella Freeman, stared at the same deluge from her two-bedroomed cottage on the outskirts of Amersham. She was always awake at dawn, one of the more ironic tricks of the advancing years being that, having arrived at a stage in life when long bouts of sleep would have been positively welcomed, they seemed increasingly hard to come by. She could remember as if it was yesterday a time when the nights had never been long enough, when the buzz of Colin's alarm would leave them groaning with reluctance at the need to rise and face the day. Sometimes the past seemed like another life to her, like a story she had once read of an interesting person who had done interesting things. And sometimes it felt close enough to touch, she reflected with a sigh, slipping one hot veiny foot on top of the eiderdown, remembering how once, long ago, before France and acrimony, Colin had liked to kiss her feet, running his tongue up and down the valleys between her toes. In truth such attentions had been more ticklish than erotic; but she had loved the pleasure of his pleasure, the sheer joy of having a man whom she adored adore her back. These days the only people who touched her were the GPs at the surgery in South Road and the young chiropodist whose services she called upon from time to time, a nice girl with dark hair like Becky's, and quick clever hands which gently worked the tools round her yellowing nails and across the outcrops of hard skin on the soles of her feet. She had a massage too, every so often, when she felt bold enough – in need of physical contact enough – to drum out thoughts of what the stringy girls at the beauty parlour must think of her saggy hide, how they must snigger, correctly, that such attentions were the closest any lonely decrepit widow in her sixties would get to sex.

From the small radio on her bedside table a weather update informed Stella of the already obvious fact that it was raining and would continue to do so throughout the Bank Holiday weekend. She slipped the foot back under the covers and turned on her side, away from the slice of dismal weather apparent between the gap in the curtains and towards the mantelpiece arrayed with cards. There were four in all, each a design of flowers. The largest was from her brother, Philip, who had taken her under his wing after her move back to England twenty years before, but since retired to a draughty cottage on the edge of the Norfolk Broads. The others were from Colin's old friend Marcel, who always wrote on the anniversary of his death, and her daughters, Anna's packed with words and assurances, Becky's short and tightly written. Had she been a bad mother? Stella wondered, glimpsing the restrained inscription inside the last card, recalling the drawn-out business of her youngest's teenage rebellion and her ineffectiveness in the face of it. Her brother and various sympathetic teachers had offered what support they could, pointing out obvious causes, like the trauma of Colin's death and the upheaval of moving back to England. But in the end nothing had constituted much practical assistance in the daily challenges Stella had faced alone, of getting Becky to do her homework, encouraging her to comply with at least the spirit of the uniform regulations and trying not to mention the unsightly red suck marks which protruded regularly over the collar of her shirt, scarring the pretty whiteness of her neck.

Stella sighed as the memories returned, as familiar as

worn photographs, clearer with each passing year, as if the longsightedness that affected her eyes affected the process of her inner vision too. Turning down the volume on the radio and pulling the lapels of her lilac bed jacket more tightly around her, she reached for a book to help while away the time. It was a courtroom thriller, full of technicalities about timing and bomb assembly which she read without managing fully to understand. The thrust of the story was good; she particularly liked the lawyer who strode around looking handsome and being brave, busily making up for a dark past so that the young girl he was defending could love him after all. Such scenarios were of great comfort to Stella, who resented deeply that in her own case a profoundly unsatisfactory past seemed to persist nonetheless in defining her, that she remained in its thrall. Living in delapidated French farmhouses in order to restore them and sell them on to Europeans living out Peter-Mayle-style fantasies had been fun at first. With the birth of Anna however, and then Becky three years later, the glamour of inhabiting building sites with temperamental water systems and sticky walls, had quickly begun to pall. In contrast, Colin, the son of parents who had lived in the same street for thirty years, genuinely believed that their somewhat unconventional lifestyle offered a unique and enriching upbringing for any child. And while it was true that the girls themselves had showed little outward signs of suffering, Stella had felt increasingly as if she was hanging on to her existence by her fingernails. Even now, two decades on, the sight of builders' dust could make her feel queer. Visiting Anna during the first chaotic months in Dorset, seeing the skips and bare paint-splashed floorboards, she had half expected Colin to come striding through a doorway, his jeans tatty and falling round his skinny hips, his dark hair flopping in his eyes, throwing his arms around and issuing commands in his diabolical French, pretending to rant, but loving every minute of it. During the last couple of years he had kept promising that each housing project would be their last, only to find a pretext – usually financial – for one more. Sometimes, in very dark moments, Stella even wondered if it wasn't concussion that had killed him so much as a wilful decision to hold his breath until his lungs burst. So that he didn't have to keep those promises. So that she, Stella, couldn't pursue her own small dream of suburban comfort and an English education for their daughters without feeling like a deserter.

She had been dozing, Stella realised, opening her eyes and seeing from her mantelpiece clock that it was nearly ten o'clock. Outside the rain was falling as heavily but from a lighter sky. Her book had collapsed shut beside her, crushing some of the pages. Reaching across it, she picked up the telephone and dialled Anna's number.

'Darling, it's Mum. How are you both?'

'Really good thanks. It's bucketing down, but we're going to an antiques market someone recommended on the other side of Skaneford – I'm still hoping to find a rocking chair for the summerhouse and maybe a little desk too, one of those small ones with lots of secret drawers . . .'

'I suppose you get it from your father,' Stella murmured, the thought escaping before she had time to rein it in.

'Get what?'

'I just meant . . . putting that house together . . . sometimes it reminds me of him.'

'Except that I have no intention of moving anywhere else,' quipped Anna laughing easily and making a face at David, who was standing at the kitchen door tossing his car keys from palm to palm. 'We've got Becky here – would you like a word?' She glared at Becky who was shaking her head furiously.

'Oh yes,' said Stella, in truth sharing some of her youngest daughter's anxiety at the prospect of conversation, various efforts over the years having illuminated the sorry fact that a desire for reconciliation was not enough to ensure its realisation. The old patterns of conflict surfaced anyway, seemingly of their own accord.

'Sorry you've not been well,' ventured Becky stiffly.

'That's very sweet of you, darling. I'm much better now, thank goodness. And I got your card – lovely poppies – so nice to know one is being thought of. And how's Joe?'

'Fine.'

'All the rage now isn't it? Men cooking and so on . . . they're on the telly all the time . . . quite the thing.'

'He's doing really well,' snapped Becky, detecting not an attempt at empathy so much as critical incomprehension.

'I'm sure he is, dear,' replied Stella, somewhat doggedly, 'I'm sure he is.'

'Anyway, I'd better go – we're off on a furniture hunt, though it looks to me as if they've got quite enough already,' she added, in a bid to be light-hearted but receiving a beady look from David for her pains. He had given up on his pose in the doorway and was sitting behind a newspaper on the sofa, shaking the pages noisily. Though he had brushed aside all her apologies about the alarm, Becky guessed that a lot of this barely concealed impatience was to do with her, that he was counting down the hours until the following morning when she would disappear back to London.

'One thing before you go, Becky dear . . . your birthday . . . is there anything special you would like? After all, it's quite a milestone, isn't it, getting to thirty?'

'I guess it is,' Becky murmured. 'I can't think of anything off-hand. A cheque would be nice of course, or vouchers, they're always handy. Now I really *have* to go,' she insisted, even though David looked at last properly settled behind the paper and Anna was heaping fat spoonfuls of fresh coffee into a cafetière. 'Bye.' She dropped the receiver with a groan. Whereupon Anna spun round, slamming the lid on the coffee pot.

'Why do you have to be like that?'

Becky blinked in astonishment. 'Like what?'

'Like you were – you barely spoke.'

'Yes we did . . . and anyway you didn't exactly chat for hours, did you?'

'That was because she asked to talk to you.'

'Correction. You suggested she talk to me and she felt she had to say yes. Being related to someone doesn't mean you've got to like them, you know Anna.'

'I'll try to remember that, Becky. In the meantime you might care to remember that as your mother she deserves respect.'

'Respect? When all she's done is sit on her bottom for twenty years, living off the life insurance policy of a man she didn't love, picking holes in me for recreation . . .'

'Hey, calm down, both of you,' interjected David, prompted at last to peer over the top of the paper by the realisation that the conversation was in danger of growing seriously heated.

'I am calm,' Anna retorted, slopping coffee into three mugs and then marching out of the room.

'She's tired I think,' ventured Becky, in truth a little shaken and remembering with a guilty jolt that her sister was in a state of hormonally charged emotion. 'And she's right, I was foul. I am always foul to my mother.' She slumped down on the sofa next to David. 'Polite but foul. Don't you think that's the worst thing – civility between people who are meant to be close?'

David, who had for years maintained only the most superficial and deeply courteous relationship with various relatives, including his own parents, knitted his brows in an effort to consider the matter. 'No,' he said at length, 'I don't think that's the worst thing.'

'I better go and see if she's all right.'

'You couldn't just pass over one of those coffees on the way could you? Shame to let them go cold.'

She found Anna in the utility room folding pants and socks into neat piles in the bottom of a laundry basket. 'Sorry. I am a cow to her, I know. I can't help it, it's like a' – she frowned, searching for the right word – 'a reflex. I expect her to criticise me. I feel that she is, even when she most likely isn't.'

'No, I'm the one who's sorry,' Anna insisted, deftly converting a pair of her husband's pants into a tidy blue envelope. 'Exploding like that . . . not me at all.' She shook her head. 'David and I never argue, as you know,' she added thoughtfully, 'we just walk away and calm down.'

'With the aid of the laundry?'

'Invariably.' They grinned at each other, putting the seal on the reconciliation. 'Do you want to tell David that we really are ready to go now whenever he gives the word?'

'Okay.' Becky paused in the doorway. 'By the way, shouldn't he be doing all that sort of thing these days?'

Anna made a face. 'I'm afraid running companies is not the best preparation for running households. Besides, I don't mind because he'd do it all wrong.' She tutted fondly, tugging a small crease out of a sock before tucking it deftly into its neighbour and placing it on top of the pile.

Becky left her to it, marvelling afresh not only at the generous nature of her sister, but at her ability to impose order on the outside world. And she's pregnant, she reflected, having to keep reminding herself of the fact, marvelling still more, sure that in a comparable position she would long since have been in a heap at Joe's feet sobbing for advice and sympathy about her options.

# 8

Joe peered through the porthole in the kitchen doors towards the dining room, wondering if the rumour about the restaurant critic was true. The pudding-faced, curly-haired man eating alone in the far corner, tapping somewhat gingerly at the caramelised lid of his crème brûlée, certainly looked just the type; there was a quiet arrogance to him, coupled with a heavy-lidded, slightly bored look suggestive of one who dined out all the time. Joe studied the suspect for a few moments longer, wishing he could be sure, wishing too that operations in the kitchen had gone a little more smoothly. Cooking, he had discovered, was as much a performing art as delivering the lines of a play or plucking the strings of a guitar; not just because one was following pre-rehearsed routines for the gratification of an audience, but also because the quality of the performance could vary so drastically from day to day. He had done nothing obviously wrong that night; no plate had been sent back with complaints about limp vegetables or lurking fish bones; but producing each dish had for some reason felt like a strain, as if everything was teetering on the brink of disaster. More than usually busy for a Saturday night, it had been a relief to get through the last orders and on to the desserts, most of which sat ready made in the fridge.

'Watch out – coming through.'

The girl called Trish, one of a team of three who waited at the tables, came bursting through the doors, her arms skilfully stacked with dirty crockery. 'Two coffees, one decaf espresso, one decaf cappuccino for table eight. And the fat Charlie in the corner wants a second pud,' she exclaimed with some triumph, having been a supporter of the rumour about him all along. 'Treacle tart. No cream. Though how anyone can eat treacle tart without cream beats me – I mean, it's like . . . like bread without butter, isn't it?' The rest of the staff, used to Trish, who was meek with diners but maintained a machine-gun commentary about her job and life in general within the safe confines of the kitchen, didn't bother to respond.

Joe cast a last glance through the porthole just before Trish careered back out again, using her bottom to open the doors. 'Hang on,' he called, signalling her back to check on the slice of tart, reassured to see that it was a triangle of perfection, a tempting toffee brown colour, latticed with pale strips of sandy pastry. 'Go on then – too late to do anything now. Ask him if everything was to his satisfaction.'

'Mr Jordan already has,' she retorted, referring to the owner of the restaurant who devoted so much time to patrolling tables that Joe was sure some of the customers nurtured secret desires to tell him to bugger off and leave them alone. In his own restaurant things would be different, he thought dreamily, undoing his apron and slipping into the staff bathroom to wash his hands; he would emerge after the cooking was done, approach only the foodie types who invited it, who would feel positively cheated going home without at least one discussion as to the perfect gestation period of a broad bean and whether asparagus should be steamed for two minutes or three. The Italian place had come on the market that week, for the bargain price of two hundred and sixty thousand pounds, which included the two-bedroomed flat above. He had looked round it twice already, with a pimply teenager of an estate agent who had done such a clumsy job of talking the place up that Joe was sure he was the only one to express an interest. It would mean selling Balham of course, and a bigger mortgage. His bank had refused even to discuss a loan but he had been in touch with some mortgage brokers who seemed to think they could sort something out. Although Joe knew it was foolish to get his hopes up, they kept soaring skywards of their own accord, fuelled by the wonderful thought of being his own boss at last, up to his ears in debt but at least in control of his life and doing something that he loved.

Entering the small cloakroom at the back of the restaurant, he tutted at the sight of a figure leaning against the frame of the door leading into the alleyway, his head under a cloud of cigarette smoke. 'Not quite time for that yet is it, Sam?'

'Guess not.' Sam, who was sullen and bony-faced but very able, took a greedy drag on the stub of the cigarette, pressing the cork between his lips, before flicking it out outside, an arc of glowing red in the darkness. 'You off then?'

'Yes – you won't see me till Tuesday.' Joe, now pulling out his bike leathers from a small metal wardrobe in the corner, felt a sudden rush of exultation. It was a long time since he had had any time off. His only free evening was Monday, which would for several weeks yet be taken up with his wine course – improbably, the least enjoyable of his many commitments, but one that he still regarded as essential. Though planning, eventually, to employ a sommelier of his own, knowing a bit about grapes and vintages had always struck him as a vital part of the make-up of any true restaurateur. Studying books and tasting on his own just hadn't worked. He could barely remember the names, let alone the flavours. Friends like Adrian, and David, his brother-in-law, who gargled expertly and made near-miss guesses about regions and dates before looking at the label, filled him with admiring envy.

'Something special going on, isn't there?' enquired Sam lazily. 'Anniversary or something.'

'Yes, my wife's birthday. The big three zero.' Joe made a face. 'In fact the birthday itself isn't till Thursday, but I've set everything up for this weekend so as to surprise her. She's one of those annoyingly inquisitve types – sniffing out secrets – very difficult to catch unawares. Lucien's going to hold the fort here – simplify the menu a bit – you'll hardly notice I'm gone,' he added, a small pathetic part of him hoping that the surly-faced boy would contradict him and insist that they'd be holding their breath for his return. But Sam merely shrugged, muttering, 'Have a good one then,' before disappearing back into the kitchens.

Joe made his way out of the back of the restaurant to the alleyway where he parked his bike. Several dustbins were lined along the pavement, all of them already full to overflowing. Steam was coming out of the wall vent into the kitchen, smelling faintly of fat and hanging in the air like thin mist. A sinister rustling noise behind the bins was followed by the appearance of a fat rat, which paused to twitch its nose at Joe before scuttling down a drain. Joe stared after it for a few moments, faintly appalled but telling himself he had no reason to be. He had read somewhere recently that no one in England was ever more than twelve yards from a rat, that the creatures were now so resilient and canny that the pest control people had abandoned conventional poisons in favour of special food that took their appetites away so that they unwittingly starved themselves out of existence. Thinking wryly that this particular creature had looked ready to explode with good health, he dug into his pocket for his keys and crossed the narrow cobbled street to his bike. Although it had at last stopped raining, the air felt chill and moist, as if any moment the drizzle might start again. Joe buttoned up his leather jacket and slotted his helmet onto his head, feeling as he always did when in his bike gear, both more protected from the world and more invincible. Riding the bike freed his mind up too, something of which he felt particularly in need that weekend, with all the maths on the Brixton place to mull over and the now imminent birthday treat, which he had been thinking about for weeks but only got around to organising at the last minute. He had originally hoped to use the whole of the Bank Holiday weekend, but Mr Jordan had been adamant that Lucien, his enthusiastic but somewhat clumsy assistant chef, could not manage a Saturday night alone. And then Ruth had asked him to have Jenny which had put the seal on things. Right from the beginning he had vowed never to shirk an opportunity to see his daughter. As well as the obvious pleasure of spending time with her, it seemed the least any separated parent could do to make up for the failure of providing a single and secure family home. Although Jenny had shown little pleasure at the sight of him recently, Joe reminded himself, flashing his headlight at an indecisive minivan, and frowning at the recollection of his daughter's sulkiness that weekend. Not even the sight of Johanna, generally regarded as the coolest and most favourite of her babysitters, had won her round. In spite of numerous suggestions of things they could do, she had spent most of his precious free time spreadeagled on the sofa with the TV remote, flicking through the channels and offering dull, monosyllabic responses to his attempts at conversation. Even pointing out the river delta on the bedroom ceiling had elicited only the mildest of smiles, as if she was humouring him instead of the other way round.

Joe was only two streets from home when a girl stepped in front of him, emerging from between two parked vans in a text book enactment of how not to cross a road. He had time to notice that she was scantily clad, in a tight vest top, silver stilettos and a matching shiny silver skirt that barely covered the swell of her buttocks, before the need to alter the direction of his front wheel registered in his mind. He braked and swerved, so suddenly and sharply, that the bike slid under him like a subsiding horse. Putting his foot down to try and correct this loss of balance, resulted only in pulling the thing further on top of him. He continued to slide for several yards across the wet tarmac, until eventually coming to a halt by the wheel of a parked car. Levering himself free, pleased and not a little astonished to find that his motorbike was in one piece and that he could still stand up, Joe looked back up the road to see that the girl remained exactly where she was, staring after him. Two passers-by, who had paused for the spectacle, hurried on.

'I'm fine, thanks,' he shouted.

She moved then, but very slowly, waiting for a distant car to approach and pass before crossing the road. Not shy so much as uninterested, Joe decided, watching her and letting out a gasp of astonishment as, instead of coming up to him, as he had expected, she turned on the heel of her platform boots and began to walk away.

'Hey.'

'I didn't do nothing,' she called, her voice tremulous but her stride unfaltering as she continued to walk away, the silver plastic of her skirt glittering like tinfoil in the darkness.

'Hang on . . .' It was only as Joe tried to run after her, with dim notions of proper apologies and explanations, that he felt the first twist of pain in his ankle. Unzipping his boot he saw that his ankle bone was already submerged by swelling and turning a vivid purplish blue. 'Hey,' he called, more meekly, only to look up and find that she had gone. He rode home slowly and with some difficulty, marvelling at such insouciance, but recognising that it constituted a kind of power. Later, sitting with a bag of organic petits pois pressed to his ankle, musing on Jenny whom the babysitter said had remained sullen, and on Becky, who hadn't called, Joe found himself wishing that he cared less about things, that he could be the sort of man who didn't notice other people's emotions and the often gruelling compulsion to respond to them.

The next morning Ruth arrived an hour earlier than they had agreed. Joe, still in his pyjamas, his eyes bloodshot with fatigue and his face unshaven, hobbled to the door expecting to find the paper-boy struggling to fit the Sunday newspaper through the letter flap.

'Were you still asleep?' she asked, lacing her incredulity with thinly disguised disapprobation. 'It's nine o'clock, you know.'

'Yes, I know and you said you'd come at ten.'

'Nine. I said nine,' she repeated stoutly, stepping through the door and turning to shake out her umbrella on the doorstep. She shook her head too, though her hair, recently cropped to a boyish half inch, looked perfectly dry. It had also received a fresh coating of henna, Joe noticed, seeing the shimmer of deep red amongst the brown. The observation triggered a vivid memory of Ruth bending over the basin in her bra and pants, scattering brown droplets across the basin and wall tiles as she dabbed at her hair with muddy-stained rubber gloves. He paused, struck momentarily by the intimacy of the image, contrasting so crudely with the separateness of the last six years.

'Whatever. It doesn't matter. How are you?'

'Fine thanks. Is Jenny ready?'

'Not quite.'

'Is she even up?' She peered past him down the hall, frowning at the realisation that Joe had yet to lay eyes on their daughter that morning.

'I thought I'd let her sleep.' He turned and led the way through to the kitchen, doing his best not to limp, dreading Ruth's enquiries on the subject, feeling suddenly that it would confirm the view she had of him – and which, increasingly, he had of himself – as someone who couldn't cope.

'You're limping.'

'A slight sprain. Coffee?'

She hesitated, dropping her bag onto the kitchen table and looking about her. 'Okay then. Thanks. You've got a new oven.'

'Yeah, well the old one was really past it and of course these days I need something with a little more subtlety than a blow torch.'

'Of course. Very smart,' she added, managing not to say, though he knew she wanted to, that it must have cost a lot of money. She had slung one leg over a kitchen chair and was sitting astride it, facing him over the back, looking far more complacent and at ease than she would had Becky been in the house. 'Things okay with you then?'

'Yes, fine. Great, in fact.' He paused, before adding, 'Though not, apparently, with Jenny.'

'And what on earth is that supposed to mean?' All the complacency had gone in an instant, replaced by a steeliness which Joe sensed had everything to do with a desire to protect herself rather than their daughter. He held out a mug of coffee, scalding his hand so that she could take the handle, but she ignored it.

'I just mean . . .' He set the mug down, shaking out the pain from his fingers. 'She didn't seem herself this time . . . very quiet . . . withdrawn even. I just wondered if something was going on at school or—'

'Or maybe it has something to do with the fact that this is the third time she's seen her father in as many months,' snapped Ruth, swinging herself off the kitchen chair and picking up her handbag. 'And I had to ask.'

Joe opened his mouth to deny the accusation but closed it again. He could feel his heart racing so badly that it seemed to be pummelling the inside of his T-shirt. She was right of course. Ruth was good at being right. 'I know I've not . . .'

'Damn right you haven't.'

'It's just been hard, what with the new job . . . it's not fair having her over if I'm not around . . . things won't be this hectic for ever.'

Ruth folded her arms, as if having to make a monumental effort to contain her impatience. 'Yes, well, perhaps you'd like to explain that to your daughter.'

'That is the problem, is it?'

'Of course it is Joe. What the hell else could it be? And now, if you don't mind, I'm going to wake her. We're going to Mum's and I promised we'd be there before lunch. Thanks, but I don't think I'll bother with the coffee after all.'

At the sound of Ruth's shrill voice calling up the stairs Joe felt his whole body go tense. He curled his hands more tightly round his coffee mug, wishing suddenly that she would leave, wishing too that he felt more in the mood for rushing across London and whisking his wife away on a birthday surprise.

'By the way,' declared Ruth, reappearing in the doorway, her jacket back on, 'you ought to know, I've met someone.'

Joe looked up. 'Good. I'm glad for you.'

'Sure you are.'

He smiled uncertainly, musing on the unhappy fact that divorcing Ruth had not released him from the duty of having to react to her, even if it was less frequently. 'That's great Ruth, really.'

'He's American. Over here with a firm of lawyers. Dalton and Chesapeake.'

'An American lawyer, eh? He must have money.'

'Honestly Joe, is that all you can . . . ?' She left the question hanging in the air, as if too disappointed to complete the sentence. 'I just thought you ought to know,' she continued wearily, 'that Glen and I . . . that it's serious.'

'Glen?'

'That's his name,' she said tightly, 'Glen Marshal.'

'Does he wear a badge?'

'That's it, go for the cheap crack, put me down, you always did, so why break the habit of a lifetime?' she snapped, seizing her bag off the table. 'And there was me thinking we could have a sensible discussion. Jenny, for God's sake hurry up,' she shouted, only to turn and find that her daughter was standing silently in the hall. 'Darling, there you are. Ready to go?' Jenny nodded, eyeing both her parents warily from behind the long pale brown strands of her fringe. 'Bye, Dad.'

'Come here then.' Joe set his coffee down and held out his arms. She approached slowly, the wide hems of her flares flapping round her trainers. 'Hey, sweetheart, you know Daddy loves you?' She said nothing but returned his hug with such ferocity that Joe felt a lump swell in his throat. 'We'll see more of each other soon, I promise, when things are a bit more sorted.'

Hobbling to the doorstep to wave them off, he experienced a fresh ache of helpless longing at the sight of his daughter's pale face pressed against the window, ghostly through the screen of rain. The quips to Ruth, about money and the badge, had been childish he knew, unforgivable in fact. They had slipped out without his meaning them to; a retaliation for her standing there all shiny-haired and smug, parading the fact that she, once so desperate and floundering, had got her life sorted while he seemed to have entered a new period of exhaustion and struggle. But there was Brixton, Joe reminded himself, slamming the door shut, clenching and unclenching his fists as he stared round the familiar dinginess of the hall. There was a way forward, always, if one looked for it hard enough.

# 9

—◆—

. 'It's mostly seaweed,' explained the girl cheerfully, fastening a plastic apron over her starchy white dress and scooping out a handful of the green sludge for Becky to examine. 'Full of nutrients and minerals, wonderful for invigorating the skin, getting rid of toxins and generally making you feel like a new woman. Smells lovely too, don't you think?' She held the tub out for Becky to sniff, which she did tentatively, breathing salt and tangy cucumber. 'After you've undressed – pop your clothes into one of those lockers and put the key round your wrist – take a towel and go into one of the chambers where you'll find several tubs of this seaweed extract and a shower to rinse it off afterwards.'

'So I just smear it on?' asked Becky doubtfully.

'Exactly. Use as much as you want and then relax for maybe fifteen or twenty minutes – each chamber is kept very warm and cosy – and then, when you are ready, use the hand shower to rinse it off. Afterwards some people like a plunge in the cold pool – through those doors there – but that's entirely up to you. If you need any help at any stage just press the red button next to the chamber door. Okay?'

'Great,' replied Becky, managing a smile, but wishing that Joe's birthday bonanza could have involved something fractionally more mundane, like a pedicure or a facial. Or even a manicure, she mused, starting to unbutton her shirt, distracted for a moment at the notion of having the bitten edges of her fingernails smoothed and transformed into a set of long pearly talons that she could click over her computer keyboard, like Juliette who glued on different sets to match different outfits.

The chamber was steamy with heat and very quiet. Once inside, Becky closed the door gingerly, feeling in spite of the presence of the red button next to it, as if she might be sealing herself into the place for a lifetime. Keeping her towel round her, she sat on the palette of a bed, staring gloomily at the vat of green cream and musing upon the unhappy fact that knowing one was an ungrateful wretch offered no remedy for erasing such feelings. Joe had met her off the train from Dorset, hobbling on his sprained ankle and shouting about her birthday. 'Birthday surprise,' he had called several times, brushing off her concern at his limp and waving bits of paper in her face; bits of paper which she had for one wild brief moment imagined to be airplane tickets, but which turned out to be vouchers for an Oxfordshire country hotel instead; a grand country house of a place which they had visited before, early on in the relationship when they were at the stage of planning dreams instead of wondering when they were going to come true. Appalled at her capacity for ingratitude, Becky had done her utmost to rise to the challenge of looking pleased and made no reference to an explosion of unhelpful doubts about the recklessness of celebrating something before it had actually happened. She wasn't thirty. She might never be thirty. Thursday was four full days away. By which time she might have died of food poisoning or been run over by a milk float. And if her guardian angel prevented such calamities, it left the prospect of the dreaded day itself looking bleak and empty.

With Joe's ankle there was no question of going on the bike. By the time they had crossed London on the underground to Paddington, sat on a slow train that stopped at every station and waited half an hour to be ferried to the hotel by a country taxi, Becky was a little tired of appearing thrilled. As if sensing her reticence, Joe kept asking if she was pleased, if she had guessed his plans, if she could think of anywhere more heavenly to go than the place where they had first declared their love. After the most cursory of enquiries about Dorset, he had spent the entire journey talking about Jenny, saying how worried he was, how he was going to have to make the effort to see her more often than he had been managing in the recent past. Watching him speak, seeing the tension in his broad face, the violet shadows round his eyes, Becky had struggled to stop her sympathy curdling into a secret and selfish gloom.

Walking across the handsome forecourt of the hotel, she made a fresh effort to summon up the right feelings, exclaiming at the fountain, which hadn't been working on their previous visit and at the topiarist's griffins, looking sleek and noble in spite of the rain. She exclaimed at the fine rolling views of the Cotswolds too, but rather wished she hadn't when they were shown to a room which overlooked some kind of gas tank and the side bit of the car park.

'I'll ask if we can be moved,' said Joe at once, 'it's not what they promised on the phone.'

'I don't mind, really. The room is lovely – I mean it's lovely just to be here.'

'So you didn't guess? You really didn't?'

'No, I've told you, I didn't.' Becky spoke more edgily than she meant, some of her disappointment seeping out of her. 'It's just lovely to be on our own,' she added more gently, 'there's so much I want to talk about – to tell you – stuff that happened in Dorset and about work—'

'Me too, love, me too,' he interjected, throwing himself onto the bed and reaching for the TV remote. 'Let's talk tonight, over dinner. God, I'm whacked. I've booked a table at a place not far from here – just been awarded a star – some young chef from Cornwall – does amazing things with seafood apparently.'

'Oh, I get it, you've brought me here so that you can nick a few recipes, have you?' Becky quipped, aiming to be funny but knowing the moment the words were out that she had failed. 'Joe, you know I was teasing, don't you?' She crossed to the bed and took his face between her hands, steering his hurt gaze to meet her eyes, feeling suddenly that his cheerfulness deserting them would be worse than anything, that without it what remained of her own flimsy defences would come tumbling down.

'Of course.' He kissed her nose. She slid onto the bed next to him, burrowing under his arm and resting her head on the solid familiar sanctity of his chest. 'I did think at one stage of trying to book somewhere abroad, but then with so little time . . .'

'Quite right . . . that would have been daft. This is great Joe, really.' She traced a finger along the zigzag pattern of his shirt.

'Christ, what's the time?' he exclaimed suddenly, giving her head a jolt as he swung his arm up to examine his watch. 'I almost forgot . . . you've got six minutes to get yourself to the beauty parlour on the lower ground floor. Seaweed and a hot tub or something – they said it was the latest thing. About ten quid a minute so it better be good. It's to keep you young and beautiful,' he added with a chuckle, channel-flicking to a football match while Becky had heaved herself off the bed, straightened her clothes and slipped her stockinged feet back into her shoes.

Much to her astonishment Becky emerged from her steamy sanctum feeling deeply refreshed. The girl in the white coat was waiting to greet her with a bottle of mineral water. 'Drink some of this and have a little sit down before you go – you might feel a bit dizzy otherwise.'

'Oh, I feel fine,' Becky assured her happily, 'really good in fact.' She accepted the bottle of water nonetheless and took little sips as she made her way back to the room, feeling not dizzy so much as pleasantly lightheaded and thinking that a pampering premature birthday treat might be something she would be able to enjoy after all.

Joe came to the door in a towel dressing-gown, his hair still dripping from the shower, half his face covered in shaving foam.

'How was it?'

'Weird but good, though I'm not sure I got all the green off. Do I look green?'

He laughed. 'Not particularly.'

She followed him into the bathroom and ran a bath, tipping in a stream of purple liquid from one of the many bottles of toiletries arrayed round the edge, until the water bulged with mountains of white foam. Joe rubbed a hole in the steam on the basin mirror and continued to shave while she soaked herself, pulling at his skin with one hand as he carefully ran the blade over his face with the other.

'By the way,' she said, sinking deep into the froth, 'Anna got pregnant by mistake and is going to have a termination and not tell David.'

Joe, the razor poised over a last oblong drift of white, let out a low whistle. 'Is she indeed? Blimey. And what did you say?'

'Me?' Becky made a face. 'Nothing – I mean – you know Anna, once she's made up her mind . . .'

Joe tapped the razor on the edge of the basin, shaking his head gravely. 'That's heavy stuff. People who haven't had babies . . . she's no idea what she's playing with here.' Becky, guessing that he was thinking about Jenny, found herself leaping to her sister's defence. 'Oh yes she does, Anna always knows what she's playing with. That's how she is.'

'Well I certainly hope you wouldn't keep something like that from me.' He turned to look at her, so darkly, that she shrank a little more into the bubbles.

'Don't be silly. Of course I wouldn't. And I wouldn't have an abortion anyway, would I?' she blurted, surprised, the moment the sentence was out, to find herself bursting into tears.

'No of course you wouldn't,' he began, before realising the extent of her distress and trying to put his arms round her instead. 'Hey, what is this? I didn't mean . . .' He crouched over the bath, pressing her face to his neck, not realising that she couldn't breathe. 'It was a stupid thing to say . . . I just wasn't thinking.'

'It's fine, it's nothing . . . just this bath, it's so hot . . . I need to get out . . . I'm going to faint.' He released his grip and helped to lever her upright, taking her weight as she half stepped half fell onto the bath mat.

'Poor Becky,' he murmured slipping a towel round her, 'poor Becks.' The pair of them staggered, Becky still sobbing, through into the bedroom where the air was so contrastingly cool that she could feel the goosebumps springing up on her arms and legs.

'That green stuff,' she muttered, managing to contain her sobs for a smile, '. . . knew it was weird.'

'And I'm a dunce for not guessing how something like that would make you feel,' Joe faltered, in truth uncertain whether Becky was upset about her sister's predicament, the demise of the foetus or the still somewhat hazy prospect of starting their own family. Becky equally uncertain in every regard, reached for her half-finished bottle of mineral water and sank back onto the bed.

'What you need is food,' continued Joe sternly, starting

to pull clothes out of the bag he had packed on her behalf. 'Shoes, tights, a dress . . . did I do all right?'

'Marvellous,' Becky murmured, though the dress was one she hadn't worn in years and the tights were blue and didn't match. Feeling meek and drained, she let him help her dress, putting her hands through the armholes like a dutiful child.

The restaurant, which had been recommended to Joe by Mr Jordan, turned out to be a half-hour taxi ride away. It was housed in an even grander hotel than theirs, complete with a sweeping gravel drive, stone cherubs on pedestals and marble steps leading up to a vast grey-bricked portico of an entrance. The dining room was huge, decked out with crystal chandeliers and oil paintings of haughty-looking creatures in velvet jackets with lacy collars, posing with dogs and frock-coated children.

'Jesus, whatever is this going to cost?' whispered Becky, peering with wide eyes over the top of her menu, which had no prices by way of guidance for what to choose.

'A bit.' Joe, whose own menu had the prices marked very clearly, made a face, pleased to have impressed her, but hoping that she would have the sense not to go for the lobster, the cost of which could have fed a small family for a week. The place was far more opulent than Mr Jordan had led him to believe. And far pricier too. There appeared to be no set menu, and the champagne which they had ordered as an aperitif was a stunning six pounds a glass. 'To you,' he said, firmly closing his mind to such considerations. 'And to the future . . . Becky, I have been saving some news to tell you, something exciting.'

He looked so solemn and thrilled that Becky, whose own spirits had been greatly revived by the champagne and the arrival of the bread basket, stopped chewing, swallowing the lump of bread on her tongue almost whole. 'What is it, Joe?

Is it about money? Something good? Is that why we're in this amazing place?'

He nodded, laughing confidently. 'Money certainly comes into it . . . and yes, it's good, very good indeed.'

'Tell me,' she squealed, her mind leap-frogging to mad thoughts about inheritances from unknown relatives and getting five numbers on the lottery. She held her breath until he began to speak and then let it out again very slowly, keeping her eyes fixed on his, willing her disappointment, the treacherous, selfish disappointment which had clung to her all day like a disease, not to show. Not the lottery, not a fortune left by a great-aunt, not even a pay rise. But a mortgage. Bigger than the one they had already. On a place in Brixton. A flat in Brixton. Her husband wanted her to move from their three-bedroomed house in Balham to a more expensive two-bedroomed flat in Brixton. So that he could cripple their finances even further by renovating a poxy pizza parlour on the ground floor. Throughout these thoughts Becky kept her eyes wide and staring, feeling more than she ever had in her life before that her mind was a secret box to which only she held the key. He would not know these thoughts. He must not know these thoughts. Because his eyes were alight with the happiness of real excitement and in spite of all the recent confusion of her emotions she did not have the heart to say anything that might cause the light to go out. 'Oh, Joe, how wonderful.' He continued to talk, revealing that he had not only looked at the place and talked to mortgage brokers but even gone as far as having their own home valued.

'Two hundred and forty, the guy reckoned, which only leaves a shortfall of twenty odd. If I get the rise Mr Jordan has promised at Christmas we should be able to manage it – just.'

'Which reminds me,' she said quietly, 'I'm getting a pay rise too, of five thousand pounds.'

'What?'

For a moment she thought he was going to cry. A waiter, gliding with the deftness of an ice skater, set down two huge plates, each containing intricate structures of filo pastry, prawns and oyster sauce. 'He wants to promote me, give me a proper job actually servicing clients instead of merely photocopying their letters.'

'But that's amazing, fantastic . . . Jesus, I don't know what to . . . Jesus, Becky, why didn't you say something sooner?'

'I was saving it,' she replied, her eyes glittering, while her wayward, untameable thoughts flicked over the contrasting reaction she had received from Anna, from dear Anna, who alone had understood that accepting Mike Hadfield's offer was not the straightforward thing it might seem to the outside world.

# 10

On a wet September evening five days after Becky's visit, Anna was crossing the forecourt of the petrol station next to Balcombe station, credit card in one hand and her mobile pressed to her ear in the other, when she felt a dull, cramping pain somewhere in the region of her pelvic floor. 'Could I call you back?' she asked as sweetly she could, cutting the caterer, who had been in full flow about the choice of canapés for the housewarming, off in mid-flow. 'I'm so sorry – something's come up – I'm so sorry.'

So this is a miscarriage she thought, walking awkwardly, feeling another cramping pain followed by the first warm trickle of blood between her legs. Pressing her knees together, she shuffled round to the single toilet at the back of the garage, praying that it would be unoccupied. The only other time she had been desperate enough to relieve herself within its dingy four walls, she had had to wait for several long minutes until a greasy-faced lorry driver had emerged, still doing up his flies, a newspaper under his arm, his eyes watery with cigarette smoke. He had chuckled sheepishly on seeing her, rolling the stub of his cigarette between his lips. On this occasion however the cubicle was empty, and well-stocked with lavatory paper, Anna noticed with some relief, fighting through the now constant pains in her pelvis as she slid the lock into place.

'I was getting worried about you,' announced David cheerfully, striding across the courtyard to greet her as she emerged from her car some thirty minutes later. 'Was the train late again?'

'Yes . . . that is . . . a bit . . .'

'And how is my working girl?' He slipped his arms round her waist and kissed her fondly on the lips.

'A little tired to be honest . . .'

'You know you could give it all up . . . it's not as if we need the money . . .'

'I know.'

'But you love your job, which is far more important and I wouldn't have you any other way.' He leant back, searching her face with his eyes. 'How long is it since I told you that I loved you?'

'Years and years.' She smiled.

'And that I love our life, this house, the world and every-thing in it. We were going to play tennis, remember? You're not too tired for that, I hope. I booked the court in the village for seven, as we agreed. Unless . . .' he pressed his hips into hers, 'unless you'd prefer a little lie down first, a late siesta maybe . . .'

'You've obviously had a good day.'

'I have.' He released her, trying not to grin at the thought of the clay head, which now had exactly the right slope of the forehead and the beginnings of a bridge to the nose. 'So what's it to be, sex or tennis?'

Anna looked at the flush of happiness in her husband's face, wondering whether her reluctance to shatter it arose from a desire to protect his peace of mind or her own. Emerging from the small concrete-walled room half an hour before, she had felt no overwhelming desire for sympathy. That nature had accelerated an unpleasant process for which she had been prepared to pay several hundred pounds only firmed her conviction that her judgment in the matter had been correct. Though the flow of blood had since eased, there had been a fair amount at first, including a few sinister looking clots, which she had tried not to scrutinise too closely, screwing up her eyes as she pulled on the rusty metal of the lavatory chain. The worst thing had been the stomach cramps, but after a bit they too had gradually lessened and then, quite suddenly, stopped altogether. Telling David would only make it into a big deal, she decided, meeting his impish grin with one of her own. He liked her pretty and fit and full of health. Which was how she liked herself, Anna reflected, mentally compressing what she had experienced into something along the lines of a heavy period, a sordid inconvenience which she would not have dreamed of mentioning to her husband. Though she knew that some couples liked to hold a microscope up to each other's habits, to squeeze each other's blackheads and discuss bowel movements over breakfast, she and David had always maintained a healthy respect for each other's privacy in such regards. It had always been clear to her that such separateness was integral to their happiness, to the reasons for still wanting to be together after more than ten years.

'I'll flop into a bath first,' she said lightly, 'and then I think we should keep our appointment on the village tennis court . . . my period just came,' she added quickly, seeing the flicker of disappointment in his eyes, 'so maybe best to postpone the siesta plan for twenty-four hours or so. I'll make it up to you, I promise,' she whispered, reaching up to float her fingers through the soft waves of his hair, 'Sorry darling.'

Inside, when she was halfway up the stairs, he called, 'Make more sense to have your bath after tennis wouldn't it?'

'Would it?' Anna echoed, not bothering to turn round for fear of encouraging him to persist with the logic of the suggestion. Inside her pants she could feel the improvised pads of cheap toilet roll chafing against her skin, so unbearable suddenly that she ran the last few yards to the bedroom.

Sinking into the deep hot water a few minutes later, she realised that she ached from head to toe, a deep slow ache that felt as if she had been clenching every muscle in her body for a hundred years. Heaving herself out of the water, she took two analgesics and drank three tooth mugs' worth of cold water in quick succession, standing shivering on the bath mat, her teeth chattering so much that she had to bite the rim of the mug to keep them still.

Back in the sanctuary of the bath, which was large and kidney-shaped, she pressed the palms of both hands across her abdomen, relieved to see how white and flat it looked, how innocent of the trauma that had taken place inside. She would tell Becky, of course, she decided, closing her eyes and tipping her head back to wet her hair; not over the phone but face to face when they next met; at the housewarming maybe, when the whole episode would feel as safely distant as the time her appendix almost burst, or when she mangled her arm swerving off the road . . .

'Anna? Are you still in there?'

She sat up quickly, blinking the water from her eyes. 'Hang on . . . just coming. God – I didn't realise the time.' The fish-shaped clock-radio looped round the shower head revealed that it was already quarter to seven. 'One minute . . .' She scrambled to a sitting position, slipping on the smooth bottom of the bath.

'No hurry,' David called back from the bedroom, 'it's started raining again, pretty heavily. No question of a game now. You enjoy your bath.'

She lay back down, letting her head sink until the water tickled her ears. The aching feeling was almost gone. In the bedroom she heard David open and close a drawer and then the creak of his footsteps on the landing. A few minutes later she could make out the faint strains of music coming up the stairs, one of his opera tapes, something familiar though she couldn't have said what or by whom. Humming the tune, she reached for the soap and began lathering her legs and arms, soothed both by the music and the sliding touch of her own hands.

# I I

The skating rink was very crowded, even for a Saturday morning. A particularly rowdy group of teenagers in knee-length T-shirts and woolly caps were playing a disruptive game of tag, careering into the sides and carving up the ice as they twisted and raced their way round the circuit. Several jelly-legged novices had been knocked flying, including Jenny whom Joe, somewhat wobbly himself thanks to his still tender ankle, had had to coax back onto the rink with all sorts of wild promises of rewards for bravery. Becky, left to skate on her own and still nursing resentment at being dragged from her bed to entertain her stepdaughter, watched them gloomily, wondering why Joe bothered when it was clear that neither of them were having any fun. They had only been there twenty minutes and she was already not only tired of doing her own steady, unspectacular version of staying upright, but also chilled to the bone. Compared to the teenagers cheerfully staggering or whizzing past her, jigging to the tinny chart music, their bare arms blue with cold, she felt like an ancient and wizened old crone.

It was already six weeks since her birthday. Despite her fears, the day itself had passed well enough, being redeemed from total anticlimax by her work colleagues, who appeared to know all about it (even though she had made a point of not saying anything), and who insisted on taking her out to lunch in a noisy basement wine bar. After several bottles of wine and two courses each – just as Becky was expecting

Mike to order them all back to work – a waiter appeared bearing a huge chocolate cake, decorated with squirls of cream and a single pink candle which relit every time she blew it out. They even sang to her, Mike leading the way with an impressively tuneful tenor, and all the others joining in in a more motley fashion, including several of the waiters hanging around the table to enjoy the spectacle. After the cake had been carved up and distributed Mike tapped his glass with a knife and delivered a short speech, congratulating her on her promotion and saying how she already felt an integral part of the team. When Becky pointed out that her new duties had so far involved following Geoffrey, her designated mentor, to the lavatory by mistake, and sitting in on one meeting and saying nothing, they all laughed and congratulated her again. Apart from Juliette, who had had a row with the faithful Pete and who seemed to have taken the upturn in Becky's fortunes as a personal slight to her own.

Joe had marked the occasion by arriving home with three quarters of an unwanted lemon gateau from Le Moulin and a white cardboard box tied together with red ribbon. Explaining about the surprise lunch at work, Becky cut herself a modest slither of the cake before pulling eagerly at the ribbon. Inside, nestling in white tissue paper, was a set of red underwear, the bra of the underwired push-your-assets out variety and the pants a frilly triangle of silky lace. At the sight of them she couldn't help hesitating, battling with the uncharitable notion that, while possibly a welcome indicator of passion, such a gift constituted as much a treat for Joe as for herself.

'Do you like them?' he whispered.

'I . . . yes, of course . . . I mean, wow.' She held them up so that the red satiny fabric gleamed under the kitchen light. 'Wicked,' she added, managing to sound more convinced, but feeling as she had ever since the emotional rollercoaster of their excursion to the Cotswolds, that she was saying what she thought he wanted to hear rather than what she truly felt herself. Having absorbed the news of her altered circumstances at work with almost hysterical delight over their grand dinner, once they got back to London he had seemed to take it all for granted, tapping out figures on his calculator and talking to bankers and lawyers and estate agents as if the future he was plotting had no bearing on the person with whom he would be sharing it.

Becky threaded her way through the hordes of skaters towards a gap in the crash barrier. Her ankles, laced tightly into the stiff boots, felt brittle and tender. Catching sight of Joe, still making snail's progress with Jenny on the far side of the rink, she waved, indicating her intention of taking a breather. A few minutes later she was sitting on one of the wooden benches facing the rink, burrowing her frozen fingers deep inside her pockets and sighing with relief at having the weight off her feet. Joe meanwhile, his face creased in concentration, had begun gingerly skating backwards, pulling his stiff and reluctant daughter towards him with both hands. Though used to Jenny being monosyllabic and disconnected with her, Becky was faintly shocked to see the child maintain such tactics with her father. Even before the collision on the ice Joe had spent most of that morning trying to engage her interest and elicit a smile. An embarrassment of riches had been promised for the afternoon: a takeaway pizza, ice cream, a video, popcorn, as well as the services of the long suffering Johanna, who had been bribed an enormous sum not only to cover the Saturday lunch shift but to miss the first couple of hours of an evening party as well. Thanks to David and Anna's housewarming, Becky herself would be heading west on a train, absolved from the burden of having to play any part in the proceedings. Originally there had been talk of Joe leaving things to Lucien and coming too, but the plan had fizzled out, just as Becky guessed it would. First Mr Jordan had resisted and then Joe had invited Jenny over anyway. To put the seal on things, the estate agents had also called offering a couple of weekend appointments. Joe, who had been despairing at six weeks of virtually no interest in the house and who had taken the rash step of making an offer on the Brixton property, could barely contain his excitement. Becky on the other hand, distracted by the new demands being made on her at work, had found herself mentally withdrawing from the entire process. Not because she hated the Brixton place – in fact it had proved surprisingly appealing, with high-ceilinged rooms, fresh pine floors and a green nest of a garden – but because of a deep scepticism about the whole project. If anyone proved foolhardy enough to offer the required sum for their cracked and creaking home, she simply could not envisage the dilapidated pizzeria with anything like the fervour being demonstrated by Joe. It was like he had suffered a religious conversion and left her trailing behind.

Looking up, Becky saw that Jenny was heading her way, dragging herself along by the barrier, her small face flexed in a self-conscious portrayal of reluctant effort. Stepping through the gap in the barrier, she made a big show of stamping off the ice from her boots on the rubber flooring before crossing to the bench.

'Hi, where's Joe?'

'He said to come and sit with you. He's gone to the loo.'

'Right. Having a good time then?'

'Yeah, great,' she replied, her voice toneless, her eyes fixed on her boots as she swung them back and forth under the bench.

'What video are you going to get?'

'Dunno.' She shrugged, swinging her legs faster. She was wearing make-up Becky noticed for the first time, spotting that the sandy lashes had been inexpertly coated with sticky black and that the lightly freckled pale skin appeared to have been treated to a dusting of honey-coloured powder. At a smiliar age she hadn't progressed beyond occasional clumsy efforts with Stella's nail varnish. And her father had just died, she realised, the sudden connection triggering a volley of compassion, though whether for herself as a young girl or for the pre-pubescent fidgeting next to her it was hard to be sure.

'Dad says you're moving,' declared Jenny next, managing to make the statement sound accusatory and peering out from between the slats of her fringe.

'Yes . . . well, maybe.' Becky sighed.

'Do you want to?'

'Not particularly no,' she conceded, moved by the direct-ness of the enquiry to be honest.

'Well, why are you doing it then?'

'Because Joe – because Daddy wants to . . . needs to for his work. And of course I'll be two stops nearer for my work which is nice because I've got a new job where I have to work harder.'

Jenny looked away, the mixture of boredom and disappoint-ment on her face demonstrating to Becky that whatever sliver of interest she had sparked had arleady been well and truly lost. A moment later Joe was herding them back onto the ice, saying there was only ten minutes before they would have to come off anyway as the machines were due to re-smooth the surface.

Becky arrived at Waterloo with barely time to grab a coffee from one of the barrows positioned near the entrances to the platforms before hurling herself and her overnight bag into a carriage. Having committed herself to the midday train on the somewhat flimsy pretext that Anna would appreciate some help preparing for the party, she had at the last minute found herself reluctant to go. Saying goodbye to Joe, she had wanted to keep her arms round his broad neck for ever, feeling that she was clinging on to something vital between them, something that was in danger of slipping away. Late for his lunchtime shift and with the sitter and Jenny hovering in the background, he had had to prise her free, pecking her on the nose as he did so and instructing her to have a good time.

Sitting on the train now, blowing ripples into her coffee which was hot, Becky experienced a familiar longing to see her big sister, to draw on the well of calm reassurance which had seen her through so many traumatic periods in her life. Apart from her thirtieth, when Anna had phoned to apologise for the fact that her and David's gift – an exquisite turquoise green pashmina which she planned to drape across her shoulders that night – was in the post, they had spoken just a couple of times since her August visit and then only briefly. From what Becky could gather the termination had been carried out successfully, though Anna's oblique responses had made it quite clear that she had no desire to be quizzed on the subject. She was far keener to talk about arrangements for the party, which sounded fabulous, and to counsel Becky about the challenges of her new position at Takoma Designs, generously comparing it to various far more high-powered challenges which she faced herself.

Having feared David might be delegated to the station run, Becky was thrilled to spot Anna's shiny green Saab in the small station car park as the train hissed to a stop. Her sister appeared on the platform a moment later, in a red polo neck and a cream sleeveless fleece. She looked well, her hair in a new longer style, flying dramatically round her shoulders, and her face glowing. Becky dropped her holdall and they hugged.

'Good to see you.'

'And you. Looking great – must be the new career,' she quipped, picking up Becky's bag and leading the way through the small station to the car park on the other side.

Becky groaned, hurrying to catch up with her. 'Don't

remind me. This Geoffrey guy I told you about, the one I have to follow all over the place, is even more of a computer geek than I thought, writes these brilliant codes but can't explain any of it in plain English. That's what Mike says my job is, to be the human *interface*, to translate and interpret, to help Geoffrey understand that all they want is to advertise a new logo and a couple of product lines without it taking ten hours to download . . .'

'Sounds like you're getting the hang of the jargon anyway,' put in Anna with a laugh, slinging Becky's bag into the boot of her car. 'I knew you could do it, Becks, I just knew. And how's everything else – all this Brixton business, is it really going to happen?'

Becky made a face. 'Some people are coming to look round the house tomorrow – a family of four, who'll think it's too small and a pair of newly weds just moved to London from Bristol – both medics apparently, based at St George's.'

'Well that sounds promising. And like I said on the phone, Brixton is supposed to be up and coming, just the sort of area where, if Joe can make a go of things . . .'

'If, being the operative word.' Becky rolled her eyes. 'Not all of mankind is quite as positive as you, you know . . . are we waiting for someone else?' she added, puzzled at the realisation that her sister had yet made no move to turn on the engine.

'No . . . I just . . .' Anna placed one hand on either side of the steering wheel. 'I just wanted to tell you something before we set off.'

'Right. Okay.' Becky, for some reason felt her mouth go dry.

'About this pregnancy business—'

'Oh God, Anna, I was going to ask, I wanted to ask, how it was – I mean I tried to on the phone but I kind of got the impression that you'd rather I—'

'Would you just listen a minute Becky?' While not exactly harsh, her voice was so commanding that Becky closed her mouth instantly, wishing she could shake the still persistent impression that some bad news was in store. 'Don't say a word until I've finished, OK?'

Becky nodded. Over Anna's shoulder she saw that tiny dots of moisture were being flung onto the car window by the wind, too tiny even to dribble down the glass.

Anna cleared her throat and began speaking in the low firm tones that had proved such an asset in her career. 'A few weeks ago, shortly after you came to stay in fact, I had a miscarriage. Or rather, I thought I had a miscarriage. I won't go into details but it was sufficiently severe an incident for me to assume that I no longer required a termination.' She took a deep breath before continuing. 'It was some time before I realised . . . before I was able to face up to the fact that I was still pregnant. So . . . so I went back to see the consultant who said that though he preferred not to carry out terminations on fœtuses of more than eighteen weeks himself, he could refer me to someone who would, but that in the meantime I should have a scan so that they could be more precise about the dates . . .' Anna paused again for breath, seeing in her mind's eye the screen containing the clearly defined image of the tiny four-limbed creature twisting inside her. It had sucked its thumb and then, incredibly, appeared to wave, the five digits of its fingers as clear as exclamation marks on a page. Tears had flooded her eyes. The ultrasonographer, assuming them to derive from a hitherto unacknowledged love for the half-developed infant, had tutted kindly, little knowing that what Anna was experiencing was more a kind of trapped despair, that the gesture of the baby, twisting like a fish inside her had made her think not of suckling and mother-love but of her own father, of an arm above the surface of the water, not waving but drowning.

'Anna?'

She blinked slowly and smiled, drawing on the steely calm that had empowered her to tell David that her career plans and his newfound freedom were to be qualified after all. 'And it turns out that I am nineteen weeks pregnant. As I said, although there are doctors willing to perform such late terminations I – we – have decided to make the best of it, to let nature take her course, as she seems so determined to do.'

'God, Anna, that's amazing . . . so you're still . . . ?' Becky stared at Anna's stomach, trying to detect any new contour through the bulk of the fleece.

'Pregnant,' Anna finished for her, adding quickly, 'But it's not going to change anything, we are both completely agreed on that.'

'So, David's okay about it then?' asked Becky carefully.

'Fine.' Anna started the engine and reversed smartly out of her parking space. 'We've talked it all through. Like I said, we're not going to let it change anything, I mean all the plans he has – he can and must still do them. Otherwise he'll feel resentful which would be hopeless. I haven't told work yet, but when I do I'm going to make sure they understand that I'll carry on right up until my due date and then probably take no more than a couple of months' maternity leave afterwards.' She grinned suddenly, illuminating the sunny features of her face. 'I can't tell you how excited I am about this radio phone-in project I've been working on. It could be just the break I've been waiting for. I'm not going to let anything jeopardise that. It'll just be a question of sorting myself out properly, of being organised and making sure I've got the best nanny in the universe. In the meantime,' she slowed down to check for traffic at the T-junction signposting Balcombe village, 'I intend to enjoy every minute of wearing my little black dress tonight, before I metamorphose into a total heffalump. I'm so fat already I can only just get these – my *loosest* jeans – done up.'

'Not fat,' Becky corrected her quietly, 'pregnant.'

'Fat,' repeated Anna. 'Though I've already started this antenatal exercise regime – used by all the film stars apparently – which is reputed to keep the damage to a minimum. Have to do it when David's out of sight – protect him from the pendulous boobs and bulging bum.' She laughed, giving the steering wheel a little slap. 'Who'd have thought it, eh?'

'I know, a baby, it's—'

'No, I meant all this rain, for weeks now. When September was wet I thought we'd be let off the hook for October. Not that it really matters. We've got this brilliant marquee, positioned on the main lawn, but attached to the house. It's totally storm-proof, with heaters everywhere to keep us snug. They put it up on Thursday. It's so amazingly huge that David got one of his pals from the airfield to fly over and take a few aerial photos. I'm thinking of getting one blown up and framed for the downstairs loo.'

Becky let her talk, listening with only half an ear, telling herself she should be glad but feeling, for some reason that she cared not to analyse too deeply, profoundly sad.

# 12

David stood in front of the mirror, adjusting his bow tie, which was straight, and pressing the already smooth sides of his hair more firmly behind his ears. He had used a bit of gel, not much, just enough to keep the exuberance from the waves and give a nice finishing shine. Behind him Anna was sitting at her dressing-table, humming quietly to herself as she pressed the diamond crescent earrings he had given her as a wedding present through the small holes in her ear lobes. Her hair hung down her bare back, freshly washed and silky blonde, a golden arrow to the stunning black silk of her dress, cut so low across the small of her back that you could almost see the teasing tiny shadow marking the start of the cleft in her bottom. Across the front, her breasts, heavier now because of the pregnancy, filled to perfection the space provided for them, accentuating the flattering inward curve of her still discernible waistline and the long smooth lines of her legs. Sitting careless and unguarded on her dressing-table stool, the hem of the dress had ridden up so high that on one side David could see the edge of her stocking where it met the suspender belt, next to a teasing rectangle of honey flesh. Happy with the position of her earrings, she had turned her attention to her lips, leaning forward as she ran a pink pencil carefully round the edges, pouting at the mirror as if she meant to kiss it. From downstairs came the faint hum of activity, the murmured voices of the caterers intermingling with the occasional chink of crockery and the twang of musical instruments being tuned in preparation for performance. There was a tangible sense of anticipation in the house, of excitement. Dropping his fingers from his tie, David continued to stare at his wife, unconsciously puffing his chest with pride at her beauty, wishing he could make the moment, so poised and perfect, last for ever. Sensing his attention at last, Anna caught his eye, and for an instant they stared at each other through their mirrors, two reflections meeting. Then David turned and crossed the room to stand behind her. Lifting her hair, he ran his lips across the delicate fair hairs at the nape of her neck. 'You look delicious . . . good enough to eat.'

Anna smiled, closing her eyes. 'So do you.'

Slipping the straps off her shoulders, he pressed his lips more firmly against her bare skin, taking gentle bites, and whispering, 'I don't want to lose you, I don't ever want to lose you.'

'You won't silly, you won't.' Wanting, gently, to discourage his affections, Anna tried to reach up, but the strap of her dress, halfway down her arm now, prevented her. 'David, please . . . I . . .'

'Can't I make love to my own wife?' he murmured, tugging harder at the dress, which was fastened by a side zip.

'Of course you can, any time . . . but I've just done my make-up and in five minutes the front doorbell will start ringing . . . David, careful, you'll break it . . . there's a zip . . .'

'Where, where's the zip?' he growled, 'Jesus, it's like Fort Knox this thing.'

At the sound of a knock on the bedroom door he sprang back, hastily buttoning up his jacket and straightening his hair.

Becky's muffled voice came from the passage. 'It's me – sorry – can I come in? Bit of an emergency.'

'I believe it's your sister,' he remarked drily, now tugging at his cuffs, 'with her usual classic timing.'

'Well let her in then,' murmured Anna, returning her attentions to her lower lip which was slightly smudged. David opened the bedroom door to find Becky hopping from foot to foot in a state of some agitation. She was wearing a tight emerald green minidress with a huge silver buckle slung round her hips. 'Crisis,' she wailed. David's first thought was for the belt, a shocking accessory which he would have torn off Anna in an instant, but she was in fact pointing at her hair, which was dry and full of curls on one side and a mess of wet rodent tails on the other. 'My tongs just sort of exploded – there's the most horrible smell – I think I must have blown a fuse – I was wondering if Anna' – she peered past David to confirm that her sister was actually in the bedroom – 'could lend me some? Or, failing that, a hairdryer and I'll make the best of it; although these curls are harder to do with a hairdryer and I'll probably end up looking lopsided.'

'Come here, you,' ordered Anna affectionately, getting off the dressing-table chair and gesturing for Becky to take her place. 'I'll sort you out. David can field any early arrivals, can't you David?'

'Sure.' He smiled quickly. 'I could bring you two beauties a glass of champagne too if you like.'

'Mm, we would like,' said Becky at once, before glancing at her sister for confirmation, 'wouldn't we?'

'Of course,' murmured Anna, rummaging in a dressing-table drawer.

'God, David, doesn't she look fantastic?' exclaimed Becky as he reached the door, unable to contain herself at the effortless glamour of her elder sister, 'I mean you wouldn't guess in a million years that she was pregnant, would you?'

'No, you wouldn't,' he agreed, smiling again before hurrying out of the room.

'Is he okay?'

'Yes, fine. Why?'

Becky shrugged. 'He doesn't like me, does he? I feel it more and more.'

'Of course he likes you. Now sit still,' Anna commanded, waving a small circular brush of fierce black bristles in one hand and a large professional looking hairdryer in the other. 'I can work wonders, with this thing. Oh, and by the way,' she added, having to raise her voice against the whirr of hot air, 'not a word to anyone about you know what.' She tapped her stomach with the hairbrush. 'If you don't mind.' As she talked she began expertly rolling sections of Becky's thick curtain of hair round the brush. Soon pretty curls were falling out round Becky's ears, looking far more likely to stay in place than their cousins on the other side. 'Because I haven't told work yet, or Mum for that matter.'

'Blimey, Mum, I hadn't thought about that. Do you think she'll be pleased?'

'Of course,' said Anna, a little tartly Becky felt, though it was hard to be sure above the noise of the hairdryer.

Ten minutes later, with her hair a mass of glossy ringlets and bubbles of cold champagne exploding in her nose, Becky left Anna to some last-minute orchestration of the army of people hired to help out with the evening and went for a stroll round the dramatically extended ground floor of the house. Since her arrival the doors to the kitchen and David's study had been sealed off, thus encouraging all movement in the direction of the main sitting room, where the open French windows had been seamlessly connected to a marquee large enough to host a circus. Flowers were everywhere, bulging out of huge free-standing vases and cascading out of baskets from the ceiling and walls. Grand enough for a royal wedding mused Becky, unable to resist speculating as to the huge cost of such extravagance. Scores of tables, gleaming with fresh linen and silver, had been set for dinner on one side, while on the other a huge wooden floor had been laid for dancing. Next to it, on a circular raised platform, four musicians attired in dinner jackets were testing out their instruments and fiddling with sheet music. At the sight of Becky, standing alone under the vast canopy of canvas, the drummer did a drum roll and clash of cymbals. Becky blushed, raising her champagne flute to acknowledge the tribute before retreating back into the house. Seeing no sign of Anna or David, she then wandered into the den which led off from the sitting room and which had been connected by a narrow canvas tunnel to a bouncy castle; not the chubby back garden variety which Joe had hired for Jenny's birthday a couple of years before, but a grand dome of a thing, at least twenty foot by thirty, with gold walls and a glittery ceiling. Though Anna had pointed out the heap of drenched plastic when they arrived back from the station, explaining what it was, Becky had never imagined it could be inflated to such magnificence. The sound of the rain, now pounding on the roof and mingling with the gush of the air being pumped to keep it upright, somehow only served to heighten the dramatic effect.

Looking over her shoulder to check she was alone, Becky kicked off her high heels and clambered inside. She proceeded to bounce, cautiously at first and then with greater abandon, her stockinged feet slipping and sliding between the air-filled ridges of the smooth plastic floor. With each leap she felt better, more carefree, more on top of all the things she didn't like about her life. It didn't matter that her husband seemed bent on sinking their last paltry savings into a madcap house move, that her brother-in-law despised her, that her adored sister appeared to be drowning in good fortune. It didn't even matter that she was thirty. The secret of happiness was to concentrate on the moment, she decided, bouncing harder, to have a good time whenever possible. She took one last huge leap, aiming to clear four sets of ridges and get herself back to the entrance. Instead she found herself flat on her back, breathing hard, staring at the glittering bubble of a roof overhead.

'Hey, are you okay in there?'

She struggled upright, patting at her hair, which was all over the place, and tugging at her dress, which was somewhere round her hips. 'Fine, thanks . . . I was just . . .'

'Bouncing?'

'Exactly. Bouncing.' She slithered to the edge, still yanking at the hemline of her dress, and reached for her shoes. 'I'm Anna's sister.' She stood up and held out her hand in the vague hope of restoring some impression of dignity.

'And I'm Guy Fanshawe.' He gave her hand a warm squeeze. 'Delighted to make your acquaintance.'

'And how do you know David and Anna?' Becky continued, feeling composed enough, with her shoes on and the pashmina safely back across her shoulders, to continue with the business of exchanging pleasantries.

'I don't. I came with someone else, who appears to have abandoned me already.' He cast a comical look over his shoulder, where the walls of the empty tunnel were heaving under pressure from the storm going on outside. 'What about you? Are you here on your own?'

'Yes,' she replied, feeling her heart do a little skip, aware the moment the word was out that, had her companion been squat and carrot-headed, as opposed to tall with thick dark hair and glittering blue eyes, she would have been only too glad to explain the existence of a husband, absent through the necessity of spending Saturday nights in a steamy restaurant kitchen.

'And what do you do for a living, Anna's sister, who's on her own?'

'I . . . websites . . . design them . . . that is, I help other people – clients – decide how they want them designed . . .' She gave up. 'What about you?'

'I'm in films. Screenplays. I do bit of TV too, if my agent twists my arm . . .'

He was prevented from continuing by Anna, appearing briefly in the tunnel behind them. 'Becky . . . sorry to interrupt . . . could you come here a moment? And who was he?' she enquired, once they were out of earshot.

Becky laughed. 'You should know. Your party, remember?'

'Well I don't.'

'He was Guy something – said he came with someone.'

'Well, I can't think who. Unless it's that Cindy woman who used to work with David – they arrived while I was in the kitchen. Was he nice?'

Becky shrugged. 'I don't know. We exchanged three words. What did you want me for?'

'To help,' she said sternly. 'They're arriving in droves now and we're struggling to get them into the marquee, they're all hanging round the hall like lost souls.'

She was nervous, Becky realised suddenly, relishing in the same instant the luxury of being merely a guest, of being able to enjoy the extravaganza without a single anxious thought for the machinations behind it. 'Stop worrying,' she whispered, seizing a glass of champagne off a passing tray as they entered the hall, where a fresh clutch of arrivals had just tumbled in through the door, pulling mackintoshes off their evening gear and shaking out umbrellas. Putting her mouth nearer Anna's ear, she added. 'You look beautiful and you have everything in the world any woman could ever want.'

'Silly girl,' murmured Anna, shooting her a concerned glance before switching her attentions to an elderly silver-haired man in a white dinner jacket and a bulging purple velvet cummerbund. 'Arthur, how lovely to see you.'

'And you Anna. And looking simply heavenly, if I may say so.'

'May I introduce my sister, Becky?'

'Delighted, I'm sure,' he growled, pressing wet lips to the knuckles of Becky's right hand and announcing that he was in her hands entirely and would follow wherever she led.

# 13

For dinner they were seated eight to a table, each place setting having its own italicised name card and a creamy linen napkin folded into the shape of a swan. Becky found herself positioned between a freckly-faced man called Andrew, whom she vaguely remembered from Anna and David's wedding, and the white-haired gentleman, who had taken such a shine to her that she had spent some of the time prior to the meal skipping behind flower displays in a bid to avoid his attentions. Eager to continue with these discouragements, she launched all her attention at her other neighbour, who turned out to be a finance director with a passion for talking about finance. Nodding sagely to things she found too boring to even attempt to understand, while keeping her right arm and thigh pressed as much out of reach of the stroking attentions from the wizened Lothario on the other side, Becky found herself concentrating rather more on the wine than the food. By the time the coffee and petits fours arrived, she had struck such a rapport with the young wine waiter serving their table that she had merely to catch his eye to get several fresh inches of claret poured into her glass. She knew it was claret because the white-haired gentleman eventually remarked on the fact, leading to the unforeseen benefit of stopping Andrew in full flow about pension plans and diverting the pair of them instead to a mutually rapt discussion about bouquets and vineyards. They were soon leaning across her so excludingly that Becky found herself wondering if the previous arrangement had been so unsatisfactory after all. She even tried to join in, venturing a mention of Joe's wine course. But when she couldn't remember the name of the course or a single one of Joe's growing list of favourite labels, they returned their attentions to each other.

As the band trooped onto the platform to take up their positions behind their instruments, Becky slipped away from the table, fearful that her dinner neighbours, visibly tiring of each other at last, might think of asking her to dance. Knowing from the way the ground heaved that she was seriously inebriated, she made her way carefully between the tables, gripping the backs of chairs and keeping her eye fixed firmly ahead of her on the doorway into the sitting room. The music started just as she reached it. Turning to survey the scene behind her, she was arrested by the sight of David leading Anna onto the empty dance floor. More of a golden couple, with their matching blond hair and Midas touch, it would have been hard to imagine. To complete the image they were staring into each other's eyes and holding hands like newly-weds. There was a smattering of applause and then silence as the music took off and they began to move. Not mirroring each other in a rythmic jig as she and Joe would have done, but jiving and spinning in an elaborate rock and roll that soon had the audience slapping their palms to every beat.

'Your sister can dance.'

Becky looked over her shoulder to see that Guy Fanshawe was standing just behind her in the sitting room. He was smoking a freshly lit cigarette and had a quizzical look on his face, as if he had been appraising her for several minutes. On seeing him again, she felt a small but distinct burst of relief, connected to the fact that, without quite acknowledging it, she had been looking for him all evening.

'My sister can do most things.'

'As can you, I'm sure.'

'Not like Anna.' She folded her arms, pulling her pashmina more tightly across her shoulders and returning her gaze to the dance floor where other couples were now venturing, keeping clear of David who continued to fling Anna about him with all the abandonment of a child whirling a rag doll. 'I mean, look at them, they're amazing.' For a moment she almost mentioned the pregnancy, thinking at the same time how typical it was that David, whose reaction Anna had once feared so much, had clearly accommodated the idea with ease, something else to be sorted in their totally sorted lives.

'Cigarette?'

'God, I'd love one – thanks.' The ground did one of its rolls as she stepped towards him, causing her to trip on the edge of the rush matting laid down by way of protection for the sitting-room carpet.

'Whoops.' He caught her by the shoulder. 'Steady on.'

'I'm drunk,' she confessed, inhaling so deeply on the first drag that stars danced in front of her eyes.

'So am I, a little. Do you want to dance?'

She shook her head.

'Me neither. How about a bounce then? I've just been there, it's completely empty.'

Becky giggled. 'Okay then.' A few minutes later she had abandoned her shoes and shawl and was crawling after him into the glittering plastic dome. He too had taken off his shoes, revealing a hole in the big toe, which made her giggle even more. When he realised what she was laughing at he hastily took his socks off and tucked them out of sight in his shoes.

It felt much colder inside the plastic than she remembered and also slightly damp. Through the small gap between the walls and the roof it was clear that it was still raining. The roof itself had lost a lot of its dome shape and was sagging inwards from the weight of water which had accumulated on top of it. Becky bounced, but much more warily this time, partly because the claret had made her feel giddy and unbalanced, and partly because she was aware of the multifarious perils of tumbling into the path of her companion. Clearly without any such reservations himself, Guy was springing wildly, coming closer with every landing, and with such force that Becky felt in serious danger of being catapulted out of control. Still sober enough to recognise that she should make every attempt to avoid such an eventuality, she leap-frogged over to the nearest wall and flopped back against it to catch her breath. At which point a deluge of freezing water, collected in a fold between the top of the wall and the roof, cascaded down on top of her.

'Oh fuck . . . oh Jesus . . . my dress . . . oh that is so cold.' Guy was at her side in seconds, leaping with such comic urgency that Becky, in spite of being dripping wet and with her stockinged feet immersed in a deep puddle of water, could not help bursting into laughter.

'Here, take this.' He slipped off his dinner jacket and put it round her shoulders. 'Come on let's get off this bloody thing before it collapses on top of us. What we need is a drink. And some privacy would be nice too, somewhere we could talk. You must know this house,' he urged, undeterred by Becky's silence and kidnapping an almost full bottle of red wine off a passing waiter, 'Come on, Brains, where can we go?'

Becky thought wildly of her bedroom and various other hopeless possibilities upstairs before somewhere rather less suggestive and safer came to mind. 'David's studio in the barn across the courtyard – I don't know if it's locked and it means going outside . . .'

'Let's try.' He tucked the bottle out of sight of a couple of passing guests. 'If we can slip out of here, that is,' he added, lowering his voice and confirming Becky's own view that if they were to embark on so reckless an undertaking, they should do so without anyone bearing witness to it. Not wanting to go through the kitchen which was full of catering staff, they loitered like guilty schoolchildren round the main hall before finding an opportunity to escape out of the front door. Outside a chill drizzle was falling. Scampering across the courtyard in the semi-darkness, Becky's feet received a further soaking in several puddles. By the time Guy eased open the barn door, which was not locked, her teeth were clacking with cold.

'Here, get some of this down you,' he ordered, wiping the top of the bottle and handing it across. 'This is quite a place. Clever girl, thinking of it.' He kissed the top of her head, so naturally that for a moment Becky believed that it was in fact quite normal to be half drenched, half drunk and lurking in dark corners with an attractive man. 'He makes all this stuff does he?' Guy continued, starting to examine some of David's creations in the dim light provided by one of the courtyard lanterns glowing outside.

'Didn't you know?'

'Well, yes, I did, obviously – I just had no idea of the *kind* of stuff he was into. My . . . partner . . . the er . . . person I came with—'

'Cindy?'

'Judy.' He was opening cupboard doors now and peering inside. 'She's more Anna's friend. I don't know a lot about him. Hey, come and look at this.' He reached into the back of the cupboard and pulled out a clay head, huge and grey, and as imperious as the bust of a Roman emperor. 'It's him,' he chuckled. 'Your brother-in-law.'

'God, so it is.' Becky giggled, taking another swig of wine. 'Better put it back. He'd go ballistic if he knew. He's very particular, my brother-in-law, very . . .'

'Is he now? And what are you?' he murmured, sliding the bust back into the cupboard and pulling her into his arms, 'apart from icy cold. Poor baby.' He began rubbing her back, making circles, reaching wider and lower every time. He was much slimmer than Joe – she could feel his ribs through his shirt – but so tall that the top of her head barely reached his bow tie.

'I'm . . . married,' said Becky, after giving the matter some thought.

He merely laughed, holding her more tightly and steering her to a small sitting area in the far side of the room, a new development since Becky's last visit, complete with coffee table, sofa and table lamp. 'Married or not you need warming up, Becky whoever you are.' He flicked on the table lamp and pulled her down onto the sofa next to him. 'Now tell me all about yourself, I want a potted history.' He had taken her frozen hands between his and was gently massaging the fingers, rolling them round his palms.

'That's funny isn't it? The word, I mean . . . potted . . . funny word.' She giggled, extracting one hand to take another swig of wine before offering the bottle across to him. Tipping a small amount between his lips, he lifted up her hand and placed her index finger inside his mouth as he swallowed. It made a small popping sound as Becky snatched it free. 'Guy . . . I'd better go, I think, before I . . .'

He prevented her from finishing the sentence by kissing her. 'Before you do that?' he murmured, cupping her face in his hands as she tried to pull away. 'Or this?' He kissed her again, more forcefully this time, his tongue hungrily chasing hers.

'Stop, please,' she gasped, wrenching some tiny sober sane part of herself back into consciousness. 'I'm married—'

'Yes, you did mention that.'

'And I . . . I don't know anything about you . . .' she faltered, playing for time, a part of her loath to leave him, loath to walk away from what felt like the first truly exciting thing to happen to her in months, years . . .'

'You don't know anything about me? Okay, here we go, as potted as I can make it.' He spoke very softly, keeping hold of her fingers and running them round the edge of his lips, 'Eton, Oxford, the London Film School, Granada, Hollywood – till I missed the sanity of England – Channel 4 Films, flat in Notting Hill, country cottage in Wiltshire, aged thirty-two, four serious girlfriends, nothing special at the moment – Judy is just a friend – until now, that is . . . can I stop yet? Another drink maybe?'

Becky, dazed and impressed, accepted the now almost empty bottle from him without a word. She felt as if she had stepped inside a dream, where anything was possible, where tall dark handsome men really did appear from nowhere to rescue modern damsels from the drabness of real life, with all its petty dissatisfactions and disappointments. When he kissed her again she did not resist, but bit his lips between caresses, partly because she sensed he liked it and partly to reassure herself that he would not disappear in a puff of conjuror's smoke.

Some forty minutes later, David, seeing off some guests, crossed the courtyard to peer in through the window of his studio, prompted to do so by the dim light emanating from it. Puzzled, both because he had no recollection of leaving the light on and because the door was slightly ajar, he slipped inside to investigate. It took a few moments to register that the room was already occupied, and in a manner that made interruption extremely awkward. The woman was underneath; her bare legs wrapped round her partner's waist looked silvery white, whiter even than the man's backside which was moving in the rhythmic, time-honoured enactment of copulation, faintly absurd to all but those participating in it. David froze, feeling a rush of possessive concern for his new sofa, which was of high-quality leather and which was squeaking in equally rhythmic protest at being put to a use for which it had not been designed. Aware suddenly that it was this very squeaking that had masked the sound of his arrival, and balking at the notion of voicing a complaint out loud, David began to back away. He had only gone a few feet however, when he was arrested by a glimpse of emerald green in the heap of clothes next to the sofa. In the moment it took to absorb the implications of the observation two familiar eyes peered over the man's shoulder, widening in silent horror at the sight of him. He turned and walked quickly back out into the dank courtyard, gently pulling the door shut behind him.

# 14

The fireworks started the moment it was dark, transforming the clouded sky to a glittering paintbox. Stella, hurrying home from a trip to the local shops, tightened her grip on her carrier bag. She had only gone out for a jar of Ovaltine, but had ended up buying a few other things as well: ox-tail soup, a pot of cottage cheese, a packet of treacle creams, a tub of low-fat strawberry yoghurt, a carton of grapefruit juice. Feeling her right shoulder knotting under the weight of it all, she cursed herself for not having asked for a second bag, so that she could have at least spread the load more evenly. Turning into her road, she paused to swap the shopping from one hand to the other. Up ahead, beyond the skyline of terraced houses, the orange glow of a bonfire was swelling like a sunset. Sparks of gold and silver were bursting all around it, their shards like tiny falling stars. Stella paused to watch, her heart swelling as she thought about Anna's phonecall and the news about the baby. A miscalculation, but they were going to make the best of it. Her daughter had been brusque and businesslike, warming only slightly to Stella's gasped congratulations, themselves borne out of shock more than anything. She had felt a sort of joy, but at a great distance, more like something she was watching rather than experiencing for herself. With Anna's career ambitions and Becky always so badly in need of money, the notion of becoming a grandmother had seemed too remote to bother with. To have it so suddenly transformed into reality did not, for Stella, constitute the simple thrill commonly associated with such situations. On the contrary, the news had felt more like one of the rockets whining overhead, the kind that fell ominously silent before suddenly exploding in a burst of ear-shattering sound. Grandmotherhood was the last stage in life, the twitching of the final curtains, a sign that the grim reaper was waiting just around the corner with his sharpened scythe. And Anna hadn't sounded thrilled either, not in the way that she should have, not in the way that Stella herself remembered feeling, basking under the French sun some thirty-four years before, revelling in the ripeness of her swelling body, feeling blessed and beautiful and proud. Such images had flooded Stella's mind all day, fuelling her unease, not just for her daughter but for herself, making her feel the impossibility of moving on to this last stage of her life when she had done such a poor job of accommodating the first.

It was a relief to get inside her house, to have the noise muffled by double-glazing and the comfort of a cup of tea. She switched on the radio while she drank it, slurping noisily because she was alone and trying to rub the stiffness out of her shoulder with her free hand. In the last few years there always seemed to be one kind of physical pain or another; sore feet, a headache, an aching back. Sometimes she wondered if the pain wasn't a mercurial entity that had taken residence inside her, something that could be chased from one part of her body only to make itself felt in another. Already she could feel the stiffness in her shoulder edging its way into the base of her neck, a travelling snake of tension which she knew would soon be coiled inside her head, requiring analgesics to tame it to levels of toleration.

The news bulletin on the radio was followed by a ten-minute special on problems caused by the rain, which had continued more or less unabated now for over two months. Flood warnings had been issued in twelve counties. School children in Wales were stranded in their villages; Gloucester had a fortress of sandbags round the cathedral; a teenager in North Yorkshire claimed to have caught a twelve-pound salmon in his flooded back garden. Stella switched it off and went to peer through the kitchen window, shuddering at the thought of water seeping between the floorboards of her home and wondering how on earth bonfires got lit in such soaked conditions; how anyone had the heart for it. A few loud bangs told her that one of her near neighbours had embarked on their own Guy Fawkes' celebrations, possibly the couple two doors down with three noisy boys. They were always in the garden no matter the weather, playing shouting games or whacking balls over the fences. Rugby, football, tennis, golf – she had fished every sort out of her flowerbeds at one time or another. Not up to the challenge of throwing them back, she sometimes dropped them surreptitiously onto the lawn of her immediate neighbour. At other times, when she was feeling particularly bleak, she stuffed them into the bottom of her dustbin, feeling that life was a constant battle against such unwanted detritus, that she had to build her own private wall of sandbags to keep it out.

Stella left the window and put the kettle back on, even though she wasn't sure she wanted another cup of tea. While it boiled she went upstairs to find her slippers, a wide soft sheepskin pair Anna had given her a few years before. The relief after her tight leather shoes was so joyous that she gasped out loud. It had been a difficult day, she reflected, as so many of them were now, with Philip on the East Coast and Anna buried in Dorset. Phoning the previous night, as he did every Sunday, Philip had said she should get out more, take up bridge or join a choir. Stella had replied, as she always did, that she would think about it, but all the while nursing the secret knowledge that loneliness was a habit like so much else, not easily thrown off after twenty years, just less easily camouflaged. Before going downstairs she gathered up the four greetings cards from her mantelpiece, floppy now from having been displayed for so many weeks above the heat of the gas fire, and dropped them in the wastepaper basket next to the door. Having got as far as the landing however, prompted by some dim impulse of self-pity, she turned back to retrieve them for a final read-through at the kitchen table.

The second cup of tea did not taste as good as the first and the cards, with their brief messages, looked dog-eared and sad. *Come and see us soon*, Marcel had written, as he always did, both in his August card and his Christmas one too, undeterred by the fact that in twenty years Stella never had. Stella, in her own Christmas cards, played the same game, scrawling a hollow one-line salutation below her name, as if there wasn't time to elaborate, as if she had six thousand more cards to write to dear friends scattered across the globe. *Hope to see you soon! Do look me up if ever you are over! Keep in touch!* Each year she vowed to break this last thread of contact with a dignified silence, only to crumble at the last minute, overwhelmed by a futile fear of causing offence.

The treacle creams were hard to open, with a red tag of an arrow that wouldn't pull and so many glued creases that Stella had to resort to her teeth. The biscuits spilled out onto the table in a rush, filling her tea with crumbs. She picked at the broken ones, placing the pieces on her tongue and sucking the sugar out of them till there was nothing to swallow but a soggy mush. She was on her fourth segment when the doorbell rang, not once but several times, with the sort of insolent impatience that made her want to crouch behind the sofa with her fingers in her ears. Such silly things took courage these days, she reflected bleakly, patting to check on the stability of her perm as she slipped the safety chain into place and opened the door. Through the four-inch crack she saw a dark-skinned teenager in a peaked cap and grubby anorak. When she tried to close the door he slipped his fingers into the gap.

'Please, miss, it's an emergency, honest. My friend, he's hurt himself.'

'How has he hurt himself?' Stella muttered, easing her grip on the door.

'A firework, miss, this fuckin' great thing goes off in his face an' he's jus' lying there, in the road like an' I thought I'd better get some help.'

'Look I'm sorry, I can't help, I'm busy – I . . . there's a phonebox at the end of the road.'

'But we ain't got no cash, an' there's no one out here, miss, an' we need, like, an ambulance or something. Please?' He was wringing his hands now, looking so truly distressed that Stella began, for the first time since the start of the encounter, to peer properly into the darkness behind him.

'Where is he then, your friend?'

The boy pointed behind him. Stella could just make out a slumped figure on the pavement. 'Well . . . I suppose I could call you a taxi and then . . .'

'Like I said, we ain't got no cash, miss. We need an ambulance. He's hurt real bad. See for yourself, if you don't believe me.'

Stella slipped the chain off the hook and stepped outside, taking her housekeys with her. It wasn't raining but the air felt damp and chilled. Crossing her arms against the cold she paused, debating which would be more foolhardy, to leave her door open or closed; or whether she had made a huge mistake just by coming outside. The boy, as if sensing her doubts, took several steps back. 'Are you goin' to look then?'

She followed him out onto the pavement to find that the hunched grey figure was curled on his side, moaning gently, with his hands over his eyes. In the dark it was hard to make out anything properly, beyond the fact that he did genuinely appear to be in pain.

'It's his eyes,' said the dark-skinned boy, the whites of his own eyes like pearls in the dark. 'He says he can't see, won' let me look. Man, he needs a doctor.'

'Where are your parents?'

'I live with my Mum and she works nights. Dale don't want to tell his, they'll go mad.'

'Yes, well they'll have to be told sooner or later,' said Stella briskly, sounding braver than she felt. 'I could call you an ambulance . . . or maybe even . . .' She hesitated, reaching inside herself for some instinctive sense of the right thing to do. 'I could drive you to the hospital myself. There's one not far away that has an accident and emergency department.'

'Could you, miss?' The boy's eyes widened. He was not nearly as old as she had originally supposed, maybe only thirteen or fourteen.

'Hang on while I fetch my coat. See if you can get him . . . Dale . . . onto his feet.'

A few minutes later Stella was nosing her Fiat out of her cul-de-sac and into the busy main road leading down to the roundabout. The injured Dale, his hands still fixed over his eyes, had been cajoled onto the back seat, while his friend sat next to her in the front. In the enclosed space of the car they both smelt strongly of smoke, though whether this was from contact with fireworks or nicotine it was hard to be sure. Stella drove very carefully, partly because she was afraid, and partly because of the glassy glare of oncoming headlights on the lenses of her spectacles, shimmering on the wet roads like lamps on a rippling pond. At every rustle from the back seat she tensed, still half expecting one of her companions to pin a knife to her throat and ask for the PIN number to her bank account. That they hadn't, that she was driving two strange and rather large teenagers in the dark, made her feel peculiar inside. Afraid, but better too, in a way that, curiously, seemed to make up just a little bit for all her mixed feelings over Anna expecting a baby. Slowing to turn into the entrance to the hospital, it occurred to Stella that the cause of this might be because for the first time in many years she had surprised herself, as if something stuck for a long time in the same position had been nudged out of place. Once they had parked she found two orderlies to help Dale, who was groaning worse than ever, out of the car. The last she saw of them he was huddled under a blanket on a stretcher heading for some saloon-style double doors with his friend, who had said he was called Leon, jogging alongside. It was only during the course of the walk back to the car that she realised she was still in her slippers. The once white fluffy sheepskin was grey with muddy water and so sodden that driving home she could feel them squelching as she worked the pedals.

# 15

'Thanks for coming.'

'That's okay.'

'I mean, I think it's good for Jenny when the three of us do things together, makes it seem like more a family thing, more normal. She's better this time don't you think? Less sulky.' They both stared for a few minutes at the object of their discussion, who was swimming towards them down the length of their local leisure-centre pool, employing a breaststroke that was getting more lopsided by the second. Her swimming hat, tight and bulging with hair, had been pulled very low over her forehead, setting her brow into a permanent frown. 'Goggles,' she shouted, stopping suddenly and treading water, 'I need my goggles. I left them in my bag.'

'Becks, would you mind?'

'Of course not. I need a pee anyway. Won't be long.' Glad to have an excuse to put her towel round her shoulders, Becky left the poolside and returned to the ladies locker room where she and Jenny had changed ten minutes before. She found the goggles almost at once, buried in the bottom of Jenny's rucksack next to a hairbrush. She closed the locker and then opened it again, surreptitiously checking the message menu on her mobile phone. As she had hoped and expected, a new text had arrived. *mad 4 u xxx G.* Becky, her fingers trembling, hastily punched in *mad 4 u 2 xxx B*, before slipping the phone back into her handbag, deep inside where idle eyes could not pry.

She walked slowly back out to the pool, relieved that her semi-nakedness revealed only her slightly too wide hips and not the pounding of her heart. Five years of cosy domesticity with Joe had made her forget about being in love, the sheer physicality of it, the hot flushes, the racing pulse, the dry mouth, the relentless thought processes tracking always in the same direction, always to one person. Where was he? What was he thinking? What was he doing? Was he thinking of her? Only at work, where she was now genuinely busy looking after a client of her very own, instead of sitting next to Geoffrey Hooper nodding like a gormless mute, did swathes of time slip by without images of Guy Fanshawe blocking her mind.

'There we go. Catch.' She flung the goggles into the shallow end where Jenny was now doing handstands. Joe was standing beside her, steering her ankles into a vertical position until she kicked free of his grip and came up for air.

'Are you coming back in?'

'Not sure, I've got rather cold.' Becky tugged at the corners of her damp towel. 'Maybe in a minute,' she added quickly, seeing Joe's crestfallen look, knowing that she was not playing the game of happy families that he so longed for – splashy games in the pool, being jolly. 'I'll just dangle my legs and watch for a bit.' Guilt was a complex thing, she reflected, dropping her legs into the water and musing upon the fact that just when, in the interests of concealment, she should be playing the role of affectionate wife to a tee, she found herself being curt and contrary. It wasn't as if she wasn't capable of it, she reflected wryly, recalling all the episodes of shammed contentment that she had managed in the recent past. Yet, to embark on such play-acting now would in some curious way, have felt like the ultimate act of disrespect to Joe, a final, unacceptable deception. With things so bad, the least she could do was to be honest about it, on some level anyway. That Joe was proving so easy to deceive only compounded her guilt. He had the perfect career for a philandering wife. His evening shifts were far too busy to call home and if she wanted to contact him, her mobile made it only too easy. In the three weeks since the party she and Guy had already managed to meet countless times. Working these days until seven or eight, Becky had taken to going straight to Notting Hill from the office. His flat was huge and impressive, with polished parquet floors, Persian rugs, a widescreen TV and a king-size silk-sheeted double bed. Hung round the walls were vast oil paintings, some up to eight foot long, dense textured abstractions framed in gold and silver, each one appearing to Becky like windows onto another world, all the more marvellous for being unintelligible. Agreeing the first time to meet him, she had fully expected that the fairytale feel to their one-night stand in Dorset would be shattered by the sordid reality of clandestine meetings in dingy London. Instead, it was her life with Joe that had appeared dingy: she had a shabby home, a husband who worked in greasy kitchens, who seemed bent on bankrupting himself, and who, by way of a finishing touch to such charms, appeared in recent months to have traded his libido for a love of sleep. In contrast, Guy was as fabulous looking as his flat, clearly very wealthy and so deliciously attentive to her that Becky wondered how she had stood Joe's neglect for so long.

'So you see there's no contest, really is there?' she had wailed, at last breaking the news of these seismic events in her life to Anna over a hastily arranged pizza lunch in the week a few days before. 'I mean, of course I feel terrible too – terrible and wonderful – oh Annie, what ever shall I do?'

'Stop seeing him.'

'I can't.'

'Of course you can. It's called self-control, practised by millions of faithful couples the world over. Temptation doesn't stop when you get married Becky, it just has to be resisted.'

'If you're going to be like that then I'm not talking to you.'

'Like what?' Anna speared several shrivelled olives off the top of her pizza and placed them in her mouth.

'All big sisterly and sensible.'

'You asked for my advice and I'm giving it.'

'You don't understand,' persisted Becky in a tremulous voice, 'this is serious . . . I mean I think I might be in love with Guy and he certainly makes no secret of his feelings for me.' She began to smile but she checked herself. 'Joe and I haven't been getting on well for months now, he's totally obsessed with other things, agonising more than ever over Jenny . . . and as for this Brixton business I'm so fed up with the subject I could scream. I mean, it's clearly not going to happen, unless we drop the asking price on our house, which would make the whole thing financially impossible anyway. But Joe simply can't accept it.' She slammed the table with both hands. 'I tell you Anna, he's getting so desperate I think he's going to start pulling strangers in off the street and beg them to look round the house—'

'But you knew he wanted to start his own restaurant,' Anna pointed out quietly, cutting her off in mid-flow. 'He always did. You encouraged him. So why, now it's happening are you behaving as if it's something so outrageous and unacceptable?'

'Fine.' Becky threw down her napkin and reached for her purse. 'Thanks for being so understanding.' She was on the point of hurling some money onto her side plate when Anna, suddenly chalky white, swayed forward, clutching at her stomach. 'Jesus, are you okay . . . ? Anna, speak to me, what's the matter?'

'Indigestion,' she gasped letting out a deep breath. 'Phew,

that's better. I think it's the cheese.' She pushed her plate of half-eaten food to one side. 'Don't stomp off, Becks. I didn't mean to be unsympathetic. It's just that . . . well of course I can't help feeling sorry for Joe—'

'*I* feel sorry for Joe – you've no idea how hard it is, lying to him all the time . . .'

'So tell him the truth.'

Becky laughed uncertainly. 'I might well do, but not just yet, not until he's through this bad patch – that would be just too cruel. At Christmas he's giving up this ridiculous morning job he does for his friend Adrian – that will make a bit of a difference – and by then I'm sure this whole Brixton fiasco will have fizzled out too. Someone else is now seriously interested apparently; I just wish they'd get on with it, put Joe out of his misery. So I'll let all that happen first and then see . . . wait for the right moment. Guy's starting on a new project in January. In California. He's already dropped several hints that he'd like me to join him. Sun, sand . . . God, it would be brilliant.'

'He's in films, you say.' Anna picked up a bread stick and snapped it in two, scattering crumbs across her place setting.

'A director. Between projects at the moment – but he's worked all over the place with all sorts of famous people.'

'Funny,' continued Anna absently, sucking now on one end of the bread stick, 'that David and I still haven't figured out who he came with to the party. I thought it was Cindy, but then you mentioned this Judy character whom I don't remember at all . . . God knows where he sat at dinner . . .'

At the mention of David Becky felt herself go very still. She had played the scene in his studio over in her head a thousand times, clinging to the faint thread of a possibility that he hadn't recognised her. That Anna clearly had no clue about it had provided a huge boost to such hopes. And the moment had been so brief after all, Becky reasoned, replaying it all in her mind for the umpteenth time, seeing David's frozen expression and the slither of moonlight falling through the open door behind him. And her hair had been wet. And with Guy's shoulder in the way, only the top part of her face had been visible. In addition to which, David's behaviour the next day could not have been more normal. With Anna confined to her bed with a migraine, he had helped her find things for breakfast and then driven her to the station, making pleasant smalltalk all the time, about the appalling weather and how she and Joe should come and visit again soon.

'Will you tell David, do you think,' she had ventured to Anna, 'about me and Guy?'

Her sister had folded her arms with a sigh. 'I guess you would prefer it if I didn't.'

'You guess right.'

'Well, I won't then.' Anna gestured to the waiter for the bill, adding gravely, 'And you would really leave Joe and go to California with this man?'

'I'm not sure,' Becky whispered. 'All I know is that I was utterly fed up with being unhappy, fed up with having nothing to look forward to, with feeling so alone.'

'I didn't know things were so bad . . . you should have told me.' She leant forward with sudden urgency, placing her hand over Becky's and using the soft, motherly tones which Becky realised she had been hoping to hear all along. 'Poor sweetheart, what a mess.'

Becky was jolted from her reverie by Joe, bursting out of the pool between her legs, spouting water from his mouth, his dark hair sleeked back to reveal the deep receding hairline on either side of his temples. 'If you don't get in soon it won't be worth it.' His eyes, bloodshot from the chlorine, looked at her so intently that she glanced away, feeling a twist of shame.

'Okay then.' She slipped under his arms into the water and set off on a messy crawl towards the deep end, aware out of the corner of her eye of Jenny, now blue and shivery, sabotaging an attempt of Joe's to follow along behind. Reaching the other end alone, she hung on to the side for several minutes, looking up at the crawling hands of the pool clock and thinking of the flat in Notting Hill where each hour seemed to be gobbled up in minutes.

Getting ready for bed later that night, when Jenny had at last been persuaded to go to sleep, Joe peered into the laundry basket and pulled out the red underwear he had given her for her birthday. 'I didn't see you wearing these.'

'There are a lot of things you don't see,' Becky replied lightly, her mind galloping for explanations as she made a big show of plumping her pillows.

'In fact I've never seen you wear them. I assumed you didn't like them.'

'Of course I like them . . . well, sort of . . . I mean I'm not sure they're exactly . . . me.'

'So why are they in the laundry basket?'

'Because . . . if you must know, I did put them on the other morning but they were rather itchy so I thought if I ran them through the wash a few times they might soften up a bit.'

'I see. But you should have said. You should have said at the time if you didn't like them.'

'Joe I—'

'It doesn't matter now . . . I don't want to talk about it, I'm too tired.' He got into bed and rolled to face the wall, pulling the duvet round his chin as he always did by way of preparation for falling asleep. Becky, switching on her bedside light and opening a magazine, spent a few moments silently scolding herself for having so underestimated her husband's powers of observation. He never looked in the laundry basket; he just hurled things at it and round it. And the damn things had itched as well, especially round the crotch where the frilly trim felt as hard as gauze. Guy had liked the outfit well enough though, making her parade around the sea of satin sheets before pressing her onto them, saying she was the sexiest thing he'd ever seen and he could fuck her till the cows came home. Picturing the scene, Becky stared at the motionless mound under the duvet next to her with a fierce stab of satisfaction. It seemed incredible that she had once lain awake hoping that such a lifeless heap would turn over and deign to touch her. She just didn't care any more, she decided, feeling a flood of power at the observation. It occurred to her in the same instant that in any relationship the person who cared the least was bound to be the one to exercise the most control, the one who would have the courage to walk away. She would leave after Christmas, she vowed, whatever the state of play on the bloody house or anything else in Joe's life. She would put herself first for once, chuck in her job if necessary, go to California, start having some fun again, instead of slogging through life, for all the world like one of the million grey-faced and prematurely middle-aged commuters with whom she rubbed elbows each morning, the ones she so despised. Closing her eyes, Becky let her thoughts drift to her last meeting with her lover, the most intense and satisfying so far, with both of them really coming clean about their feelings. Most touching of all, Guy had talked with real openness of Judy and the women before her, of his search for a soul mate in the hazardously superficial milieu in which he worked. Becky was the first True Thing he had found, he said, and he intended to hang on to her.

Joe meanwhile, lay awake next to his wife with his eyes closed, powerless either to fall asleep or to prevent his brain spinning its own exhausting web of thoughts. He could feel the coolness in his wife's attitude like an icy wind. He disappointed her, he knew, just as he seemed, eventually, to disappoint all the women in his life. Even Jenny these days, with her wily looks and slippery eel emotions, playing hard to get and wanting more, always more; as hard to woo as a recalcitrant lover. The business of the underwear had upset him too. It had been expensive and shouldn't have itched. That Becky had disliked the gift from the start had only dawned on him slowly. Looking back, it seemed laughable that he had ventured into a lingerie department in the belief that he could find something fun and flattering as a birthday gift, something through which to communicate to his wife that the current infrequency with which he found himself in a state of arousal bore no relation to the attraction he felt for her body. He didn't feel impotent so much as wrung out, sucked dry, empty of all hope about anything; except for a tiny dangling thread of a belief in his future as a chef. But now even that was almost gone. His offer on the Brixton place was still alive, but only just. Other players were coming into the frame, more threatening as each day went by and no purchaser for his own place materialised. It was weeks since the agents had shown anyone round. Becky, exhausted these days from coping with the pressures of her promotion, seemed loath even to discuss it. She was working so hard that Joe had begun to wish that he had said to hell with the money and talked her out of accepting it. Whenever he tried to get hold of her now she was always on another line or in a meeting. All her early enthusiasm for his own new career path felt like a dream. She didn't believe in him any more. He could feel it, so badly sometimes that he thought he might snap under the pressure of it. She was distant now, using remoteness as a punishment for his failure to make her happy. Joe pressed his eyelids together, wondering how much more he could take, wondering to whom a man turned when the woman he loved had all but closed the door.

# 16

Anna lowered the side zip on her skirt a couple more inches and tugged at the hem of her jacket. The suit, of fine yellow wool and styled by one of her favourite designers, had a luxurious look to it, setting off to perfection the creamy blonde of her hair and wide blue eyes. Yellow was definitely her best colour, she mused, turning to check on her profile in the mirror, pleased to see that the multi-faceted strategy of keeping the zip at half mast, ballooning her shirt over the waistband and having her jacket done up was still doing a remarkable job of disguising the bulge in her stomach. Similar stealthy adaptations of her wardrobe meant that, twenty-six weeks through gestation, with Christmas just two weeks away, it was still not common knowledge amongst her work colleagues that she was pregnant. The only person she had told was her head of department, to whom she had felt duty bound to explain the situation because of sorting out practical matters connected to cover and maternity leave. As she had expected, his congratulations had been subtly muted, badly in need of the reassurance, which she delivered, about how her work schedule could fit around a two-month interruption. She had argued her case coolly and efficiently, pointing out that her live series was due for its annual break anyway, and that with careful planning and a bit of extra work some of her other commitments could be recorded in advance. Fortunately, the new phone-in programme, now christened *Open Reply*, was not due on air until May, by which time she would be wholly back into her stride. Her boss had nodded approvingly, rubbing his hands with relief at having a potential problem so rapidly solved and agreeing easily to Anna's final request that the matter be kept between themselves for the time being. Because she was a born sceptic, she had explained, wanting him to believe that her reserve related to the possibility of miscarrying the child instead of the more pragmatic business of safeguarding her status in the eyes of her fellow workers. Pregnancy altered people's perceptions of ability – she had seen it, felt it herself even, scores of times. Some misguided souls, lolling round the office in tent-like maternity dresses, crooning about eating for two and suggesting straw polls to decide on a name, positively invited such reassessments. But in Anna's experience those who managed to go through the process without succumbing to such excesses often suffered similar judgements, returning after maternity leave to a subtle web of suspicion, having to work twice as hard to prove that they were just as good and committed as before.

Anna jumped as the door to one of the lavatories behind her burst open and a young production assistant came scurrying over to the line of basins.

'Hi.'

'Hi.' Anna smiled, dropping her gaze from her reflection and pretending to look for something in her handbag.

The girl returned a shy smile of her own before shaking the water off her hands and racing out of the door. Anna remained where she was, taking a deep breath and squeezing her pelvic floor muscles as hard as she could, counting slowly to ten. She had squeezed them when doing a pee as well, stopping for several seconds in mid-flow, which the book said was the highest pinnacle of pelvic excellence, to be aimed for at every stage of the pregnancy and after the birth too. Striding back out into the corridor a few moments later, she felt the baby inside her start to move, performing one of its slow somersaults that made the hairs on the back of her neck stand on end. She glanced down her jacket front half fearful of finding the buttons pinging from their already strained cotton roots.

'Anna?'

'Shelley, hello.' She straightened quickly.

'Paul sent me to find you, apparently the handbag lady is downstairs.' The girl paused, frowning at some smudged black lettering on the back of her hand, 'Melissa Gibbons, is it?'

'Vanessa, Vanessa Gibbons,' Anna corrected her, glancing at her watch. 'She's twenty minutes early. Leave her for five minutes or so and then show her up, give her a coffee and so on. By which time the others should have arrived.'

'Oh, and there was something else . . . one of them, the Irishman who makes the organic leather clothes,' she clicked her fingers in a bid to jog her memory, 'can't think of his name . . . used to go out with Dawn Havant . . .'

'Damien O'Farrell,' snapped Anna, no longer willing to hide her impatience with the girl, who in the few months since the start of her employment seemed not to have graduated beyond floating round the corridors looking star-struck.

'That's it – Damien – Jesus, what a name. I mean, after that kid in that movie who on earth would pick . . . ?' Noticing Anna's fierce gaze, she changed tack. 'He's caught in a jam apparently. Roadworks on the M4 – not sure he can be here when he said, going to keep us posted.'

'Bollocks.' Anna strode briskly down the corridor, performing quick mental calculations as to how the balance of interviewees would work without its star turn.

As things turned out she needn't have worried. A few minutes before going on air, just as she had adjusted her entire

schedule of questions, Damien, looking fashionably emaci-
ated and unkempt in one of his own tasselled weatherbeaten
leather outfits, was hustled into the studio and slotted into
a set of earphones. Anna, relying on memory, switched
back to her original question plan, allowing Damien plenty
of scope for displaying the irreverent charm and quick wit
which had made him the darling of the tabloids. The slot flew
by, providing Anna with the sole problem of controlling the
exuberance of her panel, sometimes having to remind them,
gently, that they were there to discuss their wares rather than
provide entertaining banter about their personal lives.

She was in the throes of an enjoyable post-mortem with
the producer when her mobile rang. On hearing Joe's voice,
sounding pinched and tight, her first thought was that something had happened to Becky. This momentary, reflexive fear
was quashed a moment later however when, done with a few
cursory pleasantries, he asked if he could speak to Becky
herself.

'Becky . . . I . . . well no.'

'Oh sorry, haven't you got there yet?'

'Where Joe?' asked Anna feeling more and more bewil-
dered.

'The restaurant,' he said, sounding cross. 'Becky said she
was meeting you for lunch and seeing as it's already one fifteen
I assumed—'

'I . . . of course . . . sorry Joe, I'm in a daze today.' She
made a face at the producer, who slipped away, giving her a
thumbs-up sign as he left the room. She took a deep breath.
'I am here, that is . . . in the restaurant, but Becky isn't.'

'Funny,' he muttered, 'that Juliette girl said she left forty
minutes ago. And she's left her mobile on her desk apparently,
which is why I called you rather than leave a message . . .
where is it you're meeting?'

'St Christopher's Place, just off Oxford Street,' said Anna, thinking fast and speaking slowly. 'Is there a message I could give her Joe? Or shall I just get her to call you?'

'No not really . . . though perhaps you might just mention that I'm being relieved of my duties at Le Moulin . . .'

'Oh God, Joe, I'm *so* sorry.'

He responded by laughing, rather wildly, Anna felt. 'God no, not in that sense. Just a touch off colour, that's all.' There was a noisy sniff. 'My ever-generous employer is releasing me on the grounds that my germs will infect his customers, of whom there are sufficiently few on a Tuesday for him to feel their welfare should be guarded at all costs.' He began to laugh again but ended up coughing instead. 'I was just going to tell Becks that I'm going home at two and well . . . if she could get away a bit earlier than usual tonight . . . that would be nice.'

'I'll tell her Joe, I'll tell her of course, the moment she gets here,' promised Anna, having a sudden vivid flash as to what Becky might be up to and feeling a rush of guilty compassion for her brother-in-law. 'You sound as if you could do with seeing a doctor.'

'Nah, it's just a cold.'

'Well, you take care then.'

'Hang on, there was something else . . . I've been trying to get hold of David.'

'David?'

'To talk about my er . . . business plans. Do you think he'd mind? Only it suddenly occurred to me that he might be quite a useful person to run my figures by . . . seeing as he once did that sort of thing – albeit on a rather grander scale – for a living.' He gave an embarrassed laugh, before repeating, 'Do you think he'd mind?'

'God no. Of course he wouldn't. He'd love to help,' Anna gushed. 'Call him whenever you want . . .'

'Yes, well that's the thing, I've been trying all morning and got no reply.'

'He'll have gone on a walk I expect.'

'Oh, I see . . . right . . . I don't blame him – to get a bit of space to himself, some peace, it must be nice.'

'We all need that from time to time,' she agreed quickly, injecting a special heartiness into her tone because he sounded so dejected.

'Still no sign of Becky then?'

'Er . . . no . . . I expect she's got stuck on a tube somewhere, the flooding on the Jubilee Line has affected everything. But don't worry, I'll pass on your message. Get better soon, won't you?'

The moment Joe was off the line Anna punched in the numbers to her sister's mobile, only to be greeted by an invitation to leave a message. 'I've just had your husband on the line under the illusion that we were meeting for lunch . . . honestly Becks, if I'm to be used as an alibi for your deceptions the least you could do is warn me about it beforehand . . . I hardly knew what to say. He's ill by the way and going home. Call me as soon as you can.' Snapping her phone shut, Anna switched her attention to the pile of papers on the desk in front of her, resolving to attend to them rather than the growling in her stomach. With the sickness phase well and truly past, the compulsion to eat had thankfully eased. At her last check-up the nurse weighing her had expressed surprise at the slow-down in her weight gain. A large comely woman herself, she had tutted in disappointment, while Anna had felt a secret thrill of satisfaction, mentally chalking it up as one small victory against the frightening and relentless disfiguring of her once slim body. While able to use clothes to keep up a successful disguise at work, the bathroom mirror at home told a different story. These days she only examined herself in the nude when David wasn't around, staring in horrified fascination at the balloon of stretched skin where she had once enjoyed a waistline. Recently, a faint brown line had appeared, running along the line of tiny fair hairs between her navel and groin, like a fat zip on a bulging pouch; and there were faint sandy smudges on her cheeks too she had noticed, dim birthmarks beneath the surface of the skin, giving her a weathered look that seemed to persist through even the heaviest applications of foundation.

She was still deep in concentration half an hour later when her mobile rang. Expecting it to be Becky, full of apologies, she answered brusquely. Cheating on Joe was one thing. Using her as an unwitting accomplice was quite another.

'It's me, dear,' said Stella, startled at the edge in her daughter's voice. 'Just calling to see how you are.'

'I'm fine, Mum. Absolutely fine.'

'How many weeks is it now?'

'Twenty-six.'

'And you're still feeling okay?'

'Why does everybody treat pregnancy as some kind of illness,' Anna blurted, feeling suddenly full of hunger and impatience, 'when it's just a normal experience endured by a trillion women across the world every day of the year?'

There was a hurt silence. 'Well, I didn't mean . . .'

'No, I know you didn't, I'm sorry,' Anna apologised hastily, cursing herself for having lost control, for having taken her feelings out on her hapless mother when, as she suddenly realised, it was Becky with whom she was cross. Really cross. 'But tell me about you, Mum,' she urged tenderly. 'I'm sorry I've not called for a while, things have been so busy . . . how are you? How's that horrid aching you were getting, in your fingers, wasn't it, and your poor back?'

Stella, who had in fact been looking forward to telling her eldest daughter all sorts of things, mainly about how being pregnant was something to be embraced rather than resisted, muttered instead that she was doing very nicely and that aching on all fronts had been greatly soothed by sachets of sea salt in her nightly bath.

'Sea salt? Really? That's great, that's great. I'm pleased about that.'

'And Becky?' ventured Stella. 'Have you heard from her?'

'Oh yes.' Anna took a deep breath. 'She's fine. Joe's still dead set on trying to buy this restaurant, but it doesn't look as if it's going to work out.'

'Oh dear, I see. Right then.' Stella hesitated, still not sure of her footing. 'And Christmas, that was the other thing . . . so close now . . . will it be the usual . . . ?' she faltered, feeling suddenly timid of referring to the longstanding system that involved Anna hosting the occasion for her, and sometimes Becky and Joe too, if shenanigans over sharing Jenny with Ruth permitted it.

'Yes, the usual,' Anna assured her, trying to sound bright but experiencing an uncharacteristic stab of panic at the thought of orchestrating meals and presents and jollity.

After putting down the phone she sought out her powder compact to check on the visibility of the hateful sandy smudges, which looked more obvious than ever, like the effects of someone having smeared on a few streaks of suncream and leaving the rest of the skin to tan. She dabbed fiercely with her powder puff, feeling suddenly helpless and so undesirable that it seemed a wonder she dared to go out in public at all. An article in the hairdresser's a couple of weeks before claiming that pregnancy increased a woman's beauty and libido, had made her snort out loud. The frequency with which she and David made love had nose-dived in almost exact proportion to the steady expansion of her stomach. A fact which, wisely, they had both seen fit not to discuss and for which Anna bore her husband no ill will at all. Who could blame him for not being aroused at the sight of her? When they did get around to it, David, usually a fan of illumination

136

on the proceedings, made not a murmur of protest at her new habit of switching the light off. Cloaked in darkness she could feel almost normal, though when she got truly huge she knew even that was going to be hard.

# 17

It was four o'clock when David got home, by which time the December afternoon darkness was almost total. Leaning up against the kitchen door for support, he spent a few minutes trying to lever the worst of the mud clods off his boots with a stick before giving up and kicking them impatiently onto the mat inside. After a brief burst of sun in the morning, a teasing reminder perhaps that, though on what appeared to be a permanent leave of absence, it still existed, most of the daylight hours had been squeezed out of being by heavy cloud, closing round the landscape like a grey fist. Even working under the glare of his strip lights, David had sensed its oppression, the faceless grey squares of the studio's many windows making him feel muffled to the point of smothering. To find his moods so adversely affected by the climate was both new and unsettling. During the early ten-month frenzy of reconstructing the place and settling in, he had been too busy, too excited, to notice anything beyond the fact that the days were never long enough to accommodate the wish-list of achievements he had drawn up for them. Before that, spending all day in an office, heated in the winter and air-conditioned in the summer, being taxied between meeting rooms and airports, the obstinacies and idiosyncrasies of the British climate had rarely impinged upon his consciousness. High winds might delay take-off, or the wrong sort of leaves might cause a train to sit outside a station for half an hour, but such inconveniences had been mere irritations scratching the surface of his mind, nothing like the heaviness he had felt in the weeks since the party, as if the invisible rings of low pressure circling outside had a stranglehold somewhere inside his own heart.

Given his present circumstances, to feel so negative was, David knew, both illogical and shamefully unjustified. Even if it rained every day for the next ten years he had achieved a lifestyle of which most mortals could only dream and had no business being unhappy about it. What was more, he had had the wit to realise that freedom, the potential shapelessness of an unstructured day, might prove a hard taskmaster and applied himself rigorously to the challenge of coping with it: he got up early in the mornings, ate sensibly at sensible times, took regular exercise, avoided both alcohol and television until after a self-imposed six o'clock deadline and spent at least four hours a day in his studio, with his opera tapes for company, applying to each object the habit of perfectionism which had stood him in such good stead in the world of high finance.

Analysing, as he did remorselessly, the possible causes of this downturn in his outlook, David caught himself wondering whether Anna's pregnancy, as much as the weather, had something to do with it. The initial revelation had been a shock. An enormous shock, for both of them. If Anna, returning with the news after her scan, had shown any signs of doubt herself he would have leapt on the chance to dissuade her from seeing it through. But she had been so firm and sure, so reassuring, guessing all his fears before he mentioned them, that most had dissolved in the process. As she had pointed out, early on and many times since, with the financial resources to employ the best nanny in the world there would be nothing to stop either of them from continuing to live exactly as they wanted, with both his freedom and her career as secure as they wished them to be. Convinced by such arguments, the only regular and immediate inconvenience was that Anna had taken to falling asleep the moment her head touched the pillow, reducing their once healthy sex life to the barest minimum. Whenever they did get round to making love David was aware that a part of him was holding back, fearful of penetrating too hard and causing some seepage of fluid, or pain, or both. Recognising that, given the huge physical metamorphosis being endured by Anna herself, to complain about such a thing would have been churlish, he had locked this small dissatisfaction away, burying it alongside the more baffling discontent he was nursing towards life in general and sometimes seeking solace in morning masturbations after she had left for work.

Stepping over his boots, David made for the kitchen, pausing to frown at the mottled brown patch of damp above the door lintel. The result of a faulty gutter, the builder had said, which could not be replastered until it had had a chance to dry out. Frustrated, both with the man, who had installed the guttering in the first place, and with the unsettling sensation that such ugliness could so easily contaminate the costly perfection of his home, David had been tempted to get very cross; tempted, in fact, to perform one of the rare and infamous shouting explosions which had once caused executives and secretaries to dart in and out of offices waving suggestions and sheafs of paper. Judging however, from the builder's narrowed eyes, that such an outburst would have caused the very opposite reaction, he had instead backed down, softening his voice and saying that he would watch eagerly for the drying out process to run its course.

At the sight of a red light flashing on the answering machine in the far corner of the kitchen, David felt his spirits rise. Getting away from the relentless demands of the phone had been one of the many things which he had boasted of looking forward to. Yet now, burdened as he was by nebulous and niggling glooms, he had taken to receiving any sort of interruption from the outside world as a welcome relief. With contact from old mates in the city having dwindled to almost nothing, the only regular calls he got these days were from Anna, usually to say she would be late, or asking him to do something that he didn't want to do, like speak to Mrs Costa, or go to a shop for some vital ingredient for dinner. Hearing on this occasion however, the voice of his brother-in-law, he humphed out loud in surprise.

*'Hi, David, it's me Joe . . . look, I was wondering whether there was any way we could meet some time, or whether you could spare ten minutes or so on the phone. The thing is . . . I don't know how much you might have heard through the sister grapevine, as it were, but the fact is I'm in the throes of trying to buy a small restaurant and working out how much I'm going to have to invest in the place, overheads and so on. Given your knowledge on such subjects it would be really helpful to me if I could run some figures by you, see if I'm completely off the plot . . . Look, it's just a thought. No worries if you haven't got the time. If you have, give me a call. I guess you've got our home number so here's my mobile – 07980 503705. Thanks.'*

David wrote the number down and stared at it for a few seconds, thinking not of his brother-in-law's business venture, of which he had heard brief details from Anna, but of Becky, her eyes staring and huge, her pale legs curled round the buttocks of a man who was not her husband. He remembered the green dress, crumpled on the floor, a shimmering snake skin in the half light. Leaving the scene, he had felt a shudder of indignation not just on behalf of Joe, but on his own account too. The studio was his territory. Walking round it early the next morning, noting the dried medley of footprints round the sofa, the faint ring mark of the wine bottle on the table, he had felt the indignation intensify. Seeing an open cupboard door, he had cursed furiously on finding his half-finished self-portrait at an odd angle, clearly replaced by hands other than his own. Faint fingermarks round the base of the model verified his suspicions further, fuelling the impression that his young sister-in-law had violated not only her own marriage, but something private of his as well. It was a few days before he could bring himself to take the bust back out of the cupboard, some essential aspect of his faith in it having been diminished by the notion of critical, trespassing eyes poring over it uninvited. Having fully intended to tell Anna about the incident he then hadn't, initially because of her migraine and then out of fear that she would sail into the full-blown let's-save-Becky-mode which had driven him to distraction on various occasions in the past, most notably when she ditched the hapless Cliff two months before they were due to trade rings at the altar. Becky could save herself for once, David had decided, doing his best to forget the episode but finding that the most flimsy reference could cause it to come springing back to mind. Sometimes he even caught it hovering on the edges of his sexual fantasies, an unbidden and unwelcome reminder of a type of physical engagement that he, with Anna so swollen and fragile, sometimes feared he might never know again.

'Joe? It's David. David Lawrence. Returning your call. How are you?'

'David . . . good to hear you. I'm fine . . . well, no actually, I'm full of cold at the moment, but fine apart from that. Thanks for getting back to me so quickly.'

'Not at all, not at all,' David replied warmly, the clogged nasal voice on the end of the line both adding to his compassion for the cuckold state of its owner and providing an unexpected boost to his own deflated spirits. 'It's a while since we've seen you.'

'I know. I was so sorry to miss the housewarming – Becky said it was excellent.'

'Did she . . . ? Good . . . good. Well, it certainly seemed to go all right.'

'And of course, congratulations, to you and Anna – fantastic news.'

For a moment David thought he was referring to the completion of the house. 'Oh God, the baby – yes – thanks – still taking it in ourselves, to be honest. Not what you would call the most planned of pregnancies.' He laughed, feeling increasingly more relaxed and on top of things.

'When is it due?'

'Oh months yet, thank God, some time in the middle of March.'

'You're in for such a treat . . . both of you . . . I wish I could explain . . . the feelings it opens up, being a parent and so on . . .'

'I'm sure . . . of course, it must,' said David hastily, sounding unconvinced. 'Now, about this little business venture of yours, I'm not sure quite how I can help exactly . . .'

'It was just a thought, don't worry if you're too busy.'

'Oh no, that is, I'd like to help.'

'Ideally you should see the place, but I realise that . . .'

'By all means, name the day,' urged David, surprising even himself at his enthusiasm. 'I'd be very interested. We could have a bite of lunch while we were at it, my treat of course.'

'Only if you're prepared to eat what I'm cooking,' Joe reminded him with a laugh, 'meal times I'm rather tied up.'

'Of course you are – stupid of me. Well, let's meet one morning then, look at the property and perhaps go for a coffee and a talk afterwards.'

'David, this is really extremely kind of you . . .'

'Not at all. Old work colleagues are always on at me to come up to town,' he added, justifying the half-truth by thinking that such had been the case once upon a time.

'It'll give me a chance to catch up with one or two of them as well, maybe even over a spot of lunch at your place. How about that?'

They settled upon Friday, arranging to meet at the Brixton address to save time. Putting the phone down afterwards, David felt rather pleased with himself. A reaction which lingered pleasantly throughout the rest of the afternoon and evening, until cold-showered out of existence by Anna, who, instead of congratulating him on his generosity as he had hoped, issued tight warnings about business and family being a volatile mix, best avoided at all times. David was still trying to defend himself when she launched into a series of extraordinary and highly uncharacteristic tirades about the now imminent prospect of Christmas. The subject made an unpleasant theme for dinner, and was still dominating conversation an hour or two later when they crawled into bed.

'I'll order the turkey tomorrow, from the butchers in Sidminster, and some of those organic sausages too.'

'Anna, I can do that.'

'Are you saying I can't cope?'

'Anna, don't be silly, of course you can cope. But I've got more time to do things like that, haven't I?'

'How many pounds then?'

'I beg your pardon?'

'The sausages and turkey. How many pounds of each?'

'I don't know,' he admitted, wondering dimly why a brother-in-law for whom he felt the most low-key affection should be so much easier to help than his own wife. 'But perhaps you could tell me.'

'And there's the Christmas cards, have you made a start on those?'

'Ah, so I'm allowed to do the cards at least am I?'

'And what's that supposed to mean?'

'Darling, you're all wound up, relax . . . come here.' He

tried to put his arms round her, but she remained lying on her back, her arms folded across her stomach.

'I am relaxed, thank you. I would just like to know if you will do the Christmas cards tomorrow. It's a simple enough question and quite reasonable, given that we've already missed the deadline for abroad, not to mention parcels – all the godchildren will have to make do with book tokens this year – dull I know, but there you go.'

'Book tokens are fine,' he whispered, kissing her shoulder, which felt smooth, but hard as stone, 'And I love you,' he added, beginning to kiss her with more purpose. She slowly softened under his caresses, but reluctantly, as if succumbing out of a sense of duty rather than desire.

Lying in the dark after they had made love, feeling no closer than before, David felt some of the day's gloominess return. Needing some sort of further consolation he tried to squeeze her hand, only to find that the palm and fingers were already slack with sleep.

*Dear Marcel*, Stella wrote, using not the small square of white space next to the printed greeting in the Christmas card, but a separate piece of paper. *I thought I would write to you properly this year, give you a little family news. Both the girls are doing very well. Becky has recently been promoted in her company, which designs computer sites for people. I think she enjoys it although she's never been one to tell me too much about her feelings!* Stella stared for a few moments at the exclamation mark, wondering if Marcel would possibly guess that behind its suggestion of cheeriness there lay a history of disappointment and miscommunication. The notion of imparting anything worthwhile after a gap of so long suddenly seemed so awesome and futile that it was several minutes before she could bring herself to continue.

*Becky's husband is a chef, saving up to run his own restaurant.*

*A nice man, very kind and hard-working and very keen on all this organic business which is getting very popular over here nowadays – even supermarkets are full of it.* She stopped again, wishing she could put a line through the last sentence, which was rambling and bound to be of little interest to a man like Marcel who, from what she could recall, never set foot in shops, or in the kitchen for that matter except to eat food prepared by his wife. Then she remembered that Thérèse had died of cancer a couple of years back, which might have forced an acquaintance with supermarkets after all.

*Anna,* she wrote firmly, starting a new paragraph, *is doing extremely well, presenting programmes on the radio. She does three a week, one on fashion, one on health and one about people's shopping complaints. I listen to them all, feeling very proud, as you can probably imagine. The other very exciting piece of news is that she is pregnant, expecting her first child in March. She and her husband have recently moved to a lovely big house in the country so that will be ideal – lots of space for the little one to run around in. Also her husband is now semi-retired, which means he will be able to help out a lot with the baby, which is nice as Anna plans to go back to work just a few weeks after the birth. These career girls! And me, a grandmother, I can hardly believe it!*

Stella stared at the two new exclamation marks, aware that like the first, they each told a kind of lie, suggesting a jolliness where there was mostly doubt. But then in a way the whole letter was a sort of fabrication, she reflected, sighing to herself as she read back over it, realising that it portrayed a shining ideal that felt far from the truth. She had no idea if David would want to help with the baby. She had no idea if David was pleased about the baby, or what Anna thought about it really, deep down inside. The way she had snapped on the phone that morning still burned in her mind, none of the obvious explanations about raging hormones managing quite to erase the bafflement and hurt. Becky snapped, frequently, but not

Anna, her rock of gentleness, the one good thing in the world on which she could rely.

*And what of Pierre and François?* she continued, pressing away a mounting reluctance to continue with the task she had set herself. *Such bright children, I'm sure they must have gone on to do something really fine. And what of you? How have you coped on your own? I meant to write properly after Thérèse passed away, but I'm afraid I never managed it – you know how it is, I'm sure, with life sweeping you along . . .*

Stella paused to survey the comfortable, unimaginative decor of her small sitting room, thinking with a sudden twist of self-recognition that life had not swept her along so much as passed her by. Emboldened perhaps by the shame that accompanied this realisation, instead of signing off, as she had intended, she wrote another paragraph, saying that if he was still serious about his offer she would love to visit one day soon, in the early spring perhaps, before the birth of her grandchild.

*By which time, with any luck, the tulips and daffodils will be in their prime and all this dreadful rain – have you had it too? – will seem like a bad dream.*

*With fondest regards,*
*Stella*

# 18

He follows her up the narrow stairs which creak under his feet. The carpet is so threadbare that he can see the bare boards underneath, bone-white and spattered with paint. At a turn on the first landing she pauses to look back, giving him an encouraging nod, as if she knows it is his first time, as if she guesses that the bold approach he made in the street outside masks a great terror.

The top landing is no more than five foot wide, with a door on either side: 'This is me,' she says, turning to the nearest one and slipping a key in the lock. The room is red, a cliché of a crimson boudoir, furnished with cheap heavy silks of burgundy and scarlet. In one corner there is a double bed, with a plush satin headboard and matching counterpane, its pillowed end laden with tasselled scatter cushions. Switching on a lamp she quickly crosses the room and unties the sashes to draw the red velveteen curtains, screening the grey London sky from view. Sealed thus, with only one small light for illumination, the effect is more impressive, the cheapness of the silky fabrics not so obvious. So high above street level, the heavy traffic outside is reduced to a faint drone. Only the windows, rattling in sporadic protest under the thump of the wind, remind him that the outside world exists at all.

At her insistence he has already paid her, in the doorway before they entered the building, a thin bundle of crisp notes which he had drawn from a cash machine, half an hour and a liftetime before, when the idea had still been a fantasy, something to think about rather than actually do. She had snatched the small wad with quick over-eager fingers, slipping it out of sight in some deep compartment of her shoulder bag. It was her policy, she said, so there could be no funny business. On the verge of backing out, he found himself encouraged instead by the bored shopping-list tones in which she delivered his choice of options, like it was no big deal, just a menu for customers like any other.

'Come here then handsome,' she says now, lying back amongst the wall of scatter cushions and starting to undo the buttons on her shirt. He walks towards her, reaching with fumbling schoolboy fingers for the buttons on his own shirt, aware of the bulge of his crotch, the feel of his erection pushing against the waistband of his underpants. He had known arousal would be easy, with no emotional debts to pay, no mental baggage, no demands beyond the cash. She pulls her skirt up to her hips and opens her legs. Looking at her face, he sees that she has began flicking her tongue around the edges of her lips and teeth. For a moment, he hesitates, held back by the obvious fact that she is playing a part, that to do so is part of her job. She is very young, probably no more than nineteen or twenty. Her face is heavily made-up, all its features emphasised in strong lines, including her mouth, which he must not kiss, he reminds himself, hesitating. It is only as he gets closer that he notices faint bumps beneath her skin, crudely masked with make-up.

'Are you all right?' She stops the tongue dance. Her tone is curious, a little impatient even.

'Yes, fine, thanks,' he assures her. 'Yes, absolutely fine.'

She seems to relax, slipping her shirt off her shoulders to reveal the broad pale shelf of her collar bone and small white breasts, popping from a minuscule wire-cupped bra. As he starts to touch her, she arches her back and tips her chin to the ceiling, making such a show of sexual ecstasy that he catches himself wondering if she is acting after all, whether he really does have such power in his fingertips. Then he remembers that it doesn't matter what she really feels, that what he has paid for is the privilege of just that freedom, of worrying, caring about no pleasure but his own.

She makes an erotic game of getting the rubber on and then groans as he pushes inside. 'Oh yes,' she whispers, her sticky lips pressing against his ear. 'Oh yes.'

He pushes hard, forgetting her, thinking only of the pleasure swelling inside, focusing on the monumental effort of controlling it, of releasing it only at the last possible moment of containment. It feels like an act of purity; something clear-cut, honest and true. No expectations, no demands, no repercussions. No infidelity either, at least not of the heart, which is the only place it counts.

# 19

On Thursday evening Becky arrived at the Notting Hill flat in a state of some excitement. Joe, fully recovered after just two days from his cold, had phoned to say that he was meeting Adrian for a nightcap after work and wouldn't be home until midnight at the earliest. Which meant that instead of their usual snatched couple of hours she and Guy would have an entire evening to themselves. Telling him the good news as she raced for the tube, he had sounded as thrilled as she was, suggesting she pick up a Chinese on the way over and that they go to a film together afterwards.

'It's open,' he called in response to her knock on the door. She walked in to find him lying on the sofa, surrounded by papers and ash trays of half-smoked cigarettes. A visible film of blue-grey mist hung in the air, particularly over the central area of the sofa, giving Guy the air of a man marooned in sea fog.

'Hard at work, I see,' she said, blinking away the faint sting in her eyes as she crossed the room.

He groaned. 'Scripts. The bane of a director's life.'

'And also his bread and butter,' she quipped, sweeping some space for herself amongst the papers.

'True, my love, true.' He pulled her to him and kissed her once very softly on the lips. 'Did you bring the food?'

She held up the white plastic bag containing the tin foil cartons from the Chinese restaurant round the corner. 'Egg fried rice, prawns and ginger, beef and black bean sauce and spring rolls, just as you ordered.'

'You are an angel.' He kissed her again. 'And if you want to give a last magnificent shine to your already radiant halo you could get two beers from the fridge and some knives and forks. I'm starving.'

They ate sitting end to end on the sofa, with their legs interlaced and dropping occasional rice grains and dribbles of sauce onto the papers still scattered about them. Thinking back to the contrasting shambles of Tuesday, Becky vowed never to be so rash again. Meeting Guy in the middle of the day had been a mad last-minute thing, prompted by some cheeky pleading on the phone from him and the sudden delicious thought of sliding between the silky sheets of his huge bed. In the event, the reality had some trouble living up to such expectations, since it had taken ages to get there and Guy had wanted to eat before they made love, not seeming to understand that with a meeting to get back for afterwards she barely had the time. Returning to Anna's terse message, warning that Joe had been sent home sick and was trying to get in touch, had been quite a shock. And something of a disappointment too, since she had arranged to meet up with Guy again after work that evening. To make matters even worse, Guy had responded to her hasty change of plans not with sympathy but sulkiness, muttering that she seemed to spend half her life rushing away from him. She had arrived home feeling both anxious and worn out, to find Joe slumped on the sofa with a calculator and a mug of whisky and hot lemon, talking feverishly about hopes of assistance from David and new ways of looking at the figures.

Things improved greatly the next morning, when a bunch of yellow roses had arrived at the office, along with a card saying, *Missed you last night, G.* 'Wedding anniversary,' she had mumbled, in response to Juliette's enquiring gaze. The moment their backs were turned she had torn the note into little pieces and dropped it into the shredding bin, inwardly congratulating her own sense of precaution. Silly little messages found in drawers and the bottom of handbags were what got people caught out, especially creatures like Juliette, with her big resentful green eyes, hungry for any opportunity to bring down a star more ascendant than her own.

By the following evening Joe too had rallied. A day on his own at home seemed to have performed miracles not only on his health but his spirits in general. In fact, he was more lively than Becky could remember in a long time, full of optimistic talk of the St George's medics, who had been back in touch with the estate agents, and his now imminent meeting with his brother-in-law. While pleased to see him so energised, largely for the simple selfish reason that it took the pressure off her, the thought of David seeing Joe on his own filled Becky with so much apprehension that she had phoned Anna for reassurance.

'You're being paranoid.'

'You haven't said anything, have you?'

'Of course not. Anyway, I can't help wondering what you're so worried about – I mean, you're planning to leave Joe after Christmas anyway, aren't you? So what does it matter when he finds out?'

'Because I want to do it when the time is right, on my terms,' Becky had retorted, in truth a little shocked at the insouciance in her sister's tone, having to remind herself that Anna too had a lot on her plate, what with the pregnancy on top of all the usual pressures of her job. 'Guy says the California shoot might slip to February and I'm not sure how to play the work angle and although he's hinted that it would be okay for me to move into his flat whenever I want we haven't actually talked it through properly yet and . . . it's all still so complicated. I need *time* . . . I mean, there's Christmas to be got through first – we're having Jenny for the day and then again to stay for the last week of the holidays. I just can't have Joe find out yet, I just *can't*,' she had wailed, triggering a fresh round of welcome reassurance from her sister.

The queue for the cinema snaked for several yards along the pavement. Walking to the end of it with Guy holding her hand, Becky glanced nervously along the row of faces, dreading the possibility of encountering one that she knew. It was new to venture out in the open together, albeit under cover of December evening darkness, and while recognising it as an important step along the road to the possibility of any natural, normal relationship, a part of her wished that they could stay cocooned in the luxury of the Notting Hill flat for ever.

'You don't get cinema queues in Balham, anyone staying in the street that long gets mugged,' she joked, sidling into the crook of his arm, relishing the closeness which had thickened as the evening progressed. They had made love on the sofa before coming out, slowly, amazingly, and somewhat uncomfortably, crushing script pages and empty foil cartons, so like one of the truly abandoned couples in one of Guy's scripts, that she had almost laughed out loud in exultation. 'Those flowers,' she continued, remembering the roses suddenly and squeezing his arm as they shuffled forwards in the queue, 'I can't tell you what they meant to me . . . to show that you cared like that. Bloody cheeky though.' She grinned up at him, feeling as she always did at the sight of his dark-browed, magnificently symmetric features, an acute sense of disbelief in her own good fortune

He grinned back at her. 'Yeah, you said.'

'Can't I say it again?'

He laughed. 'As often as you like.' He bent down and kissed the top of her head. 'This film we're seeing, it's supposed to be in the same genre as that script I showed you tonight, subverting the Hollywood formula into something much more surprising, more contemporary. I'll be really interested to know what you think.'

Becky beamed, flattered at this continued invitation to have some involvement in his work and trying to recall the cleverest of her thoughts during their script-reading session on the sofa. In truth it had been a struggle to pick out a coherent storyline from the paragraphs of background blurb and direction surrounding the dialogue. Glancing up at Guy, frowning and scribbling over each page, she had eventually admitted as much out loud, saying shyly that she was too thick to pass any meaningful comments. It had been quite a thrill when he assured her otherwise, pointing out that the least jaded eyes were often the best, that coming at it without preconceptions would in many ways give her the clearest view.

'Becky, I'm sorry darling, would you mind doing the honours?' They had at last reached the ticket window. 'I'm out of cash and I've come out without my wallet.' Becky, who had spent all her own cash on the Chinese, quickly got out her Switch card and slid it under the glass partition, thankful both for her inflated salary and the fact that she and Joe had separate bank accounts. 'I should have offered anyway,' she said, feeling awful on his behalf, 'instead of just assuming you would pay . . . quite wrong.' Wanting to emphasise the point still further, she used the last of her change to treat them both to some sweets, or rather Guy, since he opted for a large bag of Lemon Bonbons, which she didn't like and her cash wouldn't stretch to anything else.

Seated in the cinema watching a group of muscle-bound men marooned in a snake-infested jungle, running out of both biscuit rations and bullets to ward off ferocious animals, Becky found herself wondering which Hollywood genre it was supposed to be subverting. One by one the men died, all except for the most muscle-bound and most heroic, who bumped into a lost tribe and had orgasmic sex with the daughter of the chief. At one point, in spite of the rustling of the Lemon Bonbon packet next to her, she found herself dangerously close to falling asleep and had to massage the inside of Guy's thigh to divert herself from the temptation. Liking the attention, Guy gave up on both his sweets and the movie in favour of giving her sticky kisses, which managed to feel exciting even through the taste of stale sugar. Outside in the street he renewed his embraces with even greater fervour, begging her to come home with him, saying how cruel it was that they had yet to wake up in each other's arms. Feeling weak-kneed herself, it took every scrap of Becky's flakey willpower to convince him that such delights were best reserved until after Christmas and that what she was most in need of was a cash machine so that she could pay for a taxi home. Walking with their arms clasped around each other, pausing every few minutes to kiss, it was some time before they eventually found one. Guy stood behind her, nuzzling her neck while she fed in her card.

'I'm sorry about the film by the way. It was crap wasn't it?'

She laughed with some relief, having rather dreaded what insights she might be called upon to deliver on the subject.

'Just goes to show how even the best directors can go off the rails . . . sell out to the industry . . . hey, sweetheart, you couldn't get out an extra fifty for me, could you?'

Becky, her fingers poised over a mere thirty for herself, trying the game which always failed of getting out less than she needed in the hope that she might prove herself wrong, hesitated for just a moment. He nibbled her ear. 'Hey, if it's a problem then don't worry.'

'No . . . I . . . of course it isn't . . .'

'On second thoughts, don't.' He put his hands over hers

to prevent her punching in the numbers. 'It's not fair of me to ask, especially as it's just so I don't have to rush out of the house in the morning to get cash for the cleaning lady . . . I'm a lazy sod, ignore me.'

'No, honestly, it's no problem, really Guy . . .'

He laughed meekly, releasing her hands. 'You are very sweet, did you know that? I'll pay you back next time.'

By the time the taxi reached Balham Becky had convinced herself that Joe would be waiting to greet her on the doorstep with a volley of accusations and a rolling pin. He had said midnight and it was already five past. But there was no sign of his motorbike in the street and the dark open-curtained windows of the house told her that her luck had held after all. Once inside the house she hurried up the stairs, stuffed her smokey clothes into the bottom of the laundry basket and had a hasty bath. By the time Joe got home, some twenty minutes later she was tucked between the sheets like an angel, her eyes closed, her skin still warm and smelling of soap. As he entered the room she could feel her heart begin to race a little. From the heavy uneven tread of his feet on the stairs and the way he undressed, staggering slightly as he slid off his trousers and socks, she could tell that he was a little drunk.

'Becks,' he whispered, pressing his lips to her neck, 'are you awake?'

'Hmm.'

'Becks, I love you.'

'Hmm.'

'Becks, are you awake?'

'Now I am, yes.'

'Your hair smells of smoke, or is it me? We went to a pub and then back to Adrian's . . . we've got a deal sorted, organic vegetables for the restaurant, it's going to be organic . . . Becks, are you listening? I've got a name too. "The Green Patch". What do you think?'

'Sounds a bit earthy,' she muttered, turning onto her back with a sigh designed to suggest that she had been roused from a deep sleep. 'How about "The Green Table" or maybe "La Table Verte"? Sounds more elegant somehow.'

'God, that is good . . . "The Green Table" . . . I like that. I'll put it to David tomorrow, see what he thinks . . .'

Becky rolled over to face him. 'I'm sure you don't need David, you know,' she whispered, stroking the hair out of his eyes. 'If the house deals go through you'll manage perfectly well without him. Besides, you don't even like him very much . . .'

'I like David. When have I ever said I don't like David? He's a bright man, a useful man, I respect what he's done, I . . .'

'Yeah, okay, calm down. I'm only saying that . . . I have faith in you.' She squeezed her eyes in the darkness, glad he could not see her blush of shame.

'Do you Becks?' He spoke very softly and a little unsteadily. 'Do you really . . . because sometimes recently I've felt that . . . I've felt so apart from you . . . it's made me . . . oh God, it's made me . . . you've no idea.'

It was a few moments before she realised that he was sobbing. 'Joe, please don't . . . Joe.' Becky pulled his head to her chest feeling like bursting into tears herself from the confusion of compassion and guilt suddenly pressing inside. 'Joe, stop, you've been under so much pressure recently . . . and then being ill . . . you're just letting it all get on top of you . . . stop, my darling Joe, please.' The tears subsided almost as quickly as they had come, though he kept his head buried against her chest. His breath, heavy and regular, felt warm against her skin. Soon the slackness in his body told her that he had fallen asleep. Becky in contrast felt more wide awake than she had in her life. She kept her arms round his broad frame for a long time, cursing and marvelling at the tenderness he could still evoke in her, clinging to the notion of Guy like a drowning person gripping the edge of a raft. Was it the essence of her lover she wanted, or the idea of him? Was this tenderness love? The kind of love that lasted long after the flame of erotic passion had eased, the kind of love that good sensible people treasured like gold dust, knowing that it offered a store of riches for the years ahead, when women who ran off with film directors were worrying about face-lifts and the threat of pretty starlets?

'Oh fuck,' she whispered, besieged suddenly by fresh and ugly doubts. From nowhere the scene at the cash dispenser flickered in her mind. She had lent him money before, little bits here and there, and never yet been paid back. Though trivial the thought of it made her suddenly uneasy, made her see for the first time that her lover had faults like any man and she had better be sure she knew the extent of them.

Joe, stirred beside her. 'What did you say . . . ?'

'Nothing, Joe, nothing. Go back to sleep.'

'I'm awake now.' He heaved himself out of her arms and went to the toilet. Becky lay in bed, listening to the muffled sounds through the wall. The cistern was still flushing as he opened the door. Instead of returning to bed he leaned against the doorway of the bathroom, a huge bear of a shadow in the semi-darkness. 'I'm sorry about my . . . just now . . . breaking down like that . . .'

'Joe please, you don't have to . . .'

'I do. Listen to me. I know I've been neglecting you, that I've not been myself, I'm sorry Becky I can't tell you how sorry I am . . . but it's all going to change, I just feel it now, here.' He struck his chest with his fist. 'This restaurant, The Green or Pink bloody Table, it *is* going to happen and you'll get back the man you loved, the one you married . . . I promise, Becks, with all my heart. I love you. I will always love you.'

He crawled back between the sheets and pulled her into his arms. Becky, feeling trapped in a silent, secret nightmare of her own making, listened with a pounding heart to the familiar rustles and murmurs of his body submitting to sleep. She remembered reading somewhere that it took courage to walk out of a marriage. She wondered if what she was experiencing now was simply a lack of that kind of fortitude or something much worse, something connected to having fucked up big time and having only herself to blame. She squeezed Joe's fingers again, feeling the solidity of his hand. Guy, for all his attractions, was not solid; he seemed to drift effortlessly through life, taking each moment as it came, in a way that she admired but was not sure she could ever truly share. Even the simple matter of the California shoot was something she was still having trouble pinning him down about, the dates, even the name of the project seemed to change every time he mentioned them. The next time they met she would ask him a few straight questions, she decided, make him realise that with so much hanging in the balance a more definite commitment was called for, some sort of timeplan. Relaxing into sleep at last, she found herself on a heat-hazed Californian beach, surrounded by Guy and several other bronzed and beautifully toned male creatures who alternated between paying attention to her and firing harpoons into the sea. In the dream she felt desired and thrilled, but also very afraid, because the harpoons flew like paper darts, making no impact on the huge metallic shadows gliding beneath the surface of the water, coming closer with every turn.

# 20

Over the next few days any hope Becky might have had of clarifying her state of mind were subverted by the unignorable last-minute demands of Christmas. With clients pouncing on the imminent festive break as a deadline for even the most non-urgent of demands, she found herself skidding into shops five minutes before they closed, panic-buying inappropriate and expensive items without any real idea who they were for. At home there reigned what felt to her like a state of suspended calm, generated by Joe's assumption that all was now well and her certain knowledge that it wasn't.

For the first time in a while Jenny was due to spend both Christmas and Boxing Day with them. With Joe managing the catering side of things, Becky offered to help out with presents for Jenny's stocking and also to take sole charge of decorating the house. Desperate to compensate for all the invisible and ugly imperfections rampaging beneath the surface of her life, she took these self-assigned duties very seriously, returning every day with fresh bags of gifts and tinselled trinkets. Soon the sitting room was so heavily adorned that it began to resemble some kind of gaudy yuletide grotto. While the tree, a Norwegian pine three foot taller than their usual modest purchase, was so laden with decorations that it tilted dangerously to one side and had to be sandbagged with heavy books to prevent it toppling over altogether.

Thus distracted, it wasn't until Christmas Eve that Becky managed to see Guy. It was the first time they had met without actually being able to make love and Becky felt keenly the lack of physical reassurance that being held in his arms always offered. Their chosen rendezvous was a large wine bar in Holborn, where they huddled into a dark corner and exchanged a few furtive kisses before reaching into their bags for their presents. He handed his over first, a large bottle of eau de Cologne, still in the plastic bag from the shop in which he had bought it.

'Oh God, the price,' he groaned, snatching it out of her hands. 'Sorry.' Pink-faced with embarrassment, he laboured for several minutes to peel off every sticky trace of the label before handing it back.

'How lovely, Guy, thank you.' Becky unscrewed the lid and sniffed appreciatively at the floral scent, all the while watching with anxious eyes as he unwrapped the pair of tiny gold cufflinks she had chosen from a Bond Street jeweller the day before. They were in the shape of Greek masks, complete with tiny holes for the eyes and mouth, one tragic and one comic. 'I hope you like them,' she faltered, wondering suddenly if the compulsion to spend a week's salary had stemmed from a sudden surge of certainty in her feelings for the man sitting opposite her or precisely the opposite. Having thought she needed only to see him again to feel reassured, she was now not so sure. There was no turmoil in his life, nothing comparable to what she was going through with Joe. It made it impossible to talk about or explain. That Guy somehow seemed to remain aloof from the daily slog that afflicted other people was one of the things that attracted her to him; yet it made her feel different and isolated too, Becky realised, studying the inscrutable expression with which he was gazing at the cufflinks, wishing suddenly that they could return to the simplicity of their early courtship, before the tendrils of reality had begun their stranglehold. She wished too that Joe hadn't cried and been so loving. It had thrown everything back off balance, made her feel tender just when she was doing her best to feel nothing at all.

The cufflinks twinkled in the dim light of the small oil candle burning at their table, the holed faces looking, so Becky could not help thinking suddenly, faintly sinister. 'I thought, with your being involved with actors and so on,' she began, concerned by his silence, 'I mean, just say if you don't like them . . . I'd hate you to feel that you had to pretend . . .'

'Of course, I love them,' he interrupted, closing the little leather box at last and tracing one finger round its smooth edges. 'You are so very good to me.' He glanced at her and then looked quickly away.

'Guy? Is something the matter?'

His expression softened at once into a pose of exaggerated dismay. 'Only that, instead of spending Christmas with the woman I love I am to be incarcerated in a restaurant with several other dull film fogies without homes or families to go to – if that isn't something to sulk about I don't know what is.'

'Will you go to Dorset at all, do you think?'

He scowled. 'No, probably not . . . too much work on up here. I'll set up camp on the sofa, as usual I expect.'

'I'll call if I can.'

He smiled. 'In that case I'll have my mobile glued to my ear.'

'And we'll see each other in January, after my stepdaughter's gone.'

'January,' he echoed, looking sad.

'Talking of which,' ventured Becky, 'I was wondering, do you have any further news on dates and so on – for the shoot in California? Because the thing is, if I'm ever to make proper plans—'

'Not yet.' He lit a cigarette, frowning as the first jet of

smoke hit his eyes. 'But you'll be the first to know my sweet, I promise you that.' He sat back in his chair, making a frame with his fingers and peering at her through it, as if studying her through a camera lens. 'Becky on a beach, suntanned, rubbing oil into my back . . . I can just see it.' He chuckled, flicking the packet of cigarettes across the table by way of an invitation for her to help herself.

Becky began to take one out and then put it back again with a sigh, suddenly weary of the prospect of trying to scrub all traces of it from her system afterwards. 'No thanks, better not.' She smiled, doing her best to picture the scene he had just described, but instead seeing only the more perturbing images of the dream about the shadowy sea monsters which had lingered in her consciousness long after most dreams tended to, almost as if she hadn't been asleep at all.

Staggering in through her front door laden with the results of a final shopping spree a couple of hours later, she almost blinded herself on the sharp point of a star mobile which she had strung up under the hall light the evening before. It had been the finishing touch to the vast array of decorations now clogging every windowsill and mantelpiece of the ground floor, an eye-level, immediate, in-your-face reminder that this was, at all costs, to be a house of merriment, where the charade of Christmas cheer would be taken to new extremes. Dropping her bags to the ground, Becky could not resist giving the mobile a fierce, futile swipe, feeling some satisfaction as the tiny gold strings twisted together, snarling the stars at lopsided angles. Glimpsing the tree through the open door beside her, doing its laden, leaning tower of Pisa act, she was tempted suddenly to give that a hit too, to push it in the direction it so clearly and tediously wished to go, and then stamp all the baubles to smithereens. Christmas was all play-acting anyway, she reflected grimly, even for mortals unshackled by knots of adulterous confusion, who

164

knew if they loved their lovers or their husbands, who had a definite gameplan beyond survival from one nanosecond to the next.

It was still only nine o'clock, almost two hours before Joe would be home. Fetching all her purchases from various bags scattered about the house, she tipped them out onto the sitting-room carpet and went into the kitchen to find scissors and Sellotape. In search of a drink, she opened the fridge door and stood for a few seconds, marvelling at the numerous foil-covered pudding basins that Joe had somehow found the time to prepare during the course of the previous two days: bread sauce, cranberry sauce, brandy butter, pearly green sprouts and chubby homemade sausages, the meat bulging out of their flimsy skins. The turkey, stuffed ready for the oven, its fleshy pink body mottled with herbs and its huge thighs sporting fat strips of bacon, took up the entire bottom shelf. Becky eased out a bottle of white wine that had been wedged on top of it and seized a misted wine glass from the draining board, before returning to the sitting room. Lowering herself into a cross-legged position, she then set about sorting her gifts into orderly piles for wrapping – those for Joe's stocking, those to go under the tree, those for Jenny which Joe would want to wrap himself later. She drank steadily as she worked, wishing that the chaotic state of her life could be so easily shuffled and packaged, and resisting the urge to abandon her task and call Anna, the only person in the world with whom she would have liked to discuss the mess of her private life, but who had made it quite clear all week that she was too frantic for a heart-to-heart of any kind. She had even ruled out a quick lunch to exchange presents, suggesting with uncharacteristic curtness that they make do with bubble-wrap and consign their gifts to the post instead.

By the time the bottle was three quarters empty the Sellotape was sticking obstinately to her fingers instead of the wrapping paper. The parcels began to emerge with bulky edges and untidy folds of paper as even the most simply-shaped gifts – a CD for Jenny, a tie for Joe – appeared determined suddenly to slither out of the paper envelopes she folded round them and make off across the floor. Writing the labels, her pen kept sliding across the paper, as if bent upon inscribing some message of its own.

Finishing at last, Becky rolled onto her back with a groan. Carefully balancing the last yellowy warm half-inch of her wine on her chest, she stared through half closed eyes at the tree shimmering above her. The fairy on top was leaning in the same direction as the branches beneath, as if contemplating some sort of sky-diving freefall towards the carpet. The more Becky looked the more she longed to put the little figure straight, to warn the benign plastic face, with its cherried cheeks and silky yellow hair, that she was on the edge of a precipice and should pull back at once. The step ladder necessary to fulfil such a mission of mercy was stowed in their dusty box room of a cellar, between half used tins of house paint and a fresh pagoda of empty decoration boxes. Becky was just contemplating the awesome challenge of retrieving it when she felt strong hands slide beneath her back and legs and she was being hoisted upwards, her limbs flopping no matter how hard she tried to control them. 'Love you,' she said, or tried to say, nuzzling into the warm familiar bulk of her husband's chest, marvelling that she could have imagined ever wanting to be anywhere else.

Anna stared at her plate of food, contemplating the impossible prospect of eating it. She could feel the baby wedged up under her ribcage, crushing her stomach into what felt like a small wilted sack, incapable of expanding to accommodate one mouthful let alone a three-course meal. The ballooning had happened suddenly, almost overnight, ruling out the possibility both of making do with anything from her regular wardrobe and of continuing to conceal her condition from her colleagues. Though there had been congratulations all round, she had sensed the critical surprise at the heart of them, the detached curiosity as to how she would deal with the juggling act that lay ahead. It seemed incredible that twelve more weeks of the process still remained. The skin across her abdomen was already as tight as a drum, so stretched and so unbearably itchy, that she was sometimes tempted to tear herself to shreds with her nails.

'Anna, you haven't got any of your lovely roast potatoes.'

'I'm sure I have, Mum, thanks, under here somewhere.' She prodded her food with her fork.

'You're eating for two, remember.'

Anna blinked slowly, managing, with supreme effort, to contain her annoyance to a secret invisible tightening inside her head. 'No one thinks that any more.'

Stella humphed, as aware as her daughter that a new and painful disconnection existed between them. 'Well, perhaps they should. Don't you think, David?'

'I think,' replied David carefully, 'that Anna has cooked a fabulous meal and should eat as much or little of it as she chooses.'

Anna offered him a smile of gratitude, saying quietly, 'Cooking always dulls the appetite, you know that, Mum – you used to say as much yourself.'

'True.' Stella cut a large square of white meat and began piling it with portions of sauce and vegetables. Anna, noting the self-conscious determination of the movements, the false show of appearing busy and absorbed, was for a moment so irritated that she had to bite her cheeks to stop herself from screaming out loud. Hoping for another glimmer of spousal solidarity, she glanced across the table at David, only to find that he too was lost to the ritual of eating, working his way from the back of the plate as he always did, no gravy, leaving the meat till last. He wasn't really an ally, she thought bitterly, not any more, not since the pregnancy. While her life, her sense of self, was steadily being turned on its head, nothing had changed for her husband. It seemed laughable that she had ever worried about his freedom, when it was now clear that it was hers that was up for grabs. David would continue to do his own thing, as he always did, but in a way that was already showing signs of increasingly excluding her. She had felt it steadily in recent weeks, the pulling away, the preserving self-containment, evident even in the manner of his love-making, which had grown painfully tentative – almost reluctant – as if, confronted by this new hideously bloated version of his wife, he could not bring himself fully to connect with it. But there were other more practical signs too: like the fact that these days he never seemed to be in his studio, but was always on walks or hopping on trains up to London, coming back stimulated beyond what Anna could reasonably imagine as having resulted from lunch and a bit of number-crunching with their brother-in-law. Probing about these excursions and getting nowhere, she had felt, for the first time in their ten-year marriage, like some nagging, pitifully insecure wife, hatefully threatened by the superior power and attraction of her husband. It confirmed for her the disturbing fact that the balance between them – the crucial power-equalising balance – had gone, forced out of being by the unimaginably momentous effects of her decision to press ahead and have the child. A decision which she could now see was fast destroying the equilibrium not just of her marriage, but of her inner self as well. She, who had once prided herself on being the one to hold everything together, felt as if she was slowly being pulled apart. The strong centre she had imagined to lie at the heart of her, felt now like a void, visited only by belittling spurts of irritation and envy.

'Lovely meal, Anna darling, well done.'

'Yes, here's to the chef,' chimed Stella, raising her glass.

'Thank you.' Anna speared a Brussels sprout and forced it between her lips. Inside, the baby heaved itself into a new position. She pressed one palm against her shirt, feeling the bony limbs slide beneath her skin. Pushing her cutlery over her mound of uneaten food, she placed her right hand over her left, feeling with her fingers for the familiar comforting ridges of her scar. 'And thank you both for your presents too. Super, all of them.' As she spoke her eye was drawn to the sideboard where David's clay self-portrait now sat, placed there by her following the present-opening session which had taken place after breakfast. It was an extraordinarily good likeness, displaying with impressive and uncanny exactitude the full slope of his forehead, the firm neat line of his nose and the deep-set eyes, wide and intent, as if in a permament state of concentration. Even the hair was right, hanging in its new longer style, its ends curling well below the collar of his shirt. Her gasps of surprise and admiration had needed no theatrics to sound sincere. It was only looking at it now that Anna felt something inside her recoil under the gaze of the stony eyes, fired hard and white in the fierce heat of the kiln.

'And how are you getting on with the business of nannies?' enquired Stella, offering the question by way of a diversion from the almost overwhelming desire to comment on her daughter's still untouched pile of food. 'Any luck yet?'

'Anna's department,' said David, his mouth full. 'She'll find us a Wonder Woman, I know that much.'

'Oh yes,' said Anna quickly, even though most of her faith in the existence of such a creature had been hammered out of being by the discovery that all the bright energetic nannies she had so far contacted had no wish to live a two-hour train ride away from London night clubs and the formidable nanny network employing all their friends.

'Though there's always Mrs Costa, of course, should it come to that . . .'

'Which it won't,' put in David briskly, throwing his napkin onto his side plate and getting up to clear away the dishes.

'She's also got a daughter,' continued Anna to her mother, 'who always seems to be between jobs in London. I'm not ruling anything out.'

'Quite right dear.' Stella gave a last dab to her lips with her napkin and pushed her chair away. 'I'll take this lot out. You stay where you are,' she ordered, unable to resist adding, 'Shame you weren't more hungry.'

Left alone at the long dining-room table, the white stone face of her husband staring at her, Anna felt a shiver run down her spine, light and icy, like the tip-toeing footfall of something tiny but deeply hostile. Listening to the faint chink of crockery and murmured voices coming from the kitchen, it dawned on her that she had always been alone, that people who held other people's lives together generally were. It went with the territory of being a coper, being the one always to organise, to sweeten, to succeed. If she was Becky, she mused ruefully, she would long since have run to the phone and breathlessly poured out her woes, greedy for sisterly sympathy and advice. But she wasn't Becky, she was Anna and there was nowhere to run to. There never had been, not since France. Not since the need to be good and strong had taken hold, induced into being by the fearful hope that it was the best chance she had of making up for the failings around her, of preventing anything truly bad from ever happening again.

A few moments later David and her mother burst back into the room. He was carrying the Christmas pudding, spooning brandy to fuel its halo of a blue flame, while Stella trotted behind with pots of freshly whipped cream and brandy butter.

'How about that?' he shouted, rubbing his hands in satisfaction at his handiwork once he had set the dish down. 'Just the thing, eh?'

Anna nodded because no words would come. Because a dark sea was closing round her and she could not speak, could not describe either the pain or the panic at the notion that some buried, vital part of her might be slipping out of reach.

# 21

'Do you want the good news or the bad?'

'Oh, just the good I think,' replied Becky, opening her mouth wide for a yawn but losing the urge at the last minute. 'Not in the mood for bad . . . too sleepy.' She tipped her head back until she made contact with Joe's legs, stretched out like the rest of him along the sofa behind her. 'If it's that it's my turn to do the washing up, I know and I'll do it tomorrow I promise, Brownie's honour. I just feel right now that if I stood up I would probably fall over, not because I'm pissed like last night but because I'm so tired I can't see straight . . .' She broke off for another yawn, a proper one this time that lasted several satisfying seconds. 'It's been a good day, hasn't it? I mean Jenny really seemed to enjoy herself, I've never seen her eat so much and I think she liked her presents – my God when she saw that leather jacket you gave her I thought she was going to explode with happiness.'

'I'll begin with the good news then, shall I?'

'Hm, fire away.' Becky shifted her position on the floor so that she was facing him, leaning one elbow on the sofa.

'The St George's couple want this place after all. Brixton's mine if I want it. And David has offered to put ten grand of his own money into the project, so that I can push through the decorating and be open by the middle of spring.'

'Jesus, Joe, that's amazing.' Becky, genuinely impressed, slapped the sofa cushion under her arm, before adding, with less certainty, 'But David – ten grand – bloody hell – I mean, is that wise?'

'He's a businessman. He's going to charge interest, get a return on his investment. I see nothing wrong with it at all.'

'Okay,' she said slowly, 'well in that case that really is fantastic news . . . Joe, I'm so pleased for you – for us – I really am . . .' She faltered, overcome by a terrible confusion as to what she truly felt about anything. Drunk though she had been the night before, the warm certainty she had felt in Joe's arms as he scooped her off the floor had, if anything, intensified in the intervening hours. All day she had found herself watching him tenderly, noticing as if for the first time his gentle attentiveness to Jenny, his cleverness with all the food – scores of dishes, each one a miniature masterpiece in its own right – and scolding herself for ever having imagined she could improve her lot with another man. He had been gentle with her too, and very calm, a different creature entirely from the one who had cried and clung to her in the dark, twice now, burying his face in her chest and gripping her till she thought her ribs would snap. Except last night they had ended up making love as well, in a way they hadn't for months and months, bruising each other, so intensely at one point that Becky had lost all sense of the boundary between pleasure and pain and had had to bite the pillows to prevent herself from screaming out loud. Remembering it now, she found herself smiling. 'So we'll be moving,' she murmured, glancing round the familiar shabby furnishings of the room, and thinking that leaving them might not be so hard, that maybe there was hope for them after all. 'I wish you'd told me sooner . . . I mean, how long have you known?'

'About as long as I've known that you were having an affair. That's the bad news, by the way, in case you were wondering. That and the fact that I want you to move out. Now, preferably, but I guess that isn't exactly practical, given that it's Christmas Day. So let's say in the next couple of days, shall we?'

It occurred to Becky in the long silence that followed that all the clichés about being stunned and speechless were true. She was so shocked it felt for a moment as if he had hit her, punched all the air from her lungs with one of his huge hands.

'Joe . . . I'm so . . .'

'Oh, spare me the apologies please. I, for one, would like to try and be just a little bit grown-up about this – I mean, it's not my first time, remember? A cheating wife is familiar territory.' He tutted softly. 'Though I have to admit, it doesn't feel any nicer, second time around.' He stared at the ceiling as if he couldn't bear even to look at her.

Which was entirely reasonable in the circumstances, Becky reflected wretchedly, ransacking her mind for something good to say, some redeeming thing which might point a small finger of justification towards the way she had behaved. 'I . . . it was all going wrong anyway, the affair I mean . . . Joe . . . I was going to end it . . . I . . .'

'I don't give a fuck what you were going to do. I just want you out of my fucking life as soon as possible.' He looked at her then with such dead, despising eyes that she rocked back on her heels, dropping her gaze to the carpet.

'How?' she whispered. 'How did you know?'

'It doesn't matter.'

'It does. I want to know. It was David, wasn't it?'

He looked away, crossing his arms.

'Tell me, Joe, was it David? I have a right to know.'

He began to laugh, a dark dry sound that made the hairs on her arms stand on end. 'Oh that's good, that is.' He swung himself into a sitting position and leant towards her, pressing his face so close to hers that for one mad moment she thought he was going to kiss her. 'You have been secretly screwing someone else for *months*, slyly baring your arse for someone else to grope, letting me believe that all the tension between us was coming from me, that *I* was to blame . . .' He was spitting the words out, so fiercely that she could feel tiny flecks of saliva landing across her face. 'And then to go and say you have a *right* to know who told me. What about my fucking rights Becky? As a husband, as a decent fucking human being? What about those? Were they on your mind as you spread your legs like a . . . like a fucking tart. Oh and don't cry,' he sneered, as the tears spilled out of her, 'I mean, as the one to fuck things up you have no business weeping about it.' He stood up and stretched, almost, marvelled Becky watching him through the fog of her tears, as if he was really relaxed, as if there was nothing ahead of them but the normal ritual of washing their faces and climbing into opposite sides of the same bed. 'I'm going to the spare room. You'll probably want to get on the phone to that lover of yours – pour your heart out, check he's got room in his wardrobe for another set of clothes.'

'Joe, please . . . I was going to tell you.'

'What?' he snapped. 'What exactly were you going to tell me? That our marriage was all over, or that you had strayed from the straight and narrow and would never do it again?'

She clenched her fists, fighting to swallow away the swelling in her throat. 'I've been so confused, I knew what I was doing was wrong, of course, but you were so *disconnected*, I thought there was nothing left of us anyway and then . . . and then last night was so . . . we were so . . .'

'Last night?' he scoffed. 'That's called sex, Becky, as you, of all people, should know. That's called screwing each other senseless. And don't give me any more of that confused crap – we're all confused, Becky dear, it's called being human. It doesn't give anybody the right to behave as you have.' He paused, before adding in a quieter voice, 'And I tell you something, even if you had coughed up the truth instead of leaving me the pleasant task of finding out on my own, I still would have told you to fuck off.' He clapped his hands together. 'So there we have it. Another screwed-up marriage. So bloody what. But,' he added, slamming the wall with the palm of his hand, so violently that all the tinsel-draped pictures shuddered, 'I'm not going to let this one get to me like the last. I'm starting the rest of my life tomorrow, and all I can say is it will be a lot bloody easier on my own.' He disappeared into the hall for a moment and came back with her telephone which he threw onto the sofa. 'I suggest you do the same – start organising the rest of your life – you've probably been gagging to speak to him all day anyway. Do you do phone sex, by the way? Is that one of your things?' He shook his head, his usually gentle brown eyes flashing with such evident disgust that Becky, still huddled on the floor by the sofa, flinched as if he had hit her. 'The extent to which I don't know you is truly astonishing. It's just sad that it's taken me so long to realise it.' He slammed the door shut behind him, causing not only the pictures to shudder but the tree to sway, its laden branches tinkling in protest.

'Guy? It's me . . . oh, Guy, is that you? Oh thank God.' Becky had to press the phone hard to her ear to stop it trembling.

'Who else would it be, sweetheart? Happy Christmas! I've been hoping all day that you'd call.'

'Oh Guy, the most terrible thing has happened . . . David, my brother-in-law, has told Joe about us. We've had a terrible row – I've got to get out – could I – do you think it would be all right if I came to you, just for a bit, until I've sorted myself out?'

'To me? But of course you can.'

'I know it's pushy – and I don't want to be pushy – I mean I guess we had sort of talked about it – or at least talked round it

176

'– with all the California business – but I guess we both thought there might be a little more time to play with before . . .'

'Becky, please stop, you sound so upset.'

'I am, I am . . . oh Guy, it was dreadful, you've no idea – it's so good to talk to you . . .' Feeling the tears welling up again, she wiped her eyes and nose on her sleeve. 'Jesus – how was your fucking Christmas anyway?' She managed a laugh.

'Okay, I guess. We ate at the Savoy Grill – a good spread – talked shop mostly.'

'And now you're home.'

'Yes.'

'Can I come tomorrow?'

'Of course.'

'I'll need time to pack,' she began, her voice wavering again, as more tears welled up inside.

'Of course you will,' he said gently. 'And Becky . . . you're a good girl, always remember that.'

Clicking off the telephone Becky was dismayed to see her stepdaughter framed in the doorway, her grey eyes wide, her mouse hair sticking out at messy angles like some kind of spiky halo. She was wearing a large white T-shirt of a nightie, emblazoned across the chest with the face of a pop star Becky recognised but couldn't have put a name to.

'I heard Dad shouting.'

'Yes, well . . . he was cross.'

'With you?' She stepped into the room and began to walk across the carpet, placing one foot slowly and carefuly in front of the other as if treading some invisible tightrope.

Becky sniffed, hurriedly trying to rub all traces of tears from her eyes. 'Yup. With me.'

'Why?' Having reached the sofa, Jenny slithered onto the arm and sat facing inwards, tucking her bare feet under a cushion.

'Because I've hurt him,' said Becky quietly, heaving herself onto the other end of the sofa and hugging herself with her arms. 'I've hurt him badly and he's a good man and I shouldn't have.'

'You mean you've got another boyfriend?'

Becky nodded.

'Who you love more than Daddy?'

'Oh God, Jenny . . . if only it was so simple . . . I mean there are different kinds of love and . . .'

'The sex kind of love – is that what you've got with the other man?'

'Well, I . . .'

'That's the kind Mummy's got with Glen. They do it all the time – I hear them through the wall sometimes. I used to think grown-ups only did it when they wanted to make babies, but it's not like that, is it?'

'No,' whispered Becky, not looking at her, 'it's not.'

Jenny pulled a long strand of hair out in front of her nose and started to wind it round and round her index finger. She did it very tightly, watching with crossed eyes as the bit of finger above the hair turned yellowy white.

'I walked in on my parents doing it once,' blurted Becky, 'it was awful. I felt so embarrassed.'

'Blimey.' Jenny giggled, tucking the strand of hair back behind her ear. 'That must have been, like, *horrible*.'

Becky smiled. 'It was. Truly horrible. Definitely something grown-ups should do with the door locked.'

Jenny giggled again and slid down onto the sofa next to her. 'So what's going to happen then, between you and Dad?'

Becky bit the tremble out of her bottom lip, doing her best to sound matter of fact. 'I'm going to move out and Dad will move to his lovely new place right above his very own restaurant. It'll be great . . . you'll be able to stay with him as often as you like, because he'll be working downstairs instead of miles away. There's this great second bedroom that will be yours – it's even got its very own bathroom, an ensuite, like in hotels.'

'Yeah, Dad told me already.'

'Did he? Right. Good. Hey, we ought to get to bed.'

'I never used to like you,' she declared sulkily, making no effort to move, 'but I sort of do now.'

'And I sort of like you,' said Becky gently, steeling a glance across the sofa cushion separating them. 'But we can still be friends, see each other . . .'

'Yeah, sure, like *that's* really going to happen.'

'Yes, you're right, of course you're right, it probably won't,' Becky admitted, ashamed. 'You know, when I was your age grown-ups cocked everything up for me too . . .'

'You mean your Dad dying? Well he couldn't help that, could he?' she snorted.

'No,' agreed Becky slowly, 'no, he couldn't, but a silly part of you still thinks that deep down maybe he could have, because you're so cross and sad about it. But you're so much more grown-up than I ever was – all the things you've had to cope with already – I think you're amazing.'

'Do you?' The grey eyes met Becky's full on for the first time. 'Do you really think that or are you saying it to make me feel better?'

'I really think it. If my Mum had married someone else I think I would have murdered the poor man, or run away from home or blown up my school or something. As it was, she never even looked at another man and I still behaved really badly for about ten years and got everybody mad at me. *And* I had a wonderful big sister, which you don't, who was always there when I needed her . . .' At the thought of Anna, Becky faltered, the impressive show of adult wisdom she had managed so far crumbling at the realisation that it was just such a dose of cool, guiding comfort that she needed now.

'You want her, don't you?' exclaimed Jenny, sounding at once accusing and faintly triumphant. 'You want your big sister.'

'Yes, but not as much as I want some sleep,' quipped Becky, seeing from her watch that it was almost one in the morning and feeling suddenly wrung out with exhaustion. She got up from the sofa and reached out a hand to the child, who took it, squeezing her fingers hard.

'You'll be all right, you, because you're good and strong like your Dad, deep down where it counts.'

'So why are you going to this other man then?' she snapped, pulling her fingers free. 'I don't get it. I mean, he and Mum rowed all the time – I can still remember it – but you and he never shouted at all, not until tonight . . .' Her voiced tailed off, as if losing confidence in the theory.

Becky sighed. 'One day you'll . . .'

'Yeah, one day I'll understand, that's what grown-ups always say and I hate it.' She ran from the room and up the stairs. Becky stood and listened, waiting until the sound of scampering feet had been followed by the thump of a closing door. In the few seconds of silence that ensued she wondered if Joe could possibly be asleep. At the thought of him, lying alone in the narrow lumpy spare bed, her heart gave a violent lurch that almost sent her spinning out of the room and up the stairs to his bedside. She had been waiting for something to happen and now it had, she scolded herself, turning slowly to begin the business of switching off lamps and Christmas lights. A man whom she had fantasised about eloping with countless times, a glamorous, knee-weakeningly handsome creature with exciting prospects and connections, thought she was the One True Thing missing from his existence. If he was right, a happy and fulfilled alternative future awaited her. As one door closed another opened. Fate, in the form of her subtly malevolent brother-in-law had simply lent a hand, nudging things in the direction they had probably been heading anyway.

Fortified by such thoughts, Becky nonetheless stood staring at the golden necklaces of light strung through the branches of the Christmas tree for several minutes, her finger hovering reluctantly over the switch that would cast her and her surroundings into darkness.

# 22

It was with cautious steps and a thumping heart that Becky paid off her taxi driver the following afternoon and lugged her single large item of baggage towards the heavily panelled front door of the flat in Notting Hill. One suitcase, no matter how huge, had barely made a dent in the painful challenge of removing all evidence of her identity from the house; but instinct had warned her that there would be something essentially presumptuous, or at the very least uncool, in presenting herself on her lover's doorstep with several trunks' worth of gear. Guy was a free spirit, she had reminded herself, painstakingly selecting items from her drawers, whom she was almost certainly best advised in allowing to stay that way. They would never marry, she realised suddenly, stabbing at the door buzzer which worked in fits and starts, finding herself entirely unsurprised at the notion, as if it was something she had always known but never quite confronted head on.

A moment later she was using her body to push open the heavy door and dragging her suitcase towards the lift, which was of the antique variety, complete with a flexible black cast-iron gate that had to be teased into place before the outer door would close. The contraption laboured its way to the third floor, its creaks echoing in the silence. There was a distinct air of emptiness to the place, because of Christmas no doubt, Becky reflected, slightly shy of the clack her heels made on the marble floor. At the door of the flat she paused, pushing some air into her heavy hair and pressing her lips together to ensure there was some colour in them, hoping there was no ghost of a trace left of the vision she had confronted in the mirror that morning: the puffy red eyelids, the faint creases down one side of her cheek, where she had lain too long in one position, lost to a sleep that had been deep but utterly unrefreshing. Staggering downstairs for a coffee she had found a curt note from Joe propped next to the kettle, telling her that he was taking Jenny to the park and then to a movie. Which had made the business of leaving easier, if more poignant.

A woman of about forty, wearing a blue trouser suit and with auburn hair cut into a severe bob opened the door. 'Oh, I thought you were Guy.'

'Oh, but I . . .' Becky took a step backwards. The woman pushed her head round the doorway, as if checking whether Guy might in fact be loitering somewhere in the corridor.

'I'm Belinda. How do you do.' She held out her hand. 'Over from the States and,' she checked the corridor one last time, 'with a *serious* bone to pick with my dear brother.'

'Brother?' echoed Becky faintly, placing her hand in the woman's palm, which closed round her fingers like a steel glove. 'I'm Becky, Guy's . . . girlfriend.'

Belinda raised one eyebrow, an immaculate neat gingery curve, and opened the door wider. 'You'd better come in,' she said drily, 'if you'll forgive the mess, though why I should apologise for it when it's not mine, I hardly know.'

Feeling more awkward by the minute, Becky cautiously stepped inside the familiar wide hall. 'Guy is expecting me,' she murmured, 'and he didn't say he had a sister. Are you over for long?' Instead of answering Belinda began tugging at the drawers of an antique oak dresser next to the front door. 'He didn't tell you where he put the bloody post, I suppose, did he? I pay all the main things by standing order but I bet there's other stuff which he couldn't be bothered to forward . . . I say, is that your suitcase out there?' she exclaimed, momentarily diverted from her quest by the sight of Becky's bulging black bag visible through the still open door, sitting abandoned in the hallway.

'Yes,' Becky replied, wishing for a reason she had yet fully to understand, that she could deny all knowledge of it.

'Are you on your way somewhere then?'

'Yes, here. I was on my way here,' she admitted hoarsely, feeling that the time had definitely come to lay her cards on the table. 'Guy has invited me to move in with him. We're going to give it a try . . . together . . . see how it goes . . .' She gave a nervous laugh, which she swallowed into an even more nervous silence at the sight of the expression on Guy's sister's face. It struck her in the same instant that apart from the colour of her hair, in its ferociously angular bob, the pair of them looked very much alike; with the same wide blue eyes and generous mouth. In spite of being several years older, her slim figure, complemented by high heels and the close-fitting suit, retained echoes of Guy's other physical assets too. There was no wedding band, Becky noticed, although virtually every other finger was laden with jewelled rings and sitting prettily across her collarbone was a necklace of what looked like pearl and agate. When she began to speak one hand flew to the necklace, patting the tiny smooth stones beneath her fingertips, as if seeking some sort of comfort or support.

'Oh really . . . oh fuck, this time he has gone too far. I mean I don't mind the mess but really . . . not this.'

'What?' In spite of the heat belting from under the flat's state of the art underfloor heating, Becky could feel goosebumps breaking out all over her.

'We'd better sit down,' she commanded, leading the way into the sitting room where a large plastic black sack of rubbish was propped up against the sofa. Sticking out of the top Becky saw several stained white cartons of what looked suspiciously like the remnants of the Chinese meal they had eaten ten days before. On the table, which was stained with sticky ring marks and flecks of shrivelled rice, sat a bottle of whisky and an empty glass. 'Take this my dear,' said Belinda, splashing a couple of inches of whisky into the glass and handing it to Becky, 'because you're going to need it. Sit down, please. God . . .' She ran both hands through her hair and took a deep breath. 'This is my flat, not Guy's. There was only a gap of a few months between my last tenants moving out and my needing it so I said he could stay here for a bit.' She made a face. 'I should have known better. I know what he's like you see, which' – she hesitated, looking with some concern at Becky, who had obediently taken the glass but still not drunk from it – 'you clearly don't. I suspect, my dear, that neither of us will be seeing my brother for some time.'

'You mean,' Becky licked her lips, 'that the shoot in California . . . that it's been brought forward?'

'Is that what he told you? God, worse and worse,' she muttered, fetching another glass from the drinks cabinet and pouring herself a generous dollop from the bottle. 'There is almost certainly no shoot in California or anywhere else . . .'

'But the scripts . . .'

'Years ago Guy went to film school – a four-year course of which I think he managed two, possibly three. When he's really desperate for cash he reads film scripts for companies – they pay by the hour – a cheap way to weed out the real non-starters.' She laughed quietly. 'Which rather sums up Guy, I'm afraid.' She stared into her drink for a few moments. 'Look, Becky, I'm really sorry . . . he means no harm . . . he just gets away with what he can . . . underneath he can be very sweet, he's just never got a grip on life.'

'He wouldn't . . . wouldn't do this,' Becky whispered. She had taken a sip of her drink now and could feel it like acid in her chest and stomach, as if she was disintegrating inside. 'He told me to come and stay. He said it was all right. He knows I've left my husband.'

'Your . . . oh Jesus, this just gets worse and worse. You poor girl.' She half got up from the sofa but sat back down again, watching Becky, who was rummaging frantically in her bag, spilling fat drops of whisky over her hand.

'I'm just . . . my phone . . . I'll call him . . . I'm sure . . . you see we had something . . . really special.' She drank the whisky down in one gulp, not because she wanted it but because in her dazed state it seemed like the simplest remedy against the further embarrassment of spilling any more over herself. Feeling Belinda's pitying gaze, she looked away while the number rang, fixing her attention on her favourite of the vast canvasses arrayed around the walls, streams of turquoise and bubblegum pink flecked with miniature black squares. The oil or acrylic, or whatever it was, was so densely layered that she had always to resist the urge to touch it, to plunge her hand inside.

*'The number you have dialled is unavailable. Please try later.'*

Becky turned back to Belinda, now staring morosely into her empty glass. 'The number in Wiltshire; do you have that? Would you give it to me?'

'Wiltshire?'

'His cottage in Wiltshire, he . . .' She broke off, because Belinda was shaking her head. 'No cottage in Wiltshire?'

'Nope. Christ Becky, I am so very sorry.'

Becky got up, still gripping her mobile phone. 'He has lied to me about everything . . . everything. I can't believe it, that someone could . . . would . . . I need . . . I must call my sister . . . I will leave, obviously, but first . . .'

'Go ahead, go ahead, I'll leave you to it – I've got loads of unpacking to do – and I'll make a cup of tea.' She began sweeping at the crusty rice grains as she talked, steering them into a neat pile with one hand and then brushing them off the edge of the table and into the palm of the other. 'Did he . . . does he by any chance owe you any money?'

'Money?'

'Because he's done that before.' She stood up, still clasping her fistful of rice grains. 'If he does, I'd be happy, within reason, to reimburse you—'

'Nothing,' snapped Becky, 'he took nothing.'

'He must have liked you a lot then,' she murmured, walking quickly across the room and into the kitchen.

Becky crossed to the windows before dialling Anna's number, positioning herself with her back to the kitchen. Outside it was already dark. It had begun to rain, giving a glossy look to the lamplit buildings opposite. In the street below people and cars slid past each other. Pressing her head against the pane, Becky stared at the scene, for a few moments dizzily contemplating the feasibility of crashing through the glass and doing a sky-dive onto the tarmac below. She was as dangerously poised as the plucky-faced Christmas fairy, she reflected bleakly, picturing the tilting tree in the sitting room in Balham, wondering if it had yet toppled and whether Joe would bother propping it up if it did.

It wasn't until she heard Anna's voice that the tears, held in check by a combination of shock, the presence of Belinda – not to mention the very real fear that David himself would answer the phone – exploded out of her, so violently that for several minutes she was virtually incoherent. It took all her sister's calming ability to coax out an intelligible rendition of what had happened, a process that went more smoothly once Belinda had tiptoed up with a cup of sweet tea, and then crept away again, like a relative at a death scene. Anna was kind and practical, as Becky had known – had counted on – her being. She said at once that Becky should come and stay with them.

'But I can't,' Becky wailed, 'I've got to be at work at eight thirty tomorrow morning and I'm sorry but the thought of seeing David . . . after what he's done . . . Jesus . . .' She succumbed to a fresh bout of sobbing as the full reality of her predicament sank in.

'Now Becks you don't *know* it was David . . .'

'I do, I do. He saw us at the party – me and Guy, in his studio – I never told you because I felt so bad about it and then, when David didn't say anything to you I guess a part of me was clinging to the hope that maybe he hadn't recognised me . . . he hates me, Anna, he's always hated me, deep down, I've seen it in his eyes and now he's got back at me, just like he always wanted – and he's got Joe where he wants him.'

'Becky, he is helping Joe,' Anna reminded her, a little crisply, before adding in a gentler voice, 'Are you sure there is no possibility of going back and explaining to Joe . . .'

'Go back? Go back? You've no idea – I couldn't possibly – not ever – go crawling back – and he wouldn't have me anyway – you should have heard the things he said – I'm lost, Anna, I'm lost –'

'Well, why not camp out at Mum's then?' she suggested suddenly, her voice exuberant with the simple inspiration of the idea. 'She's staying with us till the end of the week – I know she keeps a key under a flowerpot somewhere – I could ask her right now – I'm sure she won't mind. It'll give you time to sort yourself out a bit, think what you're going to do.'

'I'm not talking to her,' muttered Becky, cringing at the suggestion, but seeing the sense of it too. It would be a long ride but Amersham was at least on a tube line.

'Well, darling, it's got to be better than a hotel . . .' Anna broke off, sucking in her breath. 'God, what a monster – this man, Guy, the way he has behaved, I still can't believe it.'

'Neither can I,' whispered Becky. 'A total fake . . . I feel such a fool.'

'Poor Becks, poor love. I'll talk to Mum for you and call you back. It will all be all right, you'll see.'

'You could stay here the night if you like,' ventured Belinda, hovering in the doorway once she realised Becky was off the phone. 'I mean, I can't help feeling partly responsible – you see Guy was terribly spoiled – our parents were always baling him out and when they died I sort of took over the role.'

'Thanks, but I'll be fine. I'm going to my mother's. My sister's going to fix it and call me back.'

'You're lucky,' she said quietly, 'having a strong family, I've always wanted that, but ours never quite worked.'

'Oh I don't think any of them quite work,' said Becky wearily, flopping into the nearest chair. 'They're all screwed up in different ways, aren't they? I mean, there's this sort of myth about the possibility of a perfect family, but it doesn't really exist for anybody. You haven't got a cigarette have you?' Belinda shook her head. 'What do you do then?' She waved an arm at the room. 'To have all this?'

'Information Technology. A big company pays me lots of money to design computer systems for other big companies. I go in with a team to install it and then train the office personnel to use it. I do a lot of work in America. Europe too, for months at a time. I keep this place as my base and for the occasional assignment at home, which is what I've got now . . . Becky, if I see Guy, if he gets in touch – which he will in the end – do you want me to—?'

It was only as she was talking that Becky noticed the cufflink box sitting on top of a spindly-legged coffee table next to her. It had been left open, like a small black mouth, its tongue of velvet studded with the tiny gold masks. 'No,' she interrupted fiercely, snapping the box shut. 'Thank you, but I don't want you to tell him anything. It's all over. It never really started.'

# 23

It takes several attempts to find the same girl. When she recognises him he is pleased. He follows her up the same steep staircase with its threadbare carpet and dingy walls. In the cheap ruby chamber he is more relaxed, makes conversation as he takes off his clothes. The notes from the cash dispenser were old this time, slotting into his palm like a pack of worn playing cards. She tucks them into the side of her bag, a little more carelessly than before, as if a small wedge of trust has eased its way between them.

Her performance is somewhat less polished. She looks tired, he notices, with dark dents at the inner corners of her eyes, where the beige face cream has not found its way. The observation distracts him. He looks over the top of her head instead, at the buttons stitched into the velveteen headboard.

'Nice,' she says, tilting her hips in time to his and summoning his gaze back to her face. She is doing her tongue trick, flicking it round her lips and teeth. Her body feels languid beneath his, almost bored.

'Do you like this?' he says, pushing harder, 'And this?' He wants to touch her, not just on the outside, but deep on the inside too, where it counts. He wants to affect her, to trace some flicker of real interest beneath the routine of her erotic response. 'Can you feel me?' he whispers.

'Yes,' she says, but her body is a receptacle and her eyes are wide empty pools.

# 24

Her mother's shoe-box of a home in Amersham was probably the last place in the world Becky would have chosen as the back-drop to begin the business of convalescing from the breakdown of her marriage. Fragile with unhappiness, she found everything about her surroundings grated against her nerves, from the laundered net curtains to the crocheted doilies cushioning the base of every pot and ornament throughout the house. There was a smell too, a cross between camomile and furniture-polish, which seemed to pervade every room, even the linen on the spare bed where she wrestled with the unfamiliar too-short sheets and blankets in a losing battle to find solace in sleep.

Though Guy was the most obvious target for her misery, the more she thought about his role in what had happened, the harder Becky found it to muster anything beyond a sort of despising pity. With the benefit of hindsight, she felt as much disdain for her own willingness to believe in his flimsy fictions as his efficacy in dreaming them up. She had wanted to be conned, had colluded by believing in wild impossible things, without making the remotest effort to dig beneath the surface and perform any sort of check-list with reality. She even felt some sort of self-flagellatory justification in the fact that, when she sat down and thought about it, it was clear that during the course of their three-month liaison he had, via various casual loans – for bottles of alcohol, food deliveries and occasional tenners – probably drained her of several hundred pounds.

Far harder to confront was the thought of Joe. The way she had treated him made Becky's stomach churn with shame and remorse. Looking back, the dim unhappiness in the build-up to her birthday seemed so trivial that she could not believe the chain of reactions it had unleashed in her. She had been married to a decent man and living a decent life and had blown it all, irrevocably, for nothing. Or rather, to be completely precise, David had blown it for her. For, while admitting her own culpability in the downturn her life had taken, her brother-in-law's complicity in the process still took Becky's breath away. Not liking her – harbouring some kind of perverse envy over Anna – was one thing, but deliberately triggering the collapse of her marriage was quite another.

Anna herself, was the only thing that kept Becky going. She phoned every day, sometimes several times, always with soothing advice and words of comfort. While tactful enough not to offer any overt defence of David's behaviour, she pointed out that things between Becky and Joe had almost certainly been doomed anyway, that few relationships could have endured the revelation – which would have come at some point, if only from Becky herself – of such a turbulent affair. That she had fallen for Guy's charade of a life in the first place was a sign she said, that Becky had been looking for a way out anyway, an indication that all was far from well. She was also extremely reassuring about Stella, saying that their mother was showing no signs of being judgemental about what had happened but was merely glad to be able to offer her own house as a refuge. In spite of such reassurances, when Stella herself ventured to the phone late one evening, two days into the crisis, Becky would have given anything for an excuse not to talk. Gratitude was called for she knew, on a grand scale. Yet what she seemed to feel instead was a kind of angry shame, firstly at this sudden enforced dependence on a person from whom she had spent two decades trying to distance herself, and secondly at the creeping fear that she might, somehow be heading for the same sad solitary existence to which her mother had fallen victim: alone and spinsterly, cast adrift in suburbia with no thrills beyond a wine bottle and each evening's paltry offerings on the television. When Stella herself seemed to perceive the same parallels, offering them up under some misguided notion of providing comfort, it was all Becky could do not to drop the receiver and run screaming from the house.

'I just mean that I know what it's like, darling, to be . . . alone. I do know, I do understand. You can stay as long as you like, I hope you know that.'

'Thanks,' Becky had gasped in a small voice, plucking tufts out of a particularly frayed piece of crochet matting positioned under the telephone, 'but I expect to be out of here by the weekend.'

'So I won't see you at all?'

'Oh, maybe for a bit – it just depends how the timing works out.'

Prompted by this exchange, Becky stepped up her hitherto rather desultory assault on the problem of finding alternative accommodation, circling possibilities in the property pages of every newspaper she could lay her hands on and sneaking out in her lunch hour to make enquiries on her mobile. Not revealing any hint of her altered circumstances at work had, from the start, felt vital; not just because she cringed at the thought of Juliette's greedy, goggle-eyed concern, but also because it helped enormously in the daily challenge of holding herself together. It helped too that she was very busy, Mike having greeted her return from Christmas by putting her in sole charge of two small but demanding accounts. She was to report to him directly, he said, delivering the command in a tone of voice that managed to suggest a huge leap forward in his opinion of her professional abilities; a voice that erased in an instant any dim notions Becky might have entertained about offering some sort of thumbnail sketch of the disastrous turn in her personal life. Her career was virtually all she had left, she had reminded herself, then and many times since, quailing at the irony that she, of all people, should find herself in such a position. That she had ever contemplated the luxury of giving up work altogether now seemed laughable. She would need every scrap of her salary to survive. Even if Joe had had money, she would have felt too guilty to take any. Trying to explain as much to Joe himself in the single terse conversation they had managed since her departure, he had only laughed harshly, saying she knew bloody well he had nothing to share except debt, and that she was most welcome to that any time.

By Friday morning Becky was beginning to feel desperate. Sitting on the long tube ride into London, exhausted from lack of sleep, new work pressures and her continuing failure to find anywhere remotely feasible to live, she found herself staring at the blank, apparently untraumatised faces of her fellow commuters with irrational and hostile envy. Earlier in the week there had been an initial adrenalin rush of shock, she realised, which had helped her cope. Whereas now there was nothing, no reserves of energy and virtually no hope. Of the few properties she had managed to see the only one immediately available and affordable was no more than a bed-sit, with greasy walls and bubbled linoleum floors. For a week or two she might have borne it, but the agents wanted a six-month contract or nothing. With Stella due back from Dorset the following day, Becky was therefore facing the unbearably gloomy prospect of seeing in the New Year with her mother. Stunned and appalled at this last thought, which struck her just as she was emerging from Hammersmith tube station into the grey drizzle that passed for daylight, Becky burst into tears. Fumbling in her bag for her phone, staggering slightly through the blur of her tears, she dialled Anna.

'Oh Becky darling, don't cry, there are worse things . . .'

'Are there, really? Well, right now I'm struggling to think of any. If it wasn't for you, Anna, I don't know what I would do.' She began to cry openly, weaving her way through the crowds of workers streaming round her, not caring about their curious stares and looks of sympathy. 'The truth is, I'm the fuck-up and you're the strong one.'

'I'm not . . . I . . .'

'You are. You always have been. I mean you've got an amazing marriage, an amazing job and in a few weeks you're going to have a baby for Christ's sake. And you know what? Sometimes I hate you for it . . . for having everything I haven't . . . at your party – looking back – I can see that I hated you a bit that night . . . in fact I think that was partly why I did what I did, with Guy . . . not that I'm blaming you or anything, I love you too much . . .'

'Becky, stop this, you're getting hysterical.'

'I am, I am and I don't care.' Dipping out of the main flow of people, Becky flung her briefcase onto the ground and slid down next to a low stone wall.

'Becky, you should know . . . nothing is what it seems, no one is.'

Digging a half-used tissue from her coat pocket, Becky blew her nose hard. 'Now *that* is something I do know. Apart from you.' She sniffed. 'Guy used to call me his One True Thing . . . such a joke now . . . Jesus . . . but that's what you are Anna, that's what you are.'

There was a brief silence on the other end of the line. 'I've got to go, Becks. A meeting, I'm sorry. I'll call you later.'

Becky listened to the click as the line went dead and then dropped her head into her hands.

'Rebecca? Are you okay?'

She looked up to see Mike Hadfield peering down at her, his pale face creased with concern. 'Oh yes,' she said, struggling to her feet, 'absolutely fine.'

'No you're not. I can see you're not. Is it family troubles? Your sister perhaps?'

To Becky's horror a fresh bout of tears came pouring out before she could stop them. 'Oh God, oh shit . . . sorry I . . . please ignore me . . .' She dabbed the worst of the dribbles off her nose between sobs, the tissue being too sodden and shredded to withstand another proper blow.

'You need a coffee,' he said sternly. The next moment he had taken her by the elbow and was steering her along the pavement. 'And maybe a paper napkin or two. I haven't got a handkerchief or I'd lend it to you. I thought you'd been looking somewhat strained this week, I assumed it was because of managing your new clients. You should have told me something else was up. Really, how can I run an efficient business if my employees are collapsing all over the shop?'

A little later Becky was sitting red-eyed but composed in front of a large steaming caffe latte. 'What about work, what will they think?'

'I phoned while you were in the Ladies. I said we had a breakfast meeting.' He beamed. 'There are some advantages to being the boss. How's that coffee?' He peered over his glasses which had steamed up slightly from the spiral of vapour rising from his own cup of espresso. 'You certainly look a little better.'

'You're very kind.'

He shook his head. 'Pure selfishness, I assure you. Need you all fit and well or the business doesn't run. Would some time off help?'

Becky began to say that it probably would and to skirt round the issues as to why when instead the whole sorry story began to tumble out of her, right down to the fact that without the lifeline of Anna's phonecalls she might have thrown herself out of a window.

When she had finished Mike sipped the last of his coffee and carefully put his cup down before speaking. 'I may not be able to do handkerchiefs, but when it comes to vacant premises I am definitely your man. I own a small place in Bayswater, a basement flat, bought for my errant son who is currently in his gap year – scaling fjords in Norway or something – but the point is, it is empty and yours should you wish to make use of it. For a price of course,' he added, seeing her expression. 'A reasonable rent. It's only small, but quite comfortable, and a lot nearer than bloody Amersham.' He let out one of his booming laughs and patted her hand. 'How you've coped this week,' he continued, suddenly serious again, 'with all that I've thrown at you, not to mention what you've been going through at home, is truly remarkable. How this sister of yours, whose praises you sing so highly, could be any stronger, I cannot imagine.'

'Oh but she is,' Becky insisted, 'and she's about to have a baby,' she added, feeling a wonderful burst of pride, quite unshackled by any of the complicated emotions which had surrounded all her early reactions at the prospect. 'And Mike, thank you so much for the offer of the flat. If you really mean it I'd like to move in tomorrow.'

'Oh, I mean it all right,' he assured her, signalling the waitress for the bill, 'I never say things I don't mean. Jamie's not due back until the autumn. I was wondering what the hell to do with the place anyway. So you see the problem-solving is mutual.'

'I see only that you have saved my life,' she declared solemnly, having to restrain herself from leaning across the table and flinging her arms round his neck.

# 25

Stella gripped the cold grey railings and stared down at the sea, which churned and heaved as the ferry cut through it, spitting froth which the wind picked up and hurled across her cheeks. Though knotted tightly, her headscarf tugged and flapped round her face as if straining to break free. She could feel the curls of her tight new perm bobbing inside, jostling together in apparent alarm at the sudden assault from the elements. Water had always made her afraid, even before Colin, particularly the sea, with its sucking immensity, dwarfing every human life and quest to specks of insignificance.

To her right she could still make out a thin ridge which just half an hour before had been Dover's celebrated cliffs, not white but grey and unimpressive in the early light of a late-February morning. Watching the ridge shrink to a pencil line, it was hard to imagine that Becky and Anna were still somewhere upon it; her big grown-up girls with their complicated lives, so apart from her now – even Anna, in her hurtful and baffling new hostile bubble of self-preservation; and Becky, ploughing on after the mess wrought by her silly affair, so grindingly determined to stand on her own feet that Stella's heart had ached to perceive it. All the years of their not getting on made no difference. As a mother, she still longed to see both her children happy, still longed for the power to take some of their pain. That she could not do so had transported her back to the aftermath of Colin's death, when the pair of them had learnt, far younger than any children should have to, that for some kinds of suffering there was no sugared medicine, no cure beyond the trudge of time.

Stella let go of the railings and turned to lean her back against them, seeking some break from the wind which was pumping down her nostrils and into her mouth, making it hard to breathe. It was making her eyes water too, so badly that she had given up blinking and wiping and was just letting the tears stream freely down her cheeks. Squinting now to make out any trace of the English coast, she wondered if this trip to visit Marcel was, as she had told herself on every one of the numerous occasions she had felt like cancelling it, the opening of a new door, or the closing of an old one. Was she running away, from her meagre life, from her children's anxieties and her ineptitude in the face of them? Or was she being brave and branching out, placing one tentative hand on the high edge of the deep trench in which she had spent twenty years trying to bury herself? It had taken courage, she knew that much, packing up, booking the car onto the ferry, buying maps for the long drive down. But then courage didn't mean something was right.

Glancing to her left she saw that she had been joined at her windy standpoint by a young couple, in padded anoraks and jeans. The man's hair was cut so short that the contours of his skull were clearly visible, making him look at once baby-headed and yet prematurely old. The girl had long dry bleached hair which whipped across her face. They were laughing, pressing into each other and kissing, not caring what attention they caused, least of all to an old woman in a headscarf with damp cheeks. It was only as the girl pulled away that Stella saw she was pregnant, heavily so, with that unavoidable hint of a waddle in her stance, her back arching slightly to accommodate the heaviness of her load. Her first, obvious thought was of Anna, with her due date just three weeks away. She was worried about her, she realised, more worried in fact than she was about Becky, who, typically, seemed to have landed on her feet, with her boss's flat and doing so well at work. She was like one of those doll toys with weighted bottoms; no matter how hard you pushed them over they always bobbed up again. Whereas Anna, deep down, had always been the more sensitive child, the one who needed structure and control and attention, the one – Stella realised with a guilty jolt – who fought to keep the peace only because she could not withstand the bitterness of confrontation.

The couple were walking away, the girl carefully distributing her weight with each step, the man with one arm looped protectively across her padded back. Staring after them, Stella found her thoughts reeling away from her daughter and back to her own pregnancy, to an older, much grimier ferry from Portsmouth to St Malo, with Anna kicking frantically inside her womb and Colin at her side, really at her side, like the young man with the skeletal head, infatuated and interested and so brimming with love that he had always to be touching or holding a part of her to be sure his good fortune was not just a dream. Instead of making her sad the memory caused a burst of fierce happiness. She knew what the couple were feeling. She knew exactly. It had happened and was a part of her, still in tact beneath the layers of other bad things. She smiled after them, not caring that they couldn't see and that they would think her mad if they could. Then she turned her face back to feel the punch of the wind, barely noticing that her scarf had slipped down to her neck and that all the stylist's careful handiwork with the dryer and curlers was being blasted to nothing.

'So she's really gone to France?'

'She's really gone. He's been inviting her for years, apparently – she said she didn't feel she could carry on refusing.'

'Dad's friend, Marcel Guillot, after all these years . . .

blimey.' Becky frowned, summoning a hazy image of a jovial man with thick dark curly hair and wide girth, who had tickled her often to the point where she had not liked it. 'His breath smelt. Do you remember that? Of garlic and onions.'

'Can't say I do. I remember her better – always cooking in that huge kitchen, with the saucepans hung round the beams – and they had a dog, a fat Alsatian called something silly . . . Boudin . . . Bobbin or something.'

'Boursin.'

'That was it.' The two sisters smiled at each other, happy to have uncovered this nugget of a memory to their mutual satisfaction.

'More wine?'

'I shouldn't.'

'Go on, just a drop.' Becky reached for the wine bottle on the coffee table wedged between their knees and carefully topped up Anna's glass. 'More salad too?'

'No I'm fine thanks, that was great.'

They were sitting in armchairs in the leg of the Bayswater flat's L-shaped living room-cum-kitchen, eating with plates and napkins on their laps. Becky had originally laid the knives and forks on the breakfast bar where she perched to eat all her hasty scraps of meals, but having seen the awkwardness with which Anna heaved herself up onto one of the high stools, she had swiftly moved the accoutrements for their supper to the coffee table instead. Even so she couldn't help noticing that her sister, normally so graceful, had managed with considerable difficulty, steering precarious forkfuls over the swell of her stomach to her mouth and showing no obvious pleasure in the process. She was wearing black leggings and a shimmering violet silk shirt which seemed to catch flecks of violet in her eyes that Becky had never noticed before. She looked blooming, but in a wide-eyed, intense way; the skin on her face shining but taut, as if it had been polished raw, as if it might crack should she smile too widely. In spite of the pretty camouflage of the violet shirt, which was distracting and voluminous, the new size of her, which seemed to have quadrupled in the weeks since they had last been face to face, was such a shock that when she took off her coat Becky had only just managed to prevent herself from gasping out loud.

'You look fabulous,' she had exclaimed instead, instinctively reaching out a hand to touch the bulge under the shirt, but pulling away quickly at the expression on Anna's face. 'Sorry . . . I just wanted . . .'

Anna rolled her eyes to the ceiling. 'You're not the only one – it's incredible – the way everybody wants to touch it, like they feel they have a *right* suddenly to touch me.'

There was a new, very faint wheeziness to her voice, Becky had noticed, as if the bulk of the baby was somehow poaching some of the air from her lungs. 'Anna I'm sorry, I didn't mean . . .'

'Go on then,' she said, all the edginess seeming to dissolve as quickly as it had appeared, 'feel if you want to, not that it's moving.' She folded her arms in a show of bored toleration while Becky gently placed the palm of her hand onto the silk shirt. 'Wow, Anna, I can't believe it . . . can you believe it?'

'Frankly, yes.'

Becky could feel the tightness of her skin through the thin silk, a tightness which while completely still, seemed nonetheless to hum with energy. She was about to remark on the fact when Anna shook her hand off. 'Okay, time's up. Let's see this place then. Sorry it's taken so long to get together, but you know how it is.' She dropped her bag and began walking round the small flat, peering behind doors and feeling the fabrics of the furnishings, which were simple but attractive and tastefully arranged. 'You have really landed on your feet, haven't you?'

'Well . . .'

'When I think what you've been through, so recently too, and here you are, a couple of months on and all sorted. Well done.'

'I'm not remotely sorted,' said Becky quietly, detecting a faint brusqueness in her sister's tone and wondering what it meant. 'I'm busy, so time passes quite well. And this place has been a godsend. But I got a taxi to drive past Joe's new place the other day, after I'd been to a meeting south of the river, and there he was, up a ladder at the front, fixing a huge plant basket thing to the wall, and the whole building looked transformed, all shiny and welcoming and I felt this terrible sense of loss, like I was seeing him on the set of his new life without me, when all along I'd envisioned being there. And all I could think was how well he's doing without me, how quickly he's pulled it all together, thanks in part, of course, to David,' she added with some bitterness.

Anna laughed sharply. 'Yes, thanks to David, who these days seems to spend more time on a train to London than I do. God, is it hot in here or is it me?' She blew at her fringe, which floated briefly out of her eyebrows before landing back where it had started.

'I'll turn the thermostat down,' Becky had offered quickly. 'You go on through.'

And she still looked hot, Becky mused now, getting up to make coffee and feeling one of the pangs of longing for a cigarette that hit her from time to time, inextricably connected to the more frequent pangs she felt for the life she had known before Guy and the treacherous mirage of something better. On the other side of the table Anna had begun rolling her sleeves up, making tidy, symmetrical folds in the violet silk until it was barely covering her elbows.

'Black or white?'

'Oh, black please,' she said, stretching out her arms to check on her handiwork. When Becky returned she was leaning back in the chair with her eyes closed, idly rubbing the scar on her now bared forearm. It looked redder than usual Becky observed, feeling a sudden inexplicable disquiet at the sight. 'Annie, are you all right?'

She blinked quickly. 'Yes. Why ever shouldn't I be? I'm always all right. All Right Anna, that's me.' Her fingers continued to stroke the faded ribbon of twisted skin, tracing the shape of it over and over again.

'It's just that you don't seem . . . yourself,' Becky ventured unhappily, feeling not just concern but a selfish resentment at her sister's curious mood. It had taken weeks of pleading to get her to the flat. She had been looking forward to a proper post-mortem on the Guy fiasco, on the rubble of her marriage, on the terrible regret about losing Joe, which, instead of fading with time, seemed to be intensifying.

'Neither would you in my condition, believe me,' she replied drily. 'The truth is, I am not myself. I am a . . . a . . . fucking house, a fucking *huge* unattractive house, one that no one would want to live in . . . David certainly doesn't want to live in it . . . I mean, like I said, he's always in London these days, which is a joke, given that the big horrible city was one of the things he was supposedly trying to get away from. But now . . .' She heaved herself up from the armchair and began another tour of the room, picking up objects and putting them down. 'He's never bloody at home, never there. It has even occurred to me' – she pressed her hand to her chest and breathed deeply in an apparent bid to compose herself – 'that he might be seeing someone else. It is a classic thing for the male to do in such circumstances – the wife becomes an ugly house so the husband seeks sexual solace elsewhere – often just temporarily but . . .'

'Anna stop it,' Becky gasped at last, 'please, I've never seen you like this.'

'No, you haven't, have you?' She smiled, suddenly dreamy, as if half amused by the notion.

'Of course David isn't seeing anyone else,' Becky continued, 'he adores you – he always has. And besides, it wouldn't make sense, would it – for him to spill the beans about me and Guy to Joe and all the while be doing exactly the same thing himself?' She raised her voice in triumph at the logic of this explanation, pleased to see that Anna too appeared to be coming to her senses.

'Of course it wouldn't.' She sighed. 'Silly me.' She breathed again, even more deeply, closing her eyes. 'Thank you Becks. You're right, I'm not myself. I'm finding it hard . . . I get so tired and I'm not used to that – you know, I never get tired, do I?' She looked so forlorn, standing in the middle of the room, her hands dangling either side of the violet silk tent of her belly, her face all pink and drawn that Becky gave a cry and ran to put her arms round her. She resisted for a moment, but then went limp. 'You're always there for me,' Becky whispered, a lump blocking her throat, 'well I'm here for you too. Always.'

'No one can be there always,' Anna replied wearily, easing herself free of Becky's grasp, 'it's just not possible. And I must get on my way or I'll miss my train. Sorry about the outburst.' She grinned, for a moment looking quite like her old self. 'Work is hell and the nanny I thought I had lined up has accepted a better offer.'

'Why don't you stay here? I could sleep on the sofa and—'

She shook her head. 'David is expecting me and besides, I need my own bed at the moment – I have a special thing I do with about thirty-six pillows that gets me comfortable enough to sleep.'

'Well at least let me call you a taxi.'

'No, there'll be loads outside – it's only nine o'clock.'

Becky watched through a chink in the sitting-room curtains as Anna slowly made her way up the wrought-iron staircase outside, pulling herself on the banister with each step. On reaching street level she paused, as if undecided as to which direction she should take. It was a relief when she finally walked away, a relief to hear the thick soles of her leather boots sounding firm and sure on the concrete.

Lying in bed a couple of hours later, Becky was dismayed to find that her general sense of unease about the evening had, if anything, grown stronger. The usually comforting swish of cars passing along the road outside, the beam of their headlights sliding along the curtains, kept her awake. She began to count them, feeling with each one that she was getting closer to something terrifying and bad. When she shut her eyes all she could think of was Anna's tight pink face and Stella, journeying south alone, to the one area in the world no one would ever have imagined her wishing to revisit. It made Becky think the ground beneath the three of them – the points of reference by which they had known each other for two decades – was shifting. It made her wonder whether more than just her marriage had fallen apart, whether something much bigger and worse was unravelling, worn out like one of Stella's frayed doilies. As the cars lessened and the darkness thickened Becky succumbed to a huge burst of longing for Joe, not just for the physical comfort of his body curled round hers, dove-tailing knees and elbows in the way they had always managed so well, but for the calm reassurance she knew he would have given had she voiced her fears out loud. Turning her face into the pillow, she wrapped her arms around her own body, seeking an echo of what she yearned for, but feeling only the keyboard of her ribcage through the thin fabric of her nightie.

# 26

Taking a beer from one of the fridges behind the bar, Joe paused with both elbows on the counter and surveyed the room, now only half full of people standing in clusters with glasses of wine, picking at the tail ends of the food. Having initially been reluctant to host any kind of opening event, he had to admit that Adrian, who was the one who had pushed him into it, had been right. The evening had gone well. Thanks mostly to Adrian's huge circle of friends, there had been no shortage of bodies to fill the space. More importantly, four members of the food press had made brief appearances at various stages, not just to sample the simple examples of his cooking spread around the tables, but also to talk to him about where he had come from and what he hoped to achieve in the future. Adrian said it was no guarantee that any write-ups would make it into print, but Joe had enjoyed the whole process so much he didn't think he minded. Sam and Trish, who had touchingly begged to be allowed to jump ship from Le Moulin with him, had both got along with the media presence as well, particularly Trish who had left some while ago on the arm of the man from the *Brixton Echo*.

Joe raised the bottle to his lips and drank steadily. He had paced himself all evening and now intended to let go. So far he had drunk only wine and he had eaten very little. He could feel the alcohol seeping into his system, relaxing him in the way that nothing else did these days. He hadn't let it get out of hand, he wasn't that stupid, nor did he want to give

Becky the satisfaction of turning him into some sad alcoholic. It was more of a calculated thing; the simple recognition that several drinks was an effective way of numbing the senses, of introducing that mental slow-down so vital to a decent night's sleep. Physical exhaustion alone – a state which had seen new extremes in recent weeks, with all the business of moving and getting the restaurant ready – was not enough to ensure oblivion, not enough to keep his mind from retracing the events of the past few months, seeking some sort of pattern by which to understand them. Sometimes, he still couldn't quite believe what had happened. All evening he had had the ridiculous notion that Becky would turn up, waltz in through the door with her dark hair swinging, announcing that it had been nothing but a bad dream, that their relationship was worth more than a fling with a lying bastard who couldn't even stick around to follow through on the mayhem he had created. Hearing the bare bones of the ensuing sorry saga from David shortly after it happened, Joe had almost felt sorry for her. Calling on the support of Stella, of all people, even for a brief period would, he knew, be something she would have found incredibly hard.

Joe closed his eyes, drained the last of his beer and reached for another bottle. Overhead, the freshly painted lemon ceiling, with its strings of angled silver-headed lights, gleamed down at him, such a far cry from the dusty webbed cracks etched between the cornices of even the most solid rooms in Balham, that he almost laughed out loud in exultation. He had made it happen. He had clung to his dream and willed it into life. Gary, who had put him onto the property in the first place, had slapped him on the back several times that night, remarking on that very fact, on how he admired someone with the power and tenacity to see the germ of an idea through to fruition. Joe blinked again at the pristine ceiling, marvelling that just the other side of it was his new bedroom, somewhat crowded with furniture, but sparkling with all the promise of a fresh start. Unpacking his belongings, he had been pleased at the ease with which he consigned what remained of Becky's stuff into spare boxes. Indeed, he had relished pressing the flaps down and taping them up, feeling that it went some considerable way towards helping him package up the six years they had spent together. Six wasted years, he reflected bitterly, lifting the bottle to his lips and catching the eye of David, who had his coat on and was threading his way, somewhat unsteadily towards the door. Joe did a thumbs-up sign and waved him over, but his brother-in-law merely nodded a farewell and continued on his way, disappearing into the gossamer mist of rain shimmering under the street lights outside. Joe watched as the closing door slowly sealed the scene from view, shaking his head and marvelling for the umpteenth time at the discovery of such an unexpected and unlikely source of support and kindness during the trauma of the previous three months. The money had of course been crucial, but David had helped in other ways too, like suggesting the construction of the bar area where Joe now stood, facing away from the main body of the restaurant and into a snug corner, so that guests could sit in soft chairs while they sipped apéritifs and perused the menu. Earlier on that evening the pair of them had sat there themselves, admiring the successful realisation of the plan, Joe sipping wine, his stomach knotted with terror, while David expertly twirled his glass, somehow managing to look the epitome of the suave businessman in spite of the thick ponytail tucked into the nape of his neck and the fact that he was in starched denims and collarless shirt as opposed to a pinstripe suit.

After a moment or two of companionable silence Joe had attempted to voice some of his gratitude out loud, only to be stopped in his tracks. 'Don't mate,' David had interrupted gruffly, 'I mean it's been good for me too you know – all this'

– he gestured at the room with his wine glass – 'it's helped me too.'

Joe had frowned in puzzlement, tussling with the concept of his brother-in-law needing help with anything. 'Really? In what way exactly?'

David had stared hard at his wine for several seconds, before blurting, 'This baby business – you've been through it – it does change things, doesn't it? I mean, in spite of what people say, it changes every fucking thing, doesn't it?' He licked his lips, the inside of which – as Joe noticed for the first time – had the dark roseate tinge suggestive of some considerable wine-drinking prior to his arrival at the party. 'These last few weeks, coming here, having the excuse to come to London, has, frankly, been a relief, because Anna is so . . . so . . . *inside* herself . . . it almost feels as if she's left me . . .' He broke off, clapping his hand to his forehead. 'Jesus, how unspeakably crass of me to say such a thing – after you and Becky – Joe I'm so sorry.'

'Don't be. It's fine.' Joe paused, struck both by the irony of the fact that this new closeness with his brother-in-law should arrive only after the only character linking their lives was no longer at his side, and the inappropriateness of the moment David had chosen for its expression. Out of the corner of his eye he could see a couple of early arrivals being fielded by Trish and Adrian. 'And as to what you were saying, about pregnancy I mean, my memories of the subject are somewhat faded . . .' He faltered, silenced by a sudden and disquieting image of Becky weeping inconsolably in the bath of the Oxfordshire country hotel. 'But when Ruth was expecting Jenny,' he continued, managing slowly to shut the image down, like the turning off of a stiff tap, 'yes, there was a bit of that. Of course it hits every woman differently – hormones and so on, whether they puke their guts out or transform into the proverbial blossoming flowers . . .'

'I know, I know,' David interjected impatiently, 'but it's like I just can't *touch* her, as if . . .'

At the sight of Adrian bearing down on them, his cheerful freckled face clearly oblivious to the possibility that he could be interrupting anything of significance, Joe had leapt gratefully to his feet. In his current state he felt too raw for confidences, too raw to accept that solid successful confident people like David might be grappling with a host of their own insoluble problems.

Remembering the moment now, and the uncertainty in David's stride, Joe felt a small twist of regret. He should have told him – should at least have tried to explain – that the slimy being, shortly to slither out of the impossibly tiny space that had once been a recognisable part of the female body, would be the start of a love of unprecedented and inconceivable dimensions; that the best and worst of his life was about to begin and there was nothing on God's earth that could prepare him for it. Remembering Jenny, asleep upstairs, Joe felt a lump swell in his throat. Through the course of the evening he had checked on her several times. Ruth had delivered her about an hour into the proceedings, declining a drink herself but not looking too stern when Jenny tried some of Joe's wine, wrinkling her pixie nose in distaste at its bitterness. It had felt important to have her there, playing a part in the small initiation ceremony into the new phase of a life which Joe hoped would accommodate her as much, if not more, than the last. She had worn a flimsy lilac dress, with pencil-thin shoulder straps that showed off her white schoolgirl plumpness, and matching slipper-like shoes, with a small heel and no back strap. Although the evening was far too cold for such an outfit, which had been bought for Ruth's brother's wedding in September, she was beginning to show an alarmingly teenage defiance of such considerations, and had bristled visibly when Ruth tried to slip a cardigan across her back before leaving. Seeing her later, curled up amongst her army of cuddly animals, wearing her faded and favourite Winnie the Pooh pyjamas and surrounded by wall posters of semi-clad boy pop stars, it had struck Joe just how caught she was between one stage of development and the next; neither a child, nor yet a Lolita, without being remotely sure she wanted to be either. Was it this that had been making her so difficult in recent months? he wondered, frowning in fond perplexity at the thought of his daughter's persistently sullen resistance to his affections and thinking this would have been something else to tell David; that her sulkiness made him love her more, that parental bonds went beyond personality or behaviour.

'Had enough of us all then?'

'Adrian, hi . . . sorry . . . most people had gone anyway . . . I was just taking time out.'

'This place is going to be good, Joe, really fucking good.' He grinned, flicking a heap of ginger curls out of his eyebrows and raising his glass of wine in toast.

'For you too, I hope,' said Joe quietly.

'For me too.' He chinked his glass lightly against Joe's bottle. 'All the help with my business, all that slave labour at dawn last year . . .' He blinked his sandy lashes slowly, looking for a moment uncharacteristically solemn. 'It's no small thanks to you that I'm now solvent, that, in fact, I can barely keep pace with orders . . .'

He was prevented from continuing by Joe's mobile, ringing from the confines of his jacket pocket. 'Sorry.' He made a face.

'I was making tracks anyway,' Adrian assured him, his cheery smile sliding back into place. 'See you.' He punched him lightly on the arm, before heading off to join the last of the leavers now filtering out into the street on the far side of the room.

'Joe?'

'Becky?'

'I'm after David. Is he there?'

'David? No,' Joe replied, curtness entering his tone as the mad hope that she had phoned to offer some sort of encouragement or congratulation flickered and died. 'He left a while ago. Why?'

'Because,' she replied, sounding suddenly desperate, 'Anna – is—'

'Having the baby?'

'Maybe. Look, I haven't got time to talk to you. Anna is ill – I've got to find David.'

'What sort of ill?'

'Something called pre-eclampsia – they think – and now she's . . . she's . . . where the hell is he? Anna said he was going to your party.'

'Yes, but he's left already, about an hour ago. Have you tried his mobile?'

'Of course I've tried his fucking mobile – he's switched it off. Where was he going? Had he decided to stay in London?'

'I don't know, I—'

'Nobody bloody knows anything.'

'Becky – if there's—'

'If he calls you,' she snapped, 'perhaps you would be good enough to tell him that his wife has such high blood pressure that she may well die, that she had to crawl to the phone to call the ambulance herself and that by the time she got to calling me she could barely speak . . . she . . .'

'Becky, I'm so—' Realising the line had gone dead, Joe stared at the phone for several seconds before slipping it back into his pocket. He had heard of pre-eclampsia, had read about it in one of Ruth's innumerable pregnancy books. Something to do with the placenta not being properly embedded into the womb. He remembered the blood-pressure thing too and the possibility of death, though whether of the baby as well as the mother he was less sure. Before locking up he tried David's number several times himself, punching the numbers with increasing desperation, thinking that the only thing worse than losing one's wife in childbirth would be living with the guilt of not having been contactable when it happened.

Becky threw the phone onto her desk with such force that it bounced, knocking over half a mug of cold coffee before ricocheting onto the floor and landing amongst the scores of screwed up balls of paper around the bin. She had been working late on a presentation to a new client. With an empty flat to go home to, such once unthinkable habits had begun to creep into her routine; as had buying microwaveable meals on the way home and puffing on Camel Lights till her throat was raw once she had eaten them. That night she had been planning a Hawaiian pizza and an entire bottle of wine – paltry treats to help make up for the curious and dispiriting discovery that the once longed-for prospect of two consecutive mornings with nothing to get up for had lost much of their allure by becoming a regular reality.

Anna's phonecall had come as she was on the point of packing up. Her voice had sounded remote, a thin thread of a sound. She explained that a mild tummy ache that morning had grown so acute that she had caught an early-afternoon train home. By which time she had a blinding headache and kept seeing flashing lights. She had called for an ambulance, she said, and wanted David, whom she had been trying on and off on his mobile for hours. Before calling Joe, Becky had tried David herself several times, leaving a string of terse messages. She had also called the hospital, squeezing out the information that Anna had been admitted to something called a High-Dependency Unit with suspected pre-eclampsia. Looking the word up afterwards in one of the innumerable reference books stacked around the office, Becky had felt her mouth go dry. Throughout her unsatisfactory conversation with Joe she had half an eye on the paragraph, scanning the infuriatingly brief and bleak description of symptoms for non-existent glimmers of reassurance.

The coffee had soaked through her notes and splashed across the open pages of the medical dictionary, looking, so Becky could not resist thinking, like droplets of dried blood. Stepping out from behind her desk to retrieve the phone, which had landed between the wastepaper basket and the door, she realised her legs were shaking. Collapsing to the floor on her knees, she pressed her face into her hands and took several deep breaths, confronting the suddenly obvious fact that she needed somehow to get to the hospital in Dorset that night. Whatever Anna was going through it was not right that she should be enduring it alone. Looking at her watch, she saw to her dismay that it was already ten o'clock, almost certainly too late to catch a train. In which case it would have to be a taxi, she decided, brushing aside any thought of what such an extravagance would cost and reaching for the phone. As she did so the door next to her opened a few inches and a hand – a slim-fingered male hand which she recognised as belonging to her boss – reached in and began groping for the line of light switches along the wall.

'Don't – please – I . . .'

'Good God, Rebecca,' Mike Hadfield exclaimed, pushing the door open properly and staring down at her, his steely eyebrows flexed in amusement and surprise, 'I thought you'd gone home hours and hours ago. Have you lost something or are you paying homage to the wastepaper basket?'

'Mike, I need a car.'

'A car. I see.' He rubbed his jaw thoughtfully. 'You mean that you have chosen this obscenely late hour on a Friday evening to regret your decision to take an entirely liquid salary package—'

'No. I mean I need a car now, to drive to Dorset because my sister has been taken seriously ill and I can't get hold of her husband and she might lose the baby, not to mention . . .' Becky swallowed hard, pressing the next thought away. 'I was going to try and get a taxi because it's so late I'm not sure there'd be a train.'

'I see.' He paused for a few moments, folding his arms and staring at something over her shoulder. Then he quickly reached into his suit jacket pocket and pulled out a single silver car key attached to a round leather key ring clearly emblazoned with the letters BMW. 'You do have a licence I suppose?' he murmured, shifting his gaze to her face and raising his eyebrows.

Becky nodded, her mouth dry. 'I passed my test years ago. But I hate driving.'

'Ah.' He swung the key ring slowly round his index finger. 'In that case perhaps you would like me to drive you?'

The offer was so unexpected and so shockingly generous that she let out a gasp of a laugh before answering. 'No – thank you – but no. Look, it was mad to ask. I'm sure I can get a taxi . . .' She began to struggle to her feet but not before the car key had landed in her lap.

'From the sounds of things you better hurry up. Here.' He pulled a business card from his pocket and scribbled a line of numbers above his name. 'My home number. Call me when you're back. I'm parked in my usual space in the basement. Do you want me to come and show you?'

'No – thanks – I'll be fine. I just . . .' Having levered herself upright, Becky stood clutching the key and her phone, torn between the desire to race out of the door and the necessity of finding the right words to express her thanks.

'Better hurry then,' he repeated.

'Mike, I . . .'

'Yes, I'm a saint. Now go. And for God's sake drive carefully. I love that bloody car. And I hope your sister's okay,' he called, starting – in spite of what she had said – down the corridor after her. By the time he reached the bottom of the stone stairwell leading to the underground car park which serviced all the offices in their block, she was several yards ahead. The place was empty apart from a sleek black vehicle parked under a reserved sign on the far side. 'It's automatic so you all you need is . . .' Mike called breathlessly, the soles of his shoes squeaking faintly on the concrete floor as he jogged after her.

'I've driven an automatic before,' she called back, tugging the door open and slipping behind the wheel. He arrived at the car to find her scrabbling under the seat for a lever with which to narrow the distance between her feet and the pedals.

'Here.' He crouched down by her knees and pressed something on the seat, causing it to slide forwards with a gentle whirring sound. 'If you've got it in Drive or Neutral it won't start. It has to be in Parking. The lights are there and the windscreen wipers there and the CD player is loaded – that button there changes the disc – and don't worry about me, I've always loved public transport . . . just joking,' he added quickly, seeing her hesitate. 'Go, I mean it. Go.'

Her last sight of him was in the wing mirror, his face greyish and crumpled, the lenses of his glasses flashing under the garish lights of the empty basement.

# 27

David squinted at the figures on the digital clock set into the dashboard, trying to convince himself that it was a damp wintry afternoon in Dorset and he was dozing next to Anna during one of her innumerable weekend naps, curling up in armchairs or round pillows and cushions like a languid cat. The images swelled and faded. David blinked, seeing again the time on the clock face and feeling the unpleasant crustiness along his eyelids. He was awake because he was cold, he realised, looking about him and absorbing the disquieting reality that he was nowhere near the comfort of his home, but twisted into an awkward self-hugging position in the driver's seat of his car. Through the window, half steamed and damp from the warmth of his breath, he could make out the dim outlines of the trees skirting the layby and the shadowy whiteness of the small van which he had almost bulldozed as he swerved off the road, finally paying heed to one of the 'Tiredness Kills Take a Break' signs he had passed on the motorway. Staring, still groggy with shock and fatigue, through the smeary glass into the blackness outside, scenes from the previous evening began to pop inside his mind: Joe's party, the first pub and the second, then the nightclub where he could recall only the smell of his own sweat and a huge sequinned ball which had spun until his head ached, eventually forcing him outside where he had retched like a dog in the gutter before staggering off in search of his car. Afterwards, dizzy and sticky-lipped from vomiting, he had crawled his way out of London, driving with the exaggerrated care of the truly inebriated, keeping the speedometer to a meticulous thirty and braking at the sight of every green light lest it should choose the moment of his approach to disappear.

Lifting his head off the car window, David gently swivelled his neck to the right and left, massaging some of the stiffness away with the palm of his hand. It was time to drive on he knew, but still he could not bring himself to reach for the ignition, not even to warm up his frozen limbs. There was something about being numb which he almost liked, something to do with the discomfort of it, a sense of being wretched and admitting to it, feeling it to the core. On the seat beside him the blank screen of his mobile phone blinked accusingly, as it had done for most of the day. Not wanting to be made to feel guilty by Anna, who had continued to make her reservations about his joint venture with their brother-in-law only too plainly known, he had switched it off the moment he set out for London. The way the evening had progressed had done little to encourage the notion of reversing the situation, knowing that he was behaving like a sad adolescent giving him little enthusiasm for hearing the fact expressed out loud in recorded messages from his wife. Such unpleasantness would happen in the end, he knew, when he eventually got home and crawled upstairs to bed. Though infrequently bared – and usually at other people – he had seen enough of Anna's coolly articulated, white-lipped anger over the years to know that it was something to be dreaded. With the innately virtuous position of being eight months pregnant to fuel her cause, David shuddered at the thought of how she would crush him, how he would be reduced to crawling on his knees for forgiveness and mercy. Unlike Anna he had no moral highground from which to defend himself, only nameless fears to which he continued, vainly, to seek a solution but which only seemed to make him think and do bad things.

\*

Becky drove so fast that she stopped glancing at the dials on the dashboard for fear of scaring herself. The car seemed not to grip the road so much as to float just above it, racing with all the streamlined power of a speedboat on a mill pond. After several experiments with the panel of buttons controlling the heating, she let warm air belt out of the ventilators and wound the window down as well, responding to a need to feel both cocooned by heat and yet vividly alert. With air blasting round her ears, there was little point in seeking distraction from the CD player, but she tried all the same, pressing the disc selection button Mike had indicated several times in a bid to find something that transcended the decade separating their tastes. Trying first Joni Mitchell and then Elton John, both of whom she liked, she eventually gave up not because she couldn't hear the music but because every lyric seemed to have a painful and uncanny relevance to aspects of the recent traumas in her own life, from the mess of her marriage to the terror and loneliness of racing across the country in the dark. Wondering about this in the wind-blasted silence that followed, it occurred to Becky that life was about love and death and not much else, that all the rest was just trimmings and diversion.

The hospital was well-signposted and with a huge car park, quite unlike her experience of equivalent institutions in London where one ended up parking down side streets and walking for miles. Inside there was such a sense of hushed orderliness that Becky at once felt her spirits rise in a sudden conviction that all would be well. At the central information desk a heavy-lidded Indian girl with streaming black hair and a beautiful white-toothed smile directed her towards the maternity unit, pointing with bangled arms down the wide corridor behind them and issuing instructions about lifts and turnings left and right. 'If it's babies that's where your sister will be,' she assured Becky confidently, before returning her attentions to a dog-eared paperback with a picture of a kissing couple on the front. Following the route, Becky found herself sufficiently composed to make a mental note of a sign to the cafeteria. It was hours since she had eaten or drunk anything and her stomach felt shrunken and growling. While waiting for the lift, some of her certainty receded at the sight of a middle-aged couple walking slowly down the corridor towards her, leaning into each other, evidently stricken by bad news. Becky stepped out of their way, trying to look sympathetic, but they walked past unseeing, the man's face pasty and tense while the woman sobbed quietly into the lapel of his jacket.

'She's still in theatre. Her blood pressure was very high – the pre-eclampsia was severe – they had to operate . . .'

'Theatre?' repeated Becky. It had taken the young midwife a while to locate the appropriate bits of paper from the huge pile on her desk. Becky had stood in front of her, chewing the already raw skin round her fingernails.

'Yes,' said the girl, her face softening. 'Dr Millet is operating. He really is the best there is. She glanced at her watch. 'It will be a little while yet, so why don't you pop down to the canteen and have a nice cup of tea and . . .'

'So she's having the baby now,' said Becky, blinking at the girl and feeling stupid. 'He's operating to take the baby out. Should I . . . could I . . . be there to . . . ?' She broke off, a rage of helplessness breaking inside her which quickly became a rush of anger against David. For letting Anna go through so much alone, for hating her enough to betray her to Joe.

The midwife was shaking her head. 'She had to have a general anaesthetic because with the high blood pressure the blood doesn't clot which means an epidural would not have been safe . . .'

'Right,' Becky murmured, not listening. 'Right.' Feeling a

pain in her hand she looked down and saw that she had been clenching Mike's car key so hard that a deep scarlet ridge had appeared in the palm of her hand. 'I might then, as you say, have a cup of tea and come back.'

The midwife looked relieved. 'I'm going off duty soon. Sister Morris will be taking over. Try not to worry,' she added, the quietness in her voice communicating better than words ever could that, while not admitting it outright, there was indeed quite a lot to worry about.

The tea was thin and scalding. Becky bought a packeted honey flapjack to go with it, which she nibbled steadily even though it was sickly sweet and her hunger had mysteriously gone, displaced by a mushrooming fear in the pit of her stomach. It struck her, sitting alone at the stained Formica table, that the last time she had maintained anything like such a vigil had been when Anna had shattered her arm in her car accident. Throughout the first day at the hospital Stella had been so visibly racked with anxiety that Becky, rusticated that week for going to the shopping mall instead of afternoon lessons, had chewed the already frayed cuffs of her school jumper in cringing frustration. When the doctor reported the obvious fact that all was well apart from the arm, which would heal with the help of a couple of pins, Stella had appalled her youngest daughter still further by throwing herself against his chest and sobbing with relief. Remembering the incident now, Becky felt a burst of guilty wonderment at her teenage selfishness, how she had managed not to care about anything beyond the sphere of her own feelings. It occurred to her in the same instant that she should perhaps make some effort to contact Stella in France. The idea held little appeal however, not just because of the panic it would cause her mother, but because to make such a call would, she knew, elevate the crisis element of the situation to a level which she herself was not yet prepared to acknowledge.

'Excuse me.'

'Yes?' Becky glanced up with a jolt to find the midwife who had been on the desk upstairs standing beside her, a long black leather coat over her starchy dress and a bubbled plastic handbag slung over one arm.

'I thought you'd like to know your sister is out of theatre. She's had a little boy. They're both fine. You can see them if you like. She's still very groggy of course – won't be allowed home for a few days – but I'm sure she'd like to see you.'

'Oh thank you – thank you—'

'Cheerio then.' The girl beamed, clearly enjoying the treat of delivering good news. 'I'm off home. Is it cold outside?'

'Cold? I . . . yes, I think so.'

'Thanks.' She made a face, popping open her bubble bag and pulling out a thick woollen hat and a pair of gloves. 'See you then. Though I'm not in until Wednesday. She might be discharged by then.'

# 28

At first Anna thought the bed was shaking. It took a while to register that it was in fact her own body, that her limbs were convulsing independently of any alternative plans she might have had for them. Even her jaw was jerking, clacking her teeth together as if she were racked with cold when in fact, if anything, she felt too warm. Her joints ached too, deeply, as though worn out by the futile strain of trying to keep her arms and legs still. From the wetness on her neck and in the creases of her ears she knew that she was crying, not for any specific reason so much as a general sense of misery. Like the twitches of her body the misery felt like an independent force, taking cruel advantage of her physically stricken state to spill out of her, pouring itself into visibility when she had no powers to rein it in.

'There now.' She felt a cool hand on her arm. 'You relax now. It's all over. Dr Millet's very pleased with you. Baby won't be in special care much longer – just till we get those sugar levels up. This shivering will pass.' She felt a tissue being wiped across her cheeks. 'Just a reaction to the anaesthetic. You think of your lovely little boy, that will cheer you up.'

Anna squeezed her eyes closed as another fit of shaking took hold. The baby was out. They had cut her open and taken it out of her. Just now, a few moments ago – or had it been a few hours? Some arms, strong brown-skinned arms with silky dark hairs, had held a swaddled bundle near her face. She had smelt hospital linen and glimpsed reddish skin specked with yellow. It had been so brief, then the bundle was gone, leaving only the linen smell and the sadness.

'We're still trying to contact Dad,' continued the voice. 'We're sure to get him soon – I'm sure he would have been here if he could.'

Anna felt the tears pouring with renewed force down her face, triggered not, as the attending midwife imagined, by a desire to see the father of her newborn child, but by a sudden longing for the way things had been. For the manageable simplicity of her existence thirty-eight weeks before, when she was confident both of what life demanded of her and her power to deliver it.

'Anna?' Becky parted the curtains and approached the bed slowly, shocked, in spite of the preparatory talk she had had with Dr Millet, at the sight of all the tubes: one out of her neck for fluid balance, one out of her arm for magnesia to stop her brain swelling and two out of her abdomen, one to drain urine, the other blood. Dr Millet a serious-faced thirtysomething, clearly schooled in the latest empower-the-patients-and-relatives-with-all-the-facts attitude to doctoring, had been impressively informative. 'Anna, you're crying,' Becky whispered, feeling a lump block her own throat as she laid a hand over her sister's and squeezed a clutch of fingers. 'Don't cry, it's all right now, it's all over now.' Still holding the hand she pulled a chair up to the bedside and began stroking the thick silvery scar running along her forearm. 'A little boy – I can't believe it – can't wait to see him – me an aunt, bloody hell . . .' She continued to stroke the arm as she talked, while Anna after shivering a couple of times, lay quite still. Only the tears gave any sign of consciousness, sliding out from between her eyelids in a steady silent stream. The hand Becky held remained limp, while the other lay carelessly across the mound of her stomach – a surprisingly large mound, so Becky could not help thinking, given that a seven-pound load had been removed from inside. 'And David will be here very soon, I'm sure – some silly cock-up I expect – a dead battery on his mobile – a flat tyre—'

'It's all betrayal in the end.'

'What?'

She turned her head to face Becky and opened her eyes. They were so badly bloodshot that the usual vivid blue of the irises was barely visible amongst the squiggles of broken veins. Becky flinched at the sight, wondering whether something clinical could have caused such damage or whether it was from all the crying. 'It's all betrayal,' she repeated, speaking more firmly. 'David has someone. He has someone else.'

'Now, I've told you before, that's just silly,' Becky scolded, aghast both at Anna's distressed state and the notion of her brother-in-law doing anything so treacherous at such a time. 'He was at Joe's party and then ran into some sort of trouble afterwards . . . pranged the car or something. He would never have anybody else, Annie, I just know he wouldn't. Like I said before, he would hardly have spilled the beans to Joe about me and Guy if he'd been committing the same crime himself, would he?' Becky was disappointed to see that these remarks caused her sister to appear, if anything, even less reassured than before. The silent weeping had suddenly grown much more noisy. She was letting out high-pitched groans between sobs, each one tearing and tortured, as if it was being wrenched from her chest by force. She was trying to talk too, flinging words which made no sense.

'Not – David—'

'No, I know,' Becky soothed, trying to keep a hold of her hand which had grown damp and slippery with perspiration.

'Me – Becky – me.'

'Annie, my darling, it will be all right. You're in shock. You've had a dreadful dreadful ordeal, you . . .'

'Me – I told Joe – me – I told him – about you and Guy

– I told him.' Even after the words were out, strung at last with sufficient coherence for their meaning to be inescapable, Becky felt a part of her mind resisting the truth. The racking sobs stopped as quickly as they had started. Anna had closed her eyes again and turned her head to face the wall, where the curtains had only been half pulled across the window, leaving a black rectangle of night sky.

'Why?' she said at last.

'Always – all your life – everything your own way.'

'That's not true,' Becky stammered, incredulous.

'You never had to face things – never really tried at things – were always forgiven – always got away with it. At school, being naughty, always a cause for concern, then later, packing in courses, starting things, dropping them, all those men, and poor Cliff – poor poor Cliff – dumped without a second thought – he used to phone me you know, for months afterwards, ask me what had happened, what he had done wrong.' In spite of a powerful urge to interject, to deny it all and say she was mad, Becky at the same time found herself spellbound, filled with dread and curiosity as to what further revelations might be in store. 'Everyone always loves you Becky – even Dad, he loved you more – because you laughed easily and didn't care and defied Mum. And after he'd gone you took over Mum too – bad Becky always the centre of attention – while I played the good fairy, passing exams, being understanding. Do you know?' she added, catching her breath, her voice suddenly urgent, and turning to look at Becky for the first time since the start of her outburst, 'my accident, the operation, all that physiotherapy – I loved it – being worried about – sometimes, I even think that I did it on purpose, that it wasn't black ice at all, but me turning the wheel towards that wall . . .'

'Don't be silly,' Becky whispered, appalled.

A long silence followed. Looking across at the window

Becky could see their reflections in it, the pale shrouded figure lying on the bed and her own dark-haired self, poised and tense on the chair beside. Playing out a scene like actors in a TV drama. The invalid and the visitor. A classic pose, yet not so, not remotely so. For nothing was as it seemed, nothing ever had been nor would be again.

'Betrayal,' Anna murmured.

'Betrayal,' Becky echoed, still with her eyes on their reflections, a detached, illogical part of her curious to see what either of them would do next, as if she really was watching a drama involving other people rather than living a scene in her own life.

'I was suffering – the pregnancy, I've hated it – I think I wanted you to suffer too, couldn't bear to see you behaving so badly and getting away with it, being made happy by it . . . sorry . . . I'm sorry. Please forgive me.' Her voice was devoid of intonation, as if she had no real expectation of forgiveness or anything else.

'Yes,' said Becky, thinking not of the role her sister had played in the break-up of her marriage so much as the extraordinary perspective she had just revealed about their childhood. Was she right or had her brain been warped by shock? Had their father loved her more? Had she misbehaved merely to gain attention? It certainly hadn't felt so at the time. On the contrary, it had always seemed obvious to her that she should envy Anna, for her effortless cooperation with the outside world, for being everybody's darling, for being prettier, cleverer, more successful . . .

'You were going to tell him anyway, weren't you? Joe, you were going to tell him.'

'Yes,' murmured Becky, 'I think so.'

'So you would have broken up anyway. You said yourself – I remember you saying – that it was all just a question of time . . .'

Becky nodded, her thoughts drifting to the now unreal memories of the run-up to Christmas, of her burgeoning sense of unease about Guy and the accompanying renewal of her affections for Joe. Looking back, the irony of such coincidences struck her as so cruel as to be almost funny. Dragging her gaze away from their ghostly images in the window, she managed a weary smile. It occurred to her in the same instant that Guy inventing a fictional version of himself was neither particularly odd nor so desperately unforgivable; he had simply – albeit to a rather extreme degree – been trying to spice things up, to sweeten the bitter taste of reality. Which was what everyone did. Anna, her, everyone. It was only the extent to which they did it that varied. The thought made her very calm suddenly, very on top of things.

'Becky? Do you forgive me.'

'Hm?' She slipped her hand back over Anna's. 'It doesn't matter now. It's all over. And I've done all right since, haven't I?'

It was Anna's turn to smile, a small tired stretch of the mouth. 'Yes, you have.'

'And you are all right too,' Becky continued more firmly. 'You have a wonderful healthy baby – Dr Millett said seven pounds is quite a weight given that he was two weeks early—'

'Becky . . . don't tell David, okay? If – when – he comes.' The red eyes blinked fast, filling with tears. 'What I said just now about what I think, don't tell him, please. I know I've no right to ask you, given how I –'

'It's okay.' Becky pressed a finger to her lips. 'Not a word, I promise.'

'Thank you . . . I just . . .' She was prevented from continuing by the parting of the curtains round them and the appearance of a midwife wheeling a small transparent plastic cot. Inside, writhed a puce-faced baby in a tight white cocoon of a wrapping, opening and closing its mouth like a fish in search of a flake of food.

'Someone here wants to see you.' The midwife, who had skin the colour of polished ebony, wide swinging hips and a huge smile, deftly scooped the baby out if its cot, and swung it into the crook of her arm. 'Would Mum like to try some suckling first before he has his bottle? He needs the bottle to help keep his sugar levels up,' she explained cosily, turning to Becky, 'then Mum's breastfeeding can take over completely.'

'I'm so tired,' murmured Anna, 'perhaps he could have the bottle first.'

Becky had stood up, unable to stop herself from reaching out and stroking the tiny limbs of her nephew. 'Oh, but Anna . . . he's . . . he's perfect. Oh my, look at those little hands, so so tiny, how adorable, oh Anna, look.' The midwife had brought the baby right up to the bedside and was bending over to show Anna. 'Could I . . . do you think I could hold him?'

'Sure – that is if Mum says so.' The midwife grinned, revealing huge ivory teeth and a heartening pleasure in what must have been an all too familiar scene.

'Of course she can,' Anna whispered dropping her head back against the pillows. Becky took the small white cotton bundle, trying to mimic the expert cradling of the midwife, but finding instead that the head flopped alarmingly from side to side, while the rest of it felt so contrastingly light that she feared she might crush the little body through gripping too hard.

'There, a natural.' The midwife beamed. 'Perhaps Mum would like you to do the bottle too?'

'I don't know,' Becky faltered, though in truth she was longing to do something to soothe the child, who had not only resumed its writhing but was also turning its fish mouth to her chest with a pitiful whimpering.

'Yes, I'd like that. Becky do the bottle,' murmured Anna, closing her eyes. 'I'm going to call him Colin,' she added, her voice so quiet that the midwife, busily shaking droplets from a small plastic feeding bottle onto her forearm, didn't seem to hear. Becky, glanced quickly at the bed.

'Oh Anna . . .'

'Shh . . .' She raised the arm with the drip in to silence her and within a few instants seemed to fall asleep, her eyelids flickering restlessly as if she was fighting the pull of oblivion, or possibly, the pull of consciousness, reflected Becky, uncomfortably aware that she no longer had any confidence in what Anna thought or felt about anything. The past, an unsatisfactory but once understood process, had opened up behind them, not understood at all but full of worrying uncertainty. Not unconditional, sisterly love, as she had always presumed, but jealousy. And telling Joe. The thought of it made her dizzy. The baby was crying hard now. He had worked his hands free of his wrapping and was clasping and unclasping his fists, reaching for something to cling to.

'Oh but he's a hungry little man,' chuckled the midwife, handing Becky the bottle. 'There we go, that's it,' she encouraged her, adjusting the angle of the teat. 'You want it more upright so there are no air bubbles and don't let him take too much at a time. He'll need little rests – put him on your shoulder and rub his back ever so gently – and when you've had a nice big burp from him you can carry on. You'll be wanting this too,' she warned, placing a white cloth on Becky's shoulder, 'in case he throws up.' Becky, feeling less clumsy by the second, eased the teat out for an instant before sliding it back between the greedy pink gums. At the feel of the rubber safely back between his lips, the blue-black eyes popped open for a moment or two, wide with relief, before resuming a frenzied sucking.

'I'll come back soon and see how you're getting on. You can put him in the cot when you're done.'

'Okay,' Becky murmured, too absorbed to glance up, all her anxieties receding at the simple pleasure of her task. 'Poor little Colin,' she whispered, 'a plastic box for a bed. How horrid. Much better here with Aunty Becky.' He had stopped sucking and fallen asleep, leaving his mouth open round the teat of the bottle, as if ready to continue feeding the instant the need should present itself. With a fine coating of fair down on his head and his blue eyes there was little to suggest any obvious physical echoes of his namesake. Yet it was of his grandfather that Becky thought most forcibly as she scrutinised the small sleeping face; not only of his death, but of his life – his personality – how it had left its mark on them all, how it continued to affect and define things twenty years after his passing.

# 29

By the time David reached Balcombe and turned into his drive a steely dawn light was filtering through the night cloud, not illuminating the countryside so much as veiling it in a ghostly shroud. The wind, which had begun cutting across the road soon after his emergence from the layby, at times buffeting the car so badly that he clutched the wheel like a trembling novice, showed no signs of abating. On either side of him clumps of crocuses and daffodils lay flattened against the grass, their leaves and flowers splayed wide, like innocents seeking protection from aerial bombardment. Behind them, hardier shrubs and trees dived and ducked under the onslaught, bending towards the car and back again, their spiked bare branches seeming to jab like accusing fingers. For the final fifty yards, David slowed to a crawl, driving with most of his body slumped over the steering wheel, peering through the windscreen like a wary stranger. Even the house looked hostile, with its usually warm yellow stone an icy grey and its windows shuttered and lifeless. Pulling up outside the front door, he glanced up anxiously at the bedroom, half expecting to see Anna's drawn face glaring down at him, her beautiful eyes ablaze with hurt and vitriol.

Before going upstairs, he went into the hall toilet, groaning quietly as he relieved himself. Catching sight of his reflection in the small basin mirror afterwards, he groaned again, this time in dismay at the sight of his pouchy red-rimmed eyes and dark unshaven cheeks. His hair was a mess too, having long since escaped from its ponytail and twisted itself into indecorous fuzzy knots. There was a speck of something pink and sticky in a particularly tangled patch near his left temple which he tried to remove only to find himself wincing with pain.

'What a fucking tosser,' he growled, turning away in self-disgust and trudging upstairs, where he had every intention of deferring whatever marital showdown awaited him by tiptoeing into a spare bedroom. He didn't mind which one. He didn't even mind if there were sheets on the bed or cases on the pillows. He was so tired he felt as if he could have slept sandwiched between sharpened nails. Going past the main bedroom however, he paused, licking his sticky dry gums and thinking with sudden and deep longing of his toothbrush.

Seeing the door was ajar, he gently eased it open and stepped inside. In the dim light it took a few instants to register that the bed was empty. David stopped abruptly and listened, half expecting to hear the gush of a tap in the ensuite bathroom. But the only sound was of something cooing in the garden. Crossing to the window, he peered outside. The wind seemed to have dropped and some hint of warm yellow had begun to seep into the daylight, showing off to better effect the deep metallic green of the countryside, steeped and soaked as it had been for most of the winter in torrential rain. Turning his attention back to the room, David noticed for the first time that the curtains were drawn and that the bed was not only empty but unslept in. So she's left me, he thought, his brain addressing the proposition in the painful slow-motion of extreme shock and fatigue.

'So she's left me.' He said the words out loud this time, absently reaching out to trace a finger round a small smudge of brown damp which had recently appeared beside the window sill. A new builder enlisted to identify the source was still hedging his bets, saying he needed to investigate several possibilities far away from the stain itself. Water was stealthy, he had explained darkly, but always found a way out in the end. Like bad feelings, thought David, remorse and misery sweeping over him as he half fell onto the bed. Feeling the small hard bulk of his mobile phone dig into his hip bone, he let out a string of profanities and levered himself upright. Slowly, reluctantly, a dim part of him savouring the last few seconds of his self-imposed exile from the outside world, he took out the phone and switched it on. The screen sprang to life at once, beeping with news of several fresh messages. Seeing, without surprise, that the first one was from Anna, David hesitated again, contemplating the awesome fact that the tiny state-of-the-art gadget sitting in the palm of his hand, no bigger than a small confectionery bar, had the power to connect him to people in virtually all corners of the globe. And yet it facilitated the breaking of contact just as easily, he reflected bleakly, musing upon the unhappy notion that, pregnant or not, Anna could banish him from her life with the touch of a button. Pressing the phone to his ear at last, because there was nothing else left to do, he braced himself for the worst.

'It's me, wondering where you are. I've got these bad tummy pains. If you get this message, please could you call . . .'

'Only me again. They're really bad now, the pains, and my head feels as if it's going to explode – I'm not sure what analgesics I can take because of the baby . . . it's bloody late David, where the hell are you?'

'Me. I don't know if it's the baby, it doesn't feel like the baby. It's not due for two weeks is it . . . I've called an ambulance . . . David please I . . .'

By the time he got to the infinitely more acerbic tones of Becky's messages David was back behind the wheel of his car and halfway down the drive. Alert now and full of a new and infinitely more terrible brand of fear, he drove fast and purposefully, all maudlin reflections on the accusatory postures of the shrubbery quite forgotten. With only a glance to either side, he swung onto the main road and squeezed the accelerator, thankful that the day was still too new even for farm traffic, or the green country bus which, as Anna liked to remind him, provided a lifeline to car-less locals, but which still had the maddening habit of hogging the lanes like a lurching elephant.

It was barely ten minutes before he pulled into the hospital car park. Once inside the building, with the heels of his brogues clicking smartly on the crisp linoleum floor, David felt some sense of control return. Openly impatient with the sleepy Indian girl at reception, he raised his voice until a spritely young man in a white coat appeared to offer him a full briefing on the circumstances surrounding Anna's admission and all that had subsequently taken place.

'So she's fine,' said David, trying as he walked to smooth the straggles of his hair back behind his ears, particularly the sticky bit which felt if anything even more thickly knotted than before.

'Your wife has been through a lot,' commented the doctor evenly, 'right now she's mainly in need of rest. The magnesia will make her a little nauseous, but in a couple of days she will start to feel much better. By the middle of next week we should be taking the stitches out and sending her home.'

'Excellent.'

'For the time being she's in what we call the High Dependency Unit. If you'd be so good as to wait a few moments I'll get one of the midwives to tell her you're here.'

'Excellent,' repeated David, resisting an urge to shake the man's hand. 'Thank you Doctor . . . ?'

'Millet.'

The doctor returned a few minutes later nodding his head and smiling encouragingly. 'If you'd like to follow me?' He set off at a brisk walk down the corridor, stopping a couple of minutes later to open the door of a large room of curtained cubicles. 'She's in the end one, next to the window.'

'Thank you. Excellent.' David strode through the ward, full of headache and contrition, determined to acknowledge and apologise for his sins before Anna had the chance to mention them herself. It had been a life and death thing, he reminded himself, checking that the sticky bit was hidden behind his ear; such experiences put things in perspective, made all the big stuff – like the fact that he loved her and she loved him – stand out. He would focus on the positives and see what transpired.

The moment he pulled back the curtains however, all intellectual certainties about life, death and anything else deserted him. Anna was lying on the bed with her eyes closed, looped to drips and wires like someone about to succumb to a terminal illness. Dozing in a chair next to her was Becky, whom he might have guessed would be there but for whom he felt unprepared nonetheless. But what really stopped David in his tracks, drying his already dry mouth and making his heart race, was the sight of the tiny infant lying in a transparent box of a cradle next to the bed. In all his thoughts of Anna, of how to explain his whereabouts, how to elicit her forgiveness, how to tell her that the realisation he could have lost her altogether had made him feel afresh the swelling ocean of passionate love which had fuelled the decade they had spent together, he had somehow overlooked the business of reacting to the child. Their child. Their baby. They had a baby. Seeing it there, so multidimensional and real, and so small, took David's breath away, made him feel that he had never once in his life looked at a human being properly, never recognised the commonplace complex wonder of what creating such a thing involved.

'So you're here,' said Becky, opening her eyes, and managing to sound curt even though she was whispering. 'She

237

wants to call him Colin,' she added, getting up from the chair. 'You're lucky either of them are alive.'

David nodded, still too stunned to reply, his gaze torn between the deathly repose of his wife and the little figure in the cot beside her.

'I'll leave you to it then, I'll be in the canteen. Congratulations by the way,' she managed, groping for a way out of the curtains, marvelling to herself that David had not uttered one word of explanation, apology or thanks. If there is a mistress, he better bloody give her up, she thought fiercely, marching through the ward and back out to the corridor.

David approached the cot on his knees. Though he wasn't exactly crying, his eyes stung and his throat was pulsing, causing strange gasps to come from the back of it. He shuffled forwards slowly, feeling the hard linoleum floor grind against his kneecaps. 'Wow – look at you – little fellow – wow.' He reached inside the cot and very carefully stroked a finger down one pink cheek, jumping when it twitched in response. A moment later the tiny hands were twitching too and the mouth was stretching into a wide, searching yawn. David held his breath, terrified he had woken him up and wondering what on earth to do if he had.

Behind him Anna opened her eyes. 'David? Is that you?'

'Oh Anna – I thought you were asleep – oh my sweet – I'm so sorry.' He threw himself towards the bed, fighting his way between the tubes. 'That I wasn't here – I'm so sorry – I went to a – I went drinking – turned my phone off—'

'Shh.' She stroked his matted hair. 'Shh, it doesn't matter, I don't want to know. You're here, I just want you here.'

David lifted his head and kissed her gently on the lips. 'Still beautiful, my Anna, still beautiful. And our baby . . . he's . . . God, he's beautiful too Anna . . . so clever of you.'

'Not clever.' She closed her eyes, flinching.

'What's the matter? Anna? Is anything the matter? Should I get the doctor?'

'No . . . I just feel sick . . . horrid taste in my mouth . . . and my tummy . . . it's starting to hurt . . . time for more painkillers.' She managed a grim smile. As if on cue, the curtain parted and a short midwife with carrot red hair and a determined smile appeared, pushing a squat trolley laden with bottles and jars. 'Good morning Mrs Lawrence. Is this Mr Lawrence? Good morning to you too sir. How are we doing in here? How's the little one? Have we decided on a name?' David and Anna looked at each other.

'I thought Colin,' she whispered, 'though I know it wasn't on your shortlist.'

David nodded, tears pricking his eyes.

'Colin and then George, after your dad.'

'Colin George.'

'Lovely,' said the midwife, still looking pleased but beginning to unscrew medicine bottles in the brisk manner of one with many things yet to do. 'The doctor will be along shortly.'

'Shall I stay?'

Anna shook her head. 'No need. Go and get some rest. And Becky too. You both need it. And David . . . please . . . please be nice to her . . . she . . . she's had a shock too.'

'I'm always nice to Becky,' he murmured, lifting a strand of hair off her temple and stroking it back behind her ear.

'No, I mean *really* nice. Okay?'

He nodded, pleased to hear a trace of feistiness in her tone. 'Anything you say, my darling, anything you say.' He kissed her on the forehead.

'And will you call Mum? The number is on the pink pad in the kitchen. "Tell her everything is fine, I don't want her feeling she's got to rush back to England.'

'Sure. Anything else?' David grinned, a rush of such

euphoria pouring through him that he had to put a hand on the back of the chair to steady himself. Where it came from exactly, he couldn't have said beyond the strongest feeling that the worst was over, that all the secret soul-searching of the last few months had found a natural conclusion. Almost, he mused, still grinning like an ape, as if he had been the one to endure all the discomfort and anxiety of the pregnancy rather than Anna. 'Anything you need from home?'

'A few things – I've told Becky.' Her voice was faint again, withdrawn.

'Right. I'll come back later on then. Take your sister home and be nice to her.' He made a goofy face, wanting badly to elicit a smile, but she had already closed her eyes. Turning his attention to the cot, he spent several seconds scrutinising the pink pixie features for any physical evidence of their parentage. Conceding reluctantly that there were none, he kissed the tip of his forefinger and pressed it gently on top of the downy head. 'Okay, little fella, looks like I'm off. You take care of your Mum now, while I'm—' David broke off abruptly, aware both that he was speaking in a manner entirely out of keeping with what he had always viewed as his personality and that the carrot-headed nurse was eyeing him with wry amusement. Whether because she guessed that he wasn't usually prone to talking such nonsense, or merely because she judged him to be a sad apology of a father, it was hard to be sure. 'We're calling him Colin,' he said, straightening, wanting in some way to assert himself, not caring that she knew this information already. He then bolted through the curtains and out into the corridor, where he offered breezy waves to a sour-faced orderly and a bemused woman in a paisley dressing-gown. He was both starving and full of energy, he realised, breaking into a jog at the sight of the lifts, filled with a sudden and mysterious capacity to love not only his tricky sister-in-law but the entire world.

# 30

'Sorry, were you asleep?'

'It's eight o'clock on a Saturday morning, why would I be asleep?'

'I'm sorry,' Becky repeated, quailing at his sarcasm, 'I just wanted to thank . . .'

'How is she?' he added, his voice suddenly kind, 'your sister and the baby – was everything all right?'

Becky took a deep breath. 'Yes. It was bad, but she – they're both fine – a baby boy. She's calling him Colin after our father.'

'That's nice.'

'He died when we were quite young.'

'I'm sorry.'

Becky took another deep breath to steady herself, aware that she was in a curiously raw state where she might say anything and regret it afterwards. She could hear the kindness in Mike Hadfield's voice and wanted to respond to it. She had spent the time, since leaving David, sitting at a grimy table in the hospital canteen, drinking thin, acrid coffee and eating her way doggedly through two flabby egg sandwiches. Still feeling hollow, she had then resorted to a Mars Bar, a new larger size one which had left her feeling shaky and faintly sick. 'Yes, well it was a long time ago,' she murmured, wishing it felt that way, wishing Anna hadn't turned everything on its head. 'Look, Mike, thank you again, for the car – it was just the most brilliant thing to do – really, really kind . . . I'll get it back to you today – this afternoon when I drive back – and then' – she hesitated, wondering how far his goodwill might stretch – 'and then I was wondering if you could possibly let me have some time off work. I know it's a real cheek to ask, with all that I've just taken on, but Geoffrey could probably hold the fort on most of it and things down here are . . . well, a little complicated and . . .'

'How long do you need?'

'Two weeks?' she whispered.

'Okay. And I guess you might as well hang on to the car.'

'What? No, Mike, no, that's the last thing I . . . I've got to come back to London anyway to get some gear, I'll drop it off . . .'

'Not that much between your sizes, is there?'

'Pardon?'

'Between you and your sister. Surely you could just use some of her stuff – no point in coming back to London if you don't have to. She obviously needs you there. So stay there. Use the car. Enjoy it. Please.'

'But . . . but what about insurance and all that?'

'It's covered for anyone to whom I choose to give the key.'

'Is it? Right. Gosh. Well . . . look, I still don't think I could . . . it's just too much.' Becky faltered, feeling that if he said anything else generous or kind she might burst into tears.

'Please.' His voice was firm, but growing very slightly impatient. 'I'd like to help. It's not a big deal. I've got Jamie's Mini Metro sitting rusting on the kerb outside, I'll be fine with that – do it the world of good to have a runaround.' He paused, before adding, 'So that's settled then,' in so conclusive a tone that Becky was unable to find the wherewithal to contradict him. 'We'll see you back at the ranch in two weeks. Good luck with everything. And if you prang the car I'll take it out of your wages.' He chuckled. 'And now, if you don't mind, I'm going to see if I can get back to sleep.'

Becky was still staring in wonderment at her phone when David bounded up to the table, rubbing the palms of his hands together.

'Let's go home for a bit, shall we? Have some real coffee . . . or maybe some champagne . . . Jesus, isn't it – isn't the whole bloody thing – just incredible?'

'Yes,' Becky murmured, slowly returning her mobile to her handbag and glancing with barely concealed distrust at this new wild and gleeful version of her brother-in-law. He looked terrible, she realised, infinitely more terrible than she had acknowledged in her dazed state upstairs. His usually glossy hair was bunched in clumps round his face and neck, as if he had showered in glue or spent several months living on a park bench; and his entire face was red and puffy, particularly round his eyes and lips, which were so painfully dry that in some places she could make out cracks crusted with specks of dried blood.

'Becky, this is a good day.' With some awkwardness he reached an arm across her back and squeezed her shoulder. 'A very good day.'

'Yes,' she agreed, nodding, but unable to resist the further observation that his breath smelt vinegary and foul.

'Shall we go then?' He tossed his car keys high in the air and caught them again.

'David – last night – where were you?' she blurted, the question spilling out of its own accord. 'It doesn't matter,' she continued hurriedly, blushing at the recollection of her promise to Anna, 'obviously it's none of my business.'

'No, it isn't,' he replied gravely, pausing to run his tongue round his mouth. 'Thank you for being here Becky. I am more grateful than I can say. Last night . . . the last few months . . . I was . . . I've been . . . in a bad place . . . but it's over now . . .

look, can we get home do you think? Anna said she's told you what she needs. You're supposed to pack a suitcase in readiness, aren't you for these occasions? But I don't think she had quite got round to it . . . God, what a thing, eh? Out of the blue like that, two weeks early . . .'

He talked without drawing breath all the way to the car park, his mood lightening with every sentence. When Becky pointed out Mike's car he let out a whoop of incredulous delight and began inspecting the hub caps. 'A friend, you say? Some bloody friend to lend you this beauty.'

'I was thinking of staying down here a while,' she ventured, 'to help out.'

'Stay as long as you like,' he replied easily, running a finger along the bonnet, 'help for Anna and so on. Brilliant.' He trotted off to get into his own car and then sat at the exit to the car park waiting for her to catch up. Although Becky knew the way back to Balcombe perfectly well, she did her best to remain right on his tail for the duration of the journey, an at times difficult feat in the thickening Saturday traffic. David too seemed to think this was the most appropriate way to proceed and kept offering her thumbs-up signs in his rearview mirror by way of encouragement.

'I'm going to call my parents and a few friends and Stella of course,' he said, once they were home. 'Would you like a word?'

Becky shook her head. 'I'll leave you to it. I'll call her later. I might have a bath if that's okay, and then I'm going to need to borrow some clean clothes . . .'

'Help yourself, I'm sure Anna won't mind. She keeps heaps of stuff in that chest of drawers in the yellow bedroom anyway.' He turned to flick through a pink pad next to the telephone before adding casually, 'Oh, and I've a favour to ask you. A hack at this lot – when I've showered, of course.' He grinned, picking up a thick strand of hair and letting it drop back into his eyes. 'Dreadful, truly dreadful. I'm fed up with it.'

'But I . . .'

'You've cut Anna's hair in the past – in Pimlico, I remember. She said you were good.'

'But that was years ago,' gasped Becky, the apparently relaxed attitude of her brother-in-law at his current state of dishevelment giving her no confidence as to how he might react to her own stylistic efforts. 'And you've got curls – that's hard.'

'Not when it's wet. When it's wet it's pretty straight. Please, it's so tangled and I know Anna preferred it short, though she's never said . . . it would be a nice surprise for her.'

'Oh God, I suppose I'll give it a go if you really want me to,' Becky relented, wanting to stay cross with him but finding she had neither the heart nor the energy to do so. If Anna was prepared to overlook his indiscretions then who was she – of all people – to bear a grudge? And he did look in such a terrible state that it was hard not to feel a sort of pity, even if it was a selfish night of debauchery that had caused it.

On the way upstairs she took a few sections out of the day's paper from the hall table. While the bath ran she lay on the bed thumbing through the magazine, mildly seeking distraction but aware that she was too tired – and too distracted already – to concentrate on anything. She was on the point of casting it aside when her eye was caught by a small article under the heading, *Green Cuisine in Brixton*.

*Newly qualified restaurateur Joe Beresford yesterday officially opened the doors of his organic restaurant, The Green Table, to the increasingly cosmopolitan and discerning palates of the residents of Brixton. As an erstwhile accountant Mr Beresford admitted that the venture was something of a gamble. 'I love good food and I love cooking,' he said. 'I particularly like using old English varieties of produce, many of which are too delicately flavoured or weird-looking to make it into the supermarkets. There are literally hundreds of examples grown on small organic farms round the country which most of the population don't get to try.' His chief supplier, Adrian Stokewell, clearly shares his optimism and enthusiasm. 'Eating out is part of the health and leisure industry. Delicious food at an affordable price should be a universal right.'*

Becky skim-read the remaining paragraph until her eyes reached a picture of Joe and Adrian standing outside the restaurant, with their arms folded and their heads tipped towards each other, as if sharing a private joke. Though small, it was a good photograph. A very good photograph, mused Becky, scrutinising every speck of it, unable to resist the notion that if she hadn't known Joe already the image might well have been enough to trigger a spark of interest in wanting to get acquainted. The pair of them looked like naughty schoolboys, full of the knowledge, so rare in adults, of how to enjoy themselves. Joe in particular looked fresh-faced and full of hope, she reflected grimly, reaching for her mobile and putting it down again, torn between a sudden need to tell him everything – not just about the trauma of Colin's birth, but of what Anna had said afterwards – and fear of how such an outpouring would be interpreted. He might think that having glimpsed evidence of his new-found success, she wanted to cash in on it; that having rejected him during the hard times she was only too keen to turn to him as first choice of confidant when things took a turn for the better. After agonising over the matter during her bath, she called the moment she got out, standing dripping a dark stain of water into her fluffy bedroom carpet, her wet fingers sliding on the tiny keys of her mobile. To find herself greeted by an answering service was such a let-down that she only just had the heart to leave a message.

'Just thought you'd like to know that David turned up and the baby arrived safely and Anna is doing okay.' She spoke briskly, the face smiling out of the photograph lying on the bed next to her reinforcing the bleak and obvious fact that while her own personal crisis might, subtly, have deepened, Joe had clearly found himself and would have no need of her again.

She cut David's hair in the kitchen, moving the table out of the way and positioning him on a chair in the centre of the room so that she had plenty of room to walk round and inspect her handiwork. He had appeared looking much refreshed, with a huge towel round his shoulders, his hair hanging in dripping rats tails. 'I found these in Anna's dressing-table – they look pretty sharp.' Becky, who had hoped that the entire project might be defeated by the absence of the correct equipment, had accepted the scissors with a scowl of resignation.

'Champagne?'

Studying the scissor blades and struck suddenly by the absurdity of the situation, she burst out laughing. 'Now that just might be a *really* bad idea. I've had about half an hour's sleep in the last twenty-four and you're proposing that I wield this very sharp implement round your ear lobes. The results could be unspeakable.'

'The results will be fine. Now take a glass and let's drink to Anna and to . . . little Colin . . . my son . . . Jesus, I still can't believe it.' His voice shrank to a growl of emotion, which he covered by chinking glasses with Becky and drinking deeply. 'Ah, bloody hell, that is good. Now, where do you want me? I'm in your hands, do your worst. All off, remember – I want it really short, like all the footballers these days.'

'Well I won't need these then, a razor would be much

more effective,' she teased, snipping at the air round his head. 'Ready?' After only two sips she could feel the alcohol bubbling in her veins, giving her just the lift she needed. 'Tip your chin onto your chest – that's it – I'm going to take it up to here – okay?' She pressed her finger into the nape of his neck, inwardly balking at the huge length of hair trailing beneath it.

'Just get on with it, will you?' he urged, trying to sip from his glass with his head tipped forwards before giving up and wedging it between his thighs instead.

Biting her lips in concentration, Becky set to work. She had cut hair quite a lot at one stage, charging a fiver to her school-friends, until someone's mother complained and put a stop to it. While singularly inept when it came to styling her own tresses, she could somehow perform the job quite well on other people. Moving the scissors along the hairline framing David's face, seeing the shape emerge – envisaging suddenly how it would and must look – she felt herself relaxing. She felt a curious sort of tenderness too, something to do with the boyish vulnerability of the soft skin along his neck, so close to the keen edge of the blade, and something, more complicatedly, to do with guilt at how she had so readily assumed he had been the one to betray her to Joe. When all along it had been Anna, she reminded herself, tightening her grip on the scissor handle until the tension passed. 'Are you sure you don't want a mirror?'

'Quite sure. God, and I don't want any more of this either,' he added, making a face as he placed his empty glass on the floor, 'or I won't be capable of driving back to the hospital. Do help yourself though.'

Becky was just shaking her head, when the doorbell rang.

'Fuck – hang on – I'll get it.' He leapt from his perch only to reappear a couple of moments later on all fours in the kitchen doorway. 'Mrs Costa,' he hissed, gesturing frantically for Becky to drop to the floor beside him, 'can't face her – not now – get out of sight for God's sake.'

Becky dutifully, but somewhat reluctantly, sank to her knees and made her way, commando style, pushing with her elbows and the tips of her toes, to where David was spreadeagled – out of sight of any windows – in the hallway. 'Is this really necessary?' she muttered, giggling in spite of herself and slithering after him into the dining room, where the curtains were still drawn.

'Totally,' he assured her, pushing the door gently closed behind them with his foot and pressing his finger to his lips. 'She's still there, prowling round, nosy old bag. She's after a job looking after the baby – been going on about it for months.'

'But you haven't got anyone yet, have you?' whispered Becky, glancing nervously at the curtained windows. 'To help with Colin, I mean.'

'No, but we're not having her. Anna was beginning to cave in, but I'm not going to. She gives me the creeps, her and that tarty daughter of hers . . . thank God you're here, Becky, that's all I can say, to help us through this first bit and then there's weeks and weeks to sort something out before Anna goes back to work. When I phoned your mother she offered to come back, but on Anna's instructions I told her she was on no account to cut her holiday short.' He laughed darkly. 'Thank God – fond as I am of the old dear, I do struggle if she's in the house for more than a couple of days. I'll take you any day.'

'I'm truly honoured,' remarked Becky drily, clambering to her feet and tiptoeing to the sideboard to peer out of the window behind. As she leant across to tweak open the curtain, she felt the sleeve of the too-baggy sweatshirt she had borrowed from a bottom drawer catch on something. Looking down, she found the nose of David's grey chiselled self-portrait hooked into her cuff and toppling dangerously near the edge of its plinth. 'Whoops, that was close.' She carefully righted the bust, suppressing as she did so a vivid and guilt-stricken image of her and Guy in David's studio on the fateful night of the party, trespassing in every sense, led on by the false allure of what they had wrongly interpreted as Fate. Something grand. When it was just sordid and deceitful, a lust for someone – for something – that did not exist. Remembering in the next instant the sudden and heart-stopping appearance of her brother-in-law at the very same scene, Becky glanced nervously across the room. But David, sitting now cross-legged on the floor, was cocking his head and frowning at the bust.

'I don't like it, you know.'

'Don't you?' she murmured, returning her attention to a chink in the curtains and spotting the object of David's fear hurrying away down the drive, her wide backside straining visibly under the confines of a tight purple coat.

'It's not . . . well, it's not me, somehow . . . I think because it's more how I want to be seen than how I really am . . .' He broke off in evident dismay at Becky, who was looking at him again and making a clumsy effort to conceal a fresh outburst of giggles.

'What?'

She shook her head, pointing with the scissors at his half-coiffed state. 'It certainly isn't you . . . if you could see yourself, half-shorn – I'm sorry, but you do look funny – and it's drying fast,' she added quickly, sucking her cheeks to stifle the giggling, aware suddenly that she was a hair's breadth away from becoming hysterical. 'I'll need some water to wet it down.' She stepped past him and tugged open the door to the hall. 'But first I'm going to make us some coffee, or you'll end up with a lopsided Mohican.' She spoke with deliberate bossiness, trying to take charge not so much of David as herself. Reality had gone berserk, she reflected, pleased to retreat to the soothing ritual of kettle, mugs and teaspoons. Returning to the dining room with two cups of coffee a few minutes later, she found David still on the carpet, flat on his stomach with arms and legs splayed wide, like a climber clinging to a rock face, eyes pinned shut against the dizzying view beneath. His hair, half cropped on one side and a mass of dry curls on the other, looked weirder than ever.

'Wakey, wakey.' She spoke tentatively, curiously touched at the vulnerability of the sight, a part of her feeling that she had no business seeing it. 'Come along,' she said, moved to boldness by the fact that he hadn't moved. 'Anna needs her nightdresses and you need this.' She prodded one of his legs with the toe of her shoe.

'Sorry.' He sat up quickly, rubbing his eyes. 'Sorry. Coffee.' He took a mug. 'Marvellous. Thank you.'

'Drink it while I finish off the job,' she commanded, leading the way back to the kitchen, where she rolled up the sleeves of Anna's voluminous sweatshirt before resuming her work with the scissors.

# 31

Stella lay on her back with her eyes closed, enjoying the cold prickle of the grass through her clothes. The air was quite still, almost unnaturally so, as if this small corner of the world had decided to hold its breath in anticipation of what the mortals crawling upon its surface might do next. The afternoon rays of the spring sun felt deeply warming not just to her hands and face, pale and papery after the long English winter, but to her entire body. The longer she lay there the more intensely aware she became of the heat soaking its way through her thick smart English clothes, a foretaste perhaps of balmy summer days to come. With her eyes closed, the sounds of the water rushing nearby seemed more intense too, gurgling over the jumble of stones half blocking the bend and then tumbling into the deep pool of the bend itself. In twenty years little had changed, except that the banks on either side were muddier than she remembered and the reeds fringing them much thicker. Somewhere in the longer grass by the water's edge she could make out the sounds of an intrepid bumble bee, stop-starting its buzz amongst the white clover heads like a sputtering engine.

Reaching out one arm, Stella searched through the grass with her fingers until she felt Marcel's hand close around hers, as smooth and warm as a leather glove. 'It is time,' he had said simply that morning, packing wine and bread into a frayed basket, together with a bundle of freshly made pâté and a wedge of soft cheese, its top smooth and chalky white, its edges bulging and yellow. 'It is time to go there.' They had set off a short while later, bumping round the lanes in his dusty Chevrolet, the branches of the trees brushing the windows, the road an arching green tunnel ahead.

David's phonecall announcing the early but safe arrival of little Colin had come a few days before, as they were sitting in the snug conservatory sipping coffee after a late lunch. He had sounded dazed, but thrilled, just as a first-time father should, Stella had thought – and said afterwards to Marcel, laughing openly, so emblazoned with joy herself that if anyone had presented her with a list of her earlier fears she would have denied them outright. He had gone on to explain the scare with Anna over high blood pressure but was quick to reassure her that all danger was well and truly past. They had picked the names of both their fathers, to keep all parties happy, he had joked, so effectively brushing over the poignancy of the decision that it had not really hit Stella until her and Marcel arrived at the riverside, when she saw again her husband's skinny frame, the wet shock of his dark hair as he swallow-dived off the bank and out of their lives. Lying on the grass remembering it now, silent tears slid out of the corners of her eyes and down her temples. Not so much from sadness as an uplifting sense of life's inexorable circles, of the dead existing still in the living, in names, in flashes of physical likeness, in memories and stories from the past. As on the ferry, but more deeply, a well of understanding spread inside her, a recognition that the love which had prompted her marriage remained a true and wonderful thing, unsullied by the unhappiness that had eventually taken over. When Colin died she felt both guilty, she realised, because it offered her the release she had sought, and yet cross, because, much as she had come to resist the direction he had chosen for her life, he had until then been its driving force. Her own subsequent existence in the safety of commuter-belt London had felt flimsy in comparison; more flimsy as each year went by.

She squeezed Marcel's hand, aware as she did so that her skin had grown clammy while his remained cool and dry.

'He was a difficult man,' he said, 'I always knew that, although I loved him. Thérèse and I, we used to say, poor Stella, what a lot she has to put up with, how well she bears it.'

'Did you? I never knew that.'

He turned onto one elbow and looked at her, squinting more wrinkles into his face at the glare of the sun. The years on the whole had been kind, thinning rather than removing his hair and adding several inches to a girth that had always bulged over the belt of his trousers anyway. The essence of the man, the sense of a quiet inner strength, coupled with a gently humorous view of the world and its woes, remained just as Stella remembered it. Although she did catch herself noting the absence of Thérèse. Seeing Marcel alone made her realise just what a double act the pair of them had been, how her teasing reprimands had given him a platform from which to shine, while his huffing, comical retorts always made it clear that the dialogue was one on which he thrived, that she was everything and all he needed.

'You will want to go home.'

'Yes, soon. David said not to cut short my stay, but I think I probably will. To see my grandchild.' Slipping her hand from his, Stella turned on her side to face him, grimacing for a moment at the pressure of the hard ground on her hip bone. 'To see little Colin.'

'And next time you will meet my grandchildren,' he boomed, leaping with impressive spriteliness to his feet and reaching out a hand to help her up. 'All seven of them. When they visit it is like in the Bible when the locusts come, eating everything in sight.' He spread his arms, still laughing. 'And now we will eat our picnic. Not here, but somewhere else I know, further along the river by a café where we can enjoy coffee and a brandy afterwards and maybe a fresh pastry for dessert. Yes?'

'Yes.' She smiled up at him as she took his outstretched hand. 'Thank you, Marcel. I would like that very much.'

As they walked back to his car, parked a few yards away on the roadside, Stella turned for one last look behind. A loose tuft of cloud, briefly veiling the sun, had cast the scene in shadow, at once removing the glisten from the surface of the water and converting it into something dark and forbidding. She shivered, pulling her jacket more tightly around her, not resisting as another image of the fateful afternoon twenty years before – the fullest yet – flooded her mind: the tartan picnic rug, Colin dancing on the river edge, egged on by Becky's too boisterous shrieking, Anna solemnly practising her acrobatics, intent on improving herself as always, and her, Stella, lying on the rug eyeing them all through sleepy eyes, batting a wasp from the half-eaten food, too idle to pack it back into the plastic bags in which it had arrived. The seeds of all that had happened, all that they had become, had been there, Stella realised, ingrained and inexorable. Yet it had been a good day. A happy day on which to die.

At a splash from the river the picture in Stella's mind shattered in an instant. She glanced back to the water with a start, her heart racing. But it was only a lone kayaker, kitted out in wet suit and helmet, dipping his oars smoothly and rhythmically as he sped against the currents of the pool and on towards the rush of rock and water beyond.

'Do you want to choose the card?'

Jenny shrugged, turning with a dismissive toss of her head to examine a pot of fluorescent felt pens on the sales counter.

'Look, they've got lots for new babies, some with safety

pins and things stuck in them – they're quite clever – and one here with a stork made from real bird feathers and . . .' Joe gave up, breathing out a slow, deep sigh of frustration at his daughter's turned back. 'I'll choose then. Blue for a boy – this will do. And you can write in it from both of us.'

'What's the point?'

'Pardon?'

She shrugged again. 'I just said what's the point. We're never going to see him are we? I mean, it's not like he's a proper cousin or anything, not now.'

'Of course we'll see him, some time,' replied Joe briskly, digging for change in his pocket and leading the way out of the shop. 'The main thing is to show support, to show that we care.'

'Well I don't,' she muttered, or seemed to mutter, for he found it hard to distinguish any of the words delivered from under the thick woollen hat and flapping anorak hood in which she had chosen that morning to package herself. It was as if she was hiding, he mused sadly, offering her his hand as they walked back along the parade of shops, as busy these days on a Sunday as any other time of the week; even the trousers, huge and slung loosely round her hips, seemed designed to conceal, conveying no hint of the curves already emerging from the schoolgirl puppiness underneath. She accepted his hand, but limply, as if she would rather have put it somewhere else, and then snatched it back a moment later as some youths, all of them similarly attired, shuffled past on the other side of the pavement.

It was a week since his party. A suddenly much more compliant Ruth had agreed to a new plan of him having Jenny to stay every Saturday night. At his busiest in the kitchen downstairs, it meant she would invariably have to make do with a video by way of entertainment, but all within the hopefully comforting context of knowing that her father was just a few yards away should she have need of him. Recognising that she might feel too shy to venture into the kitchens, Joe had also taken the precaution of installing an intercom system from the flat to the restaurant so that Jenny could summon him without having to show her face. It was a set-up for which he had very high hopes, granting as it did the regular treat of waking up with the prospect of a whole day together the next morning. An unexpected twist to the arrangements had presented itself on this occasion however when Ruth, shooing Jenny through the door the previous afternoon, had pressed a Boots bag into Joe's hand.

'Sanitary towels,' she whispered, 'started yesterday. She's got her own supplies but I thought you ought to have a stock too, just in case.'

'At eleven?' he gasped, glancing anxiously over his shoulder, feeling a pang of sympathy for the ignominy of having one's parents huddling in a doorway discussing such a thing.

'I started very early too. Some women do,' Ruth said breezily. 'It's no big deal – unless we make it one,' she added, giving him a warning look.

'Well, do I say congratulations or what?'

'Jesus, Joe, sometimes I really do *despair*,' she had hissed, before hurrying away down the stairs, clearly without the slightest notion that his request for guidance on the matter had been genuine. Joe had retreated back into the flat swinging the bag of sanitary towels as nonchalantly as he could, determined as a hands-on caring sharing father to say something. On seeing the scowling face of his daughter however, burrowing in a beanbag in her bedroom, her grey eyes flashing over the top of a magazine, he had changed his mind on the spot, playing instead the trump card he had planned to keep until the following day.

'I thought we might paint your room – any colour you want – what do you say?'

'Really? Any colour?' She had put the magazine down on the floor beside the beanbag. 'Even sicky green?'

'Sicky green. Putrid pink. Whatever you like. It's your room, you choose. We can get it now if we hurry, en route to the video shop.'

The trump card had worked but not for long, Joe reflected gloomily, recalling as they walked slowly home from the card shop, the steady dwindling of Jenny's enthusiasm first over choosing a colour and then for transferring it to the walls. While the early emergence of a menstrual cycle might provide the comfort of an explanation for such moodiness – so persistent now that he found himself struggling to remember a time without it – any effective strategy for remedying it had yet to present itself.

'Would you like a can of Coke?' he asked brightly, once they were back inside.

'No thanks. Can I watch TV?'

'I guess,' he muttered, abandoning any sense of better judgement on the matter and flicking on the kettle to make himself a coffee. Sitting at his small kitchen table a little later, doing his best to ignore the hum of the TV coming from the sitting room and the pungent smell of Jenny's half painted purple walls, Joe sought solace in some paper work, double checking the takings several times for the sheer pleasure of doing so. Although it was early days, the figures were good. Unbelievably good. Shifting the columns of numbers to one side at last, he slipped the greetings card out of its paper bag and spent several minutes studying the illustration on the front, thinking how little a cartoon of a stork with a nappy in its mouth equated to the reality of having a child.

*Wonderful news*, he wrote, gripping the Biro hard as a wave of nostalgia threatened to overwhelm him, not just for the days when Jenny had been a gurgling easy-to-please baby, but for the early promise of his time with Becky. So much hope and happiness, so many dreams. Of which one at least had come vividly true, he reminded himself quickly, glancing round his new kitchen and patting the pile of papers by his elbow.

*Glad to hear that mother and baby are doing well*, he continued, seeking refuge in the worn but comforting familiarity of the phrase before signing his name. After a pause, punctuated by a burst of canned laughter from the television, he signed Jenny's too, shying away from the thought of prompting another confrontation by summoning her to do it herself.

## 32

Anna woke with a start, catching the phone just as it rolled off her chest. She was lying on the sofa padded out with extra pillows and a duvet from one of the spare bedrooms. On the table next to her, moved like the sofa, right up to the main window so that she could enjoy the sight of the garden bathed in spring sunshine, were several trays' worth of mostly untouched drinks and snacks brought at various intervals by David and Becky, to the accompaniment of reminders about getting her strength back and fuelling her supply of breast milk. Like some kind of battery fed fowl, Anna thought glumly, glancing down with distaste at the bulges of her usually modest chest, each breast already so huge with milk that whenever she tried to pacify Colin's angry hunger cries the poor child practically choked to death at the quantities of liquid gushing into his throat. After the smoothly controlled nights in the hospital, where the nurses kindly let her sleep between feeds, managing at home was proving an ordeal beyond her worst expectations, with the baby shrieking to be suckled and then hollering just as loudly at her inept efforts to keep her spurting nipples between his lips. Five minutes on either side, the nurses had said, so both breasts were stimulated equally and the baby got the richest milk. A simple enough instruction, except for the fact her baby seemed bent upon battling with her milk supply instead of accepting it, gulping so much air in the process that after just a few seconds he was writhing to be free of her, howling and grimacing like an old man in pain. Wrung out with frustration and exhaustion after four days of these struggles, Anna had by dawn that morning, almost detached herself from the process, all her anxiety transplanted by a sort of dim fury at the child's own clumsiness to satisfy his needs. David, intermittently dozing and offering words of encouragement, had eventually persuaded her to try one of the cluster of small bottles of milk stored in the freezer, expressed with the aid of a crude pump during the latter part of her stay in hospital, when her milk supply had suddenly gushed with such a vengeance that she had woken every few hours to find her nightie and sheets soaked and smelling like the inside of a cow shed. Fetching a bottle himself and heating it in the microwave, David had skipped back into the bedroom, making a big to-do of testing drops on his forearm before handing it over for Anna to assume the more awesome responsibility of parking the toffee coloured teat in their son's mouth.

'There, that's it,' he had murmured happily, as Colin ceased his struggling and popped his eyes open with an expression of what looked like exasperated pleasure, as if questioning the pair of them as to why this simple answer to his woes had taken so long to find.

Anna shifted her position on the sofa, discomforted at the thought of the new kindness being heaped on her by her husband, wishing she had no knowledge of the penitence at the heart of it. Guilt could prompt the most incredible generosity of spirit, she reflected wretchedly, reminding herself of her resolution to accept every scrap of attentiveness with silent gratitude but fearing that her capacity to do so might not last for long. If he sneaked off to London again, she vowed, under whatever plausible pretext, she would have him followed, hire a private detective if necessary. Then at least she could confront him with facts instead of suspicions and hopefully with a clear gameplan as to how she wished to proceed. The pregnancy had somehow debilitated her; without it she would long since have called a firm of lawyers and asked David to pack his bags. Or would she? Anna wondered miserably, all her flimsy bravado dissolving at the notion of ever having to take such a step, knowing that her reason for doing so would be pride rather than lack of affection. She had always believed that the pair of them had a very special kind of partnership, based on a love that might to others seem at times distant – because of them both being so self-contained, so in need of their own space – but which was nonetheless founded on a powerful bond of mutual respect and high feeling. When all the wheels were turning it worked perfectly, more perfectly than she could ever imagine a relationship working with anyone else. And then there was the physical attraction, still simmering, Anna reminded herself, in spite of the inconvenience and undermining effects of the pregnancy. She stared at the misshapen sack that had once been her body, sighing at the recollection of how tenderly David had held her during the night, how he had wanted – incredibly – to taste her milk, managing to make the request seem passionate instead of sickly. In the last few days he had said, countless times, that he loved her. And if he did, she asked herself, what in the end did it matter if there had, as she strongly suspected, been another woman? Should it really be a problem, given all that they had shared, all that they had built together? Given Colin. At the thought of her son, Anna glanced out of the window to see Becky pushing the pram across the lawn, stopping every couple of minutes to make a funny face or spin one of the plastic multicoloured monkeys strung between its sides. She was wearing an old pair of Anna's jeans, faded from use and so long that they trailed at least an inch over the soles of her shoes, together with a thick grey polo-neck sweater which had once been a favourite until an overzealous wash cycle had matted the wool and shrunk the sleeves. Anna watched their progress until they had moved beyond the frame of the window, grateful both for the regular respites her sister was providing from her son and for her quiet accommodation of all the dreadful things she had said in the hospital – things that Anna herself had hardly known she felt until she said them. Things which even now veered between seeming fanciful and so true that to think of them took her breath away. Sometimes, in her madder moments, it felt as if the baby had somehow opened a door on the past. Right from the start – with that first little handwave from the ocean of her womb – she had felt herself pulled backwards, to thoughts – to a self – she had truly forgotten. And longed only to forget again, she reflected bitterly, hurriedly forcing a smile and a cheery salute as the pram came back into view, closer to the window this time, so close that she could see the dampness of the mud stains on the bottom of Becky's jeans.

After they had gone, disappearing towards the summer-house this time, Anna picked up the telephone handset with the intention of putting in another call to work. Reminding them of her existence throughout the coming weeks would, she was sure, be vital. A stand-in for her own programmes had already been found with dispiriting efficiency, a flame-haired unashamedly ambitious dynamo in her late twenties called Zara Hobbs, who had recently burst into the limelight from the anonymity of Radio Wales. After giving the matter some thought however, Anna returned the phone to the table and closed her eyes. She had already had two long talks with colleagues that day, trying to assess the pros and cons of a recent decision to postpone the pilot for her new programme until the autumn. Which was perfect, as one of her producers had kindly pointed out, since by then Anna herself would be back in charge of everything anyway. Anna had agreed with as much enthusiasm as she could muster, doing her best to sound convinced and on top of things, all the while deeply grateful that none of them could see her, slumped like a whale on the sofa, pink-eyed with fatigue, incapable not only of all intelligent thought processes that she had once taken for granted, but also of looking after the tiny creature which had caused them to desert her in the first place.

After David's dawn raid to the kitchen Colin had slept soundly, but only for a measly two hours, renewing his shrieks for attention just as Anna herself had finally sunk from a fitful to a satisfying sleep. Another disheartening session with her vast and uncooperative breasts had resulted in David tentatively suggesting yet another sortie to the freezer and Anna bursting into tears, ranting incomprehensibly about breast being best, the dangers of engorgement, mastitis and several other pro-lactation arguments on which she had been thoroughly lectured by the maternity nurses in the hospital. The crisis had been saved by Becky, materialising out of nowhere with mugs of tea and calmly offering to take the baby so that the pair of them could get some rest. Sensibly suggesting that Anna could pump out some more milk into a couple of empty bottles, both to relieve any discomfort and keep the whole process going for when Colin was calm enough to have another go, she took the baby, a clean babygro, a supply of fresh nappies and disappeared downstairs. There had followed a few minutes of muted crying and then silence. A deep blissful silence which had lasted until Anna awoke around midday, when her efforts to get up were thwarted by David's kind insistence that she decamp to the sitting room instead.

'Hello darling, how are you feeling?'

Anna blinked quickly, a little disconcerted to find that she had been dozing again. 'Not too bad. Sleepy. Talked to work – sounds under control – sort of.'

'Shift your legs a minute – there we are – that's better. Now I can do this . . .' Having nudged a space for himself at the end of the sofa, David placed her feet on his lap and began stroking her toes and the arch of her foot, delicately, using just the tips of his fingernails in the way that he knew she liked.

'Hmm.' Anna closed her eyes, smiling, aware as she did so that her cheeks felt stiff from lack of use. 'Becky is being wonderful, isn't she? Taking time off work and everything. And she's so good with him – they've been in the garden for hours and I haven't heard one yowl.'

David nodded. 'Becky is great. The pair of us have been getting on really well.' He squeezed her ankle adding, 'If ever I've underestimated her, I'm sorry. I think, in the past sometimes I felt as if' – he paused, laughing at the absurdity of what he was trying to say – 'as if the pair of you might, you know, be ganging up on me – being so much closer than my family, I mean – the way you talk – it can make a chap feel shut out.'

'Silly.' Anna leant forwards and ruffled his freshly cropped hair, an improvement on which she had already remarked with unbridled approval several times. 'Let's try and forget the past shall we? Some of it at least, I mean – the stuff that doesn't matter any more.'

He looked at her curiously.

'We've been apart,' she stammered. 'I want us close again.'

'Oh yes,' he breathed, stretching across her body and kissing her neck, 'so do I, darling Anna, so do I.'

Their embrace was interrupted by the creak of the door and Becky, poking her head round the edge of it. 'Sorry to interrupt. I've changed him and put him down in his cot. While you were asleep I gave him another bottle so he shouldn't need any more for a while. I'm going to pop into town now – I thought I'd treat myself to a couple of things.' She tugged ruefully at the baggy grey jumper. 'Feels a bit weird wearing your gear to be honest – no offence.'

'None taken,' said Anna, laughing with sudden and luxurious ease, feeling – with her palm on her husband's neck and silence from the cot upstairs – that the world might once again become an ordered, understandable place, where ancient feelings kept to themselves, and love, both for husbands and sisters, was a simple solid thing instead of a shifting quicksand of certainty and doubt.

'Oh and I'll get some formula milk while I'm at it, just in case you get fed up with that gruesome pump. I did a white wash too,' she called from the hall, 'including the sheets off your bed and the bag of babygros – they're on the line.' The slamming of the front door was followed by the smooth grumble of the BMW and the crunch of rubber on gravel rolling down the drive.

Sorting through racks of trousers and tops in a small boutique some thirty minutes later, Becky found herself hurrying, aware that Colin would be due another feed all too soon and doubting Anna and David's capacity to cope. She had heard the crying in the night – and every night preceding it. When, at dawn, raised voices had entered the fray she had been unable to bear it any longer and intervened, offering cups of tea as a pretext for having what she was sure would be a far more successful go at calming her nephew down. And she had, Becky reflected proudly, holding a cranberry coloured T-shirt to her chest and putting it on her to-buy pile without even trying it on. Handling her nephew felt, for some mysterious, wonderful reason, entirely natural. Even the tricky business of winding him was something she had got the hang of almost at once, finding that if she held him gently enough she could somehow sense where the painful little bubbles were blocking his insides and press in just the right places to tease them out. Watching on the rare occasions when Anna herself had a go, trying to achieve the same end with ineffectual and too-hard patting, it was all Becky could do not to snatch the baby from her arms and do it herself.

'I'll take the grey trousers and these two shirts,' she said, depositing the garments next to the till and tapping her fingers impatiently as the young girl manning it rang up the items and requested a method of payment. Becky handed her Switch card over, taking a moment as she did so to enjoy the fact that thanks to her pay increases and the apology of an amount Mike charged her for rent, she could make such purchases without having to perform depressing sums in her head beforehand. And without stuffing the odd extra thing into her bag either, she reminded herself, blushing so violently at the recollection of such habits that the girl at the till glanced at her strangely as she headed for the door.

Scurrying back towards the alleyway where she had, il-legally, parked the car, she ducked into a shop called 'Babytime,' where she purchased not just formula milk for newborns, but also an entire steriliser set with six bottles, a sailor-suit outfit and a miniature jacket emblazoned with purple elephants. Elated with herself, and – for the first time she could remember in a while – with life in general, Becky snatched the plastic-covered parking ticket which had appeared under one of the windscreen wipers and stuffed it into her handbag. She then drove very fast all the way back to Balcombe, singing along to one of Mike's Elton John CDs as she went, la-laing freely where she didn't know the words.

# 33

Sitting in the car in the bowels of the ferry, with the throb of engines pounding in her ears, Stella felt the return of the faint unease which had shadowed her throughout the long drive up through the French motorway system. At the last minute Marcel had suggested putting the car on the train to save herself the stress, but Stella had found herself resisting. Not just because of the extra money, but because of some infinitely more subtle notion connected to the sense that she was back behind the wheel of her life and wished to stay that way. She wouldn't sleep in a sleeper anyway, she reassured him, touched that instead of bullying her on the matter he set about making her a delicious picnic for the journey, stuffing his own homemade black olive rolls with shavings of fresh parmesan and wafer-thin slices of garlic salami, purchased that morning from the charcuterie in the village.

'And grapes,' he said, gently placing a huge bunch in the centre of the basket, 'because they are easy to eat when you are driving, like so,' he plucked one, fat and with dusty blue-black skin, and popped it in his mouth, grinning at her as he chewed, his teeth crunching on the pips.

It was probably being so many feet under the waterline that was upsetting, Stella told herself now, peering through the windscreen for any signs of movement amongst the cars parked in front of her and thinking of the Zeebrugge disaster, tasting for a moment the horror of trying to breathe with water flooding one's lungs. Colin, she reminded herself, had almost certainly escaped so panicked and painful an end, since it was a blow to the head that had killed him, the unhappy coincidence of a lone tooth of a rock embedded in the sediment just below his own recklessly steep dive.

It was a relief to edge her car out of the ferry mouth and feel the pulse of the sun through her smeary windscreen. She was tired from her journey, Stella told herself, driving far faster than habit or wisdom would normally dictate and eating the last remaining few of Marcel's grapes, even though they were warm and faintly winey from their long stay on the passenger seat of the car. She wanted very badly to get home, to soak the grime of the journey from her body, to parcel her dirty clothes into the washing machine, to dust the dead flies off the windowsills and revive the pot plants. About an hour short of Amersham however, belting round an unclogged section of the M25, she found herself taking a slip road off towards the west instead, propelled by an apprehension which, immune to any of the commonsense arguments she threw at it, seemed bent upon growing worse with each passing mile. They were all fine, she scolded herself, remembering the clutch of phonecalls she had put through to England since hearing of Colin's birth, keeping each one brief for fear of overburdening Marcel's telephone bill. Even Becky had sounded truly happy and relaxed, willing to chat in a way that had made Stella feel she was not just over the trauma of her marriage collapsing but even – just possibly – at a stage in life where she was able to feel some rekindling of the filial affection she had once, a long time ago, felt for Stella herself.

It was late afternoon by the time she turned into the drive leading up to the house. In the March sunshine its sandy stone and white-framed windows looked as warm and welcoming as a smiling face. After parking well out of the way of the garage doors, Stella sat for a few moments before getting out of the car, suddenly shy of her own impulsiveness, sure that all her apprehensions were no more than a feverish clumsy pretext for laying eyes on her grandson. She got out slowly, easing her legs round to the ground first and rubbing at the stiffness in her lower spine as she stood up. Taking only her handbag, she walked up to the front door, hoping that the silver BMW positioned in front of it meant David had splashed out on a new car rather than that the house was full of grand visitors.

The bell was answered after several long seconds by Becky, looking glowing with her dark hair swept into a careless ponytail and a white cloth slung casually over one shoulder. 'Mum . . . blimey . . . hi,' she exclaimed, a series of rapid and unreadable expressions flashing across her pale face before a firm grin of welcome took hold.

'Surprise,' said Stella, feeling somewhat sheepish and suddenly very worn out. 'I've come straight from Dover – two days early. I just had to see him. Little Colin. I do hope David and Anna won't mind.'

'Mind? Don't be silly.' Becky laughed a little wildly, opening the door wider. 'They'll be thrilled, of course. They're both out at the moment though – some new fish restaurant on the coast that Joe told David about apparently – and then they were going to do some shopping. I'm babysitting.' She made a face, pressing her finger to her lips and pointing in the direction of the kitchen. 'He's sleeping less already – or at least for shorter periods, and really beginning to focus on things when he's awake. Come and see.'

Stella eased off her coat, hooking it over the banister knob together with her handbag before following her daughter into the kitchen, where a large green pram was parked between the dresser and the window, its chrome frame shining in the beams of afternoon sun pouring in through the windows.

'We had a walk and now he's snoozing. I give it twenty minutes,' Becky continued, shaking her head with a knowing chuckle as she checked her watch, 'before he's awake and furious for the next bottle.'

'Oh my heavens, look at him,' whispered Stella, approaching the pram on tiptoe and peering inside. 'Oh look – the little love – oh look.'

'I know.' Becky came to stand beside her and for a few moments they both watched the sleeping infant in silent wonderment. 'Isn't he perfect?'

'He is. Perfect.' Stella reached out and gently ran the back of her hand down one cheek, which had blossomed from its newborn scrawniness into a smooth plump pink. He was lying on his back with his mouth slightly open, revealing a tiny button of a blister on the inside V of his upper lip. From sucking, Stella reminded herself, as a host of memories of her own early days of motherhood flooded her mind, the exhaustion, the joy, so utterly inextricable from the terror.

'Cup of tea?'

'Oh yes please, that would be lovely.' Dragging her eyes away from the pram, Stella pulled a chair for herself out from the table, lifting it off the floor even though her back hurt, so as not to make any sound.

'How was your holiday?'

'Good, thank you,' she replied, quite unequal to the task of beginning to communicate just how good, how momentous. 'Marcel was just as I had remembered him – very welcoming and kind.'

'Great. Shall we take our tea in the sitting room? Make the most of the peace while we can.'

'And Anna's all right is she?' asked Stella, relaxing at the feel of the warm tea in her belly and the large sofa cushions folding round the aches in her body.

'It was pretty awful,' Becky conceded, frowning at the recollection of the night of Colin's birth, ten days and a lifetime before. 'With all the pre-eclampsia business and not being able to get hold of David, but it all turned out fine in the end,' she finished quickly, not wanting to fuel either the look of alarm in her mother's eyes or her own recollections of Anna's outburst.

'Thank goodness for you, Becky dear, being able to be there and to help out so much. Has she decided on a nanny yet, do you know, or is she going to wait until she has to go back to work? I didn't like to mention it on the phone just in case she was still worried about it all.' Stella shook her head thoughtfully, recalling the tensions during her Christmas visit when broaching any subject had felt like slithering across thin ice.

'Oh, she's not worried now,' declared Becky cheerfully. 'Neither of them are.' She plucked at a piece of fluff on the sofa cushion next to her, pressing it between her fingertips. 'In fact, they have asked me to consider whether I might be able to wangle some more time off – so that I can stay on and help out for a bit longer. My boss is amazingly kind like that, believes in the importance of the family and one's personal life and so on, so I might just be able to swing it. If he says no, I might pack in work anyway for a bit – I'm pretty sure I've got enough on my CV to get back into the same business later on if I want to. Don't look like that,' she complained, some of her old impatience bubbling up at the sight of the barely concealed surprise on her mother's face. 'It works really well, the three of us – and Anna needs the help, she really does.'

The conversation was interrupted by the sound of the front door and the appearance of Anna and David, their faces flushed and smiling. 'Mum – how brilliant to see you – when I saw the car I thought I had to be dreaming.' Letting go of David's hand, she did a graceful half run across the room to where Stella was sitting on the sofa, revealing through the swing of her hips and the firm outline of her long limbs, visible under thin pink silk of her skirt, the first echoes of her prenatal elegance.

'I thought I'd surprise you,' explained Stella, beaming as her eldest daughter flung both arms round her neck, hugging so tightly that she could feel the pearls of her necklace pressing into her collarbone.

'I'm so glad.'

'And I've seen him, Anna – asleep in the kitchen – my darling, he is absolutely gorgeous, you must be so very very happy.'

'Glad not to be pregnant anyway.' Anna laughed, flopping back onto the sofa next to her mother and dropping her arms across the small swell of her stomach. 'And it was very hairy in the end, getting ill and so on. You should have seen me, stuffed full of tubes with doctors and nurses running all over the place. Quite a sight, wasn't I, Becks?'

'I wish I had . . .' began Stella, breaking off at the sight of Becky holding her hand up for silence and cocking her head in the direction of the kitchen.

'Oh God, was that him?' Anna groaned. 'Typical – two minutes after we get back.'

'Don't worry, I'll fetch him,' said Becky eagerly, hurrying into the kitchen and reappearing with a creased and writhing version of the serene bundle Stella had been admiring a few minutes earlier.

'Could I hold him?' she ventured, casting an enquiring glance at her eldest daughter.

'Of course, Mum, of course.' She gave an expansive wave of her arm. 'I'm sure you'll be a lot more use than me. See?' she exclaimed with happy satisfaction a moment later, as Colin, whether from surprise at the sudden change of custodian or from recognition at the reassuring touch of practised hands, relaxed in his grandmother's arms. Stella, thrilled and awed in equal measure, glanced proudly at the three faces arrayed around her, the lump of pure joy in her throat so hard and huge that she dare not speak for fear of it erupting out of her.

'Becks you wouldn't mind doing the bottle, would you? I'm absolutely whacked,' said Anna, a few minutes later, when Colin had resumed his fidgeting.

'Sure.'

'Is he on bottles all the time then?' enquired Stella absently, her attention focused on trying to soothe her grandson as she followed Becky out of the room. Colin had begun emitting pitiful, low bleats, bunching his knees up to his chest and stuffing his tiny fist against his mouth as if attempting to muffle his hunger with the taste of his own flesh. 'These need trimming,' she murmured, easing the tiny fist away from the mouth and studying the paper sharp edges of the miniature nails. 'How about this instead?' She slipped her own finger between the gnawing lips and chuckled with satisfaction as Colin promptly started sucking furiously and then, just as suddenly, fell asleep.

'It has been all bottles for the last few days,' Becky explained. 'Anna just couldn't cope with the whole breastfeeding thing. It was getting her really distressed, particularly the nights – they were seriously out of hand. I have read that it just doesn't suit some women and I guess she's one of them. Would you like me to take him for a bit?'

'No, I think I'll give him to Anna,' replied Stella, turning back towards the door, gently swaying her arms in time to a tune unwinding inside her head. 'I'll give him to his mother,' she repeated, more softly, before starting to hum under her breath, '*Couche bien, petit enfant, sous l'arbre vert* . . .' She glided along the hall towards the sitting room, turning briefly to smile at Becky, framed in the doorway behind her still clutching the warmed bottle. '*Sous le ciel bleu et le soleil jaune* . . .' Bit by bit the words came back to her, until, as she placed Colin in Anna's lap, the memory of the lullaby was complete inside her head.

# 34

'What you're doing, it's got to stop.'

Becky, seated in the rocking chair next to Colin's cot, looked up so sharply she cricked her neck, causing a flood of warm pain round her ears and temples. Her mother was standing in an orange dressing-gown, her steely curls wild around her face, her eyes saggy with sleep. She was wearing toeless towelling slippers, of a dull peachy shade which looked as if it might once have matched the orange of the dressing-gown. And her toenails were a peachy colour too, Becky observed with some surprise, each glossy and perfectly painted, a line of pretty gems at the end of the veiny branches of her feet. 'Mum?' She frowned, wondering for one mad moment if she could be sleepwalking.

'It's got to stop.'

Becky blinked, shifting the weight of the baby's head along her forearm as she tipped the bottle for the final half inch of the feed. 'What's got to stop?'

'Sometimes it takes other people to see things, Becky. And I see you.'

'And what do you see?' Becky whispered, staring hard at the soft fuzz of hair on her nephew's crown.

'This.' Stella flung both arms in front of her. 'You here with Colin.'

'Anna asked me,' she replied, wide-eyed with innocence, yet aware that the hand on the bottle was trembling slightly in recognition of something which her conscious mind had

275

yet to acknowledge. 'Just as we were going to bed, she asked me. If you wake first could you see to him in the night, she said. She knows I'm better without sleep. I always have been. She's not coping, Mum, she needs . . .'

'She needs to do it herself. And David. They both do.' Stella took a step towards the rocking chair, her usually placid face tensed in a way that Becky had never seen before. 'You are not letting her. You' – there was a tremor in her voice – 'you are taking him over.'

'Jesus Christ . . . I don't believe this, I just don't believe it. I was only helping . . . I . . .'

'You take people over Becky, you charm them, you always have. Like your father. He won people round. It is a huge talent – and a dangerous one – you have to use it carefully. I have not always been the wisest of mothers, I know. I have been – I am – weak. But allow me wisdom in this. You must not stay here helping Anna. Babies are hard. Anna's got to learn that. She's got to learn that so much of the pleasure comes through coping with the difficulties, that only by coping with him will she get to understand him, to love him. You must go back to your life and let her get on with hers. You are too strong for her, Becky. You've always been the strong one.'

If it had not been for the baby, now fast asleep in her arms, Becky would have laughed out loud, a disbelieving hysterical laugh connected to the fact that for the second time in the space of two weeks she was having life-long perceptions of her own character and history turned upside down. 'I was trying to help,' she repeated dully, while a small dark part of her crawled towards the admission that there were indeed other, less straightforward, less edifying, aspects to her willingness to remain under her sister's roof. She loved looking after Colin because she loved him, she told herself fiercely. And because she had a knack for it. More of a knack than Anna. Closing her eyes in an effort to seal off the direction her thoughts were taking, Becky instead found herself confronting the ugly fact that it had felt good to outshine her sister. Good. Empowering. Vengeful. Becky arrived at this final realisation with some incredulity, watching it take shape in her mind like some unwanted and hideous nightmare, something from which she longed only to run away and disown. But there was no running away, she realised hopelessly, staring the monster in the face and recognising the hitherto subsumed white heat of the rage she had felt towards Anna in the hospital; for re-scripting their past in a few mad loose sentences; for becoming a mother when it was something she, Becky, had longed for so much more; and most heinous of all, for telling Joe about Guy and ruining any reachable possibility of making her own fading dream of happy families come true.

'Becky?' Stella whispered urgently, not wanting to wake her now solidly sleeping grandchild. 'I'm not cross. I'm just . . .'

'Go away.' Becky heaved herself out of the chair and put Colin into his cot, managing to complete the action in one smooth gentle motion in spite of the turmoil inside her mind. 'Leave me alone, I don't want you,' she hissed, feeling Stella's hand on her shoulder and shaking it off.

'I know, Becky, I know,' said Stella gently, not trying to touch her again but staying by her side. 'It's been hard for you. Many things have been hard for you. Being strong inside doesn't mean you don't suffer. You've wanted your father, all these years. I couldn't be him and I think . . .' Stella paused, savouring the simplicity of the truth, realising that even the most hurtful of facts was better than repression and lies. 'And I think that you have yet to forgive me for that. I hope one day you do. It's taken me twenty years to forgive myself.' As she turned to leave the room, she added quietly, 'But this is about Anna, I promise you. Nothing to do with the trouble between us. She is hanging by a thread, Becky, and has been

277

for some time. I've only just realised myself. I want to try and help her. Which means you must go.'

'Yes. I see. Okay.' Becky nodded. 'I see that you are right. I'll leave tomorrow.'

'Becky I . . .' Stella started back across the room but her daughter flung out an arm, warning her away.

'Mum, I'm fine. Go to bed. I'm fine.'

Becky remained where she was beside the cot, clenching and unclenching her hands, holding back her tears until the faint slap-slapping of her mother's slippered heels was muffled behind the closing of her bedroom door. In the end however, no tears came. Instead, a deep unnatural calm – which she recognised as shock – descended, causing her to fold away the bag of nappies and put the milk-stained cloth in the laundry basket before walking quickly and quietly back to her room.

'I am not who I thought I was,' she told her reflection in the mirror of her bathroom, brushing her teeth a couple of hours later, driven by an inability to sleep to prepare herself for the day. She had already tidied up her room, packed away her meagre belongings and stripped the bed, folding the bottom sheet, duvet cover and pillowcases into a tidy pile on top of the counterpane. 'I am the lucky one. I am strong and dangerous.' She laughed scornfully, the white froth of the toothpaste streaming down her chin.

Leaving in the end wasn't hard. Mike Hadfield had called, she said, avoiding her mother's eye; there was some work crisis and she was required back in London at once. One of those things. A big nuisance, but inarguable. And he wanted his car back. They laughed, but nervously, giving up on their protests so easily that Becky suspected a dim part of them had known all along that the situation as it stood had not really been viable, that somewhere underneath it had been wrong. Kissing Anna goodbye, Becky saw suddenly the terrible frailty of her, so obviously messed up by a life of trying to please, so hung up on her looks and being in control, that she wondered how she could ever have viewed her otherwise. And David was messed up too she thought sadly, standing there in his crisply laundered clothes checking his watch, searching for something he could not find, something quite unconnected to making money or clay pots. When it came to leaving her nephew she gave only the briefest glance at the pram, not trusting herself to manage anything more, knowing that the smell of his milky skin was likely to send her toppling over the edge.

Stella, transformed by a pair of thick stockings and a woolly twinset from the wild-haired peach-toed woman of the night, hovered in the background saving her farewells till last. 'Stay in touch darling,' she whispered, kissing Becky's cheek, her tone full of meaning, her eyes glazed with apologetic sympathy.

'Yes, of course,' Becky muttered, appreciating the tenderness behind the embrace, but still too raw to respond to it.

Once inside the car, she wanted only to accelerate at top speed down the drive, flinging stones from her wheels at the budding rhododendrons. As it was, with three of them parked on the doorstep, waving her off, she had to make do with a gentle cruise towards the gates. It wasn't until she was almost at the gates themselves that she spotted Anna, framed in her rearview mirror, racing after her, red-faced and waving both arms.

'Stop – God – I thought you hadn't seen me.' She patted her chest, catching her breath as Becky scrabbled for the right button to lower the window. 'Just wanted to say thank you – a big thank you – for everything Becks – for being so understanding about absolutely bloody everything. We're really going to miss you, David and I. And so's Colin . . .' Tears pricked her eyes.

'You'll be fine,' said Becky gently, reaching out of the car and squeezing her arm. 'Mum will help – better than me because she's been through it with the pair of us. She'll know all sorts of tricks for sorting him out.'

'Becks, look – there's something else too – a big favour – huge, in fact, and one which I've no right to ask after all you've done already . . .'

Becky rolled her eyes in a show of fond impatience, inwardly thinking that if her sister knew the half of what she had done – or almost done – she wouldn't want a favour or anything else from her ever again. 'Whatever it is, I'd love to help. I feel so bad leaving out of the blue like this when I said I'd stay. What is it? Headhunting top London nannies or something?' she teased, thinking suddenly of what Stella had said about Anna hanging by a thread and wanting the reassurance of a smile.

'No, no, nothing like that.' Anna placed both hands on the edge of the open car window, squeezing so hard Becky could see the whites of her fingernails. 'It's David. He told me last night he's going to London tomorrow.' She paused, swallowing slowly. 'He's said it's some sort of business thing but I know it's to see her.'

'Anna, really . . .'

'I just *know*, okay? And I want you to follow him.'

The idea was so ludicrous that Becky could not resist laughing out loud. 'You have got to be joking.'

'Don't laugh, Becky, please don't laugh.' Her voice was urgent and feverish. 'I know what train he's catching – it gets into Waterloo at twelve thirty – I know you've got this work crisis thing but it would be your lunch hour—'

'And what exactly am I supposed to do?' Becky interjected, still incredulous but speaking more gently. 'Hide behind pillars? Watch him get into a taxi and then rush into the street windmilling my arms in the hope that I can find one quickly enough to follow him?'

'I've thought of that. You could have a taxi waiting, explain that you're following someone, say it's for a birthday surprise or something so it's got to be secret – I'd pay of course . . . oh look, forget it – just forget it,' she snapped suddenly, all the eagerness gone from her voice. 'I'm sorry I asked. I shouldn't have asked. It wasn't fair. Forgive me.' She let go of the car, releasing a long slow breath as she straightened herself. She had come out of the house in only a thin top and her long pink skirt and looked pinched with cold. A stiff breeze was making the skirt billow round her legs, as if bent upon hoisting her off the ground.

'Why can't you just ask him, Annie?'

'Because he would deny it. I know he would. And in a way I would want him to. And then we'd still be living a lie.' She clutched herself with her arms, twisting her lips with her teeth, as if the pain behind the sentiments made them virtually impossible to articulate. 'I need to have all the facts in order to . . . *deal* with it . . . to be strong, just so I know where I stand and can . . .'

'I'll do it.'

'Oh Becks, would you?'

'You're frozen Annie, go inside. I'll do my best, okay? And I'll call you tomorrow.'

'Just an address,' she whispered, her face back inside the window, so close that Becky could see the violet lines of the veins feeding her eyes. 'That's all I want. I'll do the rest on my own.'

'I'll do my best,' repeated Becky. She waited for Anna to step well back before driving away, her heart full of dread both at the thought of the difficulties of carrying out her promise and where any discovery she made might lead.

# 35

He goes to the same street at the same time of day, but she is not there. He waits, first outside the back door of a crumbling Victorian pub and then, self-conscious of his inactivity, against a lamp-post on the opposite side of the road. Feeling with his fingers in the pocket of his trousers, he checks that the money is there, the clean tight wad of it, more than ten times what she would be expecting for any of the tricks on her list, let alone for nothing. He knows it is conscience money, but he wants to do it all the same. To make some gesture of apology. Now that he is all right. Now that he has come through. The thought that the girl should remain mired in the dark tunnel of hopelessness in which they met, pains him deeply. It doesn't seem fair, that his life should have moved on while hers should have no prospect of doing so.

When an hour passes and still she does not appear, he shuffles down the street towards the door itself. He is staring helplessly at the column of scribbled names next to the buzzers when it opens and a dark-skinned girl in jeans and a leather coat hurries out, so focused on wherever it is she is going that she barely blinks as she brushes his shoulder. Then it is easy to reach for the door before it closes behind her and to step inside, into the dim dankness of the hall. Some graffiti has appeared on walls since his last visit, a clutch of Eastern-looking hieroglyphics, smeared in luminous yellow across one panel of the peeling paper, so carelessly that dribbles of excess paint have been left to dry beneath every word. Like tears, he thinks, before hurriedly reproving himself for such sentimentality and heading up the stairs, taking three at a time, in haste now to follow through on the task he has set himself.

He knocks quietly several times, straining his ears for sounds of occupation. It is a couple of minutes before the door is opened, not by the girl he is looking for, but by another much older woman, with sallow skin and long brittle-looking hair the colour of dead grass. She peers at him over the door chain, narrowing her eyes, which look dull and heavy-lidded. Behind her he glimpses the crimson chamber; one of the curtains has lost several hooks and hangs short of its partner, exposing a triangle of azure sky.

'Yeah?'

'I'm sorry to disturb you. I'm looking for the other girl who used to work . . . to live here. Short light brown hair, big eyes . . .'

'She's gone.' The door starts to close. Without thinking he slips his foot inside, wincing with pain at the force of it ramming against his anklebone.

'Do you know where? Only I have something for her, some . . . something she'll like.'

'Oh yeah?' The pain on his foot eases, but the voice is hard and disbelieving.

'An address maybe or a . . . ?'

'Fuck off, will you?'

'Here, well you take it then,' he says, grimacing at the new slicing pressure of the door and its frame against his foot and scrabbling in his trouser pocket for the bank notes. Even when he has the money out, all five hundred pounds of it, flapping two inches from her face, her expression remains distant, although the dark circles of her pupils seem to widen slightly. 'Oh yeah?' She speaks softly, a hint of something –

Welsh or maybe Irish, coming through her voice. 'And what do want for that then?'

'Nothing,' he chokes, suddenly sick at the futility of the entire enterprise, seeing it for what it is, a sop to his own remorse, a sticking plaster on a gaping wound. He flings the money clumsily through the door, causing the neat pack of new notes to scatter and fall like leaves into a messy heap at her feet. He turns and walks quickly away, not looking back, not even at the turn in the stairs, when the silence he has left behind is broken by a muted squeal and the sad hungry scrabbling of fingernails on the bare floor.

# 36

The scratch was long and jagged, a crude silver arrow zigzagging in the gleaming black, running from the middle of the driver's door all the way back to the panel housing the petrol cap. Becky, emerging from the house on Friday morning, almost retched in horror at the sight, before rushing into the street to check whether a mad sense of symmetry had made the vandal drag his key – or knife, or whatever it had been – along the other side of the car as well. Drawing paltry relief from the fact that this was not after all the case, she turned her back on the sight and trudged off in the direction of the Bayswater Road, worries about how she would break the news of this misfortune to her long-suffering boss adding to her already churning anxiety at the prospect of playing private sleuth on behalf of her stricken sister.

She would tell Mike about it that evening, she decided, when she dropped the car off at his house. They had settled upon this arrangement the previous afternoon, when, slightly delirious both from lack of sleep and the private trauma surrounding her departure from Anna and David's, Becky had telephoned him to announce her intention of delivering both herself and his car to work the next day. Mike, sounding surprised, had said she would be far better advised to enjoy the remaining three days of her two-week break, only then agreeing to a Friday-night delivery of the car because she insisted on it. Grateful that she would not after all face the challenge of trying to squeeze her cloak and dagger activities round Waterloo Station within the time restrictions of an official lunch hour, Becky had spent the rest of the afternoon clearing the flat of dirty clothes and soured milk, before rewarding herself with a much needed early night.

After giving the matter considerable thought, both during the early hours, when she found herself suddenly and irrevocably awake, and during the slow crawl of the morning that ensued, Becky had decided that Anna's loosely outlined scheme of having a taxi waiting was probably as good a plan as any. The right kind of cabbie might even find the whole thing rather exciting, she decided, scanning the Bayswater Road for a yellow taxi light and rehearsing in her mind what she would say. In the event it took three attempts before she found a driver willing to do as she asked, her first target claiming he was about to knock off for lunch and the second protesting that he never took any jobs that left his meter running. The third however, a prematurely balding young man with a broad cockney accent and wistful grey eyes, agreed without a murmur, as if chasing round the streets of London after other cabs was how he expected to spend every Friday lunchtime.

Arriving at the station early and feeling hopelessly conspicuous and terrified, Becky dodged between pillars near the appropriate platform, practising watching people without them seeing her. After a visit to the Ladies to compose herself, she resumed her vigil behind a pillar, chanting silent prayers to herself about platforms not being altered and David not throwing her plans into chaos by electing to use the tube. As things turned out, she spotted him almost immediately, striding at the front of the emerging crowd, wearing a long grey mackintosh and with his eyes fixed on his shoes, clearly as unsuspecting of secret surveillance as it was possible to be. It almost felt too easy, especially when, without a falter in his stride, he marched straight out towards the taxi rank in the street outside.

'It's going to be the white one, three from the head of the line,' Becky instructed her cabbie breathlessly, feeling something close to exhilaration as she ducked into her own waiting vehicle a few minutes later. 'It's got an ad for the FT on it, do you see?'

'I've got it,' he replied, slowly folding away his newspaper and sounding so contrastingly unexhilarated that Becky found herself wondering if he was quite up to the job. From the moment he started to drive however, all her doubts evaporated. In spite of innumerable hazards in the form of red lights, road works and unpredictable pedestrians, the white taxi remained safely distant but well within sight as they followed its zigzagging route up through London. It was rather a shock when, after some twenty-five minutes, it suddenly stopped. Especially as it did so in a leafy street of Georgian houses instead of outside a restaurant, as Becky had dimly been expecting; the timing of her brother-in-law's assignation – virtuous or otherwise – having led her to assume it would involve lunch. They were somewhere near Edgware, she realised, surreptitiously getting her bearings as her own cabbie deftly overtook David's and pulled up some fifty yards further down the same street.

'Hang on.' Becky peered over the back of her seat and watched as David alighted from the taxi, paid his driver and then turned towards the house directly behind him. 'Okay. Brilliant. Thank you.' Settling her own bill, which was huge, while still in the taxi, she checked again that the coast was clear before clambering out into the street. What she would do from here, other than make a note of the address, she had no idea. Walking towards the house, she was too preoccupied with a combination of grim curiosity on her own part and deep sadness on Anna's to give the matter much thought. It occurred to her however, as she neared the front door, which was grand looking and painted a rich green, that any flutters of moral indignation would be sorely misplaced. She had deceived Joe and paid her own price. Giddy suddenly at the thought, almost as if the reality of it – the vast extent of her loss – had hit her for the first time, she reached out a hand to steady herself on the wrought-iron railings running along the front of the house. As she did so the handsome door burst open and David came rushing out of it, looking both ways up the street, his face creased with irritation. At the sight of Becky, clutching the railings, the look of irritation was replaced by an expression of such astonishment that, even with a thousand questions exploding in her mind as to how to react and what to say, a distant, blissfully normal part of her brain appreciated the comedy of it.

'Bloody hell,' he said at length, walking slowly down the short path towards her, frowning as if to be absolutely certain of her identity, as if he quite literally could not believe his eyes.

'Hello, David.'

'Any luck?' A woman, dressed in a knee-length navy-blue skirt and a white shirt appeared in the doorway behind him. She had her arms folded and looked relaxed.

'No, it's gone,' David called back, only half turning his head, as if fearful that taking his eyes off Becky might cause her to vanish altogether.

'What's gone?' Becky couldn't resist looking over her shoulder, struggling as she did so with her own embarrassment and a creeping sense that all was not as it seemed. The woman, composed and staid in her uniform-like clothes and flat shoes, was not remotely what she would have expected.

'My mac. I left it in the cab. I thought it might not have gone. Becky what the hell are you doing here?'

Becky slowly lifted her hand off the railings and put it against her mouth. She could smell the metal on her fingers and there were tiny black flecks on her palms where the ancient paint had flaked under her grip. 'I think,' she said, speaking slowly, but very clearly, 'the time for the truth has come, don't you? Funny thing the truth. You just can't keep it down, no matter how hard you try. Believe me,' she managed a wry grin which faded as soon as it touched her lips, 'I know.'

'Is this a friend?' called the woman, a trace of something like concern now evident in her voice.

David, in response, turned and hurried to the doorstep. Becky watched as they exchanged a few inaudible words before the woman disappeared back inside.

'It's not fair,' she said, gripping the railings again, with both hands this time. 'It's not fair on Anna.'

'How did you get here, Becky?' He started to speak before he reached her, looking now, so she could not help observing, impressively relaxed and in control.

'I followed you,' she confessed, spitting the words out, because she felt foolish saying them. 'Anna asked me to. Anna has known all along.'

'Known what?'

'That you have someone else of course,' she sneered, every trace of admiration at his composure subsumed now by anger and disappointment.

'Someone else?' He frowned, rubbing his chin with his hand and shaking his head. 'Oh my God, really . . . this is too much. You mean . . . ?' He glanced at the door and back at her. 'She can't . . . she can't . . . really . . . Becky . . .'

'I've seen her now, David,' Becky interrupted, her voice flat and solemn. 'I've seen her.'

'You have seen . . . Christ, Becky . . .' He was shaking his head again. 'You have seen my therapist.' He began to laugh. 'Today was my last session. I'm signing myself off.'

'A *therapist*?' Although Becky's tone was one of disbelief

she knew the moment the words were out that he spoke the truth. 'Why?'

He folded his arms. 'Because, if you must know, though you have no right to, I have been unhappy. For a while now. Deeply unhappy. I didn't want Anna to know because she has had enough to cope with and I didn't want her thinking it was anything to do with her when I knew it was all to do with me.' He tapped his temple. 'In here. Mid-life bloody crisis. Had everything a man could want and wasn't happy. Prenatal depression.' He grinned. 'Happens to fathers too, you know. Since Colin it's all sort of fallen back into place. Though' – he gestured with his thumb at the house – 'it's helped me sort some other stuff out too, to do with accepting the kind of person I am, not fighting it . . . that sort of thing . . .' He broke off, looking momentarily embarrassed. 'So I'm afraid you've had a bit of a wasted journey.' He grinned again, thrusting his hands into his pockets. 'How the hell did you track me down anyway?'

'And I'm afraid you ought to have told Anna,' retorted Becky, ignoring the question. 'If you knew what she has been through – the agonies – Jesus, David, are you so wrapped up in your own feelings that you can't stop for a moment to think of hers? Anna is hanging by a thread at the moment,' she continued, aware that she was using Stella's very words, but not minding because they were so apt, so wise. 'With Colin in particular she needs help – not me or nannies – but you, both of you, sorting him out, readjusting to the shock of it *together*.'

Instead of arguing back as she had half expected, David hung his head looking bleak and deflated, all traces of the grin quite gone. 'You're right of course. I know that really. I do love her . . .'

'Well bloody well show her that you do then,' snapped Becky. 'Get on the phone now and tell her everything.

Preferably before your last . . . session.' She pushed herself off the railings and set off down the street, shaking her head in wonderment, not just at the behaviour of her brother-in-law but at the dogged way in which life continued to surprise her with its twists and turns, slithering out of reach just when she finally dared to think she had the measure of it.

Lighting a cigarette and then stamping it out a moment later in the realisation that what she really wanted was food, Becky continued walking until she found a sandwich bar. She chose a tuna salad baguette which she ate out of the bag, strolling down the street, in no hurry suddenly either to work out where she was or to find a tube station to get herself home. She was in danger of being happy, she reflected with some surprise, dropping the empty bag into a bin a little later and throwing her pack of cigarettes on top of it. It had crept up on her, out of nowhere. Because David and Anna would be all right. And so, more surprisingly, would she. Something had clicked into place. Something perhaps akin to what David had been trying to achieve through his visits to the woman in the blue skirt. Accepting who he was. She had been fighting herself, for years, Becky realised, stopping to stare at her own shadowy reflection in a shop window, seeing the likeness of her father and feeling none of her usual compunctions about celebrating it. It struck her in the same instant that what both her sister and her mother had said about her was right: the role of the hopeless, chaotic, less attractive younger sister was one that she adopted by way of camouflage, as a way of dodging all the things she was afraid of, a way of abdicating responsibility. When all along her life, her talents had been waiting patiently for her to take charge of them, to make the most of them and stop messing around, hiding behind antipathy towards a mother who had done nothing to deserve it and adulation for a sister who herself badly needed support.

It was like a curtain lifting. And it stayed lifted, not just through her lazy afternoon of window shopping and ironing in front of quiz shows, but in the evening as well, when Mike Hadfield responded to her guilty confession about the scratch on his car by inviting her in for a glass of wine.

# 37

Joe moved amongst his employees that Friday night like an automaton, barking orders in the very manner he most despised and making such a hash of one sauce that he had to bin the whole thing and start again. It took a lot for him not to enjoy cooking. Ever since he was a teenager, coming home from school to an empty house and having to fix his own tea, the process of preparing and blending foods was one that he found soothing and deeply satisfactory. He would rummage through the fridge and larder the moment he was inside the door, seeing potential in the dustiest packets and the most forlorn left-overs, taking so much trouble over it that his homework often got neglected in the process. During the dark days of marriage to Ruth and accountancy, when his attempt to conform to society's and his own preconceptions of a decent working life had shrunk his cooking activities to the occasional spaghetti bolognaise at the weekend, a small intense part of him had felt permanently deprived. As a large, sometimes clumsy man, the kitchen was where he could feel poised and deft. Without it he felt only large and – a reaction particularly encouraged by Ruth – In The Way. Becky on the other hand had seemed to understand that it was something he needed to do, never once complaining during the early years about his loss of a regular income or, later on, with all the Adrian and Le Moulin business, about the madness of the hours. In fact, looking back in recent weeks, Joe had caught himself wondering if things would have worked out better if in fact she had complained a little more – pointed out to him the price they were paying for putting her own dreams on hold, warned him that when the time came for him to need her again she might not be there.

The reason for Joe's mood that night however, related not to broodings over Becky, but to a new and frightening development with regard to his daughter. Thanks to some work bonanza of Glen's, involving a weekend for employees and their spouses at some grand country house, Jenny had arrived straight from school that afternoon to stay for the entire weekend. She had come the five stops on the bus herself, a feat of independence which she had clearly enjoyed and which had given Joe, opening the door for once to a smiling dimpled faced, high hopes for an amiable and relaxing stay. Although still in the baggy trousers, the vast shapeless top had been replaced by a faded T-shirt which he actually remembered as having bought her himself. It was a little worn and tight from use, but appeared to Joe's hungry eyes like an old friend from a familiar and happy past. Thus buoyed up, it came as something of a body-blow when, halfway through a mouthful of one of his homemade pizzas, with the puffy base she liked and huge chunks of fresh pineapple embedded into the crusty cheese on top, she announced that Glen was thinking of returning to live in the United States and taking her and Ruth with him.

Joe had forced himself to gulp a mouthful of tea before delivering a response. He spoke slowly, with only a trace of a tremor in his voice, all the while gripping the underside of his chair with his free hand, as if literally to prevent himself exploding out of it. 'And what do you think about that, Jen? How do you feel?' he asked, fighting with every syllable to keep the terror under control, saying what he knew he ought to say, the thing that would put the least pressure on her.

Jenny had shrugged, the mask of sullenness with which he

had so hoped not to have to contend sliding back into its habitual position across her face. Like a shutter closing him out, Joe thought, watching with despair tearing at his heart.

'Whatever. We'd have a cool house with a big garden and it would be near the beach. We could have a dog.'

'A dog? Really?' He looked round his small kitchen, feeling helpless. 'And when was Mummy planning on sharing some of these plans with me, do you think?'

'Dunno. She doesn't know I know. I overheard. They thought I was asleep but I wanted some milk and went down to the fridge and they were in the sitting room.' For a moment her grey eyes flared with the thrill of this small triumph over exclusion from the adult world. 'Glen's work is a posting and it's coming to an end.'

'I see,' said Joe, in fact seeing nothing but the pokiness of his flat and the prospect of defeat. He pictured the big-toothed all-American smile of Ruth's lawyer lover, with his shock of healthy yellow hair and pert body. If the man promised beaches and dogs he was sure to deliver them. 'We must think very carefully about what's best for you, Jen. Or maybe Glen's posting here will get extended,' he offered lamely, scratching round for comfort, 'that does happen, you know. But the main thing for you to know is that, however it all turns out, I will always see you as much as I can and I will always . . .' he had been going to say 'love you', but the lump in his throat was too bulging and he patted her head instead.

'These filets, did you want them sliced Joe?'

'The what? Yes . . . yes . . . quite thick, at least two inches.' Joe picked up one of the slabs of bloodied meat in front of his young assistant and demonstrated with his fingers.

'The kid on table nine wants the chicken, but in bread-crumbs instead of a sauce and with chips instead of wild rice and baked beans instead of haricots,' said Trish, bursting into

295

the kitchen behind them and flinging down her menu pad in exasperation. 'What do you want me to say?'

'Ask him if he'd like organic pizza instead. I've got loads of freshly made dough upstairs. Tell him he can have any topping he likes.'

'Okay,' Trish murmured, trotting happily back out into the dining room, casting her boss a look of admiration and amazement. '*Any* topping?'

'Any,' repeated Joe firmly, turning up the gas flame on the hob in front of him and watching with glazed eyes as the sauce preparation began to reduce, bubbling furiously round the edges as if in some hopeless quest to clamber out of the pan.

'Pineapple and ham,' announced Trish, returning a few moments later, eyeing Joe with fresh uncertainty. 'Have we got that?'

Joe grinned. 'Upstairs I have. I won't be a minute.'

'I could go,' she offered, fancying not just the chance of a small break from the bustle of the dining room but also a chat with Jenny, whom she liked.

'Thanks, but I'll do it. Louis, could you take over here for a minute? Reduce it to half a saucepan's worth and then stir the cream in. Fry the mushrooms for one minute and then put those in as well. Got it?'

Louis, a recently recruited cousin of Adrian's who had dropped out of university but already showed a remarkable aptitude for any culinary duty requested of him, eagerly seized a wooden spoon and took over as commanded.

Upstairs the flat was very quiet. Pleased that Jenny, who could be prone to the most cruel and unchildlike bouts of insomnia, had fallen asleep, Joe tiptoed past her room and fetched what he required from the fridge. On the return journey, balancing the cellophane wrapped ball of dough on top of the two plates containing the ham and pineapple, he could not resist peering inside, wanting to soothe his anxious and tender heart with the reassuring sight of her curled under her duvet; his child, no matter what torturous separations the future might hold. The thought of losing her made him sick. Yet so did the thought of fighting over her like a piece of meat, making her feel bad when she had every right to want to seize the chance of a far better lifestyle than any he could offer. And of course she would want to stay with Ruth, he thought bleakly, who'd been there so much more and done all the big stuff.

The bedside light was on, as Jenny liked it to be, having graduated from plug-in fairy lights for reassurance as a toddler, to the more solid presence of a forty watt bulb. Joe was on the point of registering this small detail of normality when he found himself confronting instead the infinitely less normal fact that the bed, while showing signs of recent occupation, was empty. 'Jen?' He took a step back into the hallway, listening hard. 'Jen?' Using his chin, he turned the main light on in her bedroom, thereby illuminating the presence of a note, scribbled with evident fierceness on a half-torn page, lying on top of the creases in her pillow.

*I am running away. Don't worry about me.*

But it was Joe who was running, almost before his eyes had got to the last word, out of the flat and down the stairs, cradling the plates and dough to his chest. In the kitchens he gabbled something, some explanation, shoved the plates at Trish, seized his mobile phone and tore out of the back entrance into the street. The police station was round the corner. He would go there first, he decided, sprinting in the direction of the main road, his heart sinking at the sight of Brixton on a Friday night, buzzing with enough people and noise to hide a hundred eleven-year-old girls, let alone one small round-faced creature with hair in her eyes and huge clothes. Then he would call Ruth, he decided, his heart pounding at the thought, while his mind reached for the flimsy hope that an eleven-year-old who asked not be worried about was clearly asking for bucketfuls of worry on a grand scale, that all she really wanted was the heart-warming attention of being found and returned safely home.

# 38

It was almost eleven o'clock by the time Becky got home. Mike Hadfield's glass of wine had turned into three or four, and been accompanied by half a dozen bowlfuls of delicious finger foods. He had picked them up from his local deli by way of something for his dinner, he explained, ignoring her protestations about having to be on her way and directing her to a drawer which contained a pack of paper napkins and plastic barrel of cocktail sticks. Glimpsing the little tubs of prawns and sausages and olives lined up on the shelves of his otherwise empty fridge, so clearly purchased in her honour, Becky had moved in something of a daze, wondering how it could have taken her so long to stumble upon the disquieting and suddenly blindingly obvious fact that her host's affection for her went far beyond the bounds of an avuncular and conscientious employer.

'I'd like to pay for the scratch on the car,' she declared, once they were seated in his sitting room. She patted her lap briskly as she spoke, wanting to re-establish some sort of firm ground on which to proceed with the encounter.

'Well you can't,' he had retorted, wagging a reproving finger as he sprawled in the armchair opposite, his eyes twinkling behind the lenses of his spectacles. 'It's not your fault. Insurance will cover it.' His voice was lazy, but his gaze so intent that she had looked quickly away, casting her eyes instead over the array of food, wondering how much of it she could eat before making a dignified escape. He was quite drunk, she realised. The first bottle of white wine in the ice bucket had been replaced by a second, and she was only on her third glass. 'Becky?'

'Yes?' She looked back at him, her eyes ablaze with studied innocence and disinterest, while inside she wished there was some way of scrambling back behind the armour of naïvety in which she had arrived.

'Would you slap me if I kissed you?'

In spite of her belated but accurate reading of the situation, the question, delivered in the same lazy laconic style as his remark about insurance, caught Becky so much by surprise that her half chewed mouthful of curried prawns almost flew onto her lap. 'Mike, please . . . don't.' She struggled furiously with her food as she talked, managing in her panic to swallow the shellfish down long before it was ready.

'I'll take that as a yes. As in, yes you would slap my face if I kissed you, as opposed to yes, I can kiss you.'

Becky couldn't help smiling. He had a way of talking that she liked, a way which, if she were in the right mood and concentrated hard enough, she might even have found quite seductive. But physically he was not remotely her type – too old for one thing and too bookish and gaunt for another. Though she had nothing against glasses per se, the eyes behind them were too grey and knowing, as if he had looked life full in the face and seen through it. He would be a hard man to surprise, or to make happy, she realised; a kind man, obviously, but somewhere inside, deeply embittered and bruised. 'I . . . I . . . think I'd better go Mike.' She stood up, tugging down the hem of her skirt. 'I am sorry if I . . . I mean, I didn't mean . . .'

'You haven't. You haven't led me on in any way. It's all me.' He smiled ruefully, looking up at her and shaking his head. 'It's all me. Forgive me for trying?'

'Of course,' she said briskly, reaching for her handbag. 'Of course. And thank you again for everything – time off, the car and so on,' she added, gabbling slightly as she got to the door, aware that he was right behind her and terrified suddenly at the imminent possibility of a fond farewell. 'See you Monday then.'

'See you Monday,' he echoed, turning the handle for her and stepping well back so as to make plain that he had no intention of making any sort of attempt at physical contact. 'Since I guess you don't want me to drive you home,' he added drily, ramming his hands into his trouser pockets as she stepped past him, almost – so Becky couldn't help thinking – as if it was the only way to ensure they would behave.

'I'll find a taxi, thanks,' she replied brusquely, cringing at the thought of the Bayswater flat and the fact of having allowed herself to become so improperly beholden to the man. Business as usual on Monday would be a strain, she reflected sadly, letting herself into the flat some twenty minutes later and feeling a twist of dismay at the prospect of having to move out of it. Still too wired up from the events of the day to think of bed, she made herself a cup of coffee and flicked on the television where several hard-bitten-policemen-style dramas seemed to be running concurrently, each one involving high body counts and heaps of unintelligible forensic evidence. Becky channel-hopped dreamily between them all, still shaken by all that had happened but aware too that the happiness which had settled inside her during the course of the afternoon remained in tact, a sweet strong feeling that she had turned a corner inside her own head and that all would be well. She had dealt with the Mike Hadfield business as best she could. More importantly, it felt good to know that Anna's dreadful suspicions about David had been unfounded, that all he had been trying to do was sort out the mess inside his own head. Which in the end was all anyone on the planet was trying to do, she reflected, yawning so deeply that her eyes filled with tears, converting the rather grim mortuary scene in front of her to a pleasing blur. She was just thinking with some longing of the half-empty packet of cigarettes she had so rashly consigned to the bottom of the waste bin in North London, when there was a muffled but unmistakeable clump of a footstep on the metal staircase outside. A moment later the sound of a milk bottle smashing sent her diving under the sofa cushions. Summoning all her courage, she then slithered to the floor and crawled – using the commando style she had practised with David – into the kitchen. Aware, through intuition rather than any physical evidence, that someone was on the other side of the front door, she remained motionless, holding her breath. After a couple of long minutes there came the unmistakeable sound of feet crunching on broken glass followed by a timid knock on the door.

'Who is it?' Becky called, shouting to expel some of her terror. 'Who's there?' She thought suddenly, with rather less terror, of Mike, picturing him slumped drunk with longing against the door. 'Mike? It's not you is it?'

'No, it's me,' replied a small reedy voice on the other side.

With trembling hands, though she knew now there was nothing to be afraid of, Becky turned the handle and let the door swing wide. 'Jenny?' Her stepdaughter had grown so much that, in spite of the immediately evident traumatic circumstances of the occasion, Becky had to swallow the urge – associated negatively in her own mind with childhood visits from rarely seen and unmissed relatives – to remark on the fact. Of more obvious cause for comment was the child's distressed and dishevelled state, her usually pale angular face puffed and pink from crying, her hair wet and tangled across her face. She was standing a few feet from the door, the broken glass from the bottle scattered all about her, the pieces glinting in the dark. 'Come in, if you would like to,' ventured Becky gently, some dim instinct, connected perhaps to her own troubled childhood, allowing her to see at once that the same desperation which had propelled her to the doorstep might well cause her to bolt from it just as quickly. 'You poor love, you look worn out. How about a hot chocolate, or maybe a sandwich, if you're hungry?' she continued, marvelling at this extraordinary finale to an extraordinary day, feeling as urgent and concerned as she would have trying to talk someone down from a window ledge. 'That's it, there we go,' she murmured, her heart performing a leap of celebration as Jenny began shuffling over the threshhold.

'Hot chocolate then?'

Jenny nodded, hunching inside her huge coat, staring round her with all the wariness of a trapped animal.

'And a biscuit, maybe. I've got some somewhere.' Becky rifled through her mostly empty cupboards, feeling that it was important to keep talking until Jenny had recovered sufficiently to say something herself. 'Got them. Double chocolate chocolate chip cookies with extra chocolate . . . or something.' She eyed her stepdaughter for a reaction. 'I dip them in ice cream on Sunday nights sometimes, when there's crap on the TV and I can't face the thought of another week of work. I know it's tough being a child at times, but I tell you, it's pretty grim being an adult as well. Here, you take the biscuits – do you want ice cream as well? No? Very wise, I usually end up feeling sick afterwards. And let's go through here and sit on the sofa. I'll bring the hot chocolate,' she added, working hard now to force the jollity, wondering whether she was quite up to the situation after all. More in the mood for a stiff gin and tonic, but once again following dim instincts connected to showing solidarity and gaining trust, she poured hot milk into two mugs and stirred in several heaped teaspoons of chocolate powder. 'There we are.' She handed over the drink and watched with a rush of tenderness as Jenny, her mouth still full of biscuit, seized the mug with both hands and pressed it to her lips. 'It's good to see you, Jenny,' she whispered. 'I've missed you.'

Jenny stopped drinking and turned to look at her stepmother properly for the first time. There were streaks of chocolate at the corners of her mouth and her eyes had begun to clear from some of the redness. 'Mum wants to go and live in America with Glen and Dad doesn't care.'

'Of course he cares,' replied Becky, swallowing the catch of surprise in her voice. 'Of course he cares.'

She shook her head violently, swinging her long fringe, stiff and dry now, briefly out of her eyes. 'I told him tonight. He doesn't care.'

'Does he know where you are?' ventured Becky, her heart twisting at the thought of Joe's panic. 'Does anyone?'

She shook her head again, more slowly this time.

'You can stay here, Jenny, as long as you like. But we ought to tell Dad you're okay. He'll be worried.'

'He won't.'

'He will, of course he will. He loves you.'

'Doesn't.'

Becky took a sip from her mug. 'He does, Jenny, so much that sometimes, when he and I were together, it made me a little bit jealous.'

The eyes, screened now back behind the fringe, blinked furiously. 'Glen's okay, I mean, he tries to be nice – buys me things and that, but I don't really like him. I don't like his . . . he has a funny smell . . . like perfume.' She twisted her mouth in a show of distaste. 'And he tries to tickle me and stuff, like I'm a four-year-old.'

'I'm sure he means well,' Becky murmured, getting up and reaching for the phone. 'I'm going to call Dad now, okay? Just to say you are all right and he's not to worry. Do you want to talk to him yourself?'

She shook her head.

'Do you want him,' Becky added, speaking much more softly, 'to come and get you?'

She was halfway through another biscuit, her fourth by Becky's calculation. 'I guess.' She shrugged. 'Whatever.'

Becky stood within easy earshot for the call, not wanting to re-ignite her stepdaughter's distress by creating the impression that the adult world was any more furtive and hostile than she thought it already. 'She's here,' she said simply, feeling exultant herself at the burst of relieved joy in the gasp with which Joe responded. 'She'd like you to come and get her.' Putting the phone down, she returned to her place on the sofa, taking a biscuit from the packet on her way and dunking it in her mug till the chocolate ran.

'You should say how you feel, Jenny, to Joe, to your mum, to everybody. Bottling up feelings, running away, does no good in the end. I know because I tried all that – for years in fact – and it got me precisely nowhere. Grown-ups find it hard to express their feelings too, you know and sometimes could do with a helpful shove from people like you along the way. If you don't want to go to America you must tell your Mum. Then . . . then they'll work something out,' she faltered, in truth wondering what sort of solution could be found and whether Joe himself would have the power to exercise any rights over what happened.

Jenny responded to this attempt at reassurance by emitting a heavy sigh and, at long last, peeling off her coat. 'Look.' She put her hand inside one of the inner pockets and pulled out a fistful of fluorescent felt pens.

'Hm, very pretty,' murmured Becky, thinking not of the pens but of Joe and how it would feel to see him again. Their last meeting had been weeks and weeks before, when she had dropped by to pick up some boxes from the Brixton flat. They had barely spoken. Now he would not only have to speak, she mused, but he would be glad and grateful, which would be nice. Very nice indeed.

'They each have a special smell,' continued Jenny, taking the lid off a brown one and beginning to draw patterns along her knuckle bones. 'You'll like this one. It's chocolate.' She offered the hand to Becky who sniffed it, exclaiming in genuine amazement at the authenticity of the scent. 'I nicked them,' she said next, patting the pens back into a bundle inside her fist and then depositing them on the table next to the half-empty packet of cookies. 'All of them. When I was out with Dad. I don't know why, except maybe . . . to see if I could.' She watched as the pens rolled away from her and then turned to look at Becky, the uncertainty in her expression edged with defiance.

Becky folded her arms and shook her head. 'You are so like me, Jenny, it's spooky.' She pointed at the pens. 'I've done that too, you see. Taken stuff.'

Her stepdaughter's eyes widened in disbelief.

'If you promise not to tell on me then I won't on you. And we'll both make a pact never to do it again. Okay?'

'Okay,' she whispered, delivering both syllables of the word very slowly, her eyes still glued to Becky's.

'Because it's really really bad and pointless and you just feel sick with yourself afterwards, don't you? And it's a kind of a thrill at the time, to do with being cross with the world and taking it out on something, but in the end you just feel rotten inside so the only person you've taken it out on is yourself.' Becky was so overcome by a fresh burst of shame on her own part at this confession that it was a little while before she realised that Jenny was no longer just nodding but crying, making pitiful mewling sounds in a bid to suppress the fact.

'Come here, you,' she said, almost in tears herself, 'and have a good howl, sometimes it's the only thing. I expect

306

Dad's been bawling too, first because he thought he'd lost you and now because he's found you again.'

'Daddy never cries,' she sobbed.

'Oh yes he does,' Becky murmured. 'Oh yes he does.' She pulled the child into the crook of her arm and gently stroked the hair off her face. The sobbing eased and then stopped altogether, becoming instead the heavy even breathing of sleep. Becky continued stroking, recalling as she did so the two occasions when Joe had wept in her arms, the first when he was still looking to her for hope, the second when he had given up on ever finding it.

# 39

David steered the pram along the edge of the verge, where the ground was bumpiest, it being one of the key revelations of a generally revelatory week that the more violent the jigging the more likely his son was to remain asleep. Anna's theory was that it was because she had charged round so much when he was inside her. David, who had always found his own eyelids closing the minute he was in a train or on an aeroplane, thought it more likely to be something genetic, inherited like the slight Anna-ish pout of his upper lip and the comical gangliness of his legs – so like David's own at a similar age that his mother, on a brief visit a couple of days before, had cried out in delight at the sight of them. It had been a pleasure to see his parents drop some of their habitual reserve. En route to a fortieth wedding anniversary of old friends in Wales, they had arrived bearing armfuls of gifts, including an entire wardrobe for a newborn, several huge toys and a set of expensive toiletries for Anna. Because mothers needed to pamper themselves too from time to time, his mother had declared, with such a beady look in her eye that David had half wondered whether Anna hadn't said something while the pair of them were brewing coffee in the kitchen.

Turning the final bend into the village, the verge shrank to a narrow strip of mud. David kept as far off the tarmac as he could, straining his ears for oncoming traffic, suddenly seeing the pram and its cargo as the smallest most vulnerable and valuable thing in the world, a pea floating on an ocean, with only his limited abilities by way of protection. It was a relief to get within sight of the triangle of the village green, as trim as a pressed handkerchief from its first cut of the year and bordered on all sides by handsome red-bricked houses with small but immaculate front gardens. Looking both ways several times, David crossed the road and headed towards the lush expanse of grass, partly to make use of its gentle bumps to keep his son asleep and partly to get to the red post box situated on the far side. The letter in his jacket pocket, a bill for services rendered by his North London therapist, could have waited, but he had wanted some pretext for getting out of the house, some focus in the awesome business of getting safely from the hour of Anna's departure to her return. She was having a hair cut and then going on for a check-up at the hospital. David had wanted badly to go with her, not just because he was still a little afraid of being left alone with Colin, but also because of the new closeness between them which he wanted to guard at all costs. She was, as Becky had rightly pointed out and he had been too wrapped up in his own traumas to see, very fragile. Already denying it hotly – riding high on a fresh bubble of confidence both about them and their ability to handle their son – he was beginning to understand that it was a fragility that went very deep and which he could never again ignore. Falling into his arms on his return from London the week before, he had felt her need of him as never before. While in some ways frightening it had also made him feel powerful and good. Confessing to his own recent turmoil and unhappiness had triggered admissions from her which had taken his breath away; not just about his imaginary lover but about herself generally and her worth as a mother. She had not known a solid family life, she said, and therefore had no faith in being able to create such a thing herself. That night they had sat up talking for so long that the habitual interruptions from their son hadn't seemed anything

309

like as arduous as usual. At Stella's suggestion, she was giving breastfeeding another go, aiming just for the evenings, and placing Colin in a slightly more upright position which he seemed to find a lot more comfortable. By the third feed of that night, when it was clear to even the most untutored eye that the baby was suckling merely for comfort, Anna, looking meek but determined, had produced a small plastic dummy and popped it into his mouth instead.

'I thought those things were bad.'

'Mum bought it. She said anything that helps me is good, whether it's breast pads to stop my shirts getting soaked, dummies or caseloads of gin. She said I had a dummy till I learnt how to stick my thumb in my mouth instead. That's why my teeth stick out a bit. Look.'

'Your teeth don't stick out at all.'

'They do a bit.' She pulled at the sides of her lips with her fingers and bared her teeth.

'Beautiful.'

'No, but he is.' They both turned to look at their son, sprawled on his back between their pillows in a blue babygro, still as loose on him as the skin on a tiny puppy. 'He terrifies me.'

'Me too.'

'I . . . I . . . didn't really want to have him, only I couldn't say because it was too terrible. And then Becky was so good with him it made me feel . . . Becky's always made me feel . . .'

'Shush.' He pressed his finger to her lips. 'You don't have to . . .'

'I want to.' She looked at him hard, as if seeing all the familiar features of his face for the first time. 'I was going to have an abortion, David. I had decided it completely. I didn't want a child, I knew you didn't, I knew we weren't ready. And then I lost some blood and thought I'd miscarried, but I hadn't. I can see I should have told you, but at the time I thought I could cope – that I would in fact cope better if I kept it to myself. When I realised I was still pregnant I had this scan and saw him on the screen and . . . and I know it sounds mad, but I thought of my father and somehow I couldn't go through with it . . . I couldn't end a life when another one, such an important one to me, had been snatched away so cruelly, before I was ready, before I knew myself or what I wanted or who I was . . .'

'I'm not sure any of us ever really know who we are,' interjected David quietly.

'Wisdom from your head doctor?' She cocked her head at him, her voice and eyes offering a hint of a teasing confidence which he knew was good, because it was a sign that they were already accommodating their crisis and moving on.

'I had everything I had ever said I wanted,' he murmured. 'It seemed too awful . . . too like failure . . . to admit that it wasn't enough. I thought it would hurt you.'

'It hurt me a lot more not telling me.'

'I see that now. I'm sorry.'

'And me, I'm sorry too . . . I kept things from you, and from myself too.' She smiled wryly. 'What a disaster we are.'

'Not any more,' he murmured, stroking first Colin's cheek and then Anna's, relishing the different softness of each.

She sighed, pressing her hand over his and closing her eyes. 'And tomorrow Mum will be gone and it will just be us. The three of us. It will probably be awful, for quite a while, but at least I know now that I've got you, that I haven't lost you.' She looked at him, blinking tears from her eyes. 'In a way David, I think we both truly need each other for the first time. And it feels all right, doesn't it? Scary but all right?'

'Very all right,' he had whispered, pulling her to him, shifting his weight carefully so as not to disturb the baby.

Some time later, when Colin was tucked up under the blankets of his cot and a couple of over-eager starlings were emitting sporadic trills from the beech tree under their window, he reached for her again, more purposefully this time so that she could feel the other need he had of her, brewing steadily inside since her return from the hospital. They made love slowly and tenderly, alert to pleasure when they should by rights have been exhausted, alert too to a brand of hope that was new and deeply shared.

Remembering the night, the sheer force of the intimacy, David leant over the pram and blew a noisy affectionate raspberry at his sleeping son. Without childcare of any kind the intervening days had been hard, each one a rollercoaster ride in its own right. Yet there was a peculiar and novel joy in the fact of going through it together, getting some things right and some things wrong, all without judging or feeling judged.

Arriving at the post box at last, David parked the pram alongside and reached into his pocket for the envelope. As he did so something else flicked out of his pocket. Looking down, David was just in time to see the glint of his house key disappearing between the wide slats of a drain, set into the edge of the road just a couple of feet from the post box. Cursing volubly, he slipped the letter inside the slot and drop-ped to his hands and knees to investigate the possibilities of retrieval. Colin meanwhile, whether in protest at having been motionless for all of two minutes, or because he sensed some element of the crisis developing outside the cosy confines of his pram, started crying. 'Hang on little chap, hang on.' Still on his knees, David reached out and began rocking the pram with one hand while continuing to grope between the metal bars of the drain with the other.

'Oh dearie me, what are we up to here, Mr Lawrence?'

David straightened slowly, composing his features into a strained smile at the sight of their cleaning lady, who had appeared out of a side road behind him, wearing a shapeless jumper that reached almost to the knees of her trousers and a pair of lime-green trainers. 'Hello Mrs Costa. And how are you?' he added, out of an entrenched compunction to be polite rather than any remote desire to receive an answer to the question. His expression hardened still further at the recollection that a series of lame excuses and broken assurances about times and dates meant that she had not in fact carried out her cleaning duties for some time.

'Looks like you've lost something . . .' she began, before breaking off in a shriek of delight at the sight of Colin. 'Oh but look at this . . . look at him, and so cross.' She put her face so far inside the hood in order to deliver these greetings that David felt a momentary spurt of sympathy for his hollering son. 'We are cross this morning, aren't we? My, my what a temper.' Taking hold of her stringy ponytail of white-blonde hair, bunched at the crown of her head with a thin rubber band, she began dancing it in front of Colin's face, letting the feathery ends brush across his cheeks. 'Oh, we like that, don't we?' she crooned, chuckling. 'My Bella used to like my hair so much she'd make me curl up with her every night so she could stroke it to go to sleep. Course, I had more in them days,' she added a little quickly, perhaps reading the distaste in David's expression. 'What've you lost then?'

'The key to the house, unfortunately,' he replied, doing his best to sound mildly irritated when in fact the extent of his predicament was fast rushing upon him. It would be another two hours at least before Anna was back, by which time Colin would be frantic for the clean nappy, the bottle of milk and the small pile of most favoured rattles which he had carefully lined up on the kitchen table. Props to get through this first prolonged spell of parenting on his own. He didn't even have his mobile, he realised gloomily, glancing up with irritated surprise to see that Mrs Costa was now reaching both her plump hands into the pram. 'Could we have a cuddle?

Would you mind? Would *you* mind, little fella, more's the point . . . oh I don't think so, no I don't think so at all . . . you bootiful bootiful boy.'

David, watching helplessly, had a sudden and vivid image of the occasion he had almost run the woman off the road on his way to collect Becky from the station ten months before. She had asked for keys to the house, he remembered, thinking with a fresh burst of panic how easily solved his current problems would have been had he complied with the suggestion and entrusted her with one of the spares hanging in the utility room cupboard.

'So, what are you going to do then – about your key?'

For a moment he had the distinct and unpleasant impression that she was enjoying herself. 'I'm not sure to be honest. Anna is out for a little while yet.'

She swung Colin expertly into the air and sniffed at his padded backside. 'He needs a change, don't you petal? I tell you what though,' she continued slowly, righting the baby and pressing him to her ample chest where he seemed, after a show of resistance, to relax, or possibly suffocate, thought David, frustrated both with the situation and his son for looking so content, 'my neighbour's got a three-month-old. Shirley Brent – she'll have nappies and powdered milk too if you need any. I'm only just down there. We could go and ask her if you like.'

David, not wanting to do any such thing, but seeing little alternative, nodded stiffly. 'That would be most kind. Thank you.' Summoning what felt like a huge amount of courage, he stepped forwards and lifted his son out of their rescuer's arms and, with only the tiniest amount of fumbling, returned him to the pram where he promptly started crying again very loudly. 'He'll be fine once we get going,' he explained, trying not to look frantic as he jigged the pram.

'He'll be fine once he's got a clean bum,' declared his

companion stoutly, taking a big sideways step to save her luminous footwear from contact with a patch of mud and leading the way towards the side road from which she had emerged.

Half an hour or so later David found himself perched with a mug of thick tea on the edge of a huge mustard-coloured velour sofa that took up most of the vacant space in Mrs Costa's front sitting room. Propped next to him between two frayed scatter cushions, blinking in surprise at his surroundings was his son, the midriff of his babygro bulging as a result of several ounces of powdered milk and a fresh, slightly too large nappy, which the amiable Shirley, busy with several small children as well as her baby, had handed over with copious clucks of sympathy and congratulation. 'The first is the hardest,' she assured David, pushing heaps of corkscrew curls out of her eyes, where they flopped back again a moment later, 'after that you don't really notice.'

'She's Catholic,' Mrs Costa had confided darkly, once they were safely back behind her front door, different only from the doors on either side of her by virtue of being painted scarlet. 'Four already and I bet it won't be long before there's another.'

David, relaxing in spite of himself, took a sip of the tea, which had been produced without any consultation as to his plans or preferences and which tasted a lot better than it looked. Refusing it would have been impossible, even if Colin hadn't been so wonderfully settled. And a slight drizzle had started up outside, he noticed, leaning back against the sofa to glance out of the front window and noting with surprise how comfortable it was.

'Nice to see a dad with his child, I like that, I have to admit,' muttered Mrs Costa, sitting down with a humph in a small armchair opposite him. 'My Bella never knew that of course, but there we are, that's men for you, isn't it?' She gave him another dark look, so dark that David, without quite knowing why, found himself groping for a change of subject.

'We're sorry, Anna and I, that you haven't made it up to the house in the last few weeks . . .'

'Yes, well there it is. I don't think I'll be able to do any more work for you either. I'm sorry, but there it is,' she repeated blowing at a curl of steam rising off her tea.

'Oh.' David, struggling to an upright position in the sofa, which seemed to be sucking him downwards, was genuinely nonplussed. He had assumed she would leap at the chance to offer to combine hoovering duties with a spot of childminding. The woman had no husband, little money and clearly adored babies. Most baffling however, was the stiff manner in which she had announced this withdrawal of her services. Almost as if it was his fault, as if he had, in some unimaginable way, offended her. And though he told himself that such an impression was either wrong or of little significance, David nonetheless found himself bothered by it. 'I'm sorry to hear that, Mrs Costa. Do you mind if I ask why?'

She delivered another fierce puff of air across the top of her mug, even though it had cooled beyond the point of releasing any steam. 'It's not my business, of course, but I have my standards. And I like Mrs Lawrence. And that's all I'm saying on the matter.'

David found himself laughing nervously. 'What matter? I really don't know what you mean. With the baby Anna would be extremely grateful if you could continue with a few hours a week – and I'm sure there will be the odd occasion when maybe a little babysitting . . .'

'What you get up to Mr Lawrence is your own business, but I don't like to be involved.' She tugged at her ponytail, looking genuinely distressed. 'The fact is . . . you may as well know, I saw you and her – the sister – I saw you, Mr Lawrence. I'm sorry but there it is. I've got my standards.'

'Becky?' David was incredulous.

'While Mrs Lawrence was in hospital too. And in her clothes too. It's not right.'

If she hadn't looked so upset David would have been tempted to laugh out loud. Instead, rather to his amazement, he recognised a certain dignity in the curious barrel-shaped woman seated opposite him, making her own small but firm stand for morality, albeit on the basis of a total misunderstanding. 'I am happy to say you are quite wrong, Mrs Costa. Anna's sister and I – Becky and I – are merely friends. Very good friends, as it happens. There is nothing more to it, I assure you . . .' He broke off, blushing at the memory of the occasion which must have confirmed any simmering suspicions, imagining how the scene – through whichever chink in the house she glimpsed it – must have looked; the pair of them crawling on the floor and giggling, him with wet hair and a towel round his shoulders. Remembering too the ungenerous impulse which had prompted such furtiveness, he blushed again even more deeply. 'That day . . . that Saturday, we were celebrating the arrival of Colin – Anna had been so ill it was such a relief – we had a bit of champagne and didn't feel up to opening the door. I can imagine how it must have looked and I'm sorry . . .'

'No, I'm sorry.' Her face, pink at the best of times, had gone a violent red. 'Jumping to conclusions . . . oh dear, oh dear . . . I've been upset myself recently . . . my daughter Bella turned up on the doorstep again, lost her job in London she says, not a penny to her name and with a bruise too, though she won't tell me where from. I've not been myself, Mr Lawrence, not at all.' She stared glumly into her empty mug for a few seconds and then suddenly burst into giggles, in a way that was so unexpected and which so illuminated what must once have been a schoolgirl impishness to her face that David found himself smiling. 'Blimey, what a business.

All our wires crossed and me on my high horse. You won't be wanting me now and that's for sure.'

'On the contrary,' he corrected her firmly, setting his empty mug down on the coaster she had carefully placed in front of him, only just managing to fit it in because the table was small and mostly taken up with piles of dog-eared magazines. 'Anna will be really pleased I've seen you and had a word. She wants you back desperately. We both do.' He stood up, scooping Colin into his arms with a confidence that felt as if it was growing by the hour. 'And thank you, so very much, for rescuing us today. I can't think what we would have done without you.' Wanting to put a proper seal both on his gratitude, he leant towards her, careful to avoid head-butting the large yellow spherical lampshade suspended above the table, and offered his hand. 'If I have ever seemed discourteous in the past, Mrs Costa, please forgive me. I too have had a few troubles. It seems as if the whole world has.'

She rolled her eyes, beaming. 'That's for sure. Oh, look, it's stopped raining for you. I'd have lent you a brolly otherwise, though he'll be all right, won't he?' She chucked Colin under the chin, 'tucked up in his pram, the little darling.'

She stood at the door to see them off, waving till they were right at the end of the road, even though she had taken the baggy jumper off and her bare arms must have felt the cold.

# 40

*Dear Marcel,*

*I thought I would send you a picture of my beautiful grandson, whom I went to see the instant I got back to England and whom I completely adore. It's a bit blurred, I'm afraid, but at least it gives you an idea. He's going to be very tall and blond, I think, not at all like his namesake, except perhaps for the eyes which are set very deep and remind me just a little bit of Colin's. But then who really knows? We all see what we want to see, don't we? Anna, after a tough start – largely I think from being so ill for the birth – is now adjusting and coping very well. She calls me at least once a day, which is very sweet, asking for advice or just to give me a run-down on what Colin has been up to. I know it won't – and shouldn't – last but I can't help liking it all the same. You were quite right about this grandparent business – all the joy with none of the woe. Would you send me some photos of yours? I would so love to have a couple for my album, if you can spare them of course.*

*The other more important purpose of this letter is to thank you for having me to stay. Colin always used to say I was very good on paper, but I can't really find the words to tell you, Marcel, what a lot it meant to me, how much I enjoyed getting to know you again, how it has helped me arrive at a peace of mind which I had given up imagining, let alone expecting ever to be mine.*

Stella put her pen down and flexed her fingers which felt stiff from having written so fast and furiously for so many lines. Craning her neck so as to get a good view of the garden without making herself visible at the window, she was just able to make out the dark curly head of Dale, bent over the fork with which she had suggested he attack the weeds sprouting through the bottom flower bed. A moment later Leon came into view, looking so vulnerable with his freshly shaven head that Stella's heart clenched at the sight of it. She had come across them skulking in the street a couple of days before, with hands in their pockets and cigarette butts in their mouths, kicking around a loose stone. At the sight of her, Dale the shyer one had started to back away, but Leon had stepped forward, flicking his cigarette to the ground and looking serious.

'What you did – the hospital and that – thanks.'

'I was glad to help.' She was on the point of walking on when a thought occurred to her. 'Are you bored?'

The pair of them had looked at each other in puzzlement.

'It's just that I could do with a bit of help in my garden – these days I can't do much of the heavy stuff.' She pressed her palm against her chest to emphasise her weakness, even though it was a while since her body had complained of anything very much. Even the stiffness after all her driving the week before hadn't taken its usual grip. A good night's sleep and a little walking the following day had seen her almost back to normal. 'Only if you've got the time, of course,' she had added carefully. 'I was thinking of next weekend. Saturday morning. I'll pay you each five pounds an hour, if you work properly and save your cigarette breaks for when the job is done.'

'Shall we?'

'I guess,' muttered Dale, looking reluctant.

'I'll expect you at ten then. Two hours should do it. Though if you're good there could be quite a lot more. At this time of the year the garden goes wild and with all the rain we've had it's worse than usual. Are you any good with a hammer and nails?'

'My Dad's a chippy,' said Dale at once, straightening his shoulders and casting a superior look at his friend.

'Good. Because I'm going to need a new fence.' And with that she had turned and gone on her way, not wholly convinced that they would actually turn up, but nonetheless feeling proud of herself for having dared to ask.

It was a risk of course, Stella mused now, watching as Dale broke off from his labours to stab the fork in the direction of his friend, popping his eyes and making a roaring noise which was loud even through the closed window. That the pair were rascals was evident from a mile off. But then there were good and bad rascals, she reassured herself, picking up her pen once more and reflecting, with the smugness peculiar to inner contentment, that without faith in human nature there would be little point in getting out of bed in the mornings.

*'As to your suggestion that I return for a longer stay in the summer, I would like, if the offer is still open, to change my mind and say yes. In fact the truth is I cannot think of anything that would make me happier . . .'*

Stella paused again, sucking the end of her pen and smiling to herself at the recollection of his large dry hand fisted round hers as they lay by the river, and of the gentle squeeze he had given her shoulders kissing her goodbye: once on each cheek in the French way, his soulful brown eyes rheumy with kindness and concern. She had forgotten what it felt like to be worried about tenderly, for oneself as opposed to for an ailment of some kind, when one was merely a nuisance.

*'I will tell Anna and Becky, in due course. They might be a little shocked to find I want to return to you so soon and at the moment they both have enough on their plates as it is. In terms of dates,*

*June would suit me best, simply because I can remember how hot it gets in July and August. But then again,'* Stella let the pen hover over the sentence, not hesitating over the moment so much as savouring it, *'the idea of some real heat rather appeals. I am in your hands entirely, Marcel. Tell me when to come and I will. By aeroplane this time and with some summer clothes.'*

Outside in the garden things had gone very quiet. On further inspection Stella was surprised to discover this was in fact because her two labourers were working rather hard, one turning over the heavy clods of soil with the fork and the other attacking the tangle of the end hedge with a pair of shears. Folding her letter into an envelope, she placed it carefully on the hall table for posting and then went into the kitchen to prepare a jug of orange squash and a plate of biscuits. The jug, the only surviving member of an ancient tea set, had to be retrieved from the back of her deepest cupboard and was so dusty from lack of use that it required a thorough wash before it could be filled. Holding it against her chest afterwards, rubbing the drying-up cloth over its familiar, faded design, Stella felt a fleeting rush of exultation, a sense of the past merging with the present, of all things existing beyond the snags and pettiness of time. Colin would be pleased for her, she realised, setting the jug down and splashing in several generous inches of orange squash. Marcel was a man he had liked and admired. What better creature for her to look to for comfort and companionship in her twilight years? She got out two glasses and opened the kitchen door to call the boys to the house. But then, registering the strength of their almost-men physiques and deciding that prudence had at some stage to take precedence over blind trust, she placed the whole lot on a tray instead and carried it outside, stepping carefully over the chipped section of the patio and the occasional treacherous lump lurking in the lawn.

# 41

It took Becky several goes before she was happy with her outfit. She settled finally upon a silky red floral skirt which flared slightly at the knee and a sleeveless ribbed black top with a high neckline and a tiny glittering silver heart stitched into the middle of the front. Though in danger of being tacky, she was especially fond of the heart motif and had a suspicion that Joe might like it too. It felt odd to be dressing for him again. Odd but deeply exciting, she mused, raising her mascara brush to her lashes, aware that the slight tremor in her hand had something to do with the thought of Joe not only admiring her black top but wanting to peel it off.

Thank God for Jenny, she thought, as she had many times already during the course of the week, the tremor worsening slightly at the recollection of Joe arriving ashen-faced and windswept on her doorstep, hugging her wordlessly, his heart thumping so hard she could feel it through his thick leather jacket. With Jenny there, badly in need of both sleep and reassurance, they hadn't talked much – they hadn't needed to, each knowing at a glance what they wanted, that somehow through the trauma of the new and terrible problem confronting Joe they were being offered a second chance.

'Can we meet?' was all he said, whispering the words over Jenny's head as he shepherded her to the door. And Becky, a lump in her throat at the sight of the pair of them, all dishevelled and clinging, like two people trying to survive a shipwreck in a storm, had nodded, wondering all the while about the pain of separation he faced and whether the love churning in her own heart could ever be enough to fill the void in his.

They had arranged to meet in a restaurant in the City, a place buried at the back of a cobbled yard which Joe, confirming the date on the phone the day before, had jokingly assured her the cabbie wouldn't be able to find. It was run by a friend, he said, another fledgling restaurateur whom he wanted to support and who was still desperate enough to be working Sundays as well as every other night of the week. Putting the phone down afterwards, Becky had been struck by the easy confidence with which Joe could now say such things, how quickly success had moved him on from the struggling self-doubt of just a few months before. The fact that she too had made comparable advances, learning to stand on her own feet at work, not to mention all the other deeper stuff which Anna had unlocked, gave her almost more hope than anything. The pair of them were balanced now, both restored as poised and solid individuals with different things to offer, existing in what felt like a parallel universe to the low ebb of mutual self-doubt and misunderstanding which had caused the marriage to run aground. She would never allow such a thing to happen again, Becky vowed, catching the slightly too interested stare of the cabbie in the rearview mirror and tugging the silk skirt further over her knees. No matter what low ebb she reached, she would always support Joe, through whatever dramas lay in store for him on the Jenny front or any other. She had a fair bit to make up to him on that score, she scolded herself, casting her mind back over the previous five years and recognising that she had always nursed a small but intense resentment towards her stepdaughter, deep down inside, buried like so many things, in a place where she imagined it could be ignored. When all along Jenny was just waiting to be loved like everybody else, so unsure and in need of it, so . . .

'Oh my God . . . could you . . . would you . . . just slow down a minute?' She leant forward and tapped frantically on the partition.

The driver looked annoyed, all thoughts of her hemline plainly forgotten. 'It's bad down there at this time of night, I was going to cut across further up . . .'

'No, it's not that, I just wanted you to . . . never mind, it doesn't matter.' Becky shook her head and turned to stare out of the window behind her, trying to relocate the point on the pavement where she had seen a person whom she was sure was Guy. With the shock of glossy dark hair and easy rolling walk it couldn't have been anybody else. He had been arm in arm with a blonde-haired woman in high heels and a long suede coat, a woman who – Becky had seen at a glance – was clearly a creature of expensive tastes; a much older creature too, possibly even in her fifties. Her hair was unnaturally fair, while her face had the soft fleshy look of a skin subjected to several decades of beauty treatments. She had felt a momentary pang at the sight of him, a reflex of pain deriving not from longing but the memory of the suffering he had caused her. Overriding it all however had been the shame. Heightened by the thought of Joe, heading like her towards the most important rendezvous of their lives, it travelled through her like a fire, burning her face and making the hairs on her arms stand on end. Could he ever truly forgive her? she wondered wretchedly, forgetting Guy and his dubious-looking escort and returning her gaze to the road ahead.

Joe was seated at a corner table waiting for her, looking, so she could not help observing, tenderness tugging at her heart as she dodged an obstacle course of tables and chairs to get to him, as nervous as a courting teenager. Tiptoeing the last few feet, she slipped her hands across his eyes and whispered 'guess who' before kissing him gently on the top of the head.

'Becksy.' He reached up and put his hands over hers, pressing so hard she could feel the tickle of his lashes on her palms.

'We need champagne and I'm going to buy it,' she declared happily, swinging into the seat opposite.

'Do we?' he said faintly, staring at her in precisely the way she had hoped he would, with a look of appreciative bewilderment and yearning. 'You look fabulous, by the way. Truly fabulous.'

Becky looked down at her top, tracing the tip of her index finger round the little silvery heart emblazoned on her chest. 'I thought you'd like it. I hoped you would. And I was right.' She beamed at him, before trying to catch the attention of the wine waiter, who was floating between two sets of new arrivals on the far side of the room.

'Becks . . . I . . . you don't think maybe . . . the champagne thing . . . maybe it's a little . . . premature?'

She blanched visibly. 'Oh God, Joe . . . sorry . . . I thought we both . . . I just thought . . .'

'And you were right to think it,' he countered eagerly, reaching across the condiments for her hand. 'I want you – I want us – Becky I really do – only right now there's something else on my mind . . .'

'Of course – Jenny – I'm so sorry darling, what you must be going through and me not even asking.' She put her hand over his, looking at the strong fist they made, thinking that it would take a global explosion to pull it apart. 'Is there anything you can do, anything at all?'

Joe shook his head. 'I've looked into the legal side of things and it looks pretty hopeless. I'd have to go to court and then I'd lose anyway, all because of some case thirty years ago apparently – Poel versus Poel – where the judge ruled that a mother being prevented from doing what Ruth wants to do would pass on all her distress and anxiety to the child. In other words, if Glen wants to take my daughter two thousand miles away from me there's fuck all I can do about it. I was hoping for something rather better before confronting them,' he concluded bleakly. 'I'm sure their silence is because they're getting all their guns ready to fire at me.'

'Joe, I'm so sorry.' Becky looked back down at the fist of their hands, racking her brains for something consoling or helpful to offer him. 'But what about Jenny, what does she want?'

He shrugged, slipping his hand free and reaching for a swig of the wine they had ordered in place of Becky's original grand thoughts of champagne. 'Last weekend I couldn't get much out of her and we've not spoken since. It doesn't take a rocket scientist to see that it's an amazing opportunity for her – big house, decent weather, new horizons – and obviously she wants to stay with her mother—' He broke off, clearing a choke of emotion from his throat. 'It seems that no matter how much of my life I get right other bits of it insist on falling apart.'

'Not me, Joe,' ventured Becky in a small voice, 'not me. I'm not falling apart, not any longer. I'm still here . . . if you want me, if you can forgive me . . .' She looked at her plate of food, something with chicken and mustard which she had ordered without really concentrating. Recalling her heady resolutions on the way there, she cursed herself for having been so pathetically naïve, for having imagined reconciliation between them could ever be so simple. Things done could not be undone. The shadow of the past darkened the present and always would. 'I wasn't going to tell you, but on the way here I saw him – Guy – the man I . . . and I want you to know that I felt nothing, Joe, except shame and a sort of rage that he had picked on me when I was so . . . when we were so . . . not that I'm saying it wasn't my fault – of course it was and I take full responsibility and am truly truly sorry and just hope and pray that one day you will find it in your heart to recognise that the love I have for you goes way beyond—'

'Becky, I slept with a prostitute. Twice. In December. Once before Christmas and then once afterwards, when you had gone. The same girl. I nearly ran her over on my motorbike. Then a bit later, on a bad day, I saw her again and I . . .' He picked his wine glass up and put it down again, looking not at her but at something far away over her right shoulder.

It was a long while before Becky spoke and when the words came out her voice sounded remote, as if it belonged to someone else. 'A bad day?' she echoed. 'In December?'

He bowed his head.

'The bit of December when we were still together . . . before you had found out . . . ?'

'Yup.' He glanced up at her and back at his lap.

'Jesus Christ, Joe . . .' She began to laugh and checked herself. 'Why . . . I mean, *why* . . . ?'

'I don't know . . . I felt . . . nothing in my life was . . . good . . . I can't explain it . . .'

'But,' Becky whispered, shock slowly soaking through her as her mind absorbed the implications of this horrible admission. 'I mean . . . maybe . . . for revenge I could have . . . but to do that when we were still together . . . before Anna had told you about Guy. Oh yes, I know it was Anna,' she murmured, seeing a faint glimmer of surprise cross his stricken face. 'I know everything now. *Everything*' she repeated, as disgust began to press through the shock, every trace of her earlier resolve and hope shrivelling to a dry husk inside. 'Jesus, Joe, I hope she was worth it, I hope she was worth all the money – what do they charge anyway? Blow jobs and fucks go for different rates, don't they? You'll have to fill me in because it would seem I've led something of a sheltered life compared to you, the sort of life where prostitutes only exist in documentaries and police dramas on the telly . . .'

'Stop Becky, please,' he pleaded quietly, closing his knife and fork over his own half-eaten food.

'Oh I'll stop all right.' She swiped her napkin off her lap and threw it onto her side plate. 'Okay, I deceived you, but at least I was dumb enough to think that I'd met someone I cared about who cared for me. But to go to a *whore*, Joe,' she spat the word, not caring that she was drawing a few curious looks from neighbouring diners. 'If sex is all you want, Joe, then you don't need me.' She pushed her chair back and got to her feet.

'Becky please, I want to explain . . . I felt . . . I felt as if I was failing – with you, with Jen, with everything – I felt as if I was failing on every front.'

Becky leant over the table and pressed her face very close to his, so close she could see the chocolaty flecks in his eyes and the downy hairs between his dark eyebrows. 'Perhaps that's because you were, Joe, perhaps that's because you were.'

He flinched as if she had slung her palm against his cheek. A few moments later, feeling hollow and nauseous, Becky was stumbling along the cobbled paving stones outside, turning down any street she came across, not daring to look over her shoulder for fear that she would find Joe racing along behind.

# 42

'How about a naming ceremony then?' said Anna, heaping rocket leaves on top of her slice of quiche and sprinkling it with several teaspoons of freshly grated parmesan, 'seeing as we don't believe in God. We could have a simple blessing type thing in the church and then a party back here afterwards.'

'Why would we want anything in the church if we don't believe in God?'

'Because churches have atmosphere. Have you ever been into St Joseph's? It's got a beautiful arched ceiling and a huge stained-glass window behind the altar. I walked there with Colin the other day and had a little look round. I felt positively guilty that we've lived in the village so long and never even bothered to go.'

'Well, I'm not sure you'll get the local vicar on your side if you start saying you want to use the House of the Lord purely as background ambience for a party.'

Anna giggled, pressing a straggling salad leaf into her mouth with her fingers. 'Okay, we'll do it all here – a little service of our own – we write the words and everything. If we wait a couple of months we'll be able to use the garden. And I think we should ask Joe and Becky to be godparents, now they're getting back together . . .' She broke off, picturing the pair of them suddenly in the midst of their grand reconciliation, about which Becky had excitedly confided earlier in the week. She had been glad for Becky, and for herself too, aware that a patching up of the marriage would help to eradicate the last traces of guilt she felt over having played something of a pivotal role in its demise. 'I know they don't believe in God either but I'm sure they'd say yes. What do you think?'

'I think,' David murmured, leaning across their place settings and pressing his lips to her forehead, 'that you will go ahead regardless, as you always do, once you've got a bee in your bonnet.' He sat back down and continued eating, eyeing her happily as he contemplated the so recently unimaginable and combined blessings of a beautiful son, a contented wife and his own peace of mind. For Anna the real turn-around seemed to have come as a result of a recent check-up, when she had emerged with a clean bill of health for her scar and the almost triumphant announcement that she might be suffering from mild Post-Natal Depression. A visit to her GP had followed, from which she emerged even more reassured, perhaps from having a simple label to pin on to her far from simple feelings. Though further counselling was offered, she declined to follow up on it and had seemed inordinately better ever since; much steadier and in control. Quite like her old self, in fact, David mused, suppressing a smile as Anna, her mouth still full of food, darted into the kitchen to fetch a pen and paper for drawing up a list of guests to witness the christening of their son.

'We could ask Mrs Costa and her daughter – what's her name?'

'Bella.'

'We could ask them to help out with the catering. I mean, we don't want it too grand do we? Just fifty or so. We could order all the food in advance from that place in Galtham, plates of nibbles and so on, nothing fancy . . .'

David picked up his wine glass and leant back in his chair, content to let her talk while he basked in the growing sense that life, thrown so badly off balance, had found a new and wonderful equilibrium. With his mother so much better, Colin seemed more settled too, sleeping for longer stretches at night and managing when he was awake to do something other than cry. The day before, sitting replete in the crook of his father's arm after his lunchtime bottle, his cherry of a mouth had opened and stretched into what David remained convinced had been a smile, even though, Anna, consulting one of her many manuals, said it didn't happen till they were at least six weeks old and was probably just wind. Mrs Costa, colliding with furniture in a neighbouring room, had promptly put her head round the door and volunteered the information that her beloved Bella was grinning like a Cheshire cat from one month old and with babies there were no rules of any kind. Anna had exclaimed in polite interest at the remark, managing at the same time to roll her eyes at David, her expression full of amusement at this further evidence of the improbable alliance now existing between her husband and their cleaner.

With the easing of so much on the domestic front, David had even found time that week to venture into his studio, where he had a grand sort-out of all his cupboards, keeping only the very best pieces and consigning the rest to black plastic rubbish sacks. Aided by his recent therapy, it had become clear to him that, no matter how great his untapped potential as an artist, working with clay – or any other solitary occupation – could not in the long term provide sufficient reason for feeling good about himself or the world. Nor, if he was completely honest, could looking after Colin. While aware that New Men were springing up all over the globe, sufficiently rock-like in their self-esteem and selflessness to wave their wives off to work and martyr themselves to the business of bringing up infants, David knew that such a huge act of devotion would only return him to the crabby unhappiness from which he so recently found release. He wanted to bring up his son, but not be bound to the process twenty-four hours a day. As a result, preliminary childcare negotiations had already begun with Mrs Costa, focusing on the number of hours she could manage once Anna returned to work. There was talk of Bella helping out as well, creating what in effect would be a joint housekeeping-cum-nanny team freeing David and Anna to pursue their respective careers. Quite what this would entail for David remained to be seen, although, inspired by the recent enjoyment of helping his brother-in-law, he was beginning to think that spending a couple of days a week in town himself might not be a bad idea. Possibly even getting more ventures like Joe's off the ground. Putting money in and seeing the fruits of his labours so soon had been fun. In addition to which he had greatly enjoyed the social interaction it provided. He simply was not designed to spend too long on his own, he reflected, glancing across Anna's shoulder and frowning at the sight of his sculpted self-portrait perched on the sideboard.

'That thing,' he said, interrupting Anna in full flow and pointing over her head, 'would you mind if we put it in the garden?'

'Why?' She swivelled in her chair, looking in surprise from the sculpture to her husband. 'It's very good.'

He scowled. 'I shouldn't have given it to you. I never really liked it. It makes me look cold . . . frozen . . . like an effigy of some sad Roman emperor who's been dead for thousands of years.'

She laughed, feeling no particular tension as her memory dipped back to the antipathy she herself had once felt towards the bust, sitting swollen and miserable at Christmas dinner – how smug it had seemed, how alone it had made her feel. It was only a memory after all, something that could be revisited at will, like her father's death and her accident, distant events buffered by the passage of time. How had she ever let it be otherwise? Anna wondered now, checking to see that Colin was still asleep in the Moses basket at her feet and then adding a couple of afterthoughts to her list. 'It will get covered in mould and bird crap.'

'I don't care. Might even do it some good . . . make it look more alive.'

'You silly,' she murmured, reaching to stack his empty plate on top of hers. 'What a thing to say.' She shook her head in mock despair, looking because she chose to – because once again she had the power to – as if she had no idea what he was talking about. The past was back in its box, and she had every intention of keeping it there.

# 43

Even as she walked the last few yards to Mike Hadfield's front door, Becky was not aware of any conscious decision having propelled her there. The BMW was parked directly outside, its scratch a silver arrow in the dark. She slowed to run a finger along it, her heart surging at the memory of the incredible kindness shown to her by the owner. Peering at her finger in the half light afterwards she saw a tiny bauble of red-black blood where a fragment of the scarred metal had snagged against her skin. She pressed it into her mouth and sucked hard, relishing the metallic taste of the blood, the minuscule distraction it offered from the huge injury inside her heart.

'I've hurt my finger,' she said, holding up her hand as he opened the door. 'Look, blood. From your car. I ran my finger down it and look.'

'Hm.' He took her wrist and gently twisted her hand to inspect the damage in the light shining out of his hall, as if he had spent all evening waiting to be confronted with just such a problem. 'A bit of blood.'

'I've sucked and sucked but it won't stop,' she whispered, raising the finger near to his lips in the half expectation that he would put his own mouth around it to staunch the tiny flow.

'A plaster,' he said hoarsely, stepping to one side and gesturing for her to come in, 'I can offer you a plaster.'

'I shouldn't have come,' she said, not moving.

'For God's sake, now you're here, come inside. It's good

to see you. It's always good to see you, Rebecca, you know that.'

Very slowly, she placed one foot over the doorstep and then the other, aware as she did so that her legs were trembling badly. Looking down she saw that there was a stain of something brown and unpleasant on her skirt. She was hot from running, and could feel her black top sticking to her skin. Her face too felt sticky, and her hair lank and stringy, all the life she had washed into it for her meeting with Joe earlier that evening quite gone. 'I'm a mess,' she muttered, letting him peel her jacket off and trying to rake some order into her hair with her undamaged hand. 'God, what must you think of me?'

'You know what I think of you,' he growled, leading the way into the kitchen and pulling a bottle of wine out of his fridge door. 'Have you eaten?'

She shook her head, remembering, like a snapshot of some-one else's life, her plate of untouched food in the restaurant and the glazed misery on Joe's face as he sat opposite.

'I'll fix you some toast,' said Mike, handing her a glass of wine and looking faintly amused at the speed with which she set about drinking it. 'Thirsty, anyway,' he murmured, carving two slices of bread and putting them into a toaster. 'Jam or marmalade?'

'Just butter please.'

'Just butter it is.' He worked the knife in quick sweeping motions, spreading the butter generously and carefully to every corner of the toast.

'Squares or triangles?'

'Pardon . . . ? Oh er . . . triangles please.'

'Good choice. Always been a triangle man myself.' He handed the plate to her and watched, sipping from his own glass of wine as she took a first cautious bite and then several more much less cautious ones.

'Why are you here, Rebecca?' He folded his arms and leant back against the fridge, crossing his right leg over his left and resting the toe of his shoe on the floor for balance. He was wearing faded brown loafers and green socks which she couldn't help thinking were an ill match. Dressed in jeans and a shapeless grey T-shirt as opposed to the crisp dark suits he wore to work, he looked younger but somehow frailer too. His cheeks and chin, evidently having made no contact with a razor that day, bristled with a fine layer of silvery stubble, which he kept rubbing with the palm of his hand, as if trying to smooth the roughness away.

'Because . . . because you like me and . . . I like you.'

He raised on eyebrow. 'Is that so?'

Becky nodded fiercely, licking the remains of some butter off her fingers, including the cut one which was already beginning to heal perfectly well without the aid of a plaster. 'Is there some more wine?' She held out her glass, regarding him as steadily as she could manage. 'I am, as you say, thirsty.'

'There's always more wine in this house.' He spoke quietly, reaching not for the fridge door but her face.

Becky remained motionless, watching the hand approach, steeling herself for the feel of his skin on hers, willing herself to want it.

'Butter,' he said, brushing a speck of grease off her chin with one finger and then withdrawing it, so quickly and lightly that she barely registered the contact. 'Just a dribble. Now for that wine. We could go into the other room, if you like . . . get comfortable.'

'I would like that very much,' she replied, the wobble returning to her legs as she tried to move them, 'very much indeed.'

They sat at opposite ends of the sofa, each turned slightly to face the other, their glasses of wine clutched to their chests. Becky, feeling the numbness of shock which had brought her this far, wearing off, drank frequently and deeply, wishing her host would do something other than watch her, his grey eyes inscrutable behind the lenses of his glasses.

'What's happened?' he said at length, leaving his seat and crossing to a small silver box of a music system housed on a shelf in the corner. A few minutes later some music, not Elton John or Joni Mitchell, but what sounded like jazz, a haunting trumpet that kept finding a tune and losing it again, began pulsing gently round the room. Becky, trying to concentrate on something other than the fug inside her own head, felt as if the notes were floating round her like the disconnected pieces of some musical jigsaw which she could have put together if only someone had told her how.

'Nothing's happened. I wanted to see you, that's all.'

'Curious, since you've spent the week avoiding me.'

'I have not,' she retorted, but feebly because she knew it was true. She held out her glass, watching with glazed eyes as he refilled it. 'That kiss . . . the one that you wanted . . . you can have it now if you like.'

He set the bottle down, laughing softly and shaking his head. 'I would like that very much, Rebecca, very much indeed. I find you deeply, compellingly' – he spoke very slowly, rolling his mouth round each word – 'attractive.'

Becky, who had been staring hard at the stain on her skirt, blushing at the compliment though she herself had invited it, looked up to see Mike drop to his knees on the carpet, his gaunt face flexed in what looked like a grimace of pain. 'Okay, okay,' he growled, starting to walk towards her on his knees. 'You want that kiss do you? Well okay, my sweet Rebecca, you shall have it.'

During the course of his approach Becky realised that she was clutching her knees with both hands, leaving a crescent of ridges where her nails were digging into her skin.

'Because I am human and cannot resist you,' he continued,

arriving at her feet. 'Especially now, all tousled and drunk. So sweet.' He put a hand to her cheek and pushed a clump of the heavy dark tresses back off her face. 'Except . . . except something tells me you are here not because you want a kiss or anything else from me, but because life has disappointed you. Is that true?' He placed the other hand on the other side of her face and steered her gaze to meet his. 'Is that true, my sweet Rebecca? Is it?' He shook his head. 'You see, I know quite a bit about your private life, thanks in part to what you yourself have told me and in part to the office grapevine. I make it my business to know because . . .' he faltered, 'because I care so much for you.' He took a deep breath, as if summoning huge physical strength to continue. 'I would like nothing more than to kiss you, to make love to you, preferably for the entire night and then maybe the next night too and the one after that . . . but keen as that desire is I'd rather like – I need to be sure – that at least some of it is reciprocated.'

'I do feel something . . .' she began.

'Something but not everything, eh? Which is probably why I have the strong and thoroughly unwelcome impression that I am standing in for someone else.' His hands were still on either side of her face, cool and very gentle. 'Love is a funny old thing, isn't it?' he whispered. 'And it doesn't get any simpler either, I can tell you.' Lifting his hands off her face at last, he sat back on his heels with folded arms. 'Believe me, I am surprising myself – such self-restraint . . .' He smiled grimly. 'I honestly didn't know I had it in me. Would you like me to drive you home now? I'm still sober enough – just – in spite of your efforts to ensure otherwise . . .'

'You haven't got any cigarettes have you?'

'I'm afraid not – one of the few vices that passed me by.'

'What about prostitution – is that a vice that passed you by too?'

He frowned, looking quizzical rather than shocked. 'Let

me see now . . . aged about sixteen and a half, drunk and certain that it was high time I lost my virginity, I spent several hours one night roaming around Piccadilly and Soho giving meaningful looks to girls in high heels. Either I was looking at the wrong girls or they didn't like the look of me.' He smiled again, even more darkly. 'Not thinking of a career switch are you?'

'Joe, my husband, went to a prostitute,' she blurted, 'while we were still together. He told me tonight, just when . . . just when I thought everything might turn out all right.'

'At least he told you,' he said after a pause.

'I wish he hadn't.'

'And the marriage broke down, as I understand it – forgive me if I'm wrong – because you . . .'

'Because I had a fling with someone else, yes,' she snapped, 'a complete jerk, as it happens, but that's another story . . .'

'No it's not,' he interjected, getting to his feet and standing over her, his voice suddenly very stern. 'It's the same story. One and the same. Two sides of the same coin. You both messed up, by the sounds of it because you wanted things you weren't getting from each other. That means there's hope. Believe me, I know.'

'What do you know?' she whispered, feeling suddenly giddy and very weary.

'I lost my wife because she fell in love with someone else – seriously, badly, catastrophically in love. There's not much you can do about that. But here, with you and . . . Joe, is it? With you and Joe it doesn't sound remotely catastrophic. Presumably he wants to get back together too, but felt he had to make a clean breast of things. You don't go to prostitutes for love Becky, you go for sex or comfort, two things I'm sure you're more than able to provide,' he added drily, disappearing into the hall and returning with her jacket.

The music had stopped, she noticed, making the silence without conversation seem very intense.

'Now let's get you home before I change my mind and rip your clothes off.' He smiled as he held out the jacket though Becky noticed that his eyes looked very sad.

'I'm sorry . . . I've been . . .'

'You've been upset . . . and a little drunk,' he added, his expression softening. 'While I – though I say it myself – have been a truly amazing gentleman, a fact for which I know I will kick myself the moment I've dropped you off, but for which I will also be extremely grateful when we meet in the lift tomorrow morning. Sex and work never mix well, at least not for long anyway. Are you going to put this on?'

She turned and slipped her arms into the jacket before following him meekly out to the car. Her head was throbbing and her mouth was beginning to feel unpleasantly furry and dry. Not knowing what else to say, overwhelmed in equal measure by mortification and relief, she sat in silence as he started the engine.

'And by the way,' he said, pausing before starting the engine, 'I won't try again. You have my word.' He slipped the handbrake off and they rolled smoothly forwards to the end of the road where he had to wait for a gap in the traffic before turning. 'What's it to be then – Bayswater or . . . where does he live?'

'Brixton,' she whispered, hope flaring inside her, so fiercely that she knew it had to be love.

'Brixton it is.' The car leapt forward with such a jerk that Becky reached out a hand to the dashboard. It was her left hand, still, after all the months apart, sporting its delicate wedding band and the tiny solitaire engagement ring Joe had found in an antique shop when supposedly on an excursion for a pint of milk. Seeing the diamond had slipped right round her finger, she quickly straightened it, quietly vowing to herself that she would get the details right this time, that she would watch so closely that things could never swerve so badly off course again.

Her driver and companion meanwhile, set his teeth together and tightened his jaw, accepting that, for him at least, it would be a long night and probably a long week too. The only hope in his heart stemmed from a feeble trust that time would eventually perform its customary miracle; that the feelings raging inside him, if left alone, would eventually fade, from a pain to an ache, and then, if he was lucky, to a mere memory, something he could dust off and pull out when he wanted, like an old and cherished photo from a bottom drawer.

# 44

Joe paid for the unfinished food and left the restaurant alone. He moved with his gaze fixed firmly upon the ground, both out of shame and the certainty that the pitying eyes of the entire world were upon him. All his life he had believed in the importance of honesty; throughout a not entirely satisfactory childhood the instruction that truth was of value had been one of the few parental tenets to hit home and by which he had subsequently tried to live his life. That he and Becky had been dishonest with each other in their marriage seemed to him to be of more, potentially lethal significance than the fact that they had, in totally different ways, sought solace in other people's beds. Yet now, looking up and down the dark street blankly for his bike, too mesmerised by unhappiness to recall where he had parked it, Joe wondered how on earth he could have been so dumb. Becky had come running to him that evening with open arms, her mind a clean receptive slate, with no knowledge of the blemishes lurking like tumours in his. He needn't have told her. It would have been better not to tell her, not to burden her with so exacting a request for forgiveness, when she had had no inkling there had been anything to forgive. What a bloody fool. What a self-indulgent madman. To think he could win such a no-win game. To risk losing the only woman he had ever truly loved. And in the same week that he was grappling with the horrific possibility of losing Jenny too.

He drove fast and ineptly. With tears blinding his vision

and steaming up his visor it wasn't hard to imagine cars were moving when they were parked or to misjudge breaks in the traffic. Turning across the front of one particular lorry, there was a split second when time seemed to stand still; seeing the vast tyres rolling towards him, Joe found himself momentarily absorbed by the idea of being swallowed between them, of letting the weight of the bike topple him over and into the black jaws of the truck. But the lorry driver braked and slammed his horn, decelerating with a reproachful hiss, allowing Joe to complete the turn in safety and continue on his way. He drove with trembling care for the remainder of the journey, clenching his toes inside his boots and his fingers round the handlebars, trembling at the notion that every second of even the most unspectacular human life was a hair's breadth away from tragedy; that destiny was forged on instants the size of pinheads, a decision to brake or not to brake, to speak or not to speak. Nothing was safe. Nothing certain. Except that one day it would all end in the blackness he had glimpsed between the lorry wheels.

Finding a hand-delivered envelope in his letter box and recognising Ruth's pinched tidy handwriting on the front of it, he groaned out loud. Clumping up to the flat in his heavy boots, his helmet under his arm, he slapped the letter hard against the wall, half hoping it would explode into illegible fragments, taking the emotional trauma facing him and his daughter with it. Before opening it, he poured himself a large whisky, so rare a choice of drink that it took him several minutes to unearth a bottle, on the lowest rung of one of his many wine racks. It was a fresh bottle too, he noted with grim satisfaction, still with the price tag on, its cap dusty from lack of handling. He took three long swigs before running his finger under the letter flap, gasping out loud as the alcohol seered the back of his throat, not dulling his emotions so much as making him feel more alert to them, more up to the vile prospect of fighting back. He would not give in easily, he vowed, shaking out the single page Ruth had written, snorting to himself at the cowardice of slipping a note through his door rather than confronting him in person.

*Dear Joe,*

*I am writing this rather than speaking to you in person because we're not always very good face to face, are we? And because what I have to say is very hard and needs a lot of thought to get the words just right.*

*Glen has been offered a job back in San Francisco, a wonderful job which he wants – and which he should accept. He has asked me to marry him and I think I'm going to say yes.*

Joe snorted again, uncharitable thoughts and images sweeping through him at the thought of Ruth as the wife of an American lawyer, living the American dream on the West Coast, a manicured life of social functions and hairdressing appointments, baking brownies between instructing the pool man to skim off a few stray leaves. Nauseous at the thought of Jenny being shoe-horned into such an existence, he drained his glass and filled it again before continuing.

*The big question mark in all this of course, is Jenny. I would like her to come with us. I want to give her the chance to experience a whole other – almost certainly easier – way of life. She's due to change schools anyway at the end of this year and so the timing would be perfect. She would make new friends and get to do all sorts of things that just don't happen in south-east London. She could come to the UK to see you every holiday, and if ever you came out we would give you access to spend as much time with her as you would*

*like. It would work, I know it would . . . except for the fact*
*that Jenny herself refuses to see it that way. She is putting*
*her foot down Joe, which leaves me with a dilemma, the most*
*terrible dilemma of my life. I know that we have moved on*
*enough for me to tell you that I love Glen in a way that I*
*never imagined I could love someone. I need him. He needs*
*me. And he needs to take this job.*

Joe had set his whisky glass on the arm of his chair by this
stage and was holding the letter in both hands in a bid to stop
the paper from shaking.

*In spite of our many differences over the years, Joe, I have*
*always known you were a wonderful father, that you loved*
*Jenny in the same heart-stopping way that I did. Without*
*her I don't think we would have lasted as long as we did.*
*And since we separated I do not really believe you could have*
*done more in terms of staying a big part of her life, given all*
*the other things you have been doing as well. Joe, what I am*
*saying, with my heart aching and my eyes hardly believing*
*the words as they spill onto the page, is that if Jenny would*
*like to remain here with you in England I will be able to live*
*with that. I cannot face a future without Glen. And I know*
*that you will post her over here for as many holidays as*
*we ask.*

It was only as Joe lowered the letter to his lap that he realised
he had been holding his breath. Remembering how cynical
he had felt about Ruth's display of sympathy over Jenny's
walkabout the previous weekend, he felt a rush of guilt. In
spite of the myriad irritations that had come to cloud his view
of her over the years, his ex-wife was an extraordinary woman,
he realised. And what she was offering was extraordinary too,

both in its selfishness – that she could make such a choice – and in its simple generosity with regard to him. After all his anxieties, it was like a miracle, a pure and fabulous gift: to have the chance to have his daughter properly at his side at last, in the flat every night instead of every other weekend; to have a regular up-and-down, push-and-pull parent-child relationship without the unnatural business of saying goodbye all the time, when so often the desire to end a visit on a good note overrode the possibility of behaving normally.

*What do you say, Joe? We always said we would share her, didn't we? Though I never in a million years envisaged it would mean what I am proposing. I can only do it because I know how much you love her, and she you. I have had her for seven years Joe, now it is your turn – if you agree, which I have a feeling you will.*

*Another thing you should know, though Jenny doesn't yet, is that I am expecting Glen's child. Obviously this has affected my decision, but not governed it entirely. Jenny would I think love a younger sibling – be warned, at the moment she's got her heart set on a puppy!*

*When you've digested this let's meet to talk about it properly.*

*Once again, apologies for not telling you in person, but I'm so emotional right now, I wanted to set things down clearly, without tears or the danger of misunderstanding.*

*With love,*

*Ruth*

Having finished the letter, Joe read it again, four times, the words and sentences – as if sharing his exultation – performing cartwheels across the page. He then got to his feet, knocking his glass of whisky off the chair as he did so. It landed with a quiet thud on the carpet and rolled for a few inches, spilling its load in a glistening crescent. Joe took a small leap over it, and then another higher one, punching the air with his fists. Not knowing how else to express his exuberance, he flicked on his CD player and began to dance, shouting the lyrics, which were of some favourite band of Jenny's, and performing huge ridiculous leaps back and forth across the room. By the third track, panting and feeling faintly foolish, he switched the machine off and went into the kitchen where he ran his head under the cold tap, letting the water pour freely down his neck and turning every so often to direct some of the flow into his mouth.

It was too late to call Ruth, but he would get hold of her first thing in the morning, he vowed, suppressing a new and sudden fear that she might change her mind. Still hot, in spite of his soaking face and shoulders, he opened one of the sitting-room windows and put his head out, taking deep breaths of the night air, which although cold seemed to lack some of its customary chill, as if heralding what the forecasters were already promising would be a balmy summer of parched lawns and uninterrupted cricket games. On the pavement opposite a man was walking his dog, tugging the creature impatiently on the lead every time it tried to stop. Joe watched, feeling some sympathy for the dog, which looked plump and resigned. After a few moments his view of the pair was blocked by a black BMW, which streaked along the road before coming to a halt in the street directly below. Joe continued to watch, first with curiosity and then mounting disbelief, as Becky emerged from the passenger side, swinging her slim legs out onto the pavement and smoothing the silky folds of her red skirt. She bent down to say something briefly to the driver before turning on her heel and appearing to make for his front door, which was set a few yards down one side of the restaurant. Sticking his body dangerously far out of the window, Joe followed her progress as far as he could, just managing to glimpse her pause for a deep breath and smooth her hair before she disappeared from view.

It was probably nothing, he told himself, hauling himself inside and racing to the bathroom for a towel. Just a fresh urge to kick him when he was down, to fire a few more venomous salvos about what he had done and why there was no hope for them. But there was always hope, he thought wildly, almost tripping over the empty whisky glass and feeling a fresh burst of elation at the sight of Ruth's letter, still open on the arm of the chair. With humans there was always hope. And she had breathed deeply and straightened her hair. Her beautiful thick jet hair which made her face so wild and pale. Forgetting the towel because there wasn't time, wanting to open the door before she rang the bell, he raced down the stairs taking three steps with each stride. She was raising her hand to the buzzer just as he flung open the door. At the sight of him she remained motionless for a few moments, her face alight with a surprise that looked more shocked than pleased.

'I saw you – from upstairs,' he gasped. 'That man – that car – who was he?' Not having meant to say any such thing, Joe pressed his face into his hands, all the hope beginning to ebb out of him.

'He's a friend,' she replied quietly, placing her raised hand over his fingers and prising them off his face. 'A very good friend. Who has helped me see that I want you more than anything in the world. What you did Joe, it doesn't matter. It must have been hard telling me. Thank you for being brave enough. I want you Joe, I want what we had.'

'So do I,' he murmured, 'more than you can ever imagine.' He pulled her to him, feeling a stab of fresh panic as she seemed, momentarily, to recoil.

'You're soaking,' she exclaimed, beginning to laugh and

then pressing herself against him nonetheless. 'Funny man, why are you so wet?'

'A long story,' he murmured, starting to laugh with her and thinking that life was not just about second chances but third and fourth ones and that from then on he would seize every slither of each one that came his way with both hands.

# 45

Seeing the marquee, open on one side and with little turrets at each of its four corners, Becky was for a moment reminded of the housewarming party and the damp bouncy castle which had formed the backdrop to her ill-fated encounter with Guy. Grateful and marvelling at how her life had moved on, a circle returning her to where she had always wanted to be, she slipped her arm across Joe's shoulders and gently rubbed her fingers across the base of his neck, which she could tell from the way he kept arching it, was stiff from the long drive down.

'Just a simple ceremony, eh?' he murmured, following the line of her gaze and checking in the rearview mirror to see how Jenny was reacting to the scene. 'What do you reckon, Jen?'

'I like it,' she declared, winding down her window and resting her head on her arms. 'Like a fairytale thing isn't it?'

'Never been known to do things by halves, Anna, has she, love?'

Becky smiled, happy these days to muse upon her striving perfectionist sister without any trace of envy, not just because she had found contentment herself, but because of her new perception of the effort behind the striving, how it hinged on a fundamental need of Anna's to keep herself and her world together. Having survived on a diet of phonecalls for three months, she was very much looking forward to seeing her, to show in whatever way she could that all the traumatic events surrounding the birth of Colin were not forgotten.

In her wilder most indulgent moments she even imagined confessing the dark shadows behind all the help she had given afterwards, inspired by the fresh start of her marriage to come clean on every other front in her life as well.

'Not done badly, has it?' remarked Joe, giving the steering wheel a fond pat as he switched off the ignition. As a soon-to-be official family of three, with a regular need to get to far-flung places for ballet lessons, sleep-overs and birthday discos, the formal acquisition of a four-wheeled vehicle had been one of the highlights of the summer. It was a Volvo Estate, bought, after much deliberation on the hazards of mixing used cars and friends, from Adrian, whose business had advanced sufficiently for him to progress to a sports car and a small fleet of vans. With Ruth and Glen on a house-hunting trip across the Atlantic, Becky and Joe were in the middle of something of a trial run with Jenny; a prospect about which they had both been equally nervous but which so far had exceeded both their expectations. Although still inclined to be moody, it was clear that these dips in her temperament bore little relation to the momentous decision she had made with regard to her future. On the contrary, it was evident that she considered the arrangement to grant her the best of all possible worlds, offering as it did the chance to move on to the same south London school as the bulk of her friends, see more of her adored father and all with the enjoyable prospect of long exotic holidays near beaches and swimming pools with her mother.

On instructions from Anna, they had arrived early, both for something of a family reunion before the arrival of the guests in the afternoon and so they could have a run-through of the ceremony, scheduled to take place in the turreted marquee later on that afternoon. During the course of the previous few weeks Becky and Joe had been sent several scripts at various stages of development, over which they had giggled irreverently, until an exquisite finalised version had arrived, held together by a tiny yellow silk ribbon and sporting so fetching a portrait of their godson that even Joe had oohed out loud at the sight of it.

During the course of the drive down the day had heated up considerably. The sky, untroubled by a breath of wind or a whisper of a cloud, seemed to shimmer with as much intensity as the small yellow disc of a sun set into it. Standing on the gravel waiting for Joe to lock the car and Jenny to scrabble out of the back, Becky stretched her arms out, luxuriating in the prickle of heat on her bare skin and the beat of the hot ground under the thin soles of her shoes.

'Isn't this great? Isn't this absolutely great?'

'All right for those of us in little party frocks,' growled Joe good-humouredly, slinging his suit jacket over his shoulder and linking arms with both his wife and daughter for the walk to the front door. 'Though you both look gorgeous and I wouldn't have it any other way.'

'Flattery will get you everywhere,' quipped Becky, exchanging looks with Jenny, with whom she had a pact of secrecy as to what the dresses, bought on a highly satisfactory excursion to Knightsbridge the weekend before, had actually cost.

Inside the house felt cool and welcoming. David and Anna came to greet them, exclaiming simultaneously that Colin was asleep upstairs preparing for his starring role in the afternoon. They both looked incredibly well, Becky observed, with Anna in a hugging pink linen dress that showed off a thoroughly reclaimed figure and David in a crisp white shirt and smart blue suit trousers. But then she and Joe looked well too, she reflected, as the four of them exchanged hugs and kisses in the hall, almost as if nothing had ever gone wrong for any of them. Or maybe they were all simply stronger because it had, she mused, noting with pleasure the new familiarity evident between the two brothers-in-law, already deep in talk about something.

'You look so pretty and so grown-up,' said Anna kindly, kissing the top of her niece's head, 'and if you want a peek at Colin he's in the bedroom at the end of the corridor upstairs. Be quiet though, won't you?' she called, as Jenny bounded off through the house to take her up on the invitation. 'You won't recognise him,' she said, returning her attention to Becky and leading the way into the kitchen, while their husbands remained chatting animatedly in the hall. 'So huge and chubby and already full of wickedness. But how are you, Becky? I mean, you look well – both of you – things are obviously working out in spite of . . . everything?' She switched the kettle on and turned to Becky with a look of tender inquisition on her face; the big sister checking up on the younger, as she always had, as if nothing had changed. While aware that there had been something of a last-minute glitch in Becky and Joe's reconciliation she had no idea what it was. And never would, Becky decided now, registering the look of intimate enquiry in her sister's eyes and choosing to ignore it. Never again would she lean on her as she once had. Perhaps because she was stronger. Perhaps because she had glimpsed her inner frailty and knew it would be unfair.

'How are you, more to the point?' she responded gently, trying now with her expression to communicate that Anna's outburst after Colin's birth was etched indelibly on her heart, that she would forever be more caring as a result of it.

'Me? I'm brilliant,' replied Anna without a blink of hesitation. 'Absolutely brilliant. We're into such a good routine now, with Mrs Costa and her daughter to help out too. When I go back to work they'll take over more or less full-time, as David too is going to have his hands full.' She lowered her voice to a confiding whisper. 'It's still all a bit hush-hush, but he's planning on launching a new chain of restaurants, two in London and two in the West Country. He's been getting

354

backers, using all his old contacts in the City – megabucks, which terrifies me, but he's loving it, which is the main thing. Having a year off has done him the world of good, but he was so ready for a new challenge.'

'So no more pots, then,' remarked Becky, reading rejection in her sister's jollity and doing her best not to be upset by it. Of course she wouldn't want reminding of her emotional explosion in the hospital, it wasn't part of how she coped with things. A shutter on their past had opened and closed, she told herself, altering them both forever, but in a way that would always be hard to acknowledge.

'No more pots,' echoed Anna gaily, 'but he's still going to use the studio – as an office – we've started having the alterations done already. I expect he'll want to show you later – it's going to be fabulous.'

'And you . . . you are all right, are you, Annie?' Becky faltered, unable to stop herself having one last go, 'because I want you to know that what happened . . . what you said in the hospital . . . I'll never forget it . . . I . . .'

'What happened in the hospital, I am happy to say, is rather a blur,' she put in, laughing, 'and I'm totally over that silly bout of depression too . . . but then that's what they say about women having babies, isn't it? That some chemical amnesia kicks in so we're all mad enough to do it again and ensure the survival of the human race. Are you black or white these days?'

Becky hesitated a moment before replying, remembering with what felt like an almost nostalgic sadness, the red-rimmed creature who had wept her heart out three months before. 'White, please, as always,' she said quietly, consoling herself with the fact – already evident in the patching up going on between her and Joe, intense one minute and easy to the point of boredom the next – that human life could not be lived at a constantly high emotional pitch. Like staring at a bright light it could only be managed in bursts, when the time was right and the eyes felt strong enough to manage the glare.

Joe took Becky's hand and led her up the stairs so that they could pay their respects to their new godson together. Placing each foot on the luxurious golden pile of the carpet, bordered on one side by a gleaming mahogany banister and on the other by silky wallpaper, a rich landscape of gold and cream and blue, Joe experienced a vivid flashback of the other, dingy staircase he had climbed, with its threadbare covers and peeling walls. With time the memory of the physical context remained far clearer than any firm recollection of the state of mind that had propelled him there. Rigorous analysis of his motives had resulted only in the conclusion that he had been seeking emptiness, something desperate to mirror the desperation he felt inside. And he certainly had found it, he thought sadly, squeezing Becky's hand in a bid to help press the image away – so tightly that Becky glanced at him in surprise.

They found Colin, oblivious to the mounting noise of preparations downstairs and the stream of visitors to his bedroom, lying flat on his back in just a nappy, with all four limbs stretched from his body like the points of a chubby star.

'We could make one of these,' Joe whispered, all the tension seeping out of him at the sight of the sleeping child, 'I mean, it isn't as if we haven't got all the know-how and necessary equipment, is it?' He glanced across the cot at Becky who was smiling and shaking her head. 'Becks,' he continued, faltering now under a rush of earnestness and remorse, 'David was telling me just now how absolutely amazing you were with Colin after he was born and I want to tell you that I did know how badly you wanted us to have a child and that with me being so skint I know I made it impossible for you to show just how much . . .'

Becky shook her head again, although this time without the accompaniment of a smile. 'No, Joe. At least . . .' She paused, wanting to get the words right. 'I did think I wanted a baby – but I can see now that it was for all the wrong reasons . . . more to do with wanting a distraction from who I was and what I really wanted out of life . . . looking for an excuse to go wild in Baby Gap.' She paused, uncertain how much to tell him. 'And as to helping out down here . . . the truth is, I did a bit too much – they thought I was helping but really I was in the way. I never told you this but in the end Mum had to tell me to piss off.'

'Stella?' Joe was incredulous.

She nodded. 'Came here straight from France to see Colin and told me to pack my things.'

'And you didn't mind?'

'Oh God, I minded all right,' she whispered fiercely, 'but I knew she was right. In fact, I think if she had told me off a bit more over the years I might have got to like her rather more, but she was so scared of being cross with us . . . because of Dad . . .' Becky broke off, shaking her head ruefully. 'Nothing like hindsight, is there? Anyway the point is, all I was doing was delaying getting back to London . . . getting back to you.' She came round the cot and put her arms round his neck. 'We will make babies, my sweetheart, one day, I promise. Think of it,' she murmured, kissing his lips between words, 'with Jen as a teenager we'll have a resident babysitter.' She grinned. 'See, what long-term plans I have for us? But in the short term I can definitely hear Mum's voice downstairs and my dear sister is desperate for us to go and practise promising to be godless godparents. Are you coming?'

'Yes – you go – I'll just be a minute.'

A look of surprised tenderness crossed her face. 'Okay. See you in a bit then.'

He watched her tiptoe down the hall and then returned his

attention to his nephew, brushing the top of his head with his fingertips and letting a host of indulgent memories of Jenny's babyhood flood his mind. Aware after a moment or two that he had an audience, he glanced up to find a rotund woman with a veiny face and a bleached ponytail standing regarding him from the doorway, arms akimbo but with a look of soppy satisfaction on her face.

'Men and babies,' she crooned, 'it gets me every time. I'm Mrs Costa, by the way. Me and my daughter Bella are helping out for the festivities. We was just putting clean towels in the bedrooms. We help with him too,' she added nodding at the baby, 'any moment we get the chance. Such a handsome little outfit he's got for this afternoon – nice and cool too, which is what you want on a day like this isn't it? Couldn't put it on before of course because he'd only get it mucky . . . ah, here she is now. Bella, did you do the end room as well where the Mum's going to be?'

Keen to extricate himself, both on account of holding up any proceedings downstairs and because he feared any more of the woman's somewhat exuberant monologue would be certain to wake his nephew, Joe took the opportunity to slip past her into the hallway. Blocking his route towards the landing however was the daughter, recently emerged from a neighbouring room, with a pile of laundered towels half concealing her face. He opened his mouth to deliver a polite but brief greeting, but closed it again, arrested by the sight of the lowering of the towels and the entire face appearing over the top of them. A young, pasty and slightly lumpen face, recognisable even without the beige face cream and heavy eye make-up, without the snake tongue darting along the edges of the lips. Joe opened his mouth again but no words came out of it. It was the girl who spoke first, saying, none of the things his pounding heart feared to hear, but simply, 'Pleased to meet you.'

'Likewise,' he stammered, swiping the sweat from his upper lip, panic still gripping his heart.

'Better get on,' chirruped Mrs Costa, padding down the hall and taking the towels from her daughter, so blissfully unaware of the silent drama exploding around her that Joe for one wild moment felt like flinging his arms round her meaty shoulders and clinging there.

'Yeah, better get on,' echoed the daughter, not looking at him and talking from behind her mousy fringe in a way that reminded him of Jenny. With the red dots in her doughy cheeks the only sign that anything was amiss, she promptly turned and trotted back down the hallway after her mother, hanging her head like a dutiful sheep.

It took Joe a few minutes to compose himself. Stopping halfway down the stairs, out of sight both of the landing above and the hall below, he took several deep breaths, covering his eyes with his hands, wishing he could rewrite the script of his recent past. The cruelty – the absurdity – of the coincidence took his breath away. Nor could he yet derive much consolation from the certainty – flooding through him within seconds of the recognition – that the girl was as unlikely to betray their past acquaintance as he was. Not with her London life behind her and her mother – such a mother too – breathing down her neck. She would have as much to lose as he had. Joe had thought he was over the shame, but it came at him now with such force that he had to grip the banisters to steady himself. Grand theories about seeking emptiness were nothing, he realised – mere indulgence – compared to the fact that he had colluded in the demise of a confused and suffering human being. A pitifully young human being too. Without make-up she looked barely nineteen. Seven or eight years older than Jenny. Sickened at the thought of a similar fate ever befalling his own beloved daughter, he groaned out loud.

'Joe? Are you all right? What are you doing up there?'

He looked down to see Becky hovering in puzzlement at the turn in the stairs. 'Are you okay?' she repeated, starting towards him with an expression of real concern on her face.

'Just hot,' he assured her quickly, running his finger round the inside of his shirt collar and hurrying down the stairs.

'They're all waiting in the marquee – there are drinks there too – a really nice fruit cocktail thing. I've temporarily lost track of Jenny but David said he saw her in the garden, talking to some dog which apparently strays over here from a neighbouring farm and likes to use their front lawn as a lavatory . . . says he's thinking of shooting it . . . are you sure you're okay?'

'Sure. Really really sure.' He put his arm round her shoulders and pressed his lips to her hair, breathing in the faint scent of lemons that seemed to linger there, regardless of the varying fragrances of shampoo that passed through the bathroom cupboard.

'Becks – can I just ask – you do like the flat, do you? And living in Brixton and so on?'

'Yes, I like the flat,' she laughed. 'And living in Brixton.'

'And you like having Jen around.'

'I love having Jen around.'

'And we will make a baby one day.'

'And we will make a baby one day.'

'And you love me . . .'

'And I love you,' she echoed.

'Then nothing else matters,' he whispered, aware still of the shame like a stone in his heart, but one that he could live with, one which, hopefully, would shrink with time. Revealing the truth about the girl would serve no positive purpose for anyone, he reminded himself. The merits of honesty, as he had discovered, were limited. 'Nothing else matters,' he repeated quietly, slipping his hand from her shoulder and linking arms for the walk across the lawn.

Jenny, spying on them from a patch of shade between a weeping willow and the summerhouse, a large ginger dog sprawled next to her and a glass of chilled orange juice in her hand, felt closer to happiness than she could remember for a long time. Seeing the pair of them smooching still made her feel weird in the stomach, but it was a lot better than not having Becky around at all. Her father was so much happier for one thing and for another, it for some reason made her feel a bit better about Glen and her mother and the whole confusing business of adult love, how unseemly it was and how unreliable. What was reliable these days, however, was the knowledge that she herself was loved; not just by her mum, but by her father and Becky and Glen too. It was clumsy at times, but it was there, a big solid thing, quite unlike the wobbly stuff they felt for each other.

'And I love you, dog,' she murmured, letting its long pink tongue lick her hand and then watching as it heaved itself upright and ambled towards the back of the summerhouse where it began sniffing eagerly in the long grass under one of the windows. Glimpsing something large and grey and envisaging an animal of some kind, possibly wounded or dead, Jenny scrambled to her feet and ran over to pull the dog away. But it wasn't an animal, it was a clay head, or rather what had once been a clay head, since it had fallen – off the summerhouse windowsill by the looks of things – and split in several pieces. Unable to resist the challenge, Jenny set about trying to reassemble the parts. Realising after a while that it was in fact an image of her Uncle David, whom on the rare occasions they met she always found stiff and a bit silly, she began to giggle. She managed after a while to balance the pieces together, but they were badly chipped and looked very precarious. Sitting back on her heels to size up her handiwork, she giggled even more as the dog, clearly wanting to contribute to the project in some way, cocked his leg on the assemblage, promptly knocking it over again in the process.

From somewhere on the other side of the willow tree someone called her name. Feeling suddenly guilty, as if she had no business seeing grown-ups in pieces on the ground, let alone covered in animal pee, Jenny hurriedly plucked some grass and scattered it over the top in a makeshift attempt to hide the evidence, before racing back up towards the house, the dog yelping at her ankles.